Taking Til

Rebekah Lee Jenkins

Dear Bonny,
Happy Reading
[illegible]

*Author's note: you may notice apologize is spelled apologise, etc. This book has been corrected to British vernacular at Til's insistence—Enjoy!

Taking Til

By: Rebekah Lee Jenkins

Cover Design: Josephine Blake of Covers and Cupcakes LLC (www.coversandcupcakes.wordpress.com)

Editing and Interior design: Alex McGilvery (www.celticfrogpublishing.com)

ISBN: 978-0-9959793-4-5

Dedication

Taking Til is dedicated to the memory of my Grandmother Kathleen Hilda Heartwell Jenkins Alston.

Chapter One

September 10, 1906, London, England

At times, Doctor Til Stone stared into the face of death and defeated it. Other times, like today, she welcomed death as an old friend. The young prostitute, dropped on the front step of her clinic in the night, was a victim of white slavery. She had bled to death from the complications of a botched abortion.

In the battle against white slavery—they were losing.

Til's heart ached at the extent of the damage. Frustration and defeat pulsed through her. Her lips thinned at the thought of filling in forms and bringing this to the attention of the police. She could raise a hue and cry about this, fill in paperwork to bring this travesty to light until her arms fell off, and it would do no good. By the time these girls ended up on Til's table, they were known prostitutes.

No chastity—no worth in the eyes of the court.

Lately, Scotland Yard had indicated they suspected these girls were dying from botched abortions performed in her clinic— a death sentence if they could connect her to this crime.

"This is the second one in two months." Shannon's jaw clenched.

"The police do nothing." Til's chest tightened as murky memories surrounding her own brush with white slavery surfaced, dragging up old terrors with it. The only thing to protect her that night had been Malcolm's fists.

Sitting down at her desk, Til rubbed between her eyes to alleviate some tension.

Shannon sat down across from her. "Is someone trying to implicate us in these crimes?"

"I believe so."

Shannon shook her head, "Who?"

"I wish I knew for sure. I have a lot of enemies, Shann." Fear tightened Til's throat as she thought about who might be behind these murders and who might hate her enough to implicate her and her clinic.

Pouring brandy into her cold tea so they could share it was an old custom. Til took a sip and then handed her the teacup.

"Cole will go mad; you here working on a murdered prostitute." Fear and contempt sharpened Til's tone.

"I can handle Cole." Shannon shot a warning look at Til.

Til knew this look. She had seen it often. A look that said she was not about to listen to any rants about her husband. Shannon had come back from Canada different. Tough. Equal. The gleam in her eye assured Til that she was a happily married woman who only knew happiness and love with Cole McDougall.

Maybe you can handle him for now, but what about when he demands more than you are willing to give? What about when he wants you to bend to his will? He will abuse his authority at some point. Every man does.

Til scrutinised Shannon for any evidence that she wasn't blissfully married. No matter how hard she looked, she failed to find anything wrong between Cole and Shannon. Recently, there was a glow about Shannon that made Til suspicious.

"Are you pregnant?" Til demanded.

"Til!" Shannon gasped. "You are outrageous!"

"Yes or no?"

"No, and I'll remind you we have an agreement. Mutual respect, remember? If I chose to have a child with Cole, I do not need your permission to do so." Shannon's eyes hardened.

"Have you decided about Brandon?" Til refused to be put in her place and pressed forward with her interrogation.

Shannon crossed her arms over her chest. "A position with Doctor White in Brandon, Manitoba, to run my own wing, a wing where I deal only with women's health, is a gift. I would be foolish to turn it down."

Til stiffened.

"I love you, I love what you have done for me, Til. We *do* want a family and we would prefer to raise them in Canada; new land, lots of cousins. You can understand that, can't you?" Shannon's eyes searched Til's for understanding. "These opportunities to run new wings of hospitals don't come around twice."

"If you get pregnant, you're vulnerable." Til tried and failed to take the fear out of her voice. "I raised you to *never* be vulnerable."

"I am with Cole," Shannon said simply. "Where a pregnancy and a baby may make me vulnerable, he will never let harm come to me."

"How do you know that?" Til leapt to her feet, turned her back on Shannon, and paced to the window. "I raised you to be strong and confident and..." Til turned to face her.

"You raised me," Shannon interrupted, "to have an utter distrust for men." Shannon stood and faced Til over her desk. "Malcolm raised me too and he is lovely. He taught me all that is good in men, and I found a man who loves and respects me. I wish you would see that. Cole could no more hurt me than he could fly to the moon. It's been two years. We're more in love now than ever."

"Love!" Til threw her hands in the air. "That's what all these women say. Queued up, wanting us to patch them up."

"Stop." Shannon shook her head. "Please, stop. I am done with this conversation. Babies and Brandon— we'll let you know."

Til pressed her hand to her heart at the thought of Shannon leaving.

"What happened to us?" Til asked Shannon.

"I grew up and you've had a two year temper tantrum about it." A grin tugged at Shannon's lip.

Til failed to stifle a grin. In moments, both women laughed out loud at the truth of that statement.

Finally, they stopped laughing, sipped more brandy and cold tea. Til placed her hand on her stomach, unsettled again.

"Are you all right?" Shannon's eyes swept over her aunt.

"My stomach is off and no wonder!" Til frowned. "Facing dead prostitutes first thing in the morning would put anyone off."

"I disagree with that diagnosis." Shannon sipped tea. "When were you planning to tell me you're pregnant, Til?"

Til looked at Shannon as if she had peeled off her blouse.

"What?" Til's stomach clenched. She pressed her hand to her mouth.

"Til. I know you, and I know a pregnant woman when I see one." Shannon's smile broke across her face like sunshine on a cloudy day.

Blood draining from her face, Til grabbed the calendar on her desk and started calculating. Her head snapped up and she looked at Shannon.

"I'm late," Til gasped. "I was so busy recruiting these new doctors I lost track of time! I thought I had just gone off eggs."

"We may need more doctors to step in while you are indisposed."

"Indisposed!" Til harrumphed. "I've never been indisposed in my life."

"You are pregnant, Til." Shannon smiled slyly. "This baby will change your life. Furthermore, you are Malcolm's wife. He will expect to have some input in how much you work, now that you are carrying his child."

"Input!" Til howled. "His child! What are you talking about? It is *my* body. I *have* to work." Til's breath caught in sheer terror. The thought of being dependent and then let down, returning to the slums, was her greatest fear. "You've taken leave of your senses."

"Never mind all that. You're going to be a mother." Shannon's smile of delight beamed at Til.

Icy fear raced over her as she thought about the whole ramification of this.

Forty! Pregnant!

Til knew she would need a team of servants, no, not a team —an army. Malcolm would be delighted, of course, but marriage and a child was his dream, not hers. Thoughts of how her life would change, of the vulnerability of being pregnant, bearing that child, and relying on Malcolm to make sure they had what they needed while she was 'indisposed' flicked across her face as she looked at Shannon.

"Til, you look as though you just bit into a lemon! This is good news! Congratulations! I wish you and Malcolm every happiness. You will be the worst mother in the world, but Malcolm will make up for it," Shannon teased her and moved to hug her aunt. "Remember Til, this baby won't be old enough to sign contracts for at least ten years. Of course, if you have a boy, he won't need to."

Til's mouth opened and then clamped shut. For the first time in this clinic she was speechless. "Don't say anything please. Let me tell Malcolm. It's so early I should wait."

"Do *not* wait!" Shannon reprimanded her. "He'll be delighted after all these years of waiting for you and this baby. I'm so thrilled! This is good news Til. I'm so happy for you." Shannon beamed at her.

"Don't get any ideas. You don't need to follow suit," Til snapped. "Don't put your career on hold yet."

"Til, you must learn to calm down and let things happen. I'll have a baby if I want one." Shannon patted her shoulder.

"Calm down! Let things happen!" Til sputtered in horror. "Thinking like that I would still be in the slums. I don't let things happen, Shannon, I make things happen. I never want to hear those words from you again. *Let things happen*." Til pointed her finger at Shannon, "Listen to me now, this is very important. Cole doesn't need to think he has a say about whether you have children or not. It changes your life, not his."

"I am pretty certain it would change both of our lives," Shannon dared to correct Til.

Til wasn't sure what to think of back-from-Canada Shannon. She had left timid and malleable. Now that she was home, licensed as a doctor and practicing medicine with her own qualifications, she often asserted herself and forced Til to look at life through new eyes.

Til disagreed with fervour.

"There is nothing to think about, Til. This is good news, and in our field, what we do here, we get precious little of it. I'm thrilled for you. Do you want a girl or a boy?" Shannon's smile lit up the examination room.

"I don't care. A girl of course!" Til sat down heavily. She picked up the newspaper and started fanning herself. "I can't even fathom this; honestly, I thought it couldn't happen."

Shannon patted her shoulder. "I'm thrilled. You and Malcolm need a baby. Your lives are too structured. This is the best news I've heard all day."

"Don't be daft," Til huffed. "Everyone needs a structured life! Otherwise, it's chaos. Come on. Back to work. Let's get this sorted." Til frowned as she double checked the calendar and then tossed it across the desk.

Two weeks late. How could I have missed that?

As the calendar dropped down beside the newspaper, Til's eyebrows drew together with concern. On the front page, the headlines screamed—Nora Blackburn missing.

God blind me, Nora Blackburn! Not Madeline Blackburn's niece! Oh, please no.

Til snatched the newspaper up off the desk. Her eyes raced over the article. East End... last seen on August 31st, 1906.

Crikey! She's been missing for almost three weeks!

Hands trembling, she put down the newspaper.

"Are you all right?" Shannon's eyebrows drew together in concern.

"Yes." Til tried and failed to shake off the worry about Nora Blackburn.

"Who's Nora Blackburn?" Shannon peered over Til's shoulder.

"Lady Harper's niece." Til's heart pounded in her throat.

This girl is no coincidence. This girl was sent for me. Only me...

"How awful! I must write to her at once." Shannon's brow furrowed worrying about her friend. "She must be frantic."

"I'll send a note as well." Til forced the words past the knot of fear that strangled her.

The last Blackburn that was very nearly abducted involved... stop! Don't think of it. It's in the past. It has to stay in the past.

Til straightened up and together they returned to the examination table and the poor, broken young woman who lay there. Shannon detailed the injuries while Til wrote them down.

"If you hadn't taken me, Til, I wonder where I would have ended up," Shannon murmured. She left her hand for the briefest of moments on the dead girl.

Til looked at her gorgeous niece and shuddered. Til knew exactly where she would have ended up and it made her sick that she had found only Shannon. Til lay awake at night wishing she could have saved her other siblings or their children. Her heart broke as she thought of her baby brother. Six months old the night she fled.

What had happened to Jimmy? An orphanage?

"Maybe the police will care about this girl and investigate." Shannon removed the girl's skirt to survey more of the damage. "The letter 'B' is branded on her left hip, like the other ones," Shannon said with the professional indifference of a doctor.

Til stopped writing, she moved to Shannon and looked at the brand for herself. Their eyes met and then they returned to the gruesome detailing of what this girl had endured.

"Can you think of who 'B' might be?" Shannon tilted her head to the side as she re-examined the brand. "Is this the work of the Bristol Butchers?"

"That would make the most sense." Til scrambled to think of ways to protect Shannon. "From now on, you'll have to have Cole escort you here. Until we know what this is all about. You'll need his protection."

"What about you?" Shannon's eyes widened in alarm.

"I'll talk to Malcolm and he'll walk with me. We must be very careful, Shannon, no risks." Fear pooled ice cold in the bottom of Til's stomach.

"Is this personal somehow?" Shannon's tone sharpened as she spoke, her head tilted to the side.

"There are things about my past, Shannon. Things I don't speak of." Til swallowed hard. Her eyes flicked over Shannon.

"Til, are you in danger?" Shannon's voice escalated with fear.

"I'm not exactly sure," Til lied smoothly.

Oh, Shannon! If I told you the whole story, it will look like I clawed to the top right over 'B'.

Chapter Two

September 10, 1906, Toronto Constabulary, Canada

Detective Sergeant Asher Grayson loosened his tie, then flung it across his cluttered office.

Sol Stein, his partner for the past two years, despised clutter and dramatics. Grayson's life was chock full of both.

"I'm not sure what the protocol is on expressing condolences on a divorce." Sol shook his head as he tried to tear his gaze away from the pile of dirty clothes in the corner of the office.

"No need for condolences. It was mutual, and it's done." Grayson pulled on a clean shirt and started to button it.

"What about Ella?" Sol frowned.

"Cora didn't tell you anything?" Grayson's eyebrow arched as he lifted his chin to fasten the top button on his shirt.

"Cora never breaks a confidence." Sol's eyes shone with pride whenever he talked about his beautiful wife, Canada's first female lawyer.

"I let her tell the judge that I was the one who committed adultery and that I abandoned her. As you know, both statements were lies." Grayson slid a tie around his neck.

"Why then?" Sol's tone indicated disapproval for lying to a judge.

"If we told the judge she had committed adultery it would destroy her reputation." Grayson adjusted the knot of his tie and pulled his collar down.

"She did commit adultery." Sol's head tilted in confusion.

"She did. However, I didn't want her reputation destroyed. She is raising Ella." Grayson tucked the tails of his shirt into his pants.

Sol's forehead furrowed. "You're the innocent party and she takes the baby. How does that sit with you?"

"I couldn't take a nursing baby from her mother, it's inhumane. I've seen the pain of a mother losing a child and I couldn't do that to Melinda. At any rate, I am not the innocent party," Grayson growled. "Melinda is like most normal women, she is extremely needy. She wanted a man that would be at her beck and call. I am not that man. She warned me, she begged me. I didn't listen. It's over. This divorce is essentially my fault. Not for the reasons we gave the judge, but because she wanted undivided attention and I had a job to do. So, we said abandonment because it was as close to the truth as we could get."

"I'm sorry to hear that." Sol's ears reddened with embarrassement. "I just assumed you would take Ella."

Grayson sighed as he pulled on his jacket and then sat down.

"What would I do with a nursing baby?" Grayson held out his hands in supplication.

Sol's ears deepened to purple with embarrassment.

Grayson cleared his throat and picked up a letter from the stack in front of him. "It's done, so on to the business of the day."

"Royce is out two months and already we have one girl branded with 'B' again." Sol leapt on the change of subject.

Grayson's eyes narrowed. "Just one?"

"Yes, one so far," Sol said ominously. "But, if Royce intends to pick up where Eli Pitman left off, there will be more."

Grayson leaned forward to reach for more correspondence. "Eli Pitman, I was hoping we were done with that name and that prostitution ring. Now that Royce is out, what about Adeline Pitman? Sorry, I mean Martin. Is she in any danger do you think?"

"Judge Martin has a man there as a butler who is actually his own private bodyguard. She thought he might be overreacting. I don't think he is." Sol crossed his arms over his chest.

"Any husband would take those precautions with his wife," Grayson agreed. "Honestly, Stein, I still shake my head in amazement at how Cora took Eli Pitman down. A woman lawyer having Eli Pitman hanged for his crimes, I still can't believe it."

"She is incredible." Sol nodded his agreement.

"Good thing she has you to keep her alive; she tends to make powerful enemies." Grayson picked up a letter opener and sliced open an envelope, skimmed it and tossed it to the far corner of his desk.

"I don't let her out of my sight, and I think my reputation precedes me," Sol said.

Grayson nodded in agreement. "It does for sure. You've heard I am on the first ship east?"

"I have. I am your replacement while you're in London." Sol leaned forward.

"Good. Lady Blackburn has hired me to find her granddaughter, Nora Blackburn. I rank higher than the Superintendent and so he is to work with me and give me any assistance I need. The police there have paperwork regarding dead prostitutes dying of botched abortions connected to a woman's clinic. It is run by a doctor, a woman doctor..." Grayson opened a file on his desk. "Yes, here it is. Her name is Til Stone."

Sol paced over to the window and scanned the street. "That is unusual isn't it?"

"As soon as I have spoken to Lady Blackburn, I intend to bring her in for questioning." Grayson's eyes narrowed as he skimmed through the file regarding Til Stone.

"What does that have to do with the prostitutes here?" Sol turned back to speak to Grayson.

"Same brand of 'B' according to the reports she has filed." Grayson's jaw clenched as he looked over the medical examiners' reports at the extent of damage the girls had suffered.

Sol and Grayson's eyes met over the open file.

"You think Royce is somehow connected to this doctor in England? That seems very unusual."

"All I know is that the Blackburns have had a brush with kidnapping in the past. It was all hushed and swept under the rug. They had two maids, Odelia Shipley and Matilda Bertram, who were caught up in it. Is Til Stone Matilda Bertram? Is the 'B' that is branded on these poor children 'B' for Bertram?" Grayson crossed his arms over his chest. "I can't find anything out and the police there are uncooperative. It is the brand that connects everything. So, I'll interrogate Doctor Til Stone. You find Royce and figure out where he's operating. No question in my mind he's picked up Eli's old ring. While you're doing that, make sure Cora, Adeline, and Hope House are protected. Assign extra men if you need to."

"You know nothing about her? There is no record of Til Stone?" Sol frowned.

"It seems like she was hatched out of an egg. Absolutely no background information on her *at all*. She lands on the scene at the London Royal Free School of Medicine for Women."

Sol's eyebrow arched in disbelief. "Really?"

"Apparently, she was so brilliant, a women's group, this National Union of Women's Suffrage Society got a hold of her and sponsored her through to be a doctor. Powerful group of women, I say."

Sol sighed.

"Exactly." Grayson took a deep breath to steady his nerves. "I'm not sure I have the fortitude to deal with another powerful group of women."

"It's your turn," Sol said dryly.

"Once she was a doctor, she went further to be a surgeon." Grayson resumed reading from the file. "She is active in the Women's Social and Political Union but not a big role."

"Hmm. Why is she sending in paperwork that could possibly implicate her? She could falsify documents and hide the truth," Sol asked. "That would be typical in a situation like this. She faces a death sentence if they can prove she botched these abortions."

"Or it's the perfect cover." Grayson rubbed tension from between his eyebrows. "She can claim she had nothing to do with this and went so far as to try to involve the police. The police are corrupt. I have no doubt. She likely knows this too. At any rate, I intend to find out. If Doctor Til Stone is trading in girls, I *will* destroy her."

"Just remember. She is innocent until proven guilty. Keep a cool head." Sol shot Grayson a hard look.

"About that." Grayson straightened his shoulders and closed the file on his desk. "I want to apologise for my actions last week. I really thought..." Grayson stopped speaking to gather his thoughts. "I thought I saw Katherine, which is ridiculous. She was stolen so many years ago. The girl on the dock looked so much like her, I lost my head." Embarrassed, Grayson cleared his throat. "It won't happen again."

Sol shrugged. "No need to apologise. It's done. It's a terrible thing, losing a sibling."

"She was stolen on a Thursday." Grayson crossed his arms over his chest. "I didn't walk with her; I wanted to play baseball with my friends. It was twenty-five years ago." Grayson shook his head. "Every day, I think if I had been there, would they have taken her? Could I have protected her? It never goes away. Wondering where she is, what happened to her. It tears me apart. Just heading this department to take down white slavers doesn't seem like enough."

"It's the best you can do," Sol said simply.

"I can't find Katherine, but I might be able to alleviate the suffering of Nora Blackburn. They may have taken other girls too. How many girls can I save if I *break* Til on the first day?" Grayson asked Sol.

Sol stood up and faced him across the desk. "Let me know how I can help. As soon as I track down Royce, I'll be in touch."

***

The next day, rain pelted the grey streets as Grayson made his way to the docks. After he bought his ticket to London, he sat down to wait for the ship to board. He looked over the crowd waiting to board the ship. Melinda stood awkwardly at the entrance to the ship station. He frowned and made his way to her side through the crowd of people.

"Can we speak before you go?" Melinda shifted Ella in her arms.

"Of course. I have half an hour before I have to board." Grayson led her to the corner of the room. Melinda settled down with sleeping Ella in her arms. He sat across from her and glanced at his pocket watch. Hurt clouded her eyes. Guilt made him feel hot and cold.

How many times have I looked at my pocket watch instead of her?

"I'm sorry about the lies." Melinda fidgeted with Ella's blanket. "I am so sorry that everything had to end that way." She fought back tears. "I am sick that I had to lie to a judge and accuse you of adultery. I couldn't sleep through the night; my conscience was bothering me so much. I just had to apologise one more time, before you go. Asher, I'm very sorry."

The lying bothers you but not the adultery?

Grayson's chest tightened in anger. He took a deep breath before he spoke. "I'm sorry too." He refused to hurt her further.

I am devastated that you are walking away with my baby daughter.

"I came here to beg you to stay." A tear slipped down Melinda's cheek. "I have a bad feeling about you leaving. You always bury yourself in work when you are hurt... I think..."

Grayson stood up. "It's done." He cut her off.

"Nora," Melinda said flatly.

"Nora," Grayson confirmed.

"If that's the case, and you *are* going, we didn't discuss terms. I think it would be best if you didn't come back and expect to be her... father." Melinda's face crumpled.

Grayson's jaw tightened in fury. "She's my daughter. I could take her today and not a court in the land would stop me. The law says she's mine."

"Until she needs to be fed and then the law of nature says she's mine." Melinda's eyes filled with tears.

Grayson grit his teeth. The pain of walking away from Ella, of leaving her behind, stabbed through his heart.

Melinda dashed tears away that slid down her cheek. "Babies need attention more often than fifteen minutes every three days."

His hard, dark grey eyes met her hurt blue ones.

"I could come back and pretend to be her uncle." Grayson scrambled to try to find a solution to this situation that would let him see his precious daughter and still find Nora Blackburn.

"I'll think about it. I'll see how Archie feels about that." Melinda pressed a handkerchief to her lips.

"Archie doesn't have an opinion on our child, Melinda," Grayson growled at her.

"He'll be raising her, Asher." Melinda's eyes flashed in fury. "He'll have lots of opinions in the years ahead. He's a good man. She's going to be a happy little girl. She already is. But, lately he's been talking about leaving Canada and relocating to Baltimore. He has family there; however, we're still just talking. It depends on the scandal I face from this divorce. His family is very religious..." Her voice trailed off.

He's talking but you'll end up doing whatever he wants. You won't have a choice.

The pain of his baby daughter being brought up in another man's house, where he would never see her, nearly took him to his knees. Torn between finding Nora Blackburn and walking away from Ella gutted him.

"I begged you to come home and be a husband and father and you wouldn't," she reminded him, as if she knew exactly what he was thinking about.

"Melinda, it's over." Grayson scrubbed his hands over his face.

"Even if you find Nora, even if you do the impossible and find her, it won't bring *her* back you know." Melinda's words of truth bit into him. "Katherine is gone, and I see how your guilt is killing you and driving you to do things you shouldn't."

Fury roared through him at her simple statement. Grayson dropped his hands from his face and looked at Melinda in disbelief.

"I will look for her until the day I die." He could barely get the words past the tight fist of emotion in his throat.

"She's gone," Melinda said as her eyes filled with tears for him. "Ash, she's destroying your life. You must get through this. You have to *stop looking*. It's over Asher. Finding Nora won't bring her back."

Grayson's knuckles were white as he strangled the hard back of the chair instead of her. He towered over her as he spoke. "If you were a man, saying such a thing to me, I would pound the life out of you."

Pain and suffering flashed across her eyes. He backed off. Intimidating Melinda wouldn't help anything. He didn't want to hurt her. This had gone on way too long as it was.

"I am not a man." More tears spilled out of Melinda's eyes and he cursed himself under his breath.

"I'm sorry, Mel, I shouldn't have said that to you. I am very sorry." Grayson sat down.

She waved her hand at the apology, indicating she was ready to move forward. "The only thing we're good at is hurting each other."

"We were good at a few other things." Grayson's eyebrows raised suggestively.

Melinda frowned at him. "That doesn't matter now. I want to say this to you." Melinda stood up.

He had to tilt his head back to look at her. It was an odd feeling because Grayson was over six feet and couldn't remember the last time he had to tilt his head back to look anyone in the eye. She faced him without fear because he had on occasion raised his voice to her but never his hand.

"Let her go." Melinda trembled as she spoke. "Promise me. You will *let Katherine go*. This obsession is destroying you and any happiness you could ever have. Her absence ripped us apart and you are losing your daughter trying to find her. You have to stop," Melinda begged him.

"I will never stop," Grayson whispered. "I can't stop Mel. I just can't."

Melinda took a step back. "Then I should say good bye, Asher Grayson."

Grayson stood up, tried to clear the emotion from his throat. "Good bye, Melinda."

Grayson wanted to take Ella in his arms one last time. Melinda, with one final act of kindness, handed him Ella. He turned away from her and walked to the windows that looked out over the harbour to have a moment of privacy with his baby daughter. His eyes filled with tears as he kissed Ella's perfect cheek. His beautiful blonde- haired, blue- eyed daughter, who was already the spitting image of Melinda, blinked at him. He cradled her against his chest.

He breathed in her scent until she started to fuss. He wiped his tears on the baby blanket and turned to hand her back to Melinda.

Melinda took Ella into her arms.

"When you get home, maybe we can talk about you being an uncle."

"That would be the best, I appreciate that." Grayson grit his teeth at the thought of another man making decisions that impacted him and his relationship with Ella.

Melinda's gaze flicked up to his and then away. "I will check with Archie, but I think, in this world, a girl can't have enough men to protect her."

"Thank you." Grayson's voice was husky with sadness as he dropped his empty arms to his side. "If you need me Melinda, I'll be there for you in a second. If Archie turns out to be mean or if you ever feel unsafe, I am a telegram away. While I'm in England if anything happens, contact Sol."

"Archie is a good man." Melinda bristled defensively as she cradled Ella against her. Ella calmed down in her mother's arms. "I hope you have a safe trip and think about what I said."

"I'll think about what you said." Grayson adjusted the baby blanket around Ella's face.

"Liar." Melinda's lips trembled with sadness.

Grayson left one last kiss on Ella's cheek and one on Melinda's. Her eyes met his before he turned from her and boarded the ship with the salty taste of Melinda's tears on his lips.

Chapter Three

Seething, Odelia Shipley Bristol entered the back room of her brothel, 32 Blue Street, London. She squared her shoulders as she opened the door to confront Andy Bristol, new head of the Bristol Butchers. He sat in Bobby's chair, Alys right beside him, in Odelia's chair.

The loss of power shook Odelia to the core. Her chest tightened, her eyes narrowed. Alys, in Andy's bed, held all the power over the women, over Odelia herself. Odelia's nails bit into her palms at the thought. Her power was gone; she would never get it back. Not now.

This is my brothel! How dare you!

Beautiful and deadly, Alys's glittery green eyes swept over Odelia. She smirked.

"Where were your men?" Odelia ignored Alys. She directed her comment to Andy. "Mol was arrested this afternoon."

Alys leaned over and whispered into Andy's ear. He chuckled and put his hand on her thigh. He whispered something back. His hand moved up.

Odelia knew what it felt like to have a man as powerful as Andy Bristol run his hand up her thigh. She knew the power he wielded and the force behind that touch. Power and force that would be at Alys's disposal now. Odelia's heart pounded with fury and frustration as the position of superiority she enjoyed as wife of Bobby Bristol crashed and burned all around her. Andy was the new head of the gang, but the women would answer to this Alys. This viper dressed as a strumpet. She didn't even *try* to look respectable. She was nearing forty but didn't look a day over thirty. Alys licked her lips like the cat that got the cream as her eyes travelled the length of Andy. His hand moved up higher; Odelia cleared her throat.

"Arrested?" Andy dragged his attention from Alys to face Odelia.

"Yes, arrested." Odelia tried not to hiss at him; she failed.

"You want your girls protected, you pay for that protection." Andy shot Odelia a hard look.

"What?" Blood drained from Odelia's face. "We're family."

"No, we're not." Alys corrected her as she trailed her fingertips down Andy's forearm.

Andy, distracted, turned from Odelia back to Alys.

"Bobby's dead." Alys tilted her head, kept her eyes on Andy as she adjusted a necklace that nestled between her breasts. Like a crow distracted by the shine of gold, Andy's gaze was dragged to the necklace and the décolletage that it rested on.

Alys turned her attention to Odelia. "You're nothing now. You pay like everyone else."

"How much to hire muscle?" Odelia fought the bile that rose in her throat at this disgusting display of power that Alys rubbed her face in. This posturing was Alys's way of letting Odelia know she had been replaced. Not just replaced—defeated.

Andy pressed his lips to Alys's neck and dragged himself away from her. He gave Odelia an exorbitant number for his protection. Her current prostitution ring could never come up with that number, not under any circumstance.

"I can't, it's too much." Odelia could barely form the words.

Andy shrugged. "Three squares in jail."

"You'd never—" Odelia gasped as she pressed her hand to her heart. As if the pain of losing Bobby wasn't enough. To lose everything she had worked for, in one fell swoop, devastated her.

Andy turned his attention back to Alys, effectively dismissing Odelia. "Alys." He nodded in the direction of the stairs that led to their bedroom. "Upstairs."

"Be right there, love." Alys smiled suggestively.

Andy left the women alone in the back room where deals were made, lives were ended, and money was lost or taken.

"Odelia." Alys's voice hardened to flint as she faced her rival. "No man, no protection, facing jail."

Odelia grit her teeth as she heard the contempt in Alys's voice. She wanted some grovelling. Odelia tried and failed to swallow her pride. Not trusting herself to speak, she waited for the attack.

"Funny isn't it? You bought and sold me, when you were at the top of the pile, and now I have the power to do the same to you." Alys tilted her head as she drove home the point. "You're done now."

Odelia could barely swallow the bile that rose in her throat as Alys circled her like a shark; a beautiful, vicious, hungry shark.

"I never should have..."

"Shut it. I don't want to hear your lies or your sniveling. You will work for me." Alys spoke smoothly. "I don't want to watch my back. I need you out of London."

"Out of London!" Odelia's breath caught in her throat.

"Royce is finally out of prison. He needs a shipment and a fresh face to run his ring, someone the Toronto police don't know."

"What will he want in return?" Odelia swallowed hard, terrified of the answer. Royce was well known as a brutal man, a known rapist, an assassin — merciless. Reports from Toronto had reached his family all the way back in London. He hadn't mellowed with age. If anything, now that he was going to run the Pitman prostitution ring, he had exorbitant demands of double the girls and younger.

Odelia shuddered at the thought of the price she would pay for his protection. The very idea of sharing Royce's bed made her shake in fear.

"You take a shipment over, I send the girls to you; you place them in brothels and collect the money," Alys instructed.

"What will he want from me then?" Odelia's voice dipped low with fear.

"He has a woman." Alys smirked.

Odelia nearly wept with relief.

"Now, if you're smart, you'll take her place." Alys moved to the stairway.

Odelia shivered at the thought. "Why isn't his own woman running the ring?"

Alys turned back and rolled her eyes. "She's too young, can't be trusted."

"Is that all?" Odelia longed to grip the back of the chair but didn't want to look weak. She swayed with worry because Royce would want more than that. There would be a catch.

"He wants ten thousand pounds, and Til Stone." Alys's eyes glittered with triumph as she spoke the words.

"What?" Odelia's head snapped up.

"You heard me." Alys's hard green eyes watched Odelia, "Unfinished business, he says."

Odelia stiffened in outrage. "How do I get Til Stone to Royce with ten thousand pounds?"

Andy Bristol shouted down the stairs at Alys. She jumped to comply. Andy owned Alys and with a sinking feeling, Odelia knew, she would go from the ownership of Bobby to the ownership of Royce. At this point, there was no choice, no other option.

"She'll want Nora Blackburn to be returned safely I think." Alys tossed her hair back and lifted her chin. "A ransom note will instruct Til to deliver the money to Royce in Toronto."

"That's madness," Odelia gasped. "Til won't do it; she doesn't care about the Blackburns."

A slight tick jumped in Alys's eyelid. "She'll care."

"She's a toff," Odelia hissed. "She won't..."

"You do as I say or take your chances on the streets." Alys jabbed her finger into Odelia's face. "Sound familiar? Same options you gave me, when I was fifteen years old."

Odelia swallowed hard.

"With no Bristols to protect you." Alys's eyes narrowed into green slits of rage. "Decide. I have to get up those stairs."

Odelia straightened up. Her chest tightened with fear as, she knew with every certainty, she was looking into the eyes of a cold-hearted killer. Alys would kill anyone who stood in her way. If Odelia didn't take this chance, she'd be dead too.

"What do I do?" Odelia finally gave up her pretence of strength and grasped the hard back of the chair to hold herself up.

"Tomorrow night, meet me here when we have more time." Alys held her hand out.

Odelia looked at her open hand, confused.

"Give me your key," Alys demanded.

"This brothel is mine. It was a gift from Bobby." The blood drained from Odelia's face.

"Mine now." Alys's jaw clenched. "A gift from Andy, the new head of the Bristol Butchers."

"Bobby gave this to me," Odelia repeated as if it would matter what a dead man gave his wife.

Alys shrugged. "Bobby's dead. It's mine now. It doesn't matter."

It will always matter.

Odelia produced a key from inside her corset. Her hand shook as she handed it to Alys.

Alys turned on her heel and raced up the stairs to Andy without a backward glance.

Odelia's eyes slid over the empty chair Bobby used to reign from. She remembered a time when she could lean over and whisper suggestions in his ear and he would agree. He ran the gang, but she could turn him. She mourned the loss of him and the end of her power. Tonight, she realised, her mourning period had to come to an end.

Odelia rested her forehead on the table. She didn't cry. There was no time for weakness. She needed to think, not feel, even though her heart ached at the thought that this place was no longer hers and never really had been.

Slowly, the thought of leaving her memories here in London to run a new ring started to lift her spirits. The idea of a new gang and a powerful man at her disposal started to slip around her mind. Eli Pitman's old ring was being revived and why not be part of that? Royce wanted her to run the prostitution ring but didn't want her in his bed. Tension eased out of her shoulders as she thought about that. She wouldn't have the same amount of power if she wasn't his woman, but some power was better than no power. Toronto, a whole ocean away from Alys, opened up new opportunities. Odelia had scrambled to the top before, she could do it again.

Chapter Four

Rain drummed gently on the windows of Malcolm and Til's dining room. Flames danced on top of the candles and flooded the room with soft light. Til examined the silverware for spots. She ran her house like she ran her clinic, scrupulously clean.

Til frowned at a piece of paper that peeked out of a drawer of the sideboard. She pulled the drawer open to tuck the newspaper away; the headlines caught her eye. Bobby Bristol — shot dead. The report detailed gruesome facts about derringers and broad daylight.

Memories of the Bristol brothers caused bile to rise in her throat. She swallowed hard. Hands shaking with fear, she folded the newspaper and tucked it away.

Nora Blackburn missing, three dead prostitutes branded with 'B' in her clinic, and Bobby Bristol dead. Til's blood ran cold at the thought of one of these events, but all three — no coincidence. How long before she and Malcolm would be in danger? She bit her lip in fear.

You are not thinking about this tonight.

Tonight was for them, to celebrate this baby. Shannon had been right; she needed to share this news with Malcolm as soon as possible. Plans needed to be made, staff hired sooner rather than later.

Til studied her reflection in the mirror, pleased at the effect. Soft light illuminated the copper and gold of her hair. She had purchased a new gown of gold and cream silk chiffon, heavily embroidered and crusted with glittering stones, far too extravagant. She had removed her corset so that the gown was too revealing to wear anywhere but their own dining room.

Til poured brandy for Malcolm and then placed a gift box on his gleaming white, gold rimmed dinner plate. Her hand hesitated for a moment as she caressed the gold trim on the plate. Some days it was impossible to believe how far they had removed themselves from the slums. Years of hard work had paid off. Tonight was a celebration of all they had achieved and all they looked forward to in the future.

Malcolm cleared his throat and leaned against the door frame. Til looked up at him in the dim light. He took her breath away, still, after all these years. A tall and broad man, he nearly filled the doorway.

"What's all this then?" Malcolm's face lit up as his eyes travelled the length of her.

"I have something for you." Til smiled as she ignored the nagging concern in the back of her mind in case it was too soon, and she lost this baby too. She refused to dwell on the times her body failed her.

Malcolm crossed the room and took the little gift box from her hand. He tilted his head in confusion as he opened the box.

"Remember you pointed these cufflinks out because you thought the amber stone was the same colour as my eyes?" Til bit her lip.

"I remember." Malcolm took his cufflinks out of his shirt and was about to replace them when Til laid a hand on his forearm.

"Wait, I had them engraved."

Malcolm examined them. "August 26, 1906. What does that mean?"

Til leaned close and whispered against his neck, "That is the night we conceived this baby."

"Baby!" Malcolm's eyes widened in surprise and then misted with unshed tears.

"Yes, baby." Til slid her arms up around his neck.

Malcolm gathered her against him. "Til! Are you sure? Are you well?"

"I'm well," Til assured him.

Malcolm kissed her until she was breathless.

"I have something for you." He kissed her one last time and then pulled away.

"Did Shannon tell you?" Til couldn't keep the disappointment out of her voice.

"No, she didn't." Malcolm went to the safe in the wall and opened it; he pulled out a folded piece of paper. "I bought this for you a few years ago and I've been waiting for this occasion to give it to you."

Til noticed he tactfully didn't mention that he had purchased this the last time she conceived.

She carefully opened the envelope and pulled out a deed.

"What is this?" Her eyes searched his.

"Read it." Malcolm encouraged her.

"I don't understand." Til's eyebrows drew together in confusion. "This looks like a deed to a house."

"The cottage, by the sea, you love it there; I purchased it the year we went, after you were released from prison, to give to you. I wanted us to have summers at the sea with our babies."

Happiness bloomed in Til's heart as Malcolm spoke.

"Malcolm!" Til's eyes glittered with tears. "I don't know what to say. We've gone every summer and you didn't tell me it was our own property!"

"You're giving me a baby; I'm giving you a measly cottage. I'd say I'm getting the better deal." Malcolm grinned, "When is our baby due?"

"May." Til smiled. Malcolm's excitement was contagious. Slowly, fear about being a new mother at her age started to let go of her heart.

"We'll go to the cottage for the summer." Malcolm's arms tightened around her.

"A whole summer!" Til sputtered. "What about my clinic and your work?"

"Til," Malcolm sighed. "We've worked our whole lives to get to this point, year in, year out. The summer of 1907 is going to be for us. You have hired two new doctors and even if Shannon and Cole decide to go to Canada, your new doctors can run your clinic in your absence. I am going to take some leave from the firm and if there is any problem with that, I'll quit and start my own firm in the autumn."

"I don't know. Not working is terrifying." Til bit her lip.

Malcolm caressed her cheek with his fingertips before he cradled her jaw with his hand and kissed her again. "We're not going back to the slums. We can take a summer off and enjoy the baby, and all this work, it'll wait for us."

"I'm frightened of poverty, you know that." Til shuddered in his arms.

"It will never happen. I promise." He kissed her again as if sealing a vow.

Til molded against him.

"As of today, I want your work days cut in half. These twelve-hour days and six days a week are over." Malcolm's arms tightened around her.

Til bristled.

"Don't," Malcolm warned. "This is my child."

"This is *our* child." Til tried to draw away.

Malcolm didn't allow it. "Let me say this." Malcolm held her by the upper arms. "You're not twenty. You're forty. A healthy forty, but forty. I want you to take care of yourself and not be over extended. No more early mornings or late nights."

Til's eyes narrowed. "That should be my decision, Malcolm."

"I held you when you lost the last two pregnancies." Malcolm refused to budge. "I want your word; you'll stop when you're tired."

"I'll think about it," Til relented. Her memories of losing those two babies were fresh in her mind.

Malcolm let her go so he could place his hand over her still flat womb. "This baby is a gift, a blessing. I want you to enjoy this pregnancy and enjoy being a mother. You deserve this happiness, Til. Don't think of this as giving up work, think of this as shifting into different work. You don't have to worry about money. You've given the women's rights movement, including the birth control movement, twenty years; your best years. It's time for us now. It's time to have a healthy pregnancy. Please promise me you will be careful. I would forbid you to work if I thought for a second you wouldn't pull out one of your many contracts and take me to court," Malcolm teased her.

"I'll restructure my staff." Til conceded as she placed her hand over his. "I'll get this sorted, tomorrow."

"Good."

"In the meantime, I was hoping we could celebrate this good news instead of you being heavy handed," Til huffed.

"In our usual fashion?" Malcolm's eyebrows shot up.

"Of course." Til loosened his tie.

"It's safe?"

Til tossed his tie into the corner of the dining room. Malcolm detangled from her embrace and quickly locked the dining room door.

"You're sure?" He turned back to look at her.

"Absolutely." Til smiled at Malcolm before she pounced.

***

The maid brought breakfast to Til in bed.

Malcolm shot his new cufflinks through the cuffs of his shirt.

Til, pale on the bed, waved her breakfast away. The maid gave Malcolm a concerned look. He inclined his head to the door indicating they needed some privacy.

He sat down on the bed beside Til. He tenderly wiped her face with a cool cloth and then took her hand in his.

"You look peaky; you should stay in bed today." Malcolm wiped her forehead again.

"I have a clinic to run," Til moaned in frustration.

"Shannon will take over." Malcolm smoothed the hair back from her forehead.

"Shannon is abandoning me for Brandon, Manitoba; probably pressured by Cole," Til said waspishly.

Malcolm sidestepped this rant as he had a stack of clients waiting; he needed to get going.

"I'll be late tonight. You are not to wait up. I am going to find out why those prostitutes are branded with 'B' and being dumped at your clinic."

"No, you are not." Til protested weakly from the bed.

"I am hiring more security." Malcolm ignored her. "I think Cole should quit work as a constable and work in the clinic to ensure Shannon's safety and indeed your own."

Til's stomach rolled. She curled into an unhappy, nauseous ball on their bed.

"Probably a good idea to have Cole at the clinic," Til grudgingly agreed. This pregnancy, particularly early morning, was sapping her strength.

"I'm sending Shannon a telegram that you are indisposed. I will ask her to come today, do an assessment and you can tell her how the staff needs to be restructured. Think about hiring another doctor to take over your patients. No need to have the clinic short staffed. Then you just work as you feel able."

"You're very high handed this morning." Til's eyes flashed with anger. Frustrated, she tried to sit up, but her stomach clenched and demanded that she lay back down.

"Til, I've known you since that night... that terrible night and I have loved you since that night. All these years, I've watched you run yourself into the ground. Women's rights, contraception, chloroform in childbirth, the list goes on. Crikey! Now, hear me. While you were only wearing yourself down, that was up to you." Malcolm leaned forward, placing a very large, hard hand on her abdomen. "This is *my* baby. So, you *will* restructure the clinic today. You *will* work half the hours and you will rest. I mean it." Malcolm kissed her on the forehead. "You demand too much, you work too hard. Stay in this bed until you are really feeling well enough and then read a book by the fireplace."

"Lay in bed and read. That is a recipe for poverty!" Til howled from the depth of the pillow.

"My baby, my rules," Malcolm demanded.

"My body!" Til crowed at him.

"That belongs to me too." Malcolm pressed his lips to her forehead, her cheekbone and then her neck. "According to the law."

"A law that needs to change!" Til pushed him away and heaved into the chamber pot.

Malcolm's eyes softened with sympathy as she finally stopped vomiting and lay back down on the bed. Weak, white and spent.

"The thing is, Til, the laws of nature are not something you can protest and change. You are a woman and as such, you need special consideration from time to time."

Til rolled her eyes in defiance. "I've spent my entire life fighting that."

"This time, this pregnancy demands that you are cared for." Malcolm wiped her chin with his handkerchief.

"What are you on about?" Til huffed. She reached for the chamber pot again. Finally, she handed it to Malcolm, laid down and pulled a pillow over her head.

"Exibit A," Malcolm said dryly. "You're a pregnant woman and pregnant women need to stay in bed and rest sometimes."

"Weak women, women who contribute nothing to society!" Til raged into the pillow.

"No, not weak women! Women who are doing the most noble job of all." Malcolm pulled the pillow away and smiled down at her. "Motherhood," Malcolm said reverently. He grinned as his words provoked her, set her off.

"Motherhood is not the most noble job!" Til hissed at Malcolm. "It is not!"

"Til, it's what you are put here to do," Malcolm said solemnly.

"I am warning you, Malcolm." Til pointed a finger at him.

"Stop fighting, Til. It's time to stop measuring yourself against men." Malcolm adjusted the pillow behind her head. "You are a forty-year-old pregnant woman."

"Malcolm! Stop saying that like I'm some sort of fossil!" Til struggled away from him.

"Don't ruin this for me. I've been waiting for this baby for a long time. The thought of a pregnant wife that I get to spoil is a highlight of life. I want you to love every minute. You are pregnant, that must be *so* exciting. You get to know this baby before I get to. Enjoy this." Malcolm kissed her cheek.

"You're daft." Til sat up. Her body betrayed her; she had no strength left to fight. She furiously accepted it as he piled pillows behind her back. "I can't stay home. I can't stop work. I can't bear this. I'll be in slum housing by the end of the week."

"I know you're afraid, Til. So, let me make this very clear." Malcolm tucked her in. He took her hand in his and gave her a long hard look. The teasing portion of their discussion was over.

"Stop talking to me as if I were a two-year-old having a temper tantrum," Til hissed at him. "I hate when you look at me like that."

"Stop acting like a two-year-old having a temper tantrum, then." Malcolm squeezed her hand in his. "You are vulnerable right now, and I know that makes you terrified. I know you. I know that you are just scared. I gave you that cottage for a reason. A place for you to take yourself and the baby to escape the memories here. I am *happy* to work. You're not going to end up back in the slums if you take a day off. I would never let that happen." Malcolm stroked Til's face as she started to soften. "You don't need contracts to protect yourself from me and you know it. I love you." Malcolm leaned forward and kissed her gently. "You try me, but I do love you. So, have a good rest, old thing, and try to enjoy this."

Til's eyes glittered with unshed tears. "You remember, how bad it was and how hard..."

"It's never going to happen again." Malcolm pulled the covers over her. "Ever. I'd sign contracts if you like. I have money set aside for this very occasion. You never have to work another day of your life unless you chose to. If you want to devote every second to this baby, you can."

Til pressed her face into the pillow. "I've come too far. I can't stop now... the women's rights movement..."

"They'll plod on without you for now." Malcolm adjusted the covers across her shoulders.

Til's eyes filled with tears. "I have always worked and yet, I am terrified to lose this baby."

Malcolm pressed his lips to her cheek. "You won't, but maybe I should stay home and look after you."

"Both of us staying home, laying in bed! Are you incurable?" Til gasped. "Go to work. Someone needs to work while I'm laying here completely useless. Send Shannon and make sure Cole comes with her. I'll be fine."

"Get a good rest. If you need anything at all, send me a telegram." Malcolm opened the door and turned back to look at Til. "I love you."

"I love you too." Til curled around a pillow. "Malcolm, promise me you will not go to the Bristols."

"I need to know why they are dumping dead prostitutes at your clinic. If Bobby Bristol is dead, there is a new boss..." Malcolm's jaw clenched in worry.

"It's more than that." Til's stomach finally let her sit up, her voice edged in fear. "Nora Blackburn is missing."

"Nora Blackburn is missing?" Malcolm echoed Til's statement. "Prostitutes are being dropped at your clinic that are branded with 'B'..."

"Bobby Bristol is dead." Til's face fell.

Malcolm's breath caught. "That means... you've lost—"

"I can't even think about that." Til cut him off as fear curled around her heart like a vice.

"It could be..." Malcolm's voice trailed off. He stopped talking as Til's face paled with fear.

"All that happened years ago, Malcolm." Til tried to sound brave.

"I'll get to the bottom of this! Today." Malcolm straightened up.

"Don't you dare. You're not twenty anymore, Malcolm," Til warned him as her stomach churned from the baby or the fear, she wasn't sure which. "Leave it to the bobbies. Please."

"No need to worry." Malcolm grit his teeth, a muscle jumped in his jaw. "Have a good rest. Put this out of your mind. I'll handle this... Oh! Wait!" Malcolm came back to the bed, he opened Til's robe. Her eyes widened as he pulled her nightgown aside and he pressed his lips to her abdomen. "Bye baby. I'll be home late tonight. I love you."

"Malcolm, it's a speck. A speck that doesn't have ears yet!" Til ran her hands through his hair as he kissed her abdomen again and she smiled at him fondly.

"Yes, but it's *my* speck and I want this speck to know that I absolutely love him or her already."

Til's heart softened. "I love you." Til pulled him down to kiss her one last time before he left for work.

"I love you more." Malcolm smiled down at her and kissed her hard.

Til smiled at him as he finally tore himself away.

Chapter Five

Rain slicked the cobblestones of London when Grayson made his way off the ship. He took a hackney cab to his apartment on Malborough Street, right across from Doctor Til Stone's clinic. After dumping his luggage, he rushed to the police station at King's Cross. As the driver slapped the reins down, Grayson laid his head back and tried to ease the tension in his shoulders. He wished he had slept better the night before. Rubbing his eyes, he checked his pocket watch; it was not even nine a.m. yet. His mind ticked through all the things he wanted to accomplish today.

The reception at the King's Cross Police Station was as frosty as he expected. He ended the introductions early by asking where his office was. The other constables, unhappy that a detective sergeant from Canada had been called in, were brisk and cool. Grudgingly, they showed him to an office and stood by for instruction.

"Can you bring me up to speed with what your constables have found out regarding Nora Blackburn?" Grayson asked the men assembled in his office.

Superintendent Graves took a deep sip of tea. He slowly and carefully placed his teacup back on its saucer.

Hot impatience snaked through Grayson. They had a missing girl to find and they were treating the disappearance of Nora Blackburn as if she were a missing golf club.

Constables Lark and Hugh shifted in their chairs and waited for their superior to speak.

"All we know is Nora Blackburn was last seen on Blue Street. There is a brothel there, 32 Blue is the name of the establishment."

"Who owns the brothel?" Grayson wrote down the address and underlined the word brothel.

"It is run by the Bristol Butchers."

"Sounds ominous." Grayson watched Graves for a sign of concern, nothing showed on his face. The lack of affect concerned Grayson straight away.

"The Butchers are in the midst of a shuffle." Graves sighed heavily. "Bobby Bristol was gunned down recently; it looks as though the dust hasn't settled yet, ghastly business." Graves shook his head. "The gang is restructuring; we expect his brother, Andy Bristol, is taking over as head of the Butchers."

Grayson's eyes swept over the evidence in front of him. He picked up a letter.

"That was sent by Lady Blackburn two days ago. She addressed it to you; we didn't open it."

Grayson looked at them in open disdain.

A young girl's life is at stake and a piece of evidence landed on their desk and they didn't open it!

He slid his finger under the envelope flap and carefully opened it.

"This is a ransom note." Grayson's eyes narrowed at them. "Nora Blackburn will be returned in exchange for ten thousand pounds, in Toronto on November 2nd, 1906." Grayson's blood ran cold as he looked at the warehouse and the dock number. "Dock 318, Warehouse 619. We know, two years ago, a prostitution ring was being run out of that dock and warehouse... A man named Eli Pitman..." Grayson's voice trailed off. The men in front of him didn't care, not at all.

Graves shrugged, "Silly girls in the wrong place at the wrong time."

Fury burned through Grayson at his words. The pain from the day his sister was taken was still so fresh in his mind, he couldn't see past it.

Were the men like this when his father went to ask them to investigate? Would Katherine have been found had the men who ran the constabularies cared more?

No wonder Lady Blackburn had hired outside help.

"Constable Lark, I want you to find out who *owns* 32 Blue Street. I want to know every owner of that property for the past twenty years and I want their full criminal record by six p.m. tonight." Grayson checked the calendar and his pocket watch. "Time is of the essence. If the ransom needs to be paid in Toronto, we have a lot of work to do. Nora Blackburn is likely already on a ship and we're too late to stop her from being taken to Canada. I will send a telegram to my men today to let them know she is on her way to Canada. Constable Hugh, I want a full background check of this Til Stone before the end of the day. I could find out almost nothing about her from Canada. Who is she and what is her history?"

"Usually we're done for the day at..." Constable Hugh pointedly looked at the clock on the wall as if it was too late to start an assignment like that.

"It's only ten in the morning. I'm sure if you get straight to it, you can have something for me by the end of the day." Grayson grit his teeth. "This is an investigation into a *missing girl*. There is no end of the day for her. There won't be for you either. You work until that information is on my desk."

"I say! We were instructed to assist, not take orders. I will remind you, I am the superintendent here..." Graves stood up and frowned at Grayson.

"Of course you are, but I am a detective sergeant and your chief has instructed you to cooperate. He wants this solved, immediately. We have no time to lose. If your day ends at five, then I suggest you work fast."

The constables looked at each other in alarm as they scrambled for the door.

"And just what will you be doing?" Graves asked imperiously.

"I'm going to interview Lady Blackburn, and then I'm bringing Til Stone in for interrogation."

"Oh." Graves opened his mouth to speak and then closed it.

"Kindly ensure that I have an interrogation room ready for me at around three p.m. today."

Before bolting from the building, he sent the entire ransom note to Sol. He could envision his men pouncing on the information and mobilising immediately.

Grayson arrived at the Blackburn's house, a Mayfair mansion, within the hour.

"You don't have an appointment? I'm sorry sir, Lady Blackburn prefers not to be disturbed in the mornings." The butler looked down a long nose at Grayson.

"I am the detective who is looking into Nora Blackburn's disappearance." Grayson's jaw clenched with the effort of speaking respectfully. "I don't have time to make appointments and bow to gentry. I'll see her now. Let her know."

"Lady Blackburn does not receive visitors without written confirmation first." The butler sniffed. "I will ask if she will receive you or if she prefers for you to make an appointment."

"I'm trying to find her granddaughter before she is packed onto a ship and sent God knows where."

"Quite. As you have not requested permission in writing, I can only ask if she is available." The butler repeated and then left him fuming.

Grayson paced and checked his pocket watch as he waited for the butler to return.

How does anyone operate at this slow a speed?

The butler finally re-entered the entrance way. "She can spare you ten minutes of her time."

Grayson rolled his eyes as he followed the butler to Lady Blackburn's drawing room. Curtains closed, she was head to toe in black mourning attire. Tea was already laid out, the butler pointedly did not offer him a chair.

"Detective Grayson, this is most... unexpected." Lady Blackburn waved a fan in front of her face as if she were about to swoon.

"I came as soon as I could." Grayson fought the urge to pace around the room in frustration.

"I expected you could resolve this matter without any intervention from me. Just find her." Lady Blackburn placed her fan beside her on the settee.

"I am trying." Grayson's tone was clipped. A headache started to pound behind his eyes. "I need you to clarify some things for me. I have a few questions I hope you can answer."

Lady Blackburn shook her head, pressed a handkerchief to her mouth and settled back on the settee. She made an elaborate show of asking the maid to pour tea.

"I'll try. This latest kidnapping has been so traumatic."

Grayson pulled out his notepad and pencil.

"You know about the two young women involved; rabble from the slums." Lady Blackburn picked up a teacup and took a delicate sip.

"Please tell me the whole story." Grayson poised to begin writing.

"It happened the winter before my daughter Madeline was engaged to be married." Lady Blackburn put down her teacup. "Let's see. She was married in 1882, so I remember it was the late autumn before that. It would have been 1881."

"What happened?" Grayson's mind whirled as he wrote.

"An elaborate scheme; most unsettling, most vulgar, Mr. Grayson." Lady Blackburn shook her head. Grayson found himself wondering if the black lace that covered her head would slide off.

"Could you be more specific?" Grayson yearned to reach across the tea service and shake the story out of her. The day was ticking away and this old doddery woman was stretching his patience past the limit.

"The two girls were hired as scullery maids." She took a long slow sip of tea. "The scandal is fresh in my mind. I sent you their names already, Odelia Shipley and Matilda Bertram. I'll have the maid come with the employment records. Just a moment."

Grayson paced around the drawing room. Lady Blackburn was not about to be rushed. Finally, fifteen minutes later, the maid appeared with a ledger book.

Lady Blackburn looked through employees from the time period. She finally adjusted her spectacles and pressed her fingertip to a name. "Yes, here it is. Matilda Bertram and Odelia Shipley, hired as maids, November the 3rd, 1881... Yes, that is right. Matilda was assigned to start the fires in our daughter Madeline's bedroom."

Matilda... Til...

"Within a week of coming here, we were informed, by Matilda, that Odelia had schemed to have Madeline abducted. Her boyfriend, one Bobby Bristol, was going to pounce on her en route to her engagement ball. Can you imagine the scandal if they had succeeded!" Lady Blackburn pressed a hand to her chest.

Not 'how terrible if dear Madeline had been abducted by butchers; just the scandal that would befall the family if the criminals had succeeded. As if abduction only happened to the lower classes.

"The police laid a trap and sure enough, Odelia and this Bobby, as well as other dregs from the slums, were in place to snatch her away." Lady Blackburn reached for a frilly handkerchief.

"So, the police caught Odelia and Bobby along with other gang members. What happened then?" Grayson tried to peer into the ledger book without being noticed.

"They were arrested. Somehow, they got off." Lady Blackburn's eyes narrowed in anger. "It's my suspicion that the police of the constabulary are being *paid to look the other way*." Lady Blackburn whispered it as if this was so impossible she shouldn't be overheard making such a scandalous claim. "I believe the police are possibly *corrupt*, Detective Grayson." Lady Blackburn pursed her lips together in disapproval. "That is why I have hired you."

Grayson agreed but said nothing. His only goal was to take down Til Stone, Odelia Shipley, and find Nora Blackburn before she was stolen out of London.

"The attempted kidnapping was so vulgar, so distressing. We were still reeling from it. You wouldn't believe what that upstart Matilda did."

"I can't imagine." Grayson's jaw clenched in fury. Matilda or Til or whatever she called herself was his prime suspect and from what he could tell she had no bottom, no level she wouldn't sink to in order to scramble to the top.

Lady Blackburn nodded her head, "She dared to come to us for money."

"How much?" Grayson's knuckles whitened as he gripped the pencil.

Lady Blackburn took a slow sip of tea as she thought, "Enough to have a private tutor. She wanted to be a doctor of all things. She thought we would pay for it since she alerted us to the attempted kidnapping." Lady Blackburn's eyes hardened.

"Then what happened?" Grayson pulled another pencil from his breast pocket.

"I turned her down flat of course; one does not educate the rabble from the slums." Lady Blackburn's lips pursed with dissapproval.

"And then?" Grayson was poised, ready to jot down more information.

"We were in a difficult and delicate situation." Lady Blackburn's eyes darted to him and then dropped. "Madeline was engaged to Lord Harper's son, William, a *tremendous* match. We didn't want a fuss or anything negative surrounding her. He was settling a new area in Canada and we thought, surely, she'll be safe with him from any nefarious schemes in Oakland, Manitoba, Canada. That is where she is now." Lady Blackburn made an elaborate show of picking up her teacup. She looked out the window at the grounds as she sipped her tea. "I'm not sure how far Toronto is from Oakland, but she is Lady Harper now. I wish she lived closer. I have a granddaughter there, in Oakland."

I don't care about granddaughters in Oakland, Manitoba! Get to the point woman!

Instead of screeching at Lady Blackburn with annoyance, Grayson grit his teeth and calmly asked. "Did Matilda receive money from you and Lord Blackburn?"

Lady Blackburn shook her head.

Either Matilda and Odelia had schemed this all along or they were mortal enemies.

"How much money?" Grayson asked.

"Vast amounts." Lady Blackburn's mouth clamped shut.

"Just for her protection, education or more?" Grayson pressed.

"She claimed just for an education," Lady Blackburn huffed.

"She is highly educated. How *did* she get the money?" Grayson paced to the ledger book as if the answer was there.

Lady Blackburn snapped the ledger shut.

"She went to Lord Blackburn, bold as brass. She swept into his library and dismissed me. Me! Said she had things to discuss with him that a lady shouldn't listen to. A fifteen-year-old upstart with coal dust under her fingernails. Lord Blackburn seemed bewitched by her and gave her exactly what she wanted."

"How much money?" Grayson didn't care about the slight to Lady Blackburn's pride. He wondered exactly what happened in that office between Til Stone, who at this point in her life was Matilda Bertram, as far as he could tell, and Lord Blackburn.

"Enough money to buy an education." Lady Blackburn bristled. "*Everyone* heralds her as the most successful woman in London. Well, she got there through Lord Blackburn. I can guarantee that." Lady Blackburn's cheeks burned red.

On her back, Grayson thought but didn't say. Lady Blackburn implied it but didn't say it either. Grayson wondered about how the women's groups that sponsored her fit into this scheme, but he knew he was at the end of what Lady Blackburn knew.

"This Matilda, if she is Til Stone, and she must be as no one else fits this history, is wealthy beyond anyone's imagination." Lady Blackburn's eyes narrowed in disapproval.

"Do you think she was working with Odelia or not?" Grayson asked bluntly.

"How do I know the mind of a criminal?" Lady Blackburn took a deep sip of tea; she frowned and made a motion to the maid to refill her cup. "Carol, it's cold."

The maid moved forward to refill her teacup. Her movements were stiff with arthritis. Grayson reached for the tea pot to relieve her of the duty of pouring tea and both women looked at him as if he'd pulled down his pants. Servants filled teacups. Detectives wrote for permission to see a Lady such as Lady Blackburn. He was out of his depth and he knew it. He pulled away and was saddened to watch the maid's mangled hands manage the tea pot despite the obvious pain in her fingers. He winced.

Lady Blackburn didn't notice. "You'll have to ask Matilda Bertram when you find her." Lady Blackburn's tone sharpened.

The butler hovered to escort him out. "You are well past your allotted time, sir."

Grayson wasn't sure how he did it, but the sir sounded like an insult.

"Lady Blackburn, I guarantee, I'll be asking that and much more." Grayson ignored the butler. "May I speak to Lord Blackburn?"

"He died a year ago." Lady Blackburn's eyes filled with tears.

Grayson wondered if those tears were real. What did women of this class *really* think or feel? How much was a constant show? What sort of life was it if your husband could take any maid he chose and there wasn't a thing you could do about it?

"I'm sorry for your loss," Grayson said. He could hardly wait to get to Til's clinic and drag her into an interrogation room.

Lady Blackburn simpered. "Thank you."

Grayson cleared his throat; he knew women like her, women who traded in attention as if it were currency. He had no patience for weak, needy women. This one had taken enough of his time already.

"If you think of anything else, please send a telegram to my office; even the smallest little detail, you never know." Grayson put his notebook back into his breast pocket.

Lady Blackburn picked up her fan. "There is one thing."

"Yes?" Grayson took his notebook back out.

"There were things missing in Madeline's trousseau. She refused to admit it. When I asked her about pieces of jewellery, she evaded the question. I never had a satisfying answer as to what had happened to them. If Matilda stole them, I don't know why Madeline would have protected her. I can't work that out *at all.* Her jewellery was worth a small fortune. I want you to promise me you will prosecute these... people... all of them, to the fullest extent of the law. I want them to pay for their crimes." Lady Blackburn's eyes narrowed as she looked up at Grayson.

"I guarantee it," Grayson promised.

Finally, he was shown out of the drawing room to track down Matilda Bertram and get to the bottom of her involvement with Odelia Shipley.

Matilda, or Til... whoever you are. You have met your match.

Chapter Six

Back at the King's Cross Police Station, Grayson combed through records involving Bobby Bristol and Odelia Shipley Bristol. The criminal investigation into Odelia revealed arrests involving theft and prostitution. Once Odelia was married to Bobby Bristol, she had two children by him. There was no further criminal activity.

No prosecuted criminal activity.

Bobby, on the other hand, was clearly a career criminal. The corruption went deep. The Bristol Butchers ran rampant in this and other jurisdictions. There was nothing on this 'Til,' however. She did go to the London Royal Free Hospital School of Medicine for Women as Til Stone, but where she had been educated before that was a mystery. There was only one current arrest that had gotten her some jail time. She had been accused of providing an abortion to the maid of one Lady Carstairs. She had been sent to jail, and then the charges had been dropped.

If she's part of the Bristols, why didn't they keep her out of jail? Hmm, the barrister who represented her was Malcolm Maddox. By all accounts, they are married, but her last name is still Stone? Was she one of those odd suffragettes who refused to be known by a husband's last name?

Grayson sighed. It was increasingly obvious that the files had been tampered with. He scrubbed his hands over his face.

What is the relationship between Til Stone and Odelia Shipley Bristol?

Pacing around his office, he grabbed his irons, a billy club, and verified that the interrogation room was readied. Taking Til Stone into custody was slightly premature, but Grayson depended on the fact that she was a woman who would be easily intimidated. His hand was forced; no one was talking; everyone was either indifferent to Nora's plight or in on it.

He sent a telegram to the press. 'Doctor Til Stone to be brought in for questioning regarding the disappearance of Nora Blackburn.' As the telegraph operator, Adams, tapped the message to the various newspapers, his eyes widened.

"Most don't... uh... tangle with the Bristols or anyone who *could* be associated with them."

"I'm not most people," Grayson growled. "Keep tapping."

The clerk's fingers trembled as he sent the message.

"Sir, you don't know who you are dealing with," Adams whispered.

"You don't seem to know who *you* are dealing with." Grayson told himself to step back as the telegraph operator looked up at him in fear. "The message went to every newspaper in the city?"

"Yes." The clerk swallowed hard.

"How long does it typically take to mobilise the press?" Grayson's tone was clipped and cold.

"Minutes. This isn't their first time with Doctor Til Stone."

"I see."

"You should be careful; she has Malcolm Maddox behind her." Adams's face creased with worry.

"We're the law. I have no intention of backing down, I'm taking Til Stone into custody; make sure the interrogation room is ready. When the press shows up, be sure they get a ringside seat." Grayson turned on his heel and called for his cab.

***

Til placed the last suture into the woman's abdomen. Enid moved forward to assist her in bandaging the incision.

"Good work," Til said to the nurses in the operating room who had assisted her. She turned from the new mother and scrubbed her hands with carbolic acid and a scrub brush. She left the operating theatre to make notes in her office.

Shannon bustled into Til's office, her eyes wide with worry. "There is someone here to see you, a detective from the police station."

"Oh, good! Send him in; maybe he has news of the branded prostitute." Til put her file away and stood as Grayson entered her office. Her eyes widened. He was the same size and build as Malcolm. Broad shouldered, dark hair, dark eyes. His biceps strained the fabric of his jacket. Til frowned as she noticed his black hair was shaggy and hung over his collar.

He needs a barber and his collar needs to be pressed.

Stubble shadowed his jaw. Huge, hard, tough, his eyes bloodshot, he looked as if he'd spent his nights drunk and in a brothel. He shut the door behind him.

His face twisted as he spoke her name, "Til Stone."

"Yes." Til lifted her chin.

"I am Detective Asher Grayson of the Toronto Constabulary. You are under arrest for kidnapping and procuring girls as prostitutes."

Til's jaw dropped open in shock.

Chapter Seven

Grayson's jaw tightened as he watched Doctor Til Stone gather her composure. Her copper and blond hair was piled high on her head; she had strange amber coloured eyes, high cheekbones. Delicate at first glance until he looked hard into her eyes. She had a look that said she would go the distance to survive. The worst sort of gorgeous woman. She knew exactly how beautiful she was, and Grayson was certain she knew how to use her fragility, her beauty, to manipulate men.

Weary and furious, patience sapped, he attacked her with his next words. "A woman doctor by day, a white slaver by night." He tilted his head and took a step forward, inviting her to defend herself against the accusation.

Til stood up taller. She straightened her shoulders and looked down her nose at him.

"Preposterous." Til held her ground.

"You're associated with the Bristol Butchers. It implicates you in kidnapping, prostitution... the list goes on." Grayson took out a pair of irons. "You'll come with me right now."

"I'm not going anywhere with you without legal representation." Til's cool English accent frosted with ice.

Grayson ignored her, he reached for her arm; she sidestepped him.

"Remember yourself, sir." Til pointed at him. "You will not arrest a surgeon on the grounds of kidnapping without sufficient evidence. This is madness!"

Grayson closed the distance between them; he took her by the upper arms. "You've been dealing with crooked cops a long time. I wonder what you will do with a straight cop that can't be bought?"

"Take your hands off of me." Til stepped back.

Grayson dragged her wrists together, slapped irons on one wrist and then the other. She struggled against him until he pinned her against the wall.

"I will have your badge for this," she vowed, her eyes flashed in fury. "I am innocent of these charges; you have this completely wrong."

"I am the most respected investigator of procurement of girls as prostitutes on two continents. Try to have my badge, I dare you," he growled against her ear as the irons locked shut.

"Prostitutes! What are you talking about?" Til gasped.

Grayson pulled opened her office door and dragged her to the front of the clinic.

"What is the meaning of this?" Shannon raced to Til as Grayson put his hand on the door that opened to the street.

"Don't follow me; wait for Cole." Til grit her teeth. "This is a complete misunderstanding. Send Malcolm at once."

Grayson opened the door. Journalists lined Marlborough Street, men with notepads and cameras on tripods were poised, gleefully anticipating the documentation of Doctor Til Stone's downfall.

Til gasped in outrage, "You will take me through the back door to avoid publicity. This is not good for my clinic."

"No." Grayson pulled her over the threshold onto the street. "The infamous Til Stone worried about her reputation? I doubt it."

"I don't care about my reputation, but I do care about the reputation of my clinic. If you sling mud at me, this clinic will have to be shut down and where will the women needing treatment go?" Til's eyes narrowed at him.

"I'm sure the Bristols will ride to your rescue and have it opened back up in minutes," Grayson sneered at her.

"The Bristols?" Her brow furrowed in confusion. Til refused to budge. "This clinic could burn to the ground and the *Bristols* wouldn't even notice. Not unless they started the fire!"

Sure, you're confused! I don't believe it.

Fury pounded through him as Til looked up at him with contempt. Katherine's face flashed through his mind, then the last shipment of girls crying as they held onto each other standing on the docks of Toronto made him feel physically sick. How could a woman like her, with all her education, all her privilege, be part of a scheme that would send hundreds of vulnerable English girls to Canada? He wanted to interrogate her right on the street.

"You're a good actress. I'll give you that." A muscle twitched in Grayson's jaw. "Let me say it's my pleasure to be the detective who is finally taking Til Stone through the streets of London to jail. Your affiliation with the Bristol Butchers, and particularly Odelia Shipley Bristol, will come to light and every newspaper in the world will know I was the one to take you down." He kept his face near hers, expecting her to blink, to drop her gaze, to show any sign of intimidation.

She gazed straight back at him, her body stiffened. "You are wrong. Think of this. Every newspaper in the world will know that you have blundered and I will have you sued for slander." Her eyes clashed with his. "Irons off, through the back streets, or I don't cooperate."

Grayson dragged her through the crowd that hounded her with questions. "Someone has abducted Nora Blackburn. The last time someone attempted an abduction, you were part of it."

"I was not!" Til's jaw dropped at the accusation. "I alerted the authorities!"

"And walked away with a fortune." Grayson leaned in as a newspaper man stepped right in front of her and knocked her off balance.

Grudgingly, he righted her and tugged her past the man with the notepad. Til haughtily ignored the questions howled at her involving her stance on birth control and what they thought of her for promoting it. Grayson dragged open the door to the hackney cab and thrust her inside. Once they were in the confines of the cab, he watched her pulse race in the hollow of her throat. "Someone has to answer for this tragedy. Talk or it will be you." Grayson watched her eyes carefully for evidence of lying. "A man who trades in girls is abhorrent, but a woman..." Grayson's eyes narrowed with disgust.

"What are you talking about? Trading in girls!" Til lashed at him. "I'm the one asking the police to *investigate* these girls. Have you not seen my documentation demanding that the police prosecute whoever is behind these murders?"

"Perfect cover," Grayson shot back at her. "You've been dealing with crooked cops who look the other way. Not anymore." Grayson leaned in closer. "I'm not crooked. You can't buy me off! You can't stop this investigation. Times up, Til."

Til's eyes narrowed at him. "You're wrong. I have dedicated my life to alleviating the suffering of women. Selling girls into prostitution is obscene. You know nothing of me, what I believe, what I stand for—"

"You're right. According to the records I have, you don't exist. Til Stone arrives on the scene in the London Royal Free Hospital School of Medicine for Women a few years after you worked as Matilda Bertram with the Blackburn family. You knew Odelia Shipley, you started that job together as maids. That's what my research verifies. Today, we will get to the bottom of who is Til Stone, who is Matilda Bertram, and where is Nora Blackburn."

Til's mouth dropped open. "Why would I know anything about Nora Blackburn?"

"The Blackburns have a ransom note requesting ten thousand pounds to be delivered to a dock and warehouse in Toronto, Canada, from you. They want you to ransom her back."

Grayson watched as the blood drained from Til's face.

"What!"

Sure, you're confused.

"Further, you were involved in the attempted kidnapping of Madeline Blackburn in 1881. This time you and the Bristols, we suspect, have succeeded. For all we know Nora could be on a ship to Toronto which is bad. Terrible, for you."

"Toronto?" Til's eyes widened in fear or confusion, Grayson couldn't be sure which one. "May I see the note? I don't understand."

Grayson banged on the ceiling of the cab. The driver slapped the reins down but they hardly moved. The crowd hemmed them in. Grayson frowned. He hadn't banked on Til Stone being so unpopular and he regretted dragging her to jail through the front of the clinic. This was a disaster.

Til turned from him and watched the men on the street.

Finally, the crowd parted so the cab could clatter down the cobblestone streets to the police station.

"Yes. Toronto. What part of the Bristol operation are you familiar with in Toronto?" Grayson demanded.

Til took a deep breath and let it out slowly. "I know nothing about the Bristols and how they operate in England, never mind Toronto. I will wait for my husband to meet me. He is a barrister but I am certain you already know that. I will not answer any further questions. Don't waste your breath."

When the cab stopped at the police station, Grayson dragged Til Stone through the corridors to the hallway in front of the interview room.

"You will wait for my counsel; I will not enter that room without protection." Til's voice sharpened in warning.

"You don't need protection from me if you are innocent," Grayson growled at her.

Til struggled harder against him. "I will not go in there with you alone."

"The superintendent being present, would that suffice?" Grayson conceded.

"No, find Malcolm and bring him here. We wait for Malcolm," Til snapped at him.

Some constables nudged each other as she struggled against him and continued to refuse to enter the interview room. They murmured as he overpowered her, picked her up easily, and carried her into the room and chained her to the table.

Til gasped as she tried to pull out of the irons tethering her to the wooden board.

"What do you know about Nora Blackburn?" Grayson demanded.

She lifted her chin, her eyes flicked over him and then narrowed to slits of fury.

"Where do you want to start, Matilda Bertram?" Grayson's eyes locked on Til.

Chapter Eight

Til's lips thinned as narrow as her eyes as they swept over Detective Asher Grayson. She looked down her nose at him and kept her mouth clamped shut.

Where is Malcolm?

A shiver of icy fear raced down her back.

Bobby Bristol dead, no protection from the Bristol Butchers. Has Odelia targeted me?

Til took a very deep breath and let it out slowly. She tested the irons that held her to the table. Secure.

"I asked you where you want to start." Grayson stood up and towered over her.

"I will speak when Malcolm is present," Til repeated.

Grayson placed falsified promissory notes from Til to Odelia for the last twenty years. "Every year, you pay her, on November 2nd, a sum of twenty pounds."

"False. I haven't had contact with Odelia Shipley for years." Til shifted in her seat to make herself more comfortable.

"So, you *are* Matilda Bertram?" Grayson tilted his head to the side.

"Not relevant. I am not speaking until Malcolm is here." Til pressed her lips together.

"Just listen then. These documents indicate you are still paying her for her help when you scammed the Blackburns out of enough money to pay for your education."

Til rolled her eyes.

"Did you come to be in Lady Blackburn's employ on November 3, 1881?"

Til remained silent.

"We can't find Malcolm. It sounds like he has been missing for a while." Grayson crossed his arms over his chest.

Til's palms slicked with sweat at the thought of Malcolm missing.

Grayson's eyes narrowed as he put pictures of the girls on the table between them. "Branded with 'B', for Bertram, that is our guess."

Til took a deep breath and willed herself to keep her mouth shut. She tried and failed. "I have nothing to do with those prostitutes; someone dumped them at my clinic already dead."

Grayson pounced on his notepad and wrote down every word she said. "Not according to the medical examiner."

"The medical examiner who gets a tidy sum from the Bristols, just like every other man in this building. Including you, I suspect," Til sneered.

"Do you refuse to be called Bertram because you run prostitutes under that name?" Grayson straightened up. "Brands of 'B' on both sides of the Atlantic."

"You have an active imagination," Til said dryly.

"You're evading me. Are you going to keep silent and let Nora Blackburn die at the hands of her captors?" Grayson's eyes burned with intensity.

"Of course not." Til pulled against the irons, frustrated when they didn't budge.

Grayson pulled open a file. He read it swiftly. "Here's what I know. A woman with your surgical skill would not botch abortions. That is the only reason I am granting you this conversation. If I thought you were some back-alley abortionist, I would have your neck in a noose by the end of the week."

Til kept her gaze levelled on him, she didn't blink.

"Who is Matilda Bertram?" Grayson shot her a hard look.

An honest look from the detective caused Til's heart to calm a bit.

He knows I didn't kill those girls. He is the only detective looking into their murders.

Til decided right there to trust him with a scant bit of information. "I don't answer to that name anymore."

"Why?" Grayson demanded.

"Not relevant to this case. Next question," she barked.

Grayson's eyes narrowed. "You worked with Odelia Shipley Bristol at the Blackburn's in 1881?"

"Yes." Til tested the irons holding her to the table again.

"You were how old?"

"Fifteen." Til spoke mutinously. Her heart hammered in her throat as the memories surrounding her employment there flashed through her mind.

"What happened in Lady Blackburn's employ?" Grayson moved closer.

Til took a deep breath and let it out slowly. "Odelia Shipley was my friend. Best friend. We grew up a couple streets apart in the worst slums in London."

"Address?"

"I lived in 9 Ann Street and she was 60 George Street." Til gritted her teeth. "You're not from here; you should shudder to hear those street names. Most people never crawl out of there."

"You're running a prostitution ring and kidnapping gentry together, I'd say you and Odelia aren't most people. That's obvious to me," Grayson quipped.

"You'd better believe I'm not most people." Til's voice hardened. "You have nothing to back that claim. If you continue with that line of questioning, I say nothing further." Til moved back as far from him as the irons allowed.

"When you lived at Ann Street your real name was Matilda Bertram?" Grayson's voice deepened.

"Not relevant to this case. Next question." Til's jaw clenched.

"I decide what is relevant, not you," Grayson roared at Til.

"When Malcolm gets here and sees me chained like a common criminal, he will beat you to a bloody pulp." Til lashed back at him.

"You were Matilda Bertram in that slum or who were you?" Grayson redirected.

"A terrified child," Til answered honestly even as she dodged the name Matilda Bertram. "I ran away and changed everything to survive. Next question."

"What were you running from?" Grayson placed his hands on the table on either side of where her hands were chained.

Til looked up at him defiantly and clamped her mouth shut.

Standing and towering over her, a muscle jumped out of Grayson's jaw. "If you don't talk, I'll add obstruction of justice."

Til stiffened in her chair. "Rules of engagement, Mr. Grayson, know this. If you bring up the name Matilda Bertram again, you will get nothing from me. Let's talk about what Odelia Shipley and Bobby Bristol attempted to do to Madeline Blackburn, shall we? I'll talk about that. I'll tell you what you want to know starting on November 3rd, 1881."

"What happened on November 2nd, 1881?" Grayson pressed.

"I will discuss nothing before November 3rd." Til raised her voice in warning. "Odelia Shipley was Bobby Bristol's girl."

Grayson backed down, picked up a pencil and started taking notes. "Bobby Bristol, he runs the Bristol Butchers."

"Ran, he *ran* the Butchers." Til leaned forward. "He would have lost control to his brother when he was gunned down on the street." Til adjusted the irons so they didn't chafe her wrists.

"How do you know about that?" Grayson's eyes locked on hers.

"Newspapers," Til answered tightly. "Those of us who crawled out never got very far, did we? I still doctor the women from the slums; try to ease their suffering where I can. They talk too. You've seen my work in birth control."

"It made you a pariah. Even today, the newspapermen were screaming for your blood." Grayson tilted his head to the side. "Everyone says you are an abomination of a woman. Such a vulgar thing to promote."

"You don't get to where I am in life by caring what people think. Certainly not a bunch of narrow-minded men! Men are of no consequence in my line of work. You only create laws and problems that inhibit what the women's rights movement is trying to promote."

"And just what is that?" Grayson rolled his eyes.

"The health of women." Til's jaw clenched with fury. "We're not here to discuss birth control; don't waste my time, it's valuable."

Grayson's eyes narrowed. "So, you use birth control to protect the girls you procure as prostitutes? Your clinic is a front to ensure working girls stay working, is that it?"

"Absolutely not," Til gasped. "I know nothing about girls being procured as prostitutes."

"Sure you do." Grayson pulled photographs of girls sold into prostitution from Canada. All branded with 'B'. All younger than sixteen years of age. Til's stomach pitched and rolled at the sight.

"This is just a few. Some refused to have their pictures taken. I respected their privacy."

"Oh my God, this is a tragedy. These girls... all stolen?" Til closed her eyes for a moment. "You think the Butchers are behind it?"

"Yes, and you." Grayson put more pictures in front of her.

"You think I could steal these... children and sell them." Til tried to catch her breath. "This is a travesty. If the Bristols are behind this, if you are right, I hope you catch them and hang them. I know nothing about any girls stolen and sold to Canada." Til shook her head in outrage at the photos of the girls. "I have sent documentation that the girls left at my clinic—"

"What happened while you were employed by the Blackburns?" Grayson cut her off. His voice sounded like an axe being dragged through gravel.

I know this tactic, I have been interrogated before!

"The Bristols planned to kidnap Madeline. I intervened, no more, no less." Til watched Grayson's eyes for evidence he believed her.

"You're lying, you were in on it." Grayson badgered her. "You walked away with a fortune. You were behind the whole scheme."

"No." Til spoke with force. "You are wasting your time on me and you know it. So, no more of this. Irons off, Malcolm in the room, I have nothing further to say." She promptly clamped her mouth shut.

Grayson paced around her and baited her with questions for an entire hour.

Til refused to speak.

Finally, furious, he unchained her from the table and dragged her out of her chair.

She fought him as hard as she could as he half pulled, half pushed her through the hallways of the station, down the stairs into the basement of the jail. Constables murmured and looked at each other as if they should step in. Any who dared got a sharp look from Grayson; they backed down. There were no separate cells for women. When she tried to resist, he picked her up and carried her through cells full of depraved men who shrieked and screamed at the sight of her.

"You wouldn't..." she gasped at him as he opened a cell in the centre of the men. Alone, but with men in cells all around her.

"This isn't right," Til hissed at him.

Grayson took her by the upper arms and dragged her into the cell. He spoke directly into her ear. "If you were a man, I would *beat* a confession out of you," his voice deepened.

Til's heart raced with fear as she looked up at him.

"I can't because you're a woman. I can, however, leave you here until you are ready to cooperate."

"I will never cooperate with you!" Til vowed.

"You don't seem to understand this. I am the authority here. You answer to me. Whatever happened before you went to the Blackburn house, whatever you are hiding might apply to this case." Grayson's eyes narrowed as he spoke. "You are withholding information from me and you are impeding this investigation. I will bring both you and Odelia down whether you are working together or not. You will not win. So, I'll leave you here until you are ready to talk. You think about the events of November 2nd, 1881 or get comfortable in this cell."

"I told you everything. Odelia and Bobby hatched the scheme, I turned them in. No more no less."

"Why did you walk away with a fortune?" Grayson slammed the jail cell door shut. "I want the truth. All of it. What happened at the Blackburns, who paid you, *why are you known as Til Stone?*"

"Never." Til shot at him. Defiantly, she stood in her cell, ignoring the men who bayed for her body all around her.

"We'll see if you still feel the same way in an hour. You don't talk in an hour, we'll see how you do overnight." Grayson turned the key in the lock.

"You wouldn't dare." Til gripped the bars that separated her from Grayson. "I will have you sacked for this!"

"I think you know who is stealing girls. I think you are protecting this person." Grayson's voice bit into her. "You will cooperate, or I will make your life as living a hell as theirs has been. What happened before the

Blackburns? How did you know Odelia and why were you in service together? What is your current involvement with the Bristol Butchers?"

"There is *no* involvement." Til balled her hands into fists.

"You have an hour to think about it." Grayson turned his back and walked away, leaving Til to the cells of men who crowed for her body.

Chapter Nine

Grayson paced in his office and checked his pocket watch. He noticed a couple enter the police station. Recognising the woman from the clinic, he quickly went to greet them.

"Where is my aunt?" The woman cut straight to the point.

"In custody. How can I help you?" Grayson escorted them into the interview room.

"There has been a huge misunderstanding." The man waited until his wife sat down before he sat down beside her.

"Maybe you can clear some things up." Grayson sat down across from the couple. "Your name please?"

"Shannon McDougall, I am Til Stone's niece."

"You are a doctor as well?"

"Yes."

"What is Til's involvement with Odelia Bristol?"

"There is no involvement with Odelia Bristol. I have never heard that name in my life." Shannon tucked hair behind her ear.

"Who was she before she was Til Stone?" Grayson poised with a pencil, ready to write down anything Shannon said.

"I..." Shannon's eyes glittered with tears. "I understand her father did something to her and she refused to be known by his name after that. My mother's maiden name was Bertram. Til's full name is Matilda, but she refuses to answer to that name. She is Matilda Bertram."

"Matilda Bertram, why did she change her name?" Grayson wrote the name down.

"You can't call her that," Shannon asserted.

"I can call her anything I want," Grayson contradicted Shannon.

The big man leaned forward, placing his shoulder between Grayson and Shannon. His intent to protect Shannon with his body was clear.

"Keep a civil tongue in your head; I will not allow anyone to speak to my wife in such a manner. We're here to get to the bottom of this. Til Stone is a trial to deal with, but she's our trial. She is innocent. There is no involvement with the Bristol Butchers. Malcolm, her husband, went to investigate why the Butchers are dropping dead prostitutes on her doorstep. We are just as confused as you are."

"And you are?"

"Constable Cole McDougall. Shannon is my wife and Til is Shannon's aunt. A thorn in my side, but she is innocent of these charges." Cole met Grayson's eyes.

"I see." Grayson looked from Cole to Shannon and then back to Cole. "If that is her given name, I'll call her Matilda Bertram."

Shannon shook her head. "If you want her to cooperate, you might try a different tactic. I don't know why she refuses to answer to the name Matilda."

"You don't seem to understand," Grayson growled at Shannon and met Cole's hard eyes. He softened his tone. "She needs to cooperate with me. I'm not done with my interrogation."

"She'll never cooperate with you, she'll rot in jail. Let me talk to her. You can be in the room," Shannon suggested.

Grayson looked at Cole who looked ready to battle him to the ground even though he was sitting in a chair. "I'll be in the room too. I'm a police officer and I want to be sure my wife is safe, from you."

"I'll get her." Grayson heard the men howling from the top of the stairs. He quickly jogged down the stairs to retrieve her.

"So." Grayson opened the cell and had to shout over the men. "Are you ready to discuss what happened on November 2nd, 1881? What caused you to run to the Bristols for protection?" He reached for her and dragged her out of the cell by her upper arm.

Til froze in his grasp and quit moving. Grayson pulled her inexorably forward.

"Keep moving or I will leave you down here," he growled in her ear.

Til stiffened in his grasp. "I didn't run to the Bristols for protection. I ran from them! Furthermore, I don't acknowledge my life before I went into service for the Blackburns. I'll tell you anything you want to know, but I won't discuss that... girl."

"Did you kill someone?" He pressed her against the wall and spoke into her ear so she could hear over the screaming of the men in the cells. "Was that the start of your criminal career?"

Til remained silent, chin tilted up, completely defiant.

Grayson dragged her up the stairs. He opened the door into the interview room where Cole and Shannon sat at the table.

"Let's talk about the Bristols and your involvement with them." Grayson opened up the interrogation.

Til swept into the interview room as if she were a queen entering her court. Turning her back on Grayson, she took over and began to issue orders.

"Cole. I need you to go and find Malcolm. I need Malcolm," Til asserted. "Take men with you, do not go alone; men you trust. Shannon, you need to go to the clinic and restructure the staff. Once you get that sorted, let me know. Tell them, I will not be returning to work for the foreseeable future." Til looked at Grayson and then back at Shannon. "Make sure my staff is up to speed. No one speaks to the newspapers, no one. Keep your eye on Mrs. Coates. She is prone to infection, Shannon, you know that. Make sure she is all right. This is all a misunderstanding. Hire more security immediately."

Imperiously, Til turned to Grayson and even in irons, she looked like a force to be reckoned with. "I answer to the name of Doctor Stone. You will conduct this interview with some respect. You may begin."

"Til, let me stay..." Shannon begged. Tears glittered in her eyes. "I don't trust him." Shannon's eyes cut to Grayson. Cole moved closer to his wife.

"He's just a man, Shann. Go, please, make sure the clinic can recover from this outrageous scandal." Til tossed her head back. Her eyes flashed with fury. She directed her attention to Cole. "Bring Malcolm to me here, I need him here."

"Til," Cole spoke gently. "We've looked everywhere. We can't find him anywhere."

"Cole, please I am begging you, keep looking," Til commanded him.

"I will," Cole promised. He stepped closer to Shannon. She moved with him as if there was an invisible string tying them together.

Shannon pressed her hand against her heart. "Please cooperate, Til. You are in no condition to be spending time in prison."

"That's enough," Til reprimanded Shannon. "There is nothing to tell. I am innocent. I am the one asking the police to investigate these girls. I have nothing to hide. Let the staff know I will be home and will need a hot meal."

"If she is not returned home by six p.m. tonight, I will be back here. She needs to be released; she is innocent of these charges." Shannon's voice shook as she faced Grayson. Cole moved closer to her side, ready to defend her.

Grayson watched Cole warily. Similar in size, a battle between them would be long and bloody. He noticed the way Cole moved with Shannon, he'd take down the entire police station if she needed him to.

"We'll see," Grayson said cooly.

Cole and Shannon hesitated at the door of the interview room.

"Just you and me, Grayson," Til spoke finally, effectively dismissing Cole and Shannon.

When the door shut behind them, Grayson turned to Til. She stiffened as he moved closer. He let her worry about what he was going to do. Her eyes locked on his, he saw resolve. She wouldn't be easy to break. If she was guilty, she didn't look it. She looked confused and furious.

Grayson took a step back for a minute. Threats and intimidation weren't working. He considered kindness as a last resort.

Grayson reached for her and she gasped. Til pulled away from him as far as she could, eyes wide, she didn't drop her gaze.

"I've known a long time. Every man with authority over a woman will abuse it," Til snapped. "You have confirmed it. You're no better than the slavers."

Grayson's jaw clenched at the insult. He reached for her irons.

"Don't you dare... you are a police officer, a detective!" Til howled at him in rage.

"Quiet," Grayson growled. He kept his eyes on hers as he held up her irons. He watched her pulse pound in her throat as he slid the key into the lock. She blinked in surprise as he gently removed the irons from her wrists. She let a tiny breath of relief out as he put the irons on the table. Finally, he held a chair out for her to sit at the table. She hesitated and then sat down. He sat down across from her.

"Please tell me what happened when you worked for the Blackburns." Careful to keep his tone soft and respectful, Grayson held her gaze.

Til swallowed hard, looked at him warily, and then took a deep breath. "Bobby Bristol was going to take over the Bristol Butchers when his uncle Oliver died. He needed money, so he asked Odelia, his girl, to work for the Blackburns and work out how they could kidnap and ransom Madeline Blackburn." Til rubbed the marks the irons had left on her wrists. "I didn't know Odelia was pregnant. As is usual among women, pregnancy made her vulnerable. She faced starving in the streets without Bobby. She would have done anything to secure her place at his side."

"That's a big risk." Grayson watched Til carefully for any evidence that she was lying to him.

"No, it really isn't." Til took a deep breath, let it out slowly. "The Bristols own the police. There is *never* enough evidence to convict them. Check their records. You'll be sickened."

"I have," Grayson said. "So, Odelia was pregnant, and applied for a position. What then?" Grayson moved them into comfortable territory by directing the investigation back to Odelia.

"Bobby needed money, Odelia wanted to be his wife. I didn't know of this until we were in service together. I would assume she was buying her place in the gang. He needed a woman to run the women. That is how it is customarily done."

"Run the women, what does that mean?" Grayson jotted down Til's words.

"Pickpockets, thieves and prostitutes, Detective Grayson. This is the real world we live in. Try to keep up," Til snapped at him.

Grayson throttled down the urge to shake information out of her.

"She needed to have some start-up capital. This was an easy way to get it. Not a big sum for the Blackburns and Madeline was engaged; they knew they would want this to be quietly brushed away. The police were on the take, they would get slaps on the wrist at best."

"What then?"

"She said she would give me some of the money if I helped her. I was the maid in charge of starting the fires; I knew when she would be leaving and which coach. I couldn't hand that girl over to them. I couldn't do it." Til crossed her arms over her chest. "It would have ruined her life and I know about ruined lives..." her gaze met his and she didn't look away. "How you never recover... I couldn't be part of such a thing."

Grayson paused as he watched Til carefully.

What happened to you?

"I see," Grayson said quietly.

"You don't see," Til rounded on him. "You don't see *at all.* Up to this point, Odelia and her family, that was *my safety*. The only safety I had after..."

Grayson didn't move; he willed her to speak.

"The only safety I had in the slums after my mother died..." Til's eyes hardened and flashed in fury. "I knew, when I looked into her eyes, that if I took money from her, I would be dead in the very streets I just escaped from. They wouldn't leave me alive to give evidence at a later date. You don't have information about a Bristol Butcher and live. Odelia was that committed to him. She truly is one of those weak women who..." Til's lips twisted in bitterness.

"Who will what?" Grayson reined in his impatience, giving her time to gather her thoughts.

"Who will compromise for a man." Til closed her eyes briefly and shook her head in disgust. "The worst sort of woman. I despised her for it when I worked it out."

"What happened then?" Grayson poised to take notes.

"I asked Lady Blackburn for enough money to get private tutoring to start again. I didn't need money as much as I needed a life off the streets. I wanted to be *permanently* removed from the streets the Bristols ran. No one seems to understand that it takes more than money — it takes education."

"So, Lady Blackburn turned you down, so you set out to speak to..."

"I went to Lord Blackburn," Til interrupted, "I asked for enough to cover my education. I needed Malcolm's protection, so I asked for enough for his education as well."

"So, you just asked and he gave it to you? How did you manage that?" Grayson tried and failed to take the accusation out of his voice. The implication that she prostituted herself for her education and Malcolm's was obvious in his inflection.

Til bristled and refused to cooperate. "It doesn't matter now."

"Of course it does." Grayson's tone hardened. "How did you get money out of Lord Blackburn? Did Lord Blackburn ask for..." Grayson refused to back down.

"Of course he did." Til's eyes blazed at him as she stood up and turned away from him.

Grayson immediately jumped to his feet and braced himself to stop her if she tried to bolt. Til paced back and forth behind the table. She kept a careful distance from him.

"And you did it... you prostituted yourself for..." Grayson followed her, backed her into a corner so she couldn't escape his watchful gaze.

"Next question." Til's jaw clenched.

Grayson redirected. "What happened to Odelia Shipley Bristol?"

"You must have investigated her." Til frowned at him as if he was too lazy to do his job. "Bobby became the head of the Bristols. He married her before she had her baby. I have been her biggest enemy ever since." Til slid past him, careful not to touch him, careful to stay out of his reach. She sat at the interrogation table and Grayson returned to his seat.

"You prostituted yourself for your education." He lashed at her.

"Men like you so easily believe the worst." Til evaded the answer. "What if I said he asked and I turned him down?"

Grayson shook his head. "Nah, you would. To get out of the slums, you would do it."

Til's tone was ice on iron. "It's neither here nor there."

"Let's say you did." Grayson's lips thinned with impatience. "So, your list of enemies is Odelia Shipley who later married Bobby Bristol, Lord and Lady Blackburn... wait. Not Lord Blackburn."

"Be professional, Mr. Grayson." Til's eyes narrowed.

"Who else hates you, Til?" Grayson pointedly refused to call her Doctor Stone.

"Most of the upper class of London, Mr. Grayson." She stiffened in defiance. "It's Doctor Stone to you."

"These promissory notes, you've been paying Odelia Shipley Bristol then?"

"Absolutely not. This is pure false documentation. I expect nothing less than evidence planted by a corrupt policeman. The truth is I parted company with Odelia after they carted her away in irons. Where they gave her a slap on the wrist and probably were guests at the wedding."

"We can verify that with bank records." Grayson reached for the falsified forms.

"Please do. I will say this. Here is what I think." Til leaned forward. "Odelia Shipley Bristol is out for revenge. Wants me to suffer because she has suffered. Recently the Bristols have had a restructure of their gang since Bobby Bristol was shot. She'll be trying to buy her place in the gang. That's how it works. Who is the new head of the Bristols? Is it Andy as I suspect?"

"Would *she* try to be the head of the Bristols?" Grayson raised his eyebrow.

"You call yourself a detective!" Til threw her hands up in the air in frustration. "A woman can't head a gang like that. The only place where women have fewer rights than in England is in a gang."

"You seem to know a lot about how the Bristols operate." Grayson's eyes narrowed at her.

"I wish I didn't." Til shot back at him.

"What does that mean?" Grayson demanded. He checked his pocket watch; he was tired of evasive answers.

"I wish I hadn't been raised in those slums where you have to stay a step ahead to stay out of their grasp." She closed her eyes for a brief moment as if remembering the slums she was raised in.

Grayson wondered if she would faint. If she did, he was in serious trouble.

"Lady Blackburn thinks you and Odelia planned the entire kidnapping scheme." He returned to the table.

"Lady Blackburn is a snob and worse, a complete simpering idiot." Til's eyes flashed. "She is a spoiled rich woman who has never had to dirty her hands in her life. She knows nothing of the slums we crawled out of. I did what I had to do to save my own life. She wouldn't understand that. She doesn't have to. My job was over with the Blackburns the moment I walked into that room and alerted them to Madeline Blackburn being in jeopardy. No jobs were available to me after admitting to that knowledge about their daughter."

"Why? If you are telling the truth, you saved her." Grayson's eyebrows drew together in confusion.

"That information would cause a scandal for their family. Odelia made her play and I trumped her, no more, no less. It's not personal and there was no emotion involved. It was the right thing for Madeline, Malcolm and me... It was a way to pay him back for his... protection. I took it. I would do it again." Til's eyes burned with intensity.

Grayson narrowed his eyes. "What protection did you need that Malcolm provided?"

"Stop being daft. What kind of protection do girls need, do you think? I needed him to keep me from being *raped* at every turn." Til's entire body tensed as she spoke those words. "He kept me safe even at the risk of his own life. He still keeps me safe. That's why I want him here. Now."

"You prostituted yourself to Lord Blackburn." Grayson hounded her.

Til rolled her eyes.

"You will answer me." Grayson leaned forward so they were nose to nose.

"I. Will. Not." Til defied him.

"Yes or no." Grayson's jaw clenched in anger.

"Or." Til's eyes clashed with his.

Grayson's face was inches from Til's. "Answer me."

"You don't need to know. It does not pertain to the facts of this case." Til didn't back down.

"A girl's life is at stake." Grayson shouted at her. "How do I know that you aren't behind it, if you would sink so low in the past? It presents a pattern."

"Stop this line of interrogation or I will say nothing further." Til's lips thinned in fury.

Grudgingly, Grayson backed off.

"I believe that Odelia is dragging up this old mess to establish some semblance of control in this gang, to carve a new place." Til's posture stiffened. "If she wants this money in Toronto, it's because she can't stay in London."

"Who would she *know* in Toronto?" Grayson demanded.

"I don't know." Til took a deep breath, let it out slowly. "I have not kept in contact with her."

"You're lying. You think you can keep information from me? I'll break you, Til," Grayson vowed as he faced her across the table.

Battle ready, Til leaned forward until they were almost nose to nose. "You can't break me. Worse than you have tried."

Grayson moved in even closer. "I can try and I daresay I would enjoy the challenge."

"You sound a lot like Lord Blackburn," Til lashed at him.

His face reddened. "I know women like you. I know about suffragettes."

"You don't know women like me." Til looked down her nose at him, her entire body stiffened. She didn't look away, she didn't blink. "There are no other women *like me*. You can't intimidate me, and you won't break me. You're out of your depth. We're done here. I'll take my leave and you can try to work out where Odelia Bristol is. I'm not touching this. Nora Blackburn is not my concern. I paid my dues to the Blackburns."

"I bet you did," Grayson sneered.

"I have no intention of tangling myself up with Odelia Bristol. I'll hire more protection and I will crack on. I have a clinic to run; you are wasting my time." Til stood up.

"You are in my custody." Grayson stood up and towered over her. Til didn't flinch. She looked up at him as if he were an errant child.

"I am having extradition papers drawn up as we speak. You're coming to Toronto and I will dangle you *as bait* to any Bristol who shows up along the way." Grayson bared his teeth. "I'd like to see how they treat their own on foreign soil with a straight constabulary to prosecute them."

Til glared at him.

"I will use you to get to Nora. You are no better than a prostitute." Grayson's voice dipped low with revulsion.

"Prostitute?" Til shook her head.

Taking Til by the upper arms, their eyes locked with loathing for each other. Grayson breathed hard with fury. "You will cooperate, I guarantee it."

Til tried to twist away, he held her easily. Her eyes met his as she struggled to no avail against him. Grayson pinned Til to the wall.

Suddenly, she stopped struggling. "Let me go, or I'll scream."

"Cooperate or it's back to the cells for the night this time," Grayson vowed.

"I am warning you one last time." Til choked on anger. "I will never return to those cells."

"You will go where ever I put you. Until I have my answers, you will do as you're told." Grayson held her against the wall.

"Help me! He's hurting me!" Til screamed at the top of her lungs. "Detective Grayson is hurting me!"

Grayson dropped his hands as two constables scrambled into the interview room.

"She's lying." Grayson held his hands out as if he had never touched her.

Tears spilled down her cheeks. "Detective Grayson is hurting me." She wept as she collapsed into the arms of a constable who scrambled to hold her up.

"This is unacceptable." Graves muscled his way into the room. He stood between Til and Grayson. "You lay a hand on her, you answer to me."

Grayson held his hands up in surrender as the men swarmed around Til.

"Would you stay here? I'm afraid for my safety." Til pressed her forehead into the shoulder of a constable, and Grayson was certain she deliberately let her voice shake. To all the male officers in the room, she sounded delicate and terrified.

Grayson rolled his eyes as he watched every man in the room leap to her aid. He was doomed. Interrogation over.

She easily manipulated these men; her femininity was a weapon she brandished with precision. This was clearly not the first time. Til Stone was a master at drawing a protective instinct out of men.

Grayson watched helplessly as they fell over themselves to ensure she had a handkerchief and a strong arm to lean on. They murmured "There, there," and "I say", and they shot him looks of contempt. One ordered tea with extra sugar; it arrived in moments.

Is this how she evades arrest? Is she a criminal or a doctor caught in a cross fire?

His eyes narrowed at her show of vulnerability.

Grudgingly, however, Grayson had to admit he had used his physical power against her. Not hurting her, but purposely intimidating her with his size and strength, overpowering her, hoping to break her, to make her confess. Grayson was convinced, watching her performance, between the two of them; she wielded far more power than he did. The men hovered around her ready to take him down if he so much as looked at her hard. He was a respected detective and she was accused of procuring girls for prostitution! For all they knew she was the criminal mastermind behind the Bristol Butchers! The police officers poured her tea and handed her fresh handkerchiefs. He shook his head.

The power of women.

More tears slid down her face. Grayson's jaw clenched at this *show* of delicacy. Til Stone was as hard as nails. He'd interrogated her and she hadn't even flinched. Even after an hour in the cells she had come out harder, with iron clad resolve to defy him.

Finally, she pretended to calm down. The constables around her, including Graves, created a wall of protection between her and Grayson.

One of the constables helpfully poured her more tea and handed her the teacup.

"There, there, I'll stay and ensure he doesn't hurt you. You are quite safe." Graves sat down beside her; he patted her narrow shaking shoulder.

"There is no need to stay." Grayson scowled. "I didn't lay a hand on her."

"I'll stay all the same." Graves shot a hard look at Grayson. "The poor dear is distraught." Grayson turned from the spectacle because try as he might, he couldn't stop rolling his eyes.

"The *poor dear* is a suspect in a white slavery ring. There are three dead prostitutes connected to her clinic!" Grayson reminded them. His concerns fell on deaf ears.

"Thankfully, Detective Grayson ruled me out as a suspect." Til spoke demurely to Graves.

"Of course he did." Graves poured her more tea.

A constable pushed Grayson aside as he placed a hot meal on the table for Til.

Steak and kidney pie! Where had they found that!

Grayson rolled his eyes.

As Til ate her pie, another officer entered the interview room. "Til Stone is requested at her clinic, new evidence has surfaced."

Chapter Ten

Til smirked as Superintendent Graves narrowed his gaze at Grayson. "Lark and Hugh will accompany you." He got up to leave the interview room. "If she has even one complaint about your conduct, Grayson, I will report you to your superior."

Til dropped her eyes to the floor, pretending to be defeated.

"I am sorry, on behalf of the men here. We do not condone what this police officer has done to you. He is from... Canada. A savage, from the frontier."

"I know. I am familiar with Canadians. An uncouth lot, for sure." Til shuddered.

"We'll come at once." Grayson reached for Til's arm.

"Get your hands off me." Til twisted out of his grasp.

"Detective Grayson, this is your last warning." Graves pointed at Grayson.

"If I were going to use physical force, she'd be black and blue by now," Grayson snapped.

"I fear for my safety," Til gasped.

"I'm reporting you. To threaten a woman with force is inappropriate." Graves shook his head.

"I didn't threaten her!" Grayson protested.

"Close enough it doesn't matter. Lark and Hugh — keep him supervised. Step in if he is rough with her. By rough, I mean, don't even let him raise his voice to her. She is distraught."

As Graves turned his back, Grayson leaned down to hiss into her ear.

"That was quite a performance. It won't work on me." Grayson led her out of the police station as he tightened his hand around her upper arm. "I am not letting you out of my sight. Don't fight me, you'll only get hurt."

"Stop threatening me with physical violence." Til looked pointedly at Graves who fumed at Grayson.

Lark and Hugh hovered behind them. Grayson dragged Til to a halt and then held her against the wall. "Stop it."

Til, on tiptoe, reached up and dragged his head down so she could hiss into his ear. "As soon as Malcolm comes back, he will deal with you to the fullest extent of the law after he has beaten you bloody for interrogating me in such a fashion."

Grayson let go of Til and followed her into the cab and instructed the driver to take them to the clinic. Til gasped as she saw another dead body on the threshold.

"Do you want to know why I won't cooperate with the police? This, this right here! The fourth girl and you do nothing. I have written reports; I have begged you to step in. How much do the Bristol Butchers pay you to look the other way? How much?" she demanded an answer from Lark and Hugh. The men refused to meet her eyes. "You are cowards and I despise you." Til turned her attention to Grayson, "You are nothing more than a bully. If you think you will bully me into some sort of compliance, you are greatly mistaken."

Grayson remained silent.

"This is the fourth girl. Fourth! These girls have suffered and died because the Bristols pay you to look the other way. What do they pay you?" Til pointed at the corrupt police officers.

Til raced to the body, dropped to her knees and fumbled at the body's wrist, trying to find a pulse. Lark and Hugh trailed behind.

"I'll dictate, you take notes. I want this murder investigated if you have to bring in police from Toronto to do it," Til commanded Grayson. "We should get Cole; you'll need a second witness. These two will hide evidence and it will be a disaster. Go immediately to find Cole McDougall," Til said to Lark who hesitated.

"You heard her, go!" Grayson barked at the constable who jumped to action.

Til pressed her ear to the girl's chest and failed to find a pulse. Enid quietly came to her side to assist.

"Enid, is the examination room ready?" Having verified the girl was dead, Til rifled through the girl's clothes, looking for the brand she knew was there. She stopped suddenly as she opened the girl's thin coat.

"Yes." Enid spoke dully.

"I'll help you get her inside." Grayson crouched down beside Til.

"There's a note on her chest." Til's eyes widened as she unpinned the note.

"What does it say?" Grayson gently gathered up the dead girl and carried her down a narrow corridor to an examintyation room.

"It says..." Til slumped against the door frame of the examination room, hands shaking on the note. "The note says 9 Ann Street." Til's lips were white with fear.

"That's the address of the slum..." Grayson's voice trailed off as Til doubled over and tried to breathe through the horror that suddenly crippled her.

This girl was sent for me. This girl is what would have happened to me if Malcolm hadn't stepped in. This would have been Shannon's future if I hadn't stolen her back from the slums. This is my past. Right here, right in front of me. I can't run from it. If I hadn't run... this is my worst nightmare and I can't wake up from it.

"Let me help you to a chair." Grayson reached out to her.

"Get away from me." Til clamped her hand over her mouth as bile rose in her throat, vomit close behind. She couldn't fight as Grayson pulled a chair into the room and helped her sit down before she fell down. He pulled the door shut.

"This is my past. Here to destroy me. Everything I've worked for." Til tried to speak past the fist of horror in her throat. "I've tried my whole life to try to stay a step ahead."

Grayson sat down opposite her and waited for her to compose herself.

"You need Cole; you can't prosecute this yourself. You are only one man." Til pressed a handkerchief to her mouth.

"I'm sure he is on his way. Now, I'll send for one of the other doctors to do an examination," Grayson said. "Who do you recommend?"

Til wiped her eyes. Enid bustled into the room with a basin and a white coat for Til.

"This girl was sent as a message for me." Til stood, visibly pulled herself together and took the white coat. She pulled it on. "I'll examine her."

She took a deep breath as Enid hovered around her, handing her a towel. Grayson got up and stood by the door, eyebrows drawn together in concern.

"If you would be so kind as to bring me some tea with lots of sugar and dry toast. I feel a little nauseous."

"Of course." Enid went to the door. "There is something shiny in her mouth, Til. I'm not sure what it is."

Til breathed as shallow as possible to keep her stomach settled.

"If you are ill, another doctor can do this examination and you can stay to see what we find," Grayson offered as he hesitated by the dead girl.

"Stand back." Til ignored his concern and moved to the girl and carefully extracted the shiny objects from her mouth. Grayson stood still across the examination table from Til.

"They're cufflinks?" Grayson tilted his head to the side.

Dread pooled in Til's stomach as she turned the cufflinks over in her hand. She gasped as she examined the back of them. Raw fear rushed through her. Screams tore up through Til as the cufflinks clattered to the floor.

Chapter Eleven

Only one thought pounded through Til's mind as she dropped to her knees.

Malcolm is dead. No, he can't be. He is. Malcolm is dead.

Til hardly noticed Shannon's arms around her as she wept. Pain sliced through Til with each beat of her broken heart. Rocking in Shannon's arms, she tried and failed to stop weeping.

Shannon's eyes filled with tears as she asked Enid to bring Til calcium carbonate and laudanum.

"Not laudanum," Til wept.

"You are distraught, and our first priority is your pregnancy." Clipped tones, professional in her assessment, Shannon measured out the calcium carbonate and held Til's jaw as she administered it. "Double dose, come on. I know. You need this Til, we are not losing this baby."

"Pregnant!" The blood drained from Grayson's face.

Til ignored him as she obediently took the spoon full of calcium carbonate. "Not laudanum. I have to finish this to the end."

"You do not," Shannon contradicted her. "I will go. I will follow these notes and I will find Malcolm." Shannon's breath caught on the name.

Til tried to see Shannon through her tears. "Half a dose of that laudanum."

Shannon ignored Til and pressed the full dose into her mouth as if she were a babe.

Til felt the drug swim through her bloodstream. She wiped her tears and held Shannon's hands in her own.

"Thank you for offering, but I have to see these clues for myself. You don't know my story."

"I know some of it." Shannon's eyes swam with tears.

Til reached out and wiped the tears from Shannon's cheeks.

"She wants me to go to Ann Street." Til closed her eyes at the thought.

"Maybe he is alive, and the Bristols are ransoming him for money." Shannon tightened her grip on Til's hands.

"He's dead," Til said. Bitterness sharpened her tone. "He wouldn't allow anyone to take these cufflinks. He would have just paid whatever she wanted. This is about more than money." Til pulled away from Shannon and pressed her hands to her heart trying to ease the ache there. "I need a moment. Please." Til's eyes met Grayson's and she was surprised to see sympathy there.

"Of course." Grayson put his hand on her shoulder briefly before he left the room.

Til pressed her face into Shannon's skirt and tried to ignore the memories of Ann Street as they engulfed her.

Drunk father, drunk landlord... a poker game. Stop. You can't think these thoughts. These thoughts weaken you. You must be strong.

Shannon wept as she rubbed Til's back. After a gentle knock, Cole entered the examination room. He crouched down and placed his hand on Til's shoulder. Til sat up and wiped tears from her eyes.

"Detective Grayson told me what happened. Til, are you all right?" Cole asked.

Til's splintered heart ached as Shannon pressed her face into his shoulder. He held her tight against him as she wept into his chest.

"Shhh, we don't know for sure." Cole rubbed her back and held her tightly. "Til, we will find him. Detective Grayson says there is a note, we know where to go." He reached out to take Til's hand in his. "We don't know anything for certain yet. Please, let's all remain calm until we know for sure." Cole gave Til's hand a hard squeeze and then murmured against Shannon's ear. "Darling. Please, don't cry. We know nothing yet."

Why did I think you were a threat to her? You would trade your life for hers.

Til pulled herself to her feet and wrapped her arms around herself. She tried and failed to tear her gaze away from Cole and Shannon. The way he held her and cared for her; Til suddenly felt foolish for all the levels of contracts she had forced him to sign. Cole McDougall would stop a bullet for Shannon and not even think twice. Grudgingly, here on the second worst day of her life, she trusted one man other than Malcolm. Til Stone trusted Cole with all her broken, bruised, aching heart. She could give Shannon the blessing to return to Brandon because there wasn't a bad bone in Cole's body. She realised as Cole wiped Shannon's tears away with his thumb and kissed her tenderly, she had been harming them. All this time. The love between a man like him and a woman like her should be celebrated. Not stifled by an old sniping aunt. Cole gently wiped tears from Shannon's eyes.

"We'll find him." Cole looked up at Til.

"I know," Til replied dully.

Watching Cole's fingertips chase Shannon's tears away brought memories of the night Malcolm dragged the Bristols off her to the surface of her mind. Fresh pain stabbed through her as she thought of how Malcolm's fingertips felt along her cheekbones, the sound of his voice as he said. "You're safe now, you're safe with me." The feel of his arms as they locked around her as she had shattered from the fear of what had happened at Ann Street and what had nearly happened at 32 Bluebell Street, on the same night.

A wash of sorrow, of cold empty loss, dragged through her. With Malcolm, Til had been complete. Her husband, lover, protector at the risk of his own life—she would never have it again.

I must find Malcolm and if Malcolm is dead, bring Odelia Shipley Bristol to justice. There is no time to think of the past... I must gather my strength. I can't stop. I can never stop.

Til wanted to ignore the voice in her head urging her to keep moving; she couldn't. The iron hard determination to survive that had surfaced in her on November 2nd, 1881 resurfaced now. She clung to the anger that came with it.

Grayson came back to the door and checked his pocket watch. Til knew he was desperate to get to Ann Street and uncover whatever horror was waiting for them there. While she was gutted by the loss of Malcolm, he was determined to find Nora Blackburn.

You can be impatient all you want. You'll wait until I'm ready.

"Detective Grayson." Til spoke in clipped tones as she brushed tears out of her eyes and smoothed her hair down. "Please inform the police that this woman was killed by the Bristol Butchers." Til exposed the left hip of the woman to show Grayson the telltale marking of 'B', just as she knew it would be. "If you would escort me to Ann Street, I believe there will be another clue once we get there." Her voice cracked on the address as she fought to present a calm veneer.

"Til, let me take you and Shannon home. Detective Grayson and I will follow the clues and we will report back to you with what we find. This is too much for you," Cole said softly. He held Shannon's hand as he moved closer to Til, preparing to intervene. "You cannot put your life or the life of your baby in danger."

And this one is bossy.

"If the Bristols wanted me dead, I would be dead now. They won't kill me in the slums." Til's breath caught. "They don't want me dead. They want me destroyed and humiliated... this is pay back and retribution." Til closed her eyes as memories assaulted her. She braced herself. "This is my past, *mine alone*. I must face it, or this will never stop. We find the next clue. Let's crack on."

"Please, Doctor Stone. You are in a fragile state. Let Cole and I proceed, please go home and rest." Grayson swallowed hard, guilt showing all over his face. "Cole and I will get to the bottom of this."

"You have no say in whether she continues or goes home. You have done quite enough." Cole stepped in between them. "I will have your badge for the inappropriate interrogation you conducted this afternoon. She is pregnant and forty."

Til winced at the label Cole threw at her.

"My sincere apologies, I wasn't aware of that." Grayson held his hands up. "I deal with white slavers every day; my own sister was stolen and it has clouded my judgement. She is safe with me. I guarantee it."

"In future, remember that you cannot treat a woman suspect the same way as a man. You shouldn't need to be told that." Cole's eyes narrowed at Grayson.

"You are absolutely right. I stand corrected." Grayson didn't try to excuse himself. "My apologies Doctor Stone. Please return home and I will report back with my findings."

Cole crossed his arms over his chest, "And."

Grayson's eyes met Cole's for a moment. "Doctor Stone, I would like to further apologise. I had no idea you were in such a delicate state."

"Let's get to the bottom of this," Til snapped at both of them.

"I'm coming with you." Shannon tossed her soiled handkerchief on the pile of dirty laundry.

"Absolutely not." Cole shook his head.

Til turned to her niece. "Shannon, would you please go to my home, have the staff make supper for the four of us. This won't take long. Cole and Grayson are going to document whatever we... find... and after that I will need you tonight, please."

Shannon's eyes filled with tears.

"Please," Til asked so softly Shannon wrapped her arms around her again. "Shannon, I can't bear for you to see what I've come from."

"You took me from the same thing," Shannon wept. "I was there in the same slums. You don't need to shield me from that." Shannon's arms tightened around Til.

"Yes, I do. I am your aunt and I love you. Cole is right. Listen to your husband."

"Til!" Shannon gasped, she pulled back to look Til in the face. Despite the horror of finding the cufflinks and what that might imply, Shannon looked at Til as if she had never seen her before. "Did you just tell me to... listen to my husband?"

"I'll probably never say it again," Til said dryly. "But today, I agree with him. It is getting late. I need a hot meal and I'll need you tonight. No need for both of us looking at all this horror." Til straightened up to her full height.

"What was in that laudanum?" Cole asked Shannon.

"I have been remiss." Til placed her hand on Cole's forearm. "Forgive me, please. Go to Brandon with my blessing. You should get as far away from this city as you can."

"I'm not leaving you now. Til, you need me to stay." Shannon's eyes filled with tears again. Cole slid his arm around her waist.

"We'll talk tonight. Cole, Grayson, would you please take me to Ann Street. Lark and Hugh can't be trusted. Maybe after you witness this mess, you'll believe I'm not part of the kidnapping."

With that statement, Til swept out of her clinic and the men had no choice but to step into place beside her. Entering the hackney cab, Til ignored the men. There was only room for her and Grayson. She kept her gaze on the streets as the cab dragged her back to Ann Street. All the way back in time, to her old home. Her heart hammered as she saw familiar sights. Memories of hunger and pain hollowed her and brought back old fears. She could feel Grayson's eyes on her. She ignored him. Valiantly, she tried to stifle sobs as they surfaced.

When Til stood in front of her old home, the one she had run from, the memories were too much to bear. Weeping, Til dropped to her knees again.

Chapter Twelve

"I'm sorry. I need a moment to..." Til vomited into the gutter as Cole leaped out of another cab a few feet away.

Grayson stood by helplessly.

"I haven't been back here since... since the night I ran." Til shuddered.

"I'll go in first," Grayson offered.

"You won't know where to look." Til tried to speak past the hard knot of terror in her throat. Her eyes swept over the broken doors and windows. Piles of rubbish and broken furniture cluttered the street by the entrance. A rat peeked out from a heap of broken crockery.

Cole crouched down by her and put his hand on her shoulder.

"I'm going in first." Grayson spoke in a tone no one contradicted. "This is still my investigation."

As Grayson entered the building, Til pulled herself together. Listening for any indication there was someone inside, she could hear nothing. Finally, she couldn't wait any longer. Standing in the doorway, Til watched as Grayson searched all of the tiny flat and there was nothing. Not a soul. Dead. Empty. A floor grey from dust, drab brown weathered wood walls and broken windows greeted her. No one had lived in this slum for a few years. Cobwebs clung to every surface. Til looked in the direction of the kitchen and physically trembled at the memories. Quickly, she turned and focused on the door to the old bedroom she had shared with all her siblings. No better memories there. Sadness dragged at her.

"How do people live like this?" Grayson directed his question to Cole. "It must be brutally cold in winter."

"They don't live. They only survive." Til replied dully. She gulped down bile that threatened to burn her throat at the thought of entering this place. She could smell the alcohol on her father's breath, she could feel the shame as the landlord's hands... she refused to allow the memories to surface completely.

"The next note will not be here." Til forced her feet to move forward to the one bedroom past the area that they had used as a kitchen. "It will be in the bedroom."

Grayson cautiously went to her side.

There, stabbed onto a piece of broken window, was a note.

Til slid her eyes shut as she looked at the broken glass. Remembered hurtling herself through the window. Tears filled her eyes as she carefully pulled the note free of the jagged glass.

"It says 32 Bluebell Street." Til's tone was rough with pain.

"You mean 32 Blue Street?" Grayson held his hand out for the note. She handed it to him. "That is the name of the brothel where the Bristols..."

"No, Bluebell Street, is the name of the street where the Bristols operated until 1890. The London County Council changed the name of the street to Blue Street in 1890."

"The name of a ship that brought prostitutes to Toronto is Bluebell." Grayson's eyes gleamed.

Til met his eyes as he assimilated another link, another clue that took them closer to Nora Blackburn.

"Odelia runs that brothel on Blue Street. I have a theory." Til took a deep breath to steady her nerves.

"Let's hear it." Grayson's words were spoken with surprising gentleness.

Cole entered the bedroom and the three of them stared at the note as she spoke.

"The brothel on Bluebell Street was given to her after she gave birth to her son, Shipley. That is hers. The structure of the Bristols is changing now that Bobby is dead. This was the place that..." Til stopped speaking as she remembered the last time she was at Odelia's brothel. All the old fear of her brush with the Bristols paralysed her for a moment. "That was where Odelia wielded all her power. I believe there is a new head of the gang; she may have lost her authority. I don't know. Only the old gang members would know her brothel as Bluebell. Malcolm was led down this path of horror first. He would remember it as Bluebell. He would try to protect me from revisiting all of this. That I'm here, looking at this note, means he's dead. Malcolm would never have allowed this to happen to me, never." Til's lips twisted with bitterness.

Grayson pulled a notebook out of his breast pocket and started writing.

"Is there any significance of the note being in this bedroom instead of the kitchen or the other room?" Grayson asked gently.

Til gasped in pain as he spoke. "My sisters were in this room." Til didn't wipe the tears that slid down her face. She held her hand to her heart. "I raced by them..." Til moved through the room as if they were still there sleeping in their beds. "I fled through this window while my sisters slept..." Til's breath caught. "While my little brother slept, here..." Til's eyes widened in horror as she pointed to the opposite wall. "It was my sisters I worried for the most." She pressed the palm of her hand against her mouth. Devestation shuddered through her.

"What happened in this room, Dr. Stone?" Grayson spoke barely above a whisper.

"I can't speak of it." Til turned from him.

Cole moved closer to her and placed a hand on her shoulder in comfort.

"It is not relevant to this case. This is intended to break me. That is all. This is her way of telling me that the past is not buried and that I will pay for it; for what happened here, for what I ran from. At the end of these clues we'll find Malcolm." Her voice caught with emotion.

"Take your time," Cole murmured.

"We should get to Blue Street right away." Til turned back and looked past him to the corner of the room. Her hands shook as she tried to look away and couldn't. "However, I fear going to the Blue Street brothel with Lark and Hugh. Those constables would deliver me to whoever is running the Bristols now on a plate."

Grayson shook his head. "You've nothing to fear from them."

"They wouldn't take me to the leader like this though." Til looked down at her expensive dress. "No. I would have to go in looking like a prostitute. Bristols like their women to know their place," Til spoke bitterly. "If Malcolm hadn't rescued me..." Til closed her eyes and shook her head at the memories.

"Why now?" Grayson's tone remained gentle as he opened the battered door for her to leave the bedroom and the memories there.

Til ignored that question as she followed him to the threshold. Shame made her heart pound. She felt hot and cold as she turned to him. "I need a moment."

"Of course." Grayson and Cole stepped out of the dilapidated room.

She closed the door on them and faced the empty room and the memories there. Til sat down and rested her back against the wall. She could hear Grayson clear his throat with impatience. She ignored him. The first time back in this room since she fled. Memories of sisters, giggling, and plaiting hair swept through her. Her breath caught on a sob as she remembered brushing Martha's hair.

"You would be so proud of your daughter, Martha," Til whispered to the memory of her little sister. "She's brilliant. An absolutely brilliant doctor. She is better than me because she shows more compassion. She is fearless; she promotes women's health like a soldier. Shannon found a good man, she's going back to Canada with him." Til's heart shattered as she spoke those words. "She has been a delight in my life. When I thought I would never have children, I found her. Too late to save you though."

Til closed her eyes, tears poured down her cheeks. "I'm so sorry about that but I saved her; Malcolm helped me save her. He is better than me, really. You know how I am, so driven. But Malcolm made time for her, made sure she always had what she needed. Anyway, her man is really good to her. He treats her the way a man should treat a woman. He loves her. But, oh, Martha, she is my heart." Til's breath caught on a sob. "I watch her work, I watch her quick mind and I thank you for her, Martha. She has made my heart sing with happiness. My life wouldn't have been complete without her in it. I was lucky to have her."

Til took a deep breath and let it out very slowly. "But I wish we could have shared her. I got to you too late." Gathering her thoughts and emotions, she traced a shoe print in the dust on the floor of the abandoned dwelling. No sun penetrated into this room; it was blazing hot in summer and icy cold in winter. Fond memories of sleeping with her sisters in a bed in the corner of the room, and of her mother tucking them in with tired hands and lines on her face which deepened with each passing year, made her weep from the loss.

Her heart broke as she whispered to her sisters she'd left behind.

"I wish I could tell you how sorry I am. I am just so sorry. I wish I knew what happened, but at the same time if you were hurt... hurt by Mr. Carn I could never live with that." With that statement, Til put her face in her hands and wept. "Alys, my dear Alys, I have thought of you every day. Did you keep Jimmy with you?" Til wiped tears from her face with her skirt. "I tried to find you; I tried to find all of you. I'm so sorry. Alys, I beg you to forgive me."

Chapter Thirteen

Finally, Til appeared through the door, eyes rimmed red with tears. She closed the door behind her, leaned against it and shut her eyes.

Grayson looked at his pocket watch.

Cole cleared his throat.

"Right then, would you ask the driver to take us to Blue Street, previously Bluebell Street, into the heart of Bristol territory." Til lifted her chin and despite her grief stood tall and braced for battle.

Once inside the carriage, dragging them inexorably forward, Til tried and failed to stop trembling as she sat beside Grayson. Archenemy just that afternoon, suddenly he'd become one of the only two men she trusted to take her to Odelia's brothel and keep her alive. The hard line of his arm against hers felt strangely reassuring. Having felt his strength and the power he kept tightly leashed, Til was grateful it would now be used for her defense. She tucked her narrow and shaking shoulder behind his, so they would fit in the small bench of the coach. Nausea clawed up inside her as she dreaded what she was about to find at the brothel Malcolm had rescued her from at the age of fifteen. She swallowed hard as the carriage ground to a halt.

Grayson climbed down and held his hands out to assist her.

"Constable McDougall and I are going in first," Grayson commanded. "Lark and Hugh, stay with Doctor Stone. We will let you know what we find."

"You might miss a clue," Til protested.

"Listen." Grayson's stance broadened, "It's clear to me now; this is all a deranged woman dragging you back to the worst time of your life. You don't need to see what is behind this door."

"Detective Grayson, I have to see this to the end." Til drew herself up to her full height

"No." Grayson stood in front of her, blocking her access to the brothel. "No. You will wait here."

Cole stood by Grayson. "If Malcolm is in there, I can identify him."

Grayson nodded in the direction of the door. "Good idea. You go in and tell us what you find; I'll stay here with her."

Cole came straight back out as Til paced beside Grayson.

"He's not in here." Cole's eyes were wide with worry.

"He'll be at the back." Til could barely get the words out as she realised where Odelia would have put the body.

In the back alley, where Malcolm had nearly killed Royce Bristol.

Her heart pounded as she remembered the fight. How Royce Bristol had put his hands on her... same place as the landlord. Til tried to pull away from Grayson's grip. His arms tightened. She stopped struggling. He was a powerful man; it was useless to fight against him.

"Please." She drew back and looked up at him. "I have to see this to the end."

"You're pregnant, I don't think you should go into that alley. Cole and I will deal with it." Grayson held her back.

Til shook her head. "Please, if there is anything I can do for him, I have to be allowed to do it."

Grayson's jaw tightened but his grip relaxed.

She pulled away and led the men to the back of the brothel on Blue Street. Sure enough, he was there, in the exact place where he had been prepared to trade his life for hers.

Til moved forward and crouched down by his still body.

A stabbing pain shot through her womb and with it the thought that she had not only lost Malcolm but very possibly his child too. Til couldn't handle the thought. She scrambled in her pocket for the calcium carbonate and took a deep swig. She curled into a ball of pain on the hard, grey cobblestones beside Malcolm's body. She pressed her face into his sleeve.

Grayson crouched down beside her. "I'll take you out of here."

"Don't you dare leave this scene," Til reprimanded him. "You have to prosecute Odelia Shipley Bristol; she's murdered him and put him here.

She is the only one I can think of who would hate me enough to do this. You must destroy this prostitution ring. Malcolm cannot have died in vain." Til tried to will the cramping pain away as the cold cobblestones bit into her hip and side. "You have to build this case and prosecute it."

"I intend to." Grayson crouched down and placed his hand on her shoulder.

"Ensure this crime scene is not contaminated." Til demanded. "Promise me you will stay until the proper documents and papers are submitted. She can't get away with this." Til put her arm around Malcolm and then gasped as she drew it back. "He's cold. Oh, my god, he is so cold." She shuddered and drew away from him.

"I'll stay." Grayson's eyes softened in sympathy as she vomited the calcium carbonate onto the street and scrambled to take more.

"What does that do?" Grayson pounced on the vial and helped her unscrew the cap. Gently, he held it to her mouth as she took a deep gulp of it.

"Prevents miscarriage." Til groaned as she rolled to her side trying to stop the pain. She willed the calcium carbonate to stay in her stomach long enough to stop the cramping pain that roared through her.

"Is it working?" Grayson's face paled in fear.

"Not yet." Til's eyes filled with tears. "I need that laudanum, too. I don't think I need a clear head for the rest of this."

"The more drugged the better," Grayson agreed grimly as he quickly untwisted the cap off the laudanum bottle. He held her head up as she took a deep gulp and then helped her lay back down.

Cole and Grayson crouched down beside Til as she lay on the cobblestones. Grayson pulled off his coat and placed it under her head.

"Thank you," she murmured as Cole put his coat around her shoulders. "We need a doctor who is not tainted by the Bristols, someone who will give evidence in court. Someone with some integrity if such a thing exists." Til spoke with the last of her strength.

As the sun set on Blue Street, Til lay on the ground and silently begged the cramping pain to stop. By some miracle, within a few minutes of the calcium hitting her blood stream, it did.

Laudenum however, was a double-edged sword, as it loosened her muscles and stopped the cramping, it unlocked the painful memories that surfaced in her mind.

Chapter Fourteen

Memories of the night Malcolm fought for her freedom threatened to gut Til completely.

That night, forced to take her chances with the possibility of rape on the streets against the certainty of violation by the men her father drank with. Her body shuddered in horror, even now, as she remembered the sheer terror of looking into Royce Bristol's eyes as they swept over her. She had been rail-thin; they all were because they all lived on the brink of starvation. No one had enough to eat until they joined a gang.

Til knew, even then, to stand tall against Royce. Any sign of weakness or begging wouldn't work.

"Are you here to deliver me safely to Odelia?" Til had asked sweetly.

Royce's brother Bobby liked Odelia at one time, did he still? Would Royce think twice about violating a friend of Odelia's?

Til's brain scrambled to form sentences. She remembered flashing him her biggest smile. If there was a shred of decency in him, she was appealing to it. She forced herself to giggle.

Royce Bristol spit tobacco juice out on the cobblestones.

"Nah, other plans for a girl like you, Matilda," Royce smiled at her like a wolf.

"You know my father would..." Til remembered trying to bluff.

"Your father's a drunk." Royce's eyes undressed her.

There was no man in Til's life that would make him pay for anything he chose to do to her. She knew it — he knew it. The only thing that would stop this assault was the power of a fist and she didn't have access to that. Nobody cared about fifteen-year-old girls from the East End. Not their drunk fathers, not the police. The mothers cared but the mothers held no power. Not against the likes of a Bristol.

"Too right," Til agreed.

Royce took a step toward her and she took a step back until her back pressed into a hard, unforgiving brick wall. Royce pinned her there with a hand on her throat.

"Hey!" A man called out from down the street.

Til looked from Royce to a young man who sauntered straight up to the two of them.

"I'm Malcolm," Malcolm said to Royce, "that's my girl there."

Royce growled obscenities at Malcolm.

"I don't want trouble." Malcolm put his hands out in surrender indicating he didn't want a fight.

Matilda's pulse pounded hard under Royce's hand on her throat. She'd never laid eyes on this young man in her life and she pleaded with her eyes for him not to leave her there.

"Mine now," Royce taunted Malcolm.

He pressed harder against her throat so she struggled to breathe. She tried and failed to drag his arm away. The more she struggled, the tighter his hand squeezed her throat.

"Let her go! I'm not asking again," Malcolm's voice hardened in warning.

Matilda fought panic as black dots danced around her peripheral vision.

"If I have to take your hand off her, I'll break it," Malcolm growled at Royce.

Royce leaned forward and spoke directly in her ear. "I'll have you when I'm done with him." He spit another stream of tobacco, then dropped her.

Til slithered away from him as she gasped for breath. She moved behind Malcolm, staying in the shadows.

Royce threw a punch at Malcolm as hard as he could. Malcolm dodged the punch and lightning fast hit Royce hard enough in the face that he staggered. He snatched a knife from his boot. Til screamed a warning as Royce attempted to sink the knife into Malcolm's abdomen. Malcolm sidestepped him and drove his fist into a kidney. Royce roared in pain as Malcolm took him down by driving his foot into the side of his knee. Once

Royce was down, Malcolm pounced on him and beat him until he stopped moving.

Malcolm hauled Royce up and spoke into his ear. "If you come after her, you'll have to come through me."

Malcolm dropped Royce on the hard cobblestones and turned his attention to Til.

"Come on." Malcolm held his hand out to Til and helped her up. "Let's get you out of here."

The memory of Royce Bristol's voice rang in her ear. "I'll have you when I'm done with him."

She remembered Malcolm half dragging, half running, arm hard around her, all the way to Odelia's. Til remembered the feeling of safety as she crawled into Odelia's home through a broken window. How Odelia's mother held her as she wept. Hand bleeding, throat bruised, cramping as the fear intensified her pain.

Odelia was the only person other than Royce who knew about that night. Of how Malcolm had nearly killed Royce Bristol to protect her. Royce had disappeared after that night. He was supposed to take over the gang, but instead, since he'd been beaten bloody by Malcolm Maddox, he lost his place to his younger brother Bobby.

"Are you all right?" Grayson crouched down beside Til.

Til's mind snapped back to the present as she squinted up at him. Til heard the impatience in his voice. He had a job to do and she was a liability, laying here, trying not to miscarry, thinking about the past. One thought pounding through her head.

Is Royce the new head of the gang now that Bobby is gone? Or is he trying to be?

"I'm all right." Til pushed her thoughts aside as she struggled to sit up. "Let's get to work."

Grayson pressed her back down. "You stay on the ground, you're still pale. What doctor do you want to supervise the medical examiner?"

"Doctor Cotter, she will be at my clinic now." Til bunched the coat under her head.

"She?" Grayson's eyebrow raised in concern.

"Yes, she," Til snapped at him. "Is that a problem?"

"Not at all. My question is this; do you think a woman doctor's word carries as much weight as a man's in court? Whoever examines him will have a target on his back. Do you want a woman to face that sort of harassment? The objective here is to have Odelia charged with murder; not just charged, convicted. You have a crooked police department and likely a crooked medical examiner. Let's do this right."

Til thought about that. "Ask Dr. Wolley to attend. Cole, he lives on my street; you know where. He owes me a favour."

"Lark and Hugh, get the medical examiner," Grayson barked at them and they leapt to comply. "McDougall, go and fetch Dr. Wolley. No one proceeds until he is here."

When Cole and the other two constables had left, Grayson found a chair in the brothel and brought it out so Til could sit and wait for the medical professionals to come.

"You're as tough as nails, Til Stone, I'll give you that," Grayson said as Til ignored the chair. On her knees by Malcolm's body, her eyes glazed with tears as she saw the note stabbed into his chest with a hat pin. No blood, the hat pin had been stabbed into him after he was already dead.

Til's eyes swept over the note. "Did you read this? The note says Matilda Bertram is— I am— on November 2nd, 1906, to bring ten thousand pounds to Warehouse 619 on Dock 318 in Toronto or Nora Blackburn dies next." Til covered her mouth with her hand. "This has to be Odelia. I fled to her that night after the attack. We were friends until we went into service together and when Bobby wanted to kidnap Madeline she expected I would help her. Payback, I guess, for keeping me safe. Anyway, when I turned her in she turned on me obviously. This is her, now, all these years later getting revenge on me," Til said bitterly. "And Malcolm has paid the price."

Was Royce with Odelia right now celebrating that Malcolm, my protector, the only man who cared if I am safe, is dead in the streets like a dog? If I show up with the money to buy back Nora Blackburn, then what? Where is Royce? In Toronto or still in these streets ready to pounce?

Til shuddered and Grayson moved closer.

"So, Odelia is the suspect?" Grayson drew her hand back as she went to take the note.

"That note is for me." Til's eyes flashed in defiance.

"And attached to a murdered man that I will prosecute Odelia, or whomever, for murdering. But leave it there; the medical examiner needs to see it." Grayson held her hand hard in his.

"She's a Bristol," Til warned. "She doesn't think the law applies to her. This has to be conducted very carefully."

"Or else someone is behind her, setting her up. Someone else killed Malcolm and Odelia is going to take the fall. The note is not signed, it could be any enemy you have." Grayson let go of Til's hand. "That's why the note stays there. I will document all this. I'll start building a case against Odelia and see if anyone else crops up as I investigate. This is murder, kidnapping, and procuring girls as prostitutes. However, it's unfortunate that she has run them all through this brothel if my guess is right." Grayson got to his feet and held his hand out to assist Til.

Tentatively, she placed her hand in his, allowing him to help her up. "Why would that matter?" Til's eyes were dark with the pain of having this discussion over Malcolm's body.

"Lesser charge if the girls that are procured are *known prostitutes.*" Grayson spat the sentence out.

Til's jaw dropped in disbelief.

"That's why they are branded! The law says they are worth less if they are known prostitutes?" She shook her head.

"I didn't write the law." Grayson held his hands up as if to ward off an attack. "I am as horrified as you. I believe she snags these girls off the streets, runs them through this brothel first and then sells them. That way the law isn't as concerned. Take a virgin off the streets and sell her, the police care about that. Take a known prostitute and everyone turns a blind eye."

Til shook with fury. "A woman is only of value in court if she is a virgin?"

"In the eyes of the law, it would appear so." Grayson's lips thinned in anger.

"No, not appear so. That is what you're saying." Til's eyes hardened. "She's used this loophole to steal girls, sell them and then ship them."

"The criminal code allows different punishments for different levels of chastity." Grayson explained, "I was shocked when I read it too."

"That puts the girls on trial first," Til gasped.

"It's despicable." Grayson's jaw clenched. "I work with suffragettes in Toronto. They are lobbying, but there are so many things that need to change for women. It is one of many. They are trying very hard to make it difficult to move women from one country to another. Honestly it's a battle." Grayson frowned. "I don't see a resolution anytime soon."

Til's eyes searched Grayson looking for insincerity in his gaze. She could find no hint of it.

As the medical examiner came forward with Lark and Hugh, Cole was quick to assist Doctor Wolley to the back alley.

"Doctor Wolley is here to supervise. This investigation involves the Bristols and we will have no information lost, stolen or tampered with." Grayson instructed the men standing there. The medical examiner's head snapped up. He looked at Constables Lark and Hugh in fear. They shuffled awkwardly.

"When we are done here, I will check ship manifests," Grayson said to Til while the men started working to gather evidence.

"If I'm to meet her in Toronto, she'll already be gone. She'll be on a boat to Toronto by now." Til moved to Grayson's side so that the medical examiner could pronounce the body dead. As he said the word, Til swayed with the pain of it and Grayson was quick to hold her up in case she collapsed.

"She's going to Toronto. That means she's in my city, and she doesn't stand a chance. I'll find her, and I *will* prosecute her. Bristol means nothing in Toronto. She's in for a surprise." Grayson growled to Til.

"I'll pack so I can come with you," Til murmured as she watched Cole take notes as they started to process the crime scene.

"Absolutely not." Grayson turned to Til.

"Grayson." Til's eyes flashed in warning as she spoke. "Get used to the fact that I don't answer to you or any man. I will meet her there with ten thousand pounds and *I will* bring her to justice. I'll be ready to go as soon as passage can be booked. We'll need to leave early next week. I'll book your ticket while I book mine."

"It's not safe for you to travel to Toronto." Grayson's tried to reason with her.

Cole moved to stand by Grayson.

"I don't need a forty-year-old woman miscarrying a baby half way across the Atlantic. My men will find Odelia in Toronto. You stay here where you are safe," Grayson pleaded with her, trying not to distract the doctors from examining Malcolm's body.

Til looked down her nose at him. "I disagree. I'm going home, but when they have a verdict about what happened, I'll expect a full report and then we can work out a strategy." Til pulled on her gloves. "I have a funeral to plan and a lot of packing to do. Cole, would you please stay with Malcolm's body, assist Mr. Grayson, until they are finished? You can tell me what the medical examiner finds out."

"How will you get home?" Cole frowned at Til.

"I'll take a hackney cab," Til snapped at Cole. "Full report, Grayson. An honest report the inspector has signed off." Til levelled her gaze at him. "A duplicate copy to be sent to me at your earliest convenience. We will not rest until justice has been served. I'd say you owe me that much for your outrageous behavior this afternoon."

Grayson's jaw dropped as Til turned on her heel and left them in the back alley of Blue Street.

***

"I'm sure she'll change her mind," Grayson said to Cole. "She'll see reason, right? She can't go across the Atlantic to take down someone who has killed more than once and is running a white slavery ring. She's a woman, a *pregnant* woman!"

"Detective Grayson, Til Stone has never believed the word *no* has ever applied to her. You are not dealing with a regular woman. If she's about to take down this white slavery ring, well, sir, if there is a woman on earth that can do it, it's her." Cole moved back to the body to keep an eye on the medical examiner.

"She's not coming to Toronto; I'm not taking Til Stone anywhere," Grayson vowed as he followed Cole to double check that no evidence was being missed; intentionally or otherwise.

"Detective Grayson, I expect you will have very little say in the matter." Cole gave Grayson a pat on the shoulder in sympathy and got back to work.

Chapter Fifteen

As the carriage clattered to Queen Street West, in the borough of Bloomsbury, Grayson rolled tension out of his shoulders. He checked his pocket watch and frowned at the thought of calling on Doctor Stone after midnight. He took a deep breath and let it out slowly at the thought of an altercation with Doctor Stone. One day in her company and he knew two things with absolute certainty. Doctor Til Stone, Matilda Bertram or whatever she answered to, was the most difficult woman he had ever encountered in his life; that being said, she was also the strongest.

She had nothing to do with the kidnappings and the procuring of girls for the sake of prostitution. Malcolm had been shot in broad daylight in the back. No witnesses, of course, which indicated the Bristol Butchers were behind it. But which one?

He struggled with the fact that while he had been determined to use her as bait to drag Odelia Bristol to justice, he couldn't. He grit his teeth as he thought of finding a different angle. He would not, under any circumstances, drag a pregnant woman to Toronto, no matter how great the stakes were. He made a mental note to send a telegram to Sol — work here is done, home on the first ship west.

As the carriage stopped at Til Stone's front door, Grayson jogged down the sidewalk and knocked politely.

Shannon opened the door; face drawn, eyes red from weeping. She ushered him into the drawing room. "Detective Grayson, where is Cole?"

Grayson's heart went out to her. This was a blow for anyone.

"He stayed with the body." Grayson cleared his throat as pain flashed across Shannon's eyes. "We wanted to be sure no evidence was tampered with."

Shannon nodded and pressed a handkerchief to her eyes. "Could I go to him?"

"I don't think a morgue is any place for a lady." Grayson shuffled awkwardly.

Shannon frowned. "I'm a doctor, sir. I have seen many dead bodies."

Grayson held his hands up in surrender. "It's late, Mrs... uh... Doctor McDougall. I assured Doctor Stone that I would come to see her with the final report from the medical examiner, but I am sure she is sleeping, and I don't want to disturb her. I understand, from today, she is in a... uh... delicate state."

"Delicate state? I don't think so." Til stood ram-rod straight in the doorway of the drawing room. "I'm pregnant, Detective Grayson, not dying."

Grayson turned from Shannon to face Til.

Til's eyes raked over him as if there might be new evidence clinging to him. She had a way of looking at a man that made him feel lacking. "Where is the report?"

Grayson handed her the paperwork.

She read it swiftly.

"Shot in the back with a derringer." Til shook her head and pressed her fingertips to her lips for a brief moment. "I knew it. Same as Bobby Bristol. Same type of gun and the gunshot wound is in the same position on the body."

"Same gun, same gunshot wound? Same killer?" Grayson raised his eyebrows.

"No." Til shook her head. "Odelia wouldn't kill Bobby. No. This is someone else."

"Who?"

"I don't know. As I said, I haven't had a thing to do with the Bristols since I parted ways with Odelia at the Blackburns."

"You're lying." Grayson accused softly. "Why didn't Bobby come after you once you were back in London with your education? Different name, same woman; he's not stupid. Why didn't he kill you years ago?"

A clock on the mantel clicked as Til and Grayson squared off in the drawing room. Shannon's eyes darted from one to the other.

Til took a deep breath. She leveled her gaze on Grayson. "I got back to the slums and Bobby came after me; yes," Til conceded. She moved to the fireplace in the room and warmed her hands against the dying embers.

"Then what?" Grayson demanded.

Shannon turned to Grayson and pleaded with him. "Mr. Grayson, this has been a trying day for anyone. Pregnant or not."

"I'm sorry." Grayson crossed his arms over his chest. "But Nora Blackburn is just one of many missing girls associated with this ring. I must know who is behind this. Doctor Stone, you are not telling me the whole truth of your involvement. You must start talking or this girl's blood will be on your hands."

Memories of Katherine surfaced in his mind as Til finished warming her hands and turned back to face him.

"Odelia was in labour, their third child..." Til's jaw clenched as she spoke.

"They only have two." Grayson corrected her.

"Right. They only have two." Til's back stiffened at his tone. "Bobby should have come for me right away. He didn't. Finally, when he did come, I was afraid to go with him, terrified."

"I can imagine." Grayson watched Til carefully.

"We struck a deal." Til lifted her chin.

Shannon closed her eyes.

Grayson held his breath. He knew Shannon was worried that her aunt was about to incriminate herself.

"I said I would assist her." Til's voice shook. "I made him give me a guarantee."

"I bet you did." Grayson's eyes narrowed.

"Don't interrupt." Til's eyes flashed with defiance. "It is not what you think. He had to guarantee my protection in the slums. So help me, I stood over her body as she nearly bled to death and I didn't treat her. I didn't assist until I got his word."

Shannon gasped in alarm.

Til shook her head. "Remember. There was an entire gang of Bristol Butchers out for our blood Shannon, you'll think me unfeeling, but I knew I wouldn't get out alive that night unless the head of the Bristols swore his protection. The baby didn't survive."

"Would that baby have lived if you had intervened earlier?" Grayson choked the words out.

"No." Til's eyes glittered with unshed tears and Grayson wondered if she was lying. "The baby was dead when I got there but I didn't tell him that of course. I listened for the fetal heartbeat. There was no sound. Nothing. I saved Odelia's life. Bobby never laid a hand on me, neither did any of his men. Other gangs knew not to interfere with me or my women in the slums from that day forward."

"Your women?"

"The doctors who work for me or with me."

"I see."

"I have had no fear in those flats from anyone, until now." Til's eyes looked tortured with memory as she kept her gaze level with his. "The truth is Detective Grayson, I have to leave England. I will not last one minute in the slums now. Malcolm dead and Bobby's protection removed... I'm a dead woman walking now."

Grayson wondered, not for the first time, if Til Stone was capable of showing weakness. Even as she told him this truth, she didn't weep, she didn't bend. She braced for battle.

"Bobby being dead is very, very bad for me, Detective Grayson, as it will be for Odelia." Til's voice hardened as she spoke.

"Who's behind it then? What else are you not telling me?" Grayson took a step forward.

"Detective Grayson!" Shannon reprimanded him.

"I don't know." Til shook her head and held her ground. "If we find out who the new head of the Bristols is, we might have a hope of working it out. Who wanted Bobby dead and who wants me in Toronto?" Til shook her head in confusion. "Up to this point I had thought Odelia, but she will have lost all her authority with Bobby dead. So, someone is behind her and who is that? It could be anyone. As I said, I have a lot of enemies. Not just the Bristols. I refuse to do abortions and that makes me a target for many powerful men. As I said, I'm out of options."

Grayson pulled his notepad out. There was silence in the room as Grayson wrote down Til's statement. "There was no blood at the scene. Malcolm Maddox was shot and then moved. Police in the jurisdiction he worked in were investigating a crime scene where a man was shot in broad daylight. I immediately ordered a door- to- door search for witnesses."

"No one is talking." Til's lips were thin with disapproval.

"Exactly," Grayson agreed.

"Now what?" Til sat down.

Grayson sat across from her.

"All we have to go on is the note pinned to Mr. Maddox's chest. The constables have combed through ship manifests; O. Ship and N. Black are on a ship manifest to Toronto via Quebec. I believe Odelia has taken Nora and she is behind the murder of Malcolm."

"Who is behind the murder of Bobby though? It's the same weapon." Til pulled her robe around her tighter.

"Same *kind* of weapon," Grayson said quietly. "Who knows? Bobby Bristol will have enemies everywhere — any rival gang would be the first place to look. All we know for sure is O. Ship on a ship manifest incriminates Odelia. Once these papers are filed and there is a warrant for Mrs. Bristol's arrest, I'll be on the first ship back to Toronto to pick her up. We know from the ransom note the Toronto part of this ring is expecting you on November 2nd, 1906. So, I'll be there in your place."

"Why would you be there in my place?" Til frowned.

"Because meeting with killers and breaking into white slavery prostitution rings is dangerous," Grayson said firmly. "You are cleared of any suspicion. I will go back and sort out the ring in Toronto. You will hire more security and continue with your clinic, I guess. I'll be leaving on the next ship out, which happens to be Tuesday; I can't leave it any later than that. It's the last ship that will get me there in time even if we run into bad weather. Before I go, I give you every assurance— I personally guarantee that this investigation will be carried out properly. Odelia *will* be brought to justice."

"If I'm not there, in that warehouse, you will never see Nora Blackburn again," Til contradicted him. "My life is in danger whether I am here or in Toronto." Til stood up indicating her decision was final.

Grayson stood and moved to the threshold of the room. "Doctor Stone, I will find another way to retrieve Nora. Before I go, please accept my apologies for my conduct this afternoon. All the evidence pointed to you, but I had no idea you were pregnant and so my interrogation this afternoon was inappropriate to say the least. Please accept my sincere apologies."

Til shrugged. "The falsified evidence was convincing. I understand."

Grayson winced.

"You made that evidence up?" Til's eyes narrowed.

"I did. I was hoping you would give something away. Again, my apologies. Good night, Doctor Stone. Doctor McDougall."

"Detective Grayson, the funeral is on Saturday, if you wish to attend before you return to Toronto." Til turned back to the fire, dismissing him.

"Thank you, I will attend for sure." Grayson nodded to Shannon and left them.

***

Shannon moved to Til and placed her hand on her shoulder as the door shut behind Grayson.

"Very wise," Shannon said sofly. "Let him handle Odelia."

"Shannon, I will handle Odelia." Til turned and frowned at her niece.

"He's not going to take you to Toronto." Shannon dropped her hand.

"Since when do I need a man to take me anywhere?" Til hissed under her breath. "Odelia Shipley Bristol wants to meet me on a dock, in a warehouse in Toronto to exchange ten thousand pounds for a young girl. There is evidence that a gang she is affiliated to is responsible for the death of my husband, father of my child. Where else would I be? Really, Shannon, it's as if you don't know me at all!"

"But you're pregnant, Til!" Shannon gasped. "You can't traipse across the Atlantic and take down a murderer and a white slaver!"

"Shannon." Til drew herself up to her full height. She looked down her nose at her niece. "What on earth does 'can't' mean? I've spent my entire life ignoring the word."

Til blew out the candles on the mantelpiece and left the drawing room. Together, they made their way to the hallway.

"This is different," Shannon pleaded. "You have a baby now. Your body is forty years old; you have lost babies in the past."

"I'll be resting on a ship!" Til opposed her as she climbed the stairs to her room.

"Resting!" Shannon huffed, she closed the door and followed her aunt up the stairway. "You'll make a makeshift clinic and be handing out birth control; you'll be arrested and probably charged with mutiny within a week at sea."

"I don't know how I raised such a complete *pessimist.*" Til turned to face Shannon on the stairwell. "Chin up, Shannon. Odelia Bristol wants to tangle with me, well, she's in for a surprise. Besides, Detective Grayson knows, and I know, Odelia didn't kill Bobby. Someone else in this gang is after me. Whoever it is hasn't played their last card and it's better if I'm in Toronto. It seems as though the police are not corrupt there. Good night, dear."

Shannon opened her mouth and shut it.

"I am asking you on behalf of my cousin not to do this." Shannon reached out, placing her hand on Til's shoulder.

"That's a low blow." Til's eyes narrowed, she took another two steps up the stairs before she turned to address Shannon again. "This baby is going to be fine. Lead by example, Shannon. That's my motto. This baby has a mother that will fight for Nora Blackburn and stop the prostitution of young girls and bring her father's killer to justice. Stop being so emotional. When there is a job to do, we do the job."

Shannon closed her eyes briefly. "You always say that. It never makes it easier to do the job."

"That's the spirit that thins the herd, my dear. If the work were easy, everyone would be doing it." Til shrugged, turned around to climb the stairs and go to bed.

"What happened between you and Lord Blackburn?" Shannon asked hesitantly.

Til inhaled sharply, straightened up and turned to speak to Shannon. "Why is everyone wanting to get to the bottom of what happened with Lord Blackburn? You are all like dogs with a bone. Let it go. I have."

"Til." Shannon closed the space between them. "It is just so obvious that you haven't. You're hurting. It's where all your anger comes from.

What happened to you? Please." Shannon's eyes filled with tears. "Tell me what happened. Let me share this burden."

Til bristled. "Nothing happened with Lord Blackburn."

"You're lying. Someone hurt you. Who was it?" Shannon pressed harder.

"The night I ran from my father's home, I took a wrong turn and landed straight into the arms of a Bristol. He very nearly raped me before Malcolm stepped in. I ran to Odelia. She let me in and her mother came to me that night. I will never forget her. One of the reasons I returned to work the same slums was to repay her kindness. Odelia and I went into service together. I worked for the Blackburns. I protected their daughter Madeline Blackburn, whom you know as Lady Madeline Harper."

"I don't understand." Shannon frowned. "You said you met Malcolm when you were a midwife..."

"I never intended to speak of this to you. I don't want to tell you everything. I didn't want you to carry that burden of knowing my age when I was on the street. It's awful. You knowing would not help anything. So, same story but later in life."

Shannon's eyes filled with tears. "You lied to me?"

"Shannon, I couldn't speak of it." Til's lips thinned at Shannon's distress. "I still can't. Forgive me. There are things I need to leave buried."

"Lady Harper lied too? She said you met at school and that she read about your clinic in a newspaper and sent for you. This is *not* her version of accounts."

"Lady Harper is exactly that, a lady." Til sighed. "As such, they do not discuss near kidnappings and any unpleasantness with anyone. Lord Harper *never* knew about any of this, so she could hardly tell you the truth for fear it would get back to him."

"That seems preposterous; it was years ago." Shannon shook her head.

"We're talking about the gentry." Til rolled her eyes. "Appearances must be maintained at all costs. It doesn't surprise me that she has never breathed a word. Her only job in her life was to come to the marriage pure and scandal free. Being abducted by the Bristols would have ended that engagement. It would have been a disaster for the Blackburns. The Bristols were banking on it. Exorbitant amounts of money to ransom her back without anyone knowing. Bobby Bristol was a clever and cunning man. Even at that age. Anyway, I owed her a favour and I sent you to do it, since I was in jail. Perfect solution. It got you out of here and away from scandal. It gave you time to heal." Til's eyes darkened at the memories.

Shannon took a deep breath.

"It's odd; she was so hard on Enid and Martha when they were found in Oakland. She said things like, 'who knows how girls end up in this position?'"

"As I said Shannon, she is gentry. She had one tiny brush with me, but what does that matter. She wouldn't know an East End slum if it jumped up and bit her. A brothel is as foreign to her as washing her own dishes. She would have had no idea what I would have been reduced to without the coins and jewellery she handed me. In her wildest imagination she would never have had a clue what Enid or Martha had been through." Til took a deep breath as she weighed her next words. "Lady Harper is like any lady, they walk a fine line. They must present a perfect, chaste, gentle facade to the world because everything they do reflects on their husbands. She was hardly going to tell you anything."

"I see. Well then, let me ask you this. Why are you Til Stone and not Matilda Bertram?" Shannon tilted her head to the side.

"I would not be called by my father's name again." Til stiffened and drew into herself to protect a deep aching hurt.

"Your father interfered with you?" The blood drained from Shannon's face. She took one step up the staircase, closer to her aunt.

"No." Til's voice dropped and cracked with emotion. "What my father did was much worse."

"Til, there is nothing worse than that. What happened? Let it out so you can start to heal," Shannon implored her.

"Shannon, it's unspeakable," Til whispered. "There are just some things you can't heal from and talking doesn't help it."

"Til." Tears poured down Shannon's cheeks as she climbed up the stairs closer to Til so she could take her in her arms. "Please, what happened?"

Til pulled herself out of Shannon's arms. "You are my niece. I am not going to go into all the details. But, the night I ran, I realised what I was up against." Til took a step back. "It was after I left the Blackburns I chose my own name, my own path. I took control of my life and decided I would never be known by a man's name. I would be known as *my own name.* I own me and I would never rely on anyone else for anything. No man would own me."

"No one can own anyone." Shannon's face creased with confusion.

"Yes, my darling girl, they can." Til's voice caught. "I am glad to know that is a foreign concept to you. Something inside me broke apart after Blackburns. I don't know how else to explain it. From that point on, I created my own name, my own separate identity. I don't need a man to provide for me. I would provide for myself. I would never allow myself to be vulnerable again. Taking a man's name says, in a way, you are his. You don't see men running around taking women's names! I can't make my thoughts or feelings clear on this. I can see on your face, you don't understand. I refuse, Shannon. I refuse to be in a position of being *owned*."

"Til, what do you know about being owned?" Shannon's lips trembled.

"Stop crying. It's in the past." Til tossed her hair over her shoulder. "I explained this to Malcolm, and he was fine with it. He cared about me, not my past."

"Til, this makes no sense. I am known by Cole's last name, I am happy to be his."

"You trust him." Til spoke sadly.

"Cole would lay down his life for me and I know it. Of course, I trust him," Shannon said simply. "Malcolm laid his life down for you, too."

Til took a deep breath. "Too late then, to take his name."

"His baby though, will you call him Stone or Maddox?"

"Him? Oh, Shannon." Til shook her head. "This is a girl."

"Til. There are some things in life you just can't choose. Stone or Maddox?

Til pursed her lips. "I'm tired, Shann. I need to go to bed."

"You should think about opening your heart, Til. You should think hard about how you want to raise this child. It's good to trust. You don't have to rely only on yourself."

"Stop it!" Til reprimanded Shannon so severely her head snapped up. "You know nothing of my past. You know nothing of what made me. You think that *twisted* me. I am not twisted or broken, I am whole and hard. Very hard. Your open, loving relationship with Cole where you share everything is lovely and unusual. History has proven to me time and again that women can be owned by men and that they can be cruel taskmasters. Men have ultimate authority in this world, and they will abuse it. Always."

"No. You are wrong, Til. It is destroying you. It *has* destroyed you. Whatever happened the night you became Til Stone has held you back, stifled your joy and threatens your future happiness." Shannon's eyes burned with intensity. "You have to find a way to trust men. Men and women need each other—"

"You are, in a lot of ways, still a girl, Shannon," Til interrupted her harshly. "Silly girls think about men coming along and completing them. I don't. Women don't need to be completed by men. Gracious!" Til threw her hands up in the air. "I failed as an aunt! You learned nothing from me! A woman should be whole all on her own before she lets a man *near* her. They should be partners; equals who bring out the best in each other. Not one owning the other or belonging to the other. How do you have the best to bring out unless you are a complete person on your own first? It's like you weren't paying attention at all." Til narrowed her eyes at Shannon to see if she was paying attention now. "It's time to grow up, Shannon. Cole could find another woman and leave you tomorrow and you would have to find your way in this life. You were raised to be educated so you would never be vulnerable. I don't want to hear any nonsense about *trusting men*. That foolishness just opens you up to a world of hurt."

"I see." Shannon clamped her mouth shut.

"You don't see, Shannon. You don't understand." Til wiped tears from Shannon's cheeks and pulled her into her embrace. "It's time for me to be in bed. I am completely exhausted."

"Of course," Shannon murmured as her eyes filled with tears again.

Til pulled her bedroom door shut behind her. She leaned against it, closed her eyes and bowed her head. Exhaustion dragged at her arms as she pulled off her robe. She pulled the heavy covers back and crawled into her empty bed. A wave of sorrow and loneliness washed over her as she reached for Malcolm out of sheer habit. As her fingers felt nothing but cold linen sheets a sob tore out of her, from a realm she had long forgotten she possessed.

In moments, Shannon slid into bed with her and pulled her into her arms. She held Til as the storm of loss tore through her.

The next morning the early October sunshine mocked her pain by cheerfully pouring in through her windows. Til buried her head in her pillow. That moment where sleep met awareness was terrible. For one moment she had forgotten about the loss of Malcolm, the revenge Odelia sought to exact. In that moment when awareness won out, her heart suffered the loss of Malcolm again. Fresh pain radiated from her heart.

Her stomach heaved with morning sickness as she moved.

Shannon knocked gently and entered the room.

"Your morning sickness is very intense." Shannon observed as she soaked a handkerchief in water and then handed it to Til. "Other than the sickness, how are you?" Shannon's tone softened.

Concern creased Til's forehead, she sat up and opened her gown. "Oh my God," Til moaned as she saw the blood on her nightgown.

Chapter Sixteen

Shannon moved her hands over Til's abdomen. "Is there cramping?" Shannon asked calmly, professionally.

"No cramping." Til's breath caught as fear pooled in her stomach.

I cannot lose this baby. I cannot face any more loss.

"We'll dose you again and wait and see. You had some cramping yesterday, so you know better than I that blood doesn't always mean miscarriage. Yesterday was a difficult day. Bed rest today," Shannon said sternly.

"I have a funeral to plan and a trip to ready myself for." Til's eyes filled with tears at the thought of burying Malcolm and the very real possibility that she might lose their baby today.

Shannon placed her hand on Til's forearm.

"I despise the limitations of pregnancy. It's not fair." Til frowned in frustration. Anger burst inside her, close on the heels of pain.

"Once you have that baby in your arms, it will all be worth it." Shannon smiled. "Aunty Til with a baby. I can't wait to see it."

"I'm not cut out for motherhood," Til snapped. "You're going to see a lot of staff being hired, is what you are going to see. Book me passage, Shannon, a ship leaves for Canada on Tuesday."

"No." Shannon poured calcium carbonate onto a spoon and pressed it to Til's lips. "You're distraught, you are not thinking clearly."

"Shannon. I don't have the energy to fight. Go to my safe and bring me all the money and papers."

"You are going to take this and drink it. Then you are going to sleep, with your feet up. I am going to make all the arrangements for the funeral. After the funeral, you are going to the cabin by the sea for a little break. Lots of books, tea and quiet."

"Have you ever known me to require books, tea and quiet?" Til rolled her eyes.

"You do now." Shannon spoke through grit teeth.

"Book me passage to Toronto on Tuesday." Til ignored her.

"Absolutely not! You are staying in this bed." Shannon's voice lowered. "Stop fighting me."

Til lay back into the pillows. "I have been thinking. You and Cole should come back with me. You have that job opportunity in Brandon. Let's all go to Canada together. Between Doctor Cotter and Enid, everything here is well in hand. Malcolm's partners at the practice will tie up any loose ends here."

"Til Stone." Shannon tucked in her aunt. "You are not going anywhere. If there is any additional bleeding today, we are going to have to discuss how we will keep you immobile in *this* bed for the duration of this pregnancy." Shannon shot a look at Til. "It's going to be harder on all of us than on you."

Til hated the tears that filled her eyes as she was forced to concede. Her body demanded rest; her mind demanded work; her heart demanded to weep. Of the three, her body and heart won.

"I can rest easy if you get the clinic sorted." Til wiped tears from her eyes as she aknowledged defeat. She hated anyone taking over work she had assigned to herself. "Make sure all the doctors know I will be absent until further notice."

"Very reasonable of you, Til," Shannon said.

"We'll hire more staff if we need to. There was one other doctor that we were thinking would be an asset to the clinic. Please hire her today." Til surrendered further.

"Cynthia Ward?" Shannon confirmed.

"Yes. I think she would do well. Would you send Enid to me?" Til adjusted the heavy bed covers. "You need to be on site to make sure the transition is smooth."

"Stop fussing. I will handle all the arrangements at the clinic." Shannon handed Til some tea with sugar in it. "Just *rest* and let me deal with it."

"I've never been good at resting. I hate other people fawning all over me. I despise it." Til's voice cracked with fury.

"Get used to it." Shannon patted her arm and then gathered her supplies.

In the quiet of the room after Shannon left, Til had no other option but to actually think about the funeral. The aching pain at the thought of Malcolm not coming home made her weep from the very depth of her soul. A place she hadn't acknowledged since she fled to Odelia's mother.

Baby Speck, how will we manage?

After laying in bed, weeping for over an hour, Til was thankful to hear a timid knock.

Eyes swollen, Til squinted through the gloom at Enid, standing by the door.

"Oh Enid, thank goodness you came. We have a lot of work to do." Til tried to sit up. Her stomach was more settled now. She reached for her cold toast and tea.

"Don't eat that, it's cold. Let me get you some hot breakfast and then I will sit with you for the afternoon. I wondered if you want me to read to you? What would be best?" Enid asked.

Where Til couldn't bend Shannon to her will, she could bend Enid. "Enid, that all sounds lovely, but I need you to book me passage on a ship to Toronto on Tuesday."

Enid blinked in surprise. "I think Shannon would..."

"Enid." Til's lips thinned as she lost her patience. "Take the money from my safe and get me first class passage to Toronto. Tuesday is the next ship. Please."

"Shannon will kill me." Enid wrung her hands together.

"Enid, I will deal with Shannon. Please. I beg you. I have to go to Canada. If I were able to stand, I would do it myself. Please." Til despised the begging tone in her voice.

"I don't like this." Enid shook her head. "But I'll do it."

Two days in bed, with no cramping, no bleeding, and her patience completely spent, Shannon returned to examine Til. Enid came along to lend moral support. She followed Shannon with a tray of tea and breakfast.

"If you feel the slightest twinge you need to get off your feet and rest," Shannon warned Til as she finished her examination. "Your body is simply adjusting, and it appears your womb hates change as much as you do. Everything looks in order here."

Enid handed Til hot tea and tucked a heavy blanket around her.

"I'll be careful." Til took a sip of tea. "Thank you for handling the preparations for the funeral. Everything is in order?"

"Of course." Shannon's eyes misted with tears.

Til's eyes immediately flooded with tears as well.

Shannon quickly turned from Til and Enid as she wiped them away. "I'm not sure how I will bear it at the funeral. Malcolm was the only father I knew. I hope Detective Grayson gets to the bottom of it and finds out who is responsible. I'm so glad you have seen sense. I am glad you aren't thinking of going to Canada. It's all just too dangerous."

Enid caught Til's eye and then promptly looked away.

***

The day of the funeral dawned grey and wet. Rain lashed against the window. Til lay in bed, hoping her morning sickness wasn't too terrible before getting up and getting ready to bury Malcolm.

Bury Malcolm.

Finally, she could put it off no longer. Her heart aching in sadness, Til pulled on her blackest of clothes because on such a day as this there was no light in her soul. Sick and numb, the baby sapped her strength. This baby that had seemed like a figment of her imagination until it made her sick. Sometimes the thought of being pregnant was so surreal she believed it was an illness she couldn't shake.

How will I raise this child alone?

Shannon, Cole, Enid, and the staff of the clinic and the staff of the barrister's firm all assembled by the grave. Detective Grayson stood off to the side, respectfully holding his hat in his hand. Til wished everyone would leave. She despised public displays of emotion and today was the worst day of her life. She wanted to drop to her knees and weep on his casket but she couldn't allow herself to.

Until the very end.

Everyone held their hands out and she murmured to Shannon she needed time before they lowered him to the ground. Everyone left; Grayson didn't go far. Irritated, she shot him a frosty look of contempt.

Couldn't a woman have a moment of peace to grieve?

"If you would be so kind as to give me a moment." Til lashed at him as he moved closer to her.

"I would." Grayson stood very near her. "Three men in the crowd are not affiliated with you or Malcolm from what Mr. McDougall tells me. I believe they are Bristols, or at the least working for them." His eyes swept the cemetery and then landed back on her.

"I just need a moment. Alone," Til demanded wildly, she barely held onto her composure.

"Of course." Grayson's eyes softened in sympathy. "I'll be just over here."

"I didn't ask for your protection," she hissed at his retreating back. "I asked for nothing from you. I *need* nothing from you."

"This is a hard day for you. I understand you are upset." Grayson turned to her, jaw clenched. "I will be on my way as soon as I see you safely home."

Til watched him walk far enough away that he was able to keep his eye on her, still give her privacy, yet close enough to assist if a rogue Bristol tried to make trouble. Teeth grit together in frustration, she turned her back on him and Cole who was also hovering.

These men will drive me mad! My last moment with Malcolm and there is no privacy, no peace. Even now Bristols are threatening me with their presence.

Til faced Malcolm's casket and took a very deep breath and let it out slowly. This limited privacy would have to do. Icy cold October rain slicked off her, but she couldn't feel it through the haze of loss and sadness that gutted her.

"Malcolm. I needed a few words before I go." Til knelt down and put her hands over his coffin where his heart might be. Her own heart splintered with sadness as she whispered to him for the last time. "I love you. I have loved you with everything that I am and have. I will always love you and I will love your baby with every breath in my body. Malcolm, we didn't talk about names." Til pressed her forehead into the wood of the coffin. "Oh my God. We never talked about names!" A wave of pain broke her. Sobs crawled up her throat. "What will I call this child? What names would you have liked? I can't do this on my own. You were supposed to be here. We were having a summer at the sea. Malcolm, I can't do this without you." Til pressed her forehead against the cold wood of the casket and wept as there was no response.

As the storm inside of her raged, resolve filled her heart as she spoke to his coffin again. "You would forbid this. I know you would. But, I am going after your killer and I won't stop until I find out who it is. I will get to the bottom of this. That is my vow to you."

***

Grayson had a hard time keeping his distance as Til spiraled into sobs by the grave. He looked pointedly at Cole who shot him a look of warning. A look that said *do not get too close.*

Finally, he couldn't watch her suffer without comfort any further. He went to her in time to hear her say... "If you hadn't stepped in, I can't imagine what would have happened to me. I thank you again. Whoever did this to you, I will destroy them. I vow to you, Malcolm, I will not rest until there is justice."

Til pressed her face back into the wood of his coffin and wept. It sounded to Grayson as if her soul was being ripped from her body.

Grayson stood back and gave her some space. With great difficulty, he didn't rush her. He didn't even allow himself to check his pocket watch or clear his throat. Out of respect for her, he waited.

Eventually, she pulled herself away from the coffin and as she struggled to get to her feet, he came to her side and placed his hand under her elbow.

"I asked you to leave me alone." Til wiped her tears and tried to move out of his reach.

"I can't," Grayson spoke gently. "I need to speak to you before I leave. I would try to give you more time, but I leave on Tuesday. May I come by to speak to you on Monday?"

"No!" Til pulled her arm out of his grasp.

"Doctor Stone." Grayson sighed wearily. "I need some answers before I leave. I think it's someone who knows about the night—"

"Get away from me!" Til howled at him.

"I think you know the real killer here." Grayson followed her as he spoke to her retreating back.

The three men Cole had identified as neither family nor friends moved to follow Til. Grayson immediately maneuvered himself so he was between the three men and her. Her eyes flashed with fury as he reached for her. He let his hand drop. He kept his body positioned to protect her from the men circling her. Sure enough, the men moved to be able to see her clearly. Grayson kept his eye on them and on Til.

She pressed a handkerchief to her eye. Her vulnerability caused him to think of Katherine. Had men stalked her as these ones stalked Til?

She thinks I'm being intrusive, but what if a detective had fought for Katherine as tenaciously as I am prepared to fight for Nora Blackburn? Would she have been found? Would our family have remained together?

He shook his head at the memory. The detectives hadn't given Katherine a thought, except to accuse her. Girls did foolish things, they said. What was she wearing? Did she have a history of flirting with strange men?

Grayson's jaw clenched in fury all these years later, a girl who was picked up and sold into slavery must have asked for it; not vocally but by her *manner* or her clothes.

Grayson dragged his mind back to the present, convinced Til Stone knew something that would crack the case wide open. Every day, every stone he unturned pointed to the night she fled. He was convinced his whole case hinged on it. She could evade him all she liked, but she *would* talk.

"I will not meet with you Monday. Stay away from me." Til walked away from him as quickly as she could.

Grayson looked to Cole who shrugged and didn't make a move to help him.

"You are surrounded by Bristols. You should get in the carriage. There are three men just over there. You are not safe here. Between Cole and I, we can get you out of here alive. You can cry in your bed like a normal woman. You are going to leave in front of me in case someone decides to shoot you in the back." Grayson watched the pain bolt across her face. "Sorry. That was insensitive of me, but, we are dealing with those who shoot people in the back."

"I despise you." Til choked on the words.

Grayson insisted on helping her into her carriage and he stayed with her even though she frowned when he got in the carriage with her.

"Get out." Her tone of voice bit into him like a wasp sting.

"Since you won't meet with me Monday, I need to know *who* is Shipley Bristol? Is he Odelia's son?"

"Yes, he is Odelia and Bobby's son." Til's face paled at the name.

"Is he the new head of the Bristol Butchers?" Grayson itched for a notepad.

"I don't know." Til crossed her arms over her chest. "I have told you everything I know, and I will remind you, sir, I have just buried my husband and it is inappropriate of you to interrogate me today. I am not speaking to you further. Today is for Malcolm, a day to acknowledge his life, and a day to try to endure my own pain. Get out of this carriage."

"I don't want to be insensitive." Grayson held up his hands in supplication.

"Get! Out!" Til shouted at him.

Grayson sighed with frustration. He had pushed her too far. Her eyes filled with tears as she covered her face with her hands.

"I fear for your safety, so I will see you safely home." Grayson tapped the roof of the carriage to let the driver know they were ready to go.

Til dropped her hands from her face. "You take far too many liberties, sir. See me home if you wish, but I have nothing further to say to you and when you leave me, I never want to see you again."

Grayson clenched his jaw in fury. "I am trying to find a missing girl."

"I am trying to survive this day!" Til's frosty tone slicked with ice.

"I'm sorry. I truly am." Grayson softened his tone.

The carriage stopped in front of her home. Grayson leaped out to give her his hand to assist her. She batted it away, scrambled down to the street and faced him.

"I meant what I said. I've told you all I will tell you. I know nothing further. What happened to me has no relevance and it is too painful to discuss with you or anyone." Til pressed her hand against her mouth and then turned on her heel and left him standing on the street.

Chapter Seventeen

Grayson lied to the butler, telling him he had an appointment, and then he settled into Til's drawing room first thing Monday morning. A spare sort of room, no extras anywhere. No pictures, no crocheted doilies. Nothing. Just practical pieces of furniture and a few books. Grayson was convinced, looking around this private space, Til was like no other woman he had ever met. Even Cora, practical as she was, had knick knacks to soften a room, to make it look warm and cozy.

Not Til.

Everything was stripped down to the barest basics.

Don't get comfortable and don't get close.

Grayson jumped to his feet as Til entered the drawing room.

"How did you get in here? I told you I have nothing to say." Til's jaw dropped as she remained standing at the threshold.

"I am asking you, please. If there is any further information that would help me find Nora Blackburn, I need to know what it is." Grayson stood and moved toward her. "I leave first thing tomorrow. You will never see me again. Whatever happened that night will stay with me, safe in confidence."

Til called for the butler. "Kindly escort this man from my home and do not allow him to return."

"May I just say a few words?" Grayson held his hands out.

"I'll call the police," the butler said.

"Tell him not to bother the police, I'll go," Grayson said. "But, before I do. May I ask you—" Grayson begged.

"No. You may not." Til interrupted him as she drew herself up to her full height.

"Listen, I'm begging you, please tell me what happened before you got to Odelia's. I think that whatever happened has a bearing on who stole Nora. I know it's painful. I would never ask you to recall these things to mind if it wasn't of utmost importance. Please Doctor Stone, a girl's life hangs in the balance and I need you to speak."

"I can't. Not to you, not to anyone." Til clamped her mouth shut.

"Why was that note on that broken window? Why *that* tenement. Why not Odelia's tenement?"

Til took a deep breath and then turned to leave the room.

Grayson's fragile grip on his patience fled. "If I find out you knew something and refused to tell me, I can charge you with obstruction of justice, even from Canada."

Til turned back, eyes glittered with angry tears. "You wouldn't."

"Doctor Stone, tears don't work on me," Grayson warned. A muscle in his jaw jumped. "I am immune. I have spent my life dealing with weeping women. First my mother and then my wife. Tell me what you know."

"You're married?" Til pounced on this personal snippet of information as if he had revealed a weakness. Her eyes flicked down to his left hand. "You're not wearing a ring."

"Was married." Grayson's tone hardened. "We are getting divorced."

Til's eyes narrowed as she shot him a look of suspicion.

"Divorced! How scandalous," Til gasped in surprise. "You committed adultery and what else? You beat her?"

"Something like that," Grayson growled.

The blood drained from Til's face. "You're a wife beater."

Grayson raised his eyes heavenward. "If you must know and I don't know why you would care, she committed adultery with the butcher from the shop where she bought supplies. I did *not* commit adultery and I have never raised my hand to a woman ever in my life. Although, you make it very difficult to remember that it is inappropriate. You *do* push me to my limits."

"How can I know if you are telling the truth?" Til dragged them back to the matter at hand. Whether or not Grayson had beaten his wife.

"You'll have to trust me," Grayson said dryly.

"Impossible. I've never trusted any man other than Malcolm and I have no intention of starting now." Til bristled visibly. "Certainly not some *shaggy Canadian*. Gracious, who knows what goes on over there on the frontier?" Til waved in the direction of Canada, her English accent ice cold.

"Oh yes, on the frontier we have *no laws at all*," Grayson growled in fury. "We're *all* a bunch of wife beaters. Especially the police, we see women beaten all the time; we laugh and look the other way."

"I don't doubt it for a minute." Til sniffed as she looked him up and down. Her eyes indicated she found him lacking. "Why did she commit adultery then?" Til asked like an interrogator.

Grayson clenched his jaw. "I work long hours. She was lonely, or so she said."

"I see." Til's eyebrows drew together. "How long of hours?"

"How is this any of your business?" Grayson lost his temper.

"You want to know every detail of my sadness and sorrows. You can share this." Til's lips thinned. "I want to know if I am dealing with a wife beater or not."

"You are not." Grayson gritted his teeth. "I have *never* hit a woman in my life."

"There are other ways to be cruel." Til's chin lifted and she angled her head in a way Grayson was starting to despise.

"I was not cruel. I just couldn't give her all the attention that she needed." Grayson clenched his jaw.

"How much attention was that?" Til pressed.

"She wanted me home by five. She wanted me to be home as much as possible, and I had a job to do." Grayson checked his pocket watch; he needed answers not an interrogation into his life.

"Home by five?" Til frowned. "I don't understand."

"Well, Til..."

"Doctor Stone to you."

"Well, Doctor Stone, I guess finally we have something in common. I have never had that sort of job and that's what she wanted. Apparently, Archie the butcher is home by five and they can live happily ever after."

Til was silent; he watched her processing this information.

"I've never been home by five o'clock a day in my life." Til finally spoke.

Til and Grayson looked at each other across the drawing room. A sudden spark of understanding between them.

"A butcher?" Til asked again. Her eyebrows arched up in surprise.

"A butcher." Grayson confirmed.

"I just can't imagine. Home by five o'clock. How extraordinary she would expect that." Til shook her head. "Anyway, that is neither here nor there I suppose. I must say though, even though I will not discuss anything further with you, the hardest thing about this pregnancy is not working twelve hours a day. I prefer it. I feel like the walls are closing in..."

Grayson met Til's eyes. "I know exactly how you feel. On the few nights I did try, I thought I would go mad."

Grayson thought for a moment that he might just be looking at the female version of himself, then he shook it off. It didn't matter. He was leaving for Toronto and Til Stone would be back to work in her clinic. Tuesday, the world would go back to the way it should be. An ocean between them was almost far enough. All this chit chat about his wife and his life was to cleverly divert the conversation away from her and onto him.

He was just about to ask her a question, to drag the conversation back to information he needed when a knock at the door interrupted them.

The butler returned to the drawing room with two constables.

She kept me talking until the police came! This woman is insufferable!

"This man is here without invitation." Til spoke imperiously to the police officers. "I would like him evicted from my home. He is not to return. Would you make this *quite clear* to him? By quite clear, I mean by whatever force necessary."

Grayson gaped at her. He had lost his opportunity to drag information out of Til. "I am a police officer and I was just leaving."

"Of course you were." They looked him up and down.

"Ensure he doesn't return." Til instructed the police.

Grayson held his hands up in surrender as the men escorted him, none too gently, from Til Stone's residence.

***

Tuesday dawned bright and cool. The weakened October sun sparkled on the Thames River as crowds of people gathered to say goodbye to loved ones. Grayson scanned the crowd wondering for the hundredth time where

Shipley Bristol was; in England or in Toronto? He seemed to have vanished off the face of the earth.

He was so caught up in his thoughts that he nearly missed her.

A striking woman, wearing black, with a mountain of luggage grabbed Grayson's attention. She was directing porters and pelting them with approximately a hundred requests.

Til Stone. In the flesh. About to board the ship to Toronto. Absolutely not, she must be stopped.

Grayson shook his head. He tried to get through the crowd to stop her from boarding but was too late. She and her mountain of luggage were loaded in record time. Of course, she was first class. He shook his head and determined to keep his distance.

Out of the corner of his eye, he noticed the same three men from the funeral following her. The tallest man had a green cravat; the other one had a tall top hat; the third was shorter and broader. Of the three, the shortest one looked the most menacing.

"I am not taking Til Stone to Toronto!" Grayson clenched his fists as he vowed under his breath.

As he watched the three men watch her and then finally follow her to her cabin, he couldn't stop himself. Like a lamb led to slaughter, he followed, he watched them, and he braced for battle.

***

Til surveyed her first-class cabin and sniffed.

It would do in a pinch.

Her bed was heaped with a beautiful jewel toned velvet quilt. The four-poster bed had matching velvet curtains to shut out light and create a warm sleeping atmosphere. A sideboard containing three types of brandy and cut glass decanters stood by the porthole. A dressing screen in the corner matched the velvet on the bed. Til was grateful that there was lots of room in case there was any need to perform surgeries or assist with birth on board. A smile tugged at her lip as she thought of Shannon saying she would have a make-shift clinic within the week. Til believed with every fibre of her being that being idle was a form of death. She demanded that everyone carry their own load in life. Anyone who refused to carry their load in life she cut out.

Til set to work reorganising her medical bags in order of possible incident— birth, surgery, and general complaints. She tucked two boxes of contraceptives behind her dressing screen because one just never knew when and where you would have to administer them. Canada had laxer laws than the United States, but stricter than England. The boxes were labelled as knitting supplies. Til smirked, she had never picked up a knitting needle in her entire life. Who had time for that? But, who knew if she would be called upon by her suffragette sisters to slip illegal contraception over the border into the United States on her way back to England?

Suddenly, the thought of returning to England made her hesitate.

Back to what?

Til sat down as sadness made her lips tremble and her heart ache. She pressed a handkerchief to her eye to catch tears that surfaced at the thought of returning to England. No Shannon, no Malcolm. What would be the point? Back to a clinic that she knew, deep down, she couldn't give the same time and attention to if she was single-handedly raising a newborn. She placed her hands on her flat abdomen.

Where should we live, Speck? I've done twenty years in those slums, and you are going to change my focus. You are going to turn my whole world upside down. I'm afraid. I only know one thing, being a doctor. I don't know the first thing about being a mother. I left my baby brother...

Til stopped the thoughts as they tried to drag her down into a pit of despair. She settled into a window seat underneath the porthole. Looking out over the river at the London skyline, she thought about the fact that there was no longer a home with Malcolm, no summer by the sea with a new baby. Her eyes filled with tears at the thought, her heart broke. Nothing but baiting Odelia Shipley Bristol and endless days of morning sickness ahead of her. And where was Royce Bristol? Cole had told her Grayson's sleuthing had revealed that Andy had taken over as head of the Bristols, not Royce.

"I'll have you when I'm done with him." Royce's statement rang in her head all the way down the years. She shuddered.

She drew her knees up and thought about that statement. No Malcolm for protection, if she faced Royce Bristol in Toronto... well, that would be terrifying. Fear caused her hands to tremble. She tucked her hair behind her ear and looked out of the window, trying to calm down. Nerves at breaking point, she jumped when there was a pounding on the door to her cabin.

Palms slick with fear, Til got up to answer it.

"What are you doing here?" Grayson stalked into the cabin and slammed the door shut behind him.

"I've been very above board, sir. I told you I was going to Toronto to deliver the money and retrieve Nora Blackburn. That is what I am doing here." Til bristled. "You won't take down Odelia and whom ever she's connected to on your own."

Grayson's jaw clenched so hard Til wondered if his teeth would break.

"I run an entire department of the Toronto Constabulary. Believe me when I tell you I can get her back without you. So, get packed up; there is still time to get off this ship."

"I will do no such thing," Til snapped in outrage.

"How do you propose to get to Toronto in one piece?" Grayson's head tilted to the side as if he were thinking of her plight. "Are you presuming that I will protect you on this ship?" Grayson crossed his arms over his broad chest, as if to remind her that she was dependent on his power. Power he could use or not use in her defence.

"I don't need your protection," Til reprimanded him. "I am in first class; there are gentlemen among me. I will speak to the captain and ask him to verify my safety."

"What do you think the captain will expect in return for your safe passage to Toronto?" Grayson towered over Til.

"I hate when you do that." She scowled up at him.

"Do what?" Tone clipped, he took a step closer.

"Threaten to beat me by towering like that." Til took a step back and he followed her.

"As much as I would love to..." Grayson narrowed his eyes at her.

Til's eyes widened. "I knew it!" Til crowed. "I knew you were a wife beater, it's written all over you!"

"Oh, would you stop accusing me of that?" Grayson growled at her. "I swear to you on a stack of medical journals, which is probably the only authority you recognise, I never raised my hand to a woman, but so help me..."

"Don't you threaten me!" Til leaped away from him.

"I am not threatening you!" A vein stood out at Grayson's temple.

"It would be best if we parted company here, Mr. Grayson." Til looked down her nose and spoke to him as if he were a wayward boy. "I expect nothing from you. If you would be so kind as to leave my cabin." Til waved her hand to indicate her space.

"Really. You want me to leave your cabin" His eyes narrowed at her, his hands clenched to fists.

"Yes, immediately."

"Did you happen to notice that the three men that were stalking you at your husband's funeral followed you onto this ship? While you were pelting the porters with hundreds of requests, they have been watching you with your mountain of luggage all afternoon. They know where you are staying." Grayson took a step forward and looked down at her. "They know where you are sleeping."

Til's pulse pounded in her throat at the thought of three men watching her, knowing her every move.

"So, do you want me to go *now*, you spoiled shrew of a woman? Or are you ready to listen to reason and return home and leave the killers and white slavers to the men?"

"When I stumble over a man, I'll alert him." Til's cold English accent was meant to slice him to ribbons. "In the meantime, I will plead my case with the captain."

"Great heavens." Grayson scrubbed his hands over his face.

"So, if you'll leave me now, I am going to alert the captain to these three renegades and you may see yourself out. One cannot go to a captain in this attire." Til brushed her hands over her skirt.

Grayson held his hands out in supplication. "I am begging you, please, don't alert the captain to anything."

"Then what? Throw myself at your mercy?" Til stiffened at the thought. "You have already said you aren't going to be presumed upon. So, out you go."

"If the captain is inappropriate with you, it is going to be a very long journey and *I* will have to deal with it." Grayson's eyelid twitched.

"Mr. Grayson, you have already abdicated yourself from these proceedings. Why would you feel you must insert yourself into this situation?" She looked down her nose at him, again.

Grayson sat down at the window seat that Til had vacated. She tapped her foot and pointed at the door. "I have already asked you to leave." Til placed her hands on her hips. "Get up and get out."

"The captain is a womaniser, has a reputation for taking advantage of women." Grayson settled in and refused to budge.

Til's face paled.

"Get packed up and get off this ship," Grayson begged.

Til shot him a look as if he were dirt on her shoe.

"You're not *prostituting* yourself for safe passage."

Til's head snapped up as if she had been hit.

"Like I did with Lord Blackburn? Is that what you mean?" Her voice dripped with fury.

"I didn't mean it like that." Grayson held his hands out in surrender.

"Get! Out!" Til demanded.

"I didn't say that!" Grayson stood up.

Til stalked to the door and swung it open. "Get out this minute or I will—"

"You'll what? Scream?" Grayson interrupted. "Who's coming to your rescue, Til?" Grayson walked to the door. "No one! Not one person on this ship cares about your safety but me. So, do not, under any circumstances, go to the captain." Grayson stepped into the hall and turned to plead his case when Til slammed the door in his face.

Furious, Til paced around her cabin.

I'll see the captain if I want to!

Chapter Eighteen

Hiding new lines as they showed up on her face, Alys Bertram painted her lips carefully. Warm autumn sunshine poured in through Andy Bristol's windows, slanted across his wardrobe. His room was too spare; it didn't suit his new station as head of the Bristol family. Smiling like a cat, she was the only one who knew she had put him there. Bobby Bristol had been a trial to deal with, his cut was too great. It had taken Alys hours of carefully planting seeds of distrust and defiance in Andy's mind. Constant reminders that it was *his* turn to run the Bristols. Why work so hard to make Bobby great wads of money? Andy slowly started to agree, but she knew with certainty he would never act on it. Alys shook her head with contempt. Removing Bobby wasn't so difficult. It was essentially a business transaction. As far as it depended on her now, the Canadian part of the ring was settled. Alys tentatively relaxed and started to plan her wedding. Marriage to Andy would secure her future.

She put her paints away and smiled. Finally, she was the woman of the head of the Bristols and she no longer had to tip toe around anyone. She intended to get pregnant right away. Men like Andy liked knowing they had a successor.

The clock chimed half past six; Alys peered into her mirror, looking for a change in her expression. She pressed her fingertips to her reflection in the glass. Tilting her head, she looked for any tell tale sign. She wondered if murder caused your eyes to change. Do you hold your mouth differently? Alys bit her perfectly painted red lip and widened her eyes. Everything she had been through had caused a certain hardness inside her that no one else seemed to notice. Her glittery green eyes blinked back at her, same as ever. Coppery hair shimmered down the side of her face.
Alys smiled at her reflection.

Who cared if any man suspected she killed Bobby? Beautiful women didn't worry about such matters!

Alys shook her head, pleased as the sun glinted and caught the copper tones of her hair.

Men are the simplest creatures on earth, almost too easy to distract.

Alys examined her face, looking for any flaw. None.

Andy entered the room and looked her over.

"Miller will be here tonight." Andy rummamged around on top of his desk. Finally, he found what he was looking for; he folded the paper and put it in his breast pocket.

"Miller?" Alys turned from her reflection in the mirror to him.

"He's from Louisiana. He's thinking about taking twelve of your best girls back with him."

"And?" Alys's pulse pounded in her throat. Andy seemed off.

"Do you have twelve?" Andy demanded.

"Only ten," Alys admitted.

"Show him the ten." Andy pawed through her closet and pulled out a red gown.

"They are slated for Toronto." Alys leaned into the mirror and brushed a fleck of black kohl off her cheekbone.

"No. Higher price in Louisiana." Andy handed her a gown.

Hot fury washed through Alys. Andy was always like this, always had the upper hand.

Andy crossed the room to her and put his hand on the back of her neck. "Make sure Miller from Louisiana is satisfied."

Humiliation snaked through her as it slowly dawned on her. "You mean you want me to..."

Andy narrowed his eyes at her. "Make sure he buys and give him whatever he wants."

"But, I'm yours... I don't do that..."

"You do as you're told." Andy's hand tightened on the back of her neck.

He had the upper hand and always would. She was here, in this bedroom, in this position and at his disposal. If she slipped up, she would easily be replaced. A long queue of women were ready to pounce if he tossed her aside. Odelia would be back across the Atlantic in a heartbeat.

Cold fear clamped icy fingers around her heart. Her hands fumbled as she pulled on the gown. Her constant terror of being thrown back to the streets caused tears to prick the back of her eyes. Andy was her insurance.

Without him, she had nothing. Her hands shook as she thought about how to handle this.

"Ready?" Andy waited by the door for her to follow him to the bar where they would entertain Miller from Louisiana.

"Of course." Alys put her fears and feelings aside. Her heart shriveled as she proceeded from the room.

Together, they went to the bar and she put on a big smile for Miller from Louisiana. Alys picked up a glass of claret and took a deep sip.

"That claret is the colour of your lips." Miller from Louisiana didn't pretend to respect her. He undressed her with his eyes and made it clear he knew she was a package deal with the girls.

He leaned forward and Alys leaned back, away from him. She caught a hard look in Andy's eyes. She bit her lip. She knew that look. Alys's face reddened with humiliation as she leaned forward and placed her hand on Miller's forearm. She was no different from the ten girls that were for sale. Any thought that she had clawed her way out of prostitution was dashed. Foolishly, she had believed that Andy cared about her. Icy cold certainty washed through her. She was exactly like the girls he sold in a different dress. A dress she hadn't even been allowed to pick out.

Alys leaned into Miller, giving him a clear view of her cleavage. He brushed a finger down her forearm. Alys didn't allow herself to shudder in revulsion. Andy smiled his approval while he turned his attention to a younger woman. Anger pulsed through Alys as he tugged the young woman down onto his lap. She swallowed bile as it rose in her throat.

Caroline, a twenty-year old from Lancashire was replacing her. Alys knew it. Andy had what he wanted; head of the Butchers and now he wanted a younger woman in his bed while he ran the crime ring. Alys's heart broke and sunk to her feet as Caroline leaned into Andy and whispered in his ear.

Alys's dreams of marriage and respectability crashed around her. She was nothing. All these years wasted. Utterly wasted.

As Miller grew bolder and stroked her face to get her attention, a seed of an idea started to form in Alys's mind. If they could get ten thousand pounds for Nora Blackburn, kidnapping was as lucrative as selling girls. Easier. Instead of picking up ten girls, you only had to snap up one.

Alys thought about what she could do with ten thousand British sterling pounds in a new city, Toronto.

Toronto sounds like a fresh start.

Andy kissed Caroline deeply, in front of her. Alys decided with cold hard clarity, she needed a new life, a life where she wasn't at the whim of a man.

Alys ignored the lips of Miller as they pressed into her neck.

I would need thirty thousand pounds. That way I could hire protection and be at the mercy of no man.

Andy wanted Caroline.

You can have him. He was never truly mine.

Clever Alys thought of who would fetch her the greatest ransom. As a solution presented itself in her mind, she smiled. It was almost too easy. She turned her attention back to Miller. Tossing her hair over her shoulder, she leaned into him. After tonight, her life as her own woman, on her own terms, would start first thing tomorrow.

Chapter Nineteen

Bright and early the next morning, as the ship sailed out of the Thames estuary, Til dressed in her finest and made her way to Grayson's cabin. Bracing herself, she knocked on his door. He answered and blinked in surprise at her.

"Doctor Stone!" Grayson scrambled to pull on a shirt.

He is dishevelled and his eyes are red. He's been drinking.

She sniffed in disapproval as she took in his appearance. A woman called to him from inside his room. Til, horrified, took a step back.

And carousing like a dog!

Grayson opened his mouth to speak; Til cut him off before he could make a sound.

"I'll make this very simple for you." Til's accent frosted with ice. "I want nothing to do with you. I am only here to make sure you are alerted to the fact that I intend to work with the constabulary and once I arrive in Toronto, I *demand* another detective is assigned to this case. I will not work with you. I am convinced you are a wife beater and now I see evidence that you are a drunk and a womaniser. You have shocked my sensibilities, sir! I've already drafted the telegram." Til presented the telegram she had carefully written out and handed it to him.

"This isn't what it looks like." Grayson buttoned his shirt, "She brought breakfast, she is a maid."

Til frowned at him. "What you do in your spare time is none of my concern. I don't care if you bed every woman on this ship, just as long as you don't stumble *drunk* into mine," Til snapped at him.

"You can rest easy. There is not enough alcohol in the world where I could ever be drunk enough to make that mistake." Grayson scrubbed his hands over his face.

Til sniffed. "Good, see that this is taken care of today."

Grayson softened his tone. "Listen, Doctor Stone, I want to apologise for what happened yesterday." He stepped into the hallway with her and pulled the door shut.

"Would you button your shirt?" Til reprimanded him. "Can we have some semblance of dignity here?"

Grayson complied. "I wanted you to see reason and get off this ship. Now that leaving the ship is no longer an option, I am here to promise you that I will protect you from any and all harm."

Til frowned and looked down her nose at him.

Grayson gritted his teeth, adjusted his collar and continued. "There is no reason for you to risk your safety by alerting the captain. I will keep you safe." Grayson tried to flatten down his hair which made it stand up even higher.

Til rolled her eyes and shook her head. "I don't think you understand what *I am* saying." Her English accent sharpened. "Once this telegram is sent, I will stay out of your way until we get to Toronto and you can point me in the direction of another detective to work with. I will not, under any circumstances, speak to you again. This is as far as we go."

"I never said that you prostituted yourself. I never said that at all." Grayson shook his head. "Whatever happened when you were in Lord Blackburn's..."

"Why are you still talking?" Til hissed at Grayson. "I am not going to discuss that night with you or anyone. You accused me of prostituting myself for my education. I don't owe you an explanation. I don't need to defend myself to you! I know how the police view prostitutes. I know very well! I came from the streets and I have worked in behalf of the women of those same streets. I will *not* work with you and we will *not* speak again. Kindly send this telegram and you may slip the name of the officer who will meet me at the dock under my door. No need to knock. That will be all."

"You cannot just change the detective who is assigned to this case by demanding it!" Grayson towered over her. "You can't change how the constabulary does things. This is not how it works. This is my division, this is my job, and there *is* no one else."

Vibrating with fury, Til locked eyes with Grayson and didn't back down. "Find someone immediately or I go after Odelia without *any* support from the Toronto Constabulary. I will disembark in Toronto and I will disappear. If you don't think I will, prepare to be stunned and amazed."

"I am begging you to see reason." Grayson held his hands out in supplication.

"Send this telegram." Til's voice was clipped. "Report back by a *note under my door*. Do not disturb me by knocking because my door will never open to you again. This is our last conversation."

"Please." Grayson's lips thinned with the simple request.

Til brushed past him, opened the door to his cabin, and spied the woman who had tell tale whisker burn on her face and neck. She *was* fully clothed, and Til did for a split second think she may have slightly overreacted. However, he didn't need to be kissing maids!

Gracious!

"I'm his wife," Til snapped at the girl.

The girl's jaw dropped open as Til slammed the door shut behind her.

Til shot Grayson a hard look as she brushed past him.

"Was that really necessary?" Grayson put his hands on his hips.

"You're a rake." Til turned to face him, lifting her chin defiantly. "Send this telegram and give me the reply. *Immediately.* There will be no further discussion on this subject."

"Doctor Stone..." Grayson sputtered.

Til turned on her heel and left him without a backwards glance.

***

Early the following morning, Til was woken by someone pounding on her door.

She struggled to see in the darkness. She fumbled for matches to light a candle so she could see the time.

"Who is it?" Til called out as she dropped the match and tried to find another one.

"Grayson."

She refused to reply; she rolled over and pulled a pillow over her head.

"There is a woman below decks in labour. Things aren't going well. The entire floor is awake, she is in agony."

Til pushed the pillow away and got up. She opened the door to a flustered Detective Grayson.

"She needs a doctor," he repeated unnecessarily. "Would you assist her?"

"If this is a trick," Til warned as she pulled a robe around her nightgown.

"Absolutely not." Clearly distraught, Grayson's tone sounded panicked.

"I just need a moment to change and grab my bag." Til turned on her heel, shut the door on Grayson, and quickly pulled on a dress. She nibbled on hard tack to settle her stomach as she picked up her bag for delivery and turned back to the door. She took a deep breath and opened it to follow him below decks.

He held out his hand for her bag.

"You may as well let me carry that, you have a long night ahead of you," he offered kindly.

"I'll carry my own bag, thank you." Til tightened her grip on her doctor's bag. She stiffened at his outstretched hand.

"Suit yourself." Grayson's eyes narrowed.

Together they raced down flights of narrow stairs to the bowels of the ship. The moaning and screams were getting louder as they got to the cabin where the woman was in labour.

***

Grayson expected Til to turn up her nose at the scene in front of her. He thought she might scoff at the two weeping women trying to alleviate the suffering of the young woman screaming in labour on the bed. He waited for her to be superior and difficult— her general pain in the neck self. Instead, she turned into a compassionate doctor right before his eyes. She set her bag down, pulled out a mask and immediately slipped it onto the woman's face before she even said a word.

"All right now, let's take the edge off that pain, shall we?" Til's tone, low and soothing, caused the occupants of the room to relax. She was a professional; no fear, no fuss. The mask on the woman caused her to stop shrieking.

"Just a little pain medication, love, you're all right." Til's voice was authoritative but gentle and soft. "If you wish, I can look after her now and you can all get some rest to take over when the baby is born." Til dripped something onto the mask and Grayson held the door open.

"Thank you." Tears filled the eyes of the women. "Can you save her?"

"She's in good hands." Til promised. "Are you her mother?"

"Yes." The oldest woman wrung her hands in fear.

"I am a midwife. Maybe you've heard of me? My name is Til Stone. From the women's family planning clinic?"

"Yes, I have." The mother of the girl dropped her eyes to the floor. "Thank you for coming to help."

"What is her name, please?" Til asked as she turned her attention back to her patient.

"Joan. She is only nineteen. She is exhausted..." The mother's voice escalated in fear.

"I promise she is in good hands." Til smiled at the mother.

"I'm the midwife." An older woman stood by Til. "Moira O'Hare. I have been here since the beginning. This has been a particularly long and difficult birth. Now the contractions have started to slow."

"I see that. I can get things moving a bit," Til promised. "You look very tired. If you want to stay you are welcome, but I can handle things from here."

"I hate to leave a patient, Miss." Miss O'Hare touched Joan's arm.

"I know, however, she will need you tomorrow, so you may want to rest now."

"Thank you." Miss O'Hare's shoulders slumped in exhaustion. "I am just down the hall if you need me. I've been here for twenty hours and I am completely worn out."

"Have a good rest." Til smiled as the midwife left with the girl's mother.

The door shut behind them; only the three of them remained. Grayson fought panic that he was one of the three. This was no place for a man!

"Grayson, I'm going to need your help. Come and stand here, I need you to put one drop of this onto the mask every sixty seconds. Can you manage that?" She didn't look at him, she clearly expected immediate compliance.

Grayson jumped to do as he was asked even though the thought of assisting a woman in childbirth made all the blood drain from his face.

"I've never, ever... I'm not sure if I'm the best choice here," Grayson sputtered.

Til ignored Grayson's concern as she carefully handed him a vial. "One drop. Count down from sixty seconds and then another drop."

"Right." Grayson's hands shook with worry.

"After that next drop we have sixty seconds to wash our hands." As soon as Grayson administered the drop they quickly went to the basin of fresh hot water.

"You could have listed all your credentials. Told them you are a surgeon, gynecologist, doctor, you introduced yourself as a midwife." Grayson tilted his head. "Why?"

"Unfortunately, my education distances me from the women I treat." Til finished washing and scrubbing her hands. She reached for a fresh towel. "I don't want it to, but it does. The women often feel inferior and in birth we need to be a team. We need to work together and they have to trust me. In birth we are sisters."

Grayson nodded. "I see." There was more to Til Stone than he thought. There was a sliver of heart under all the ice.

"Well, sisters, but with you here, I suppose that doesn't fit." Til's lip twitched.

She enjoys my discomfort. Harpy!

Grayson peeled off his vest, he heard his pocket watch clunk as he laid the vest down by the basin.

"Will I need my pocket watch to time anything? Like the drip on the mask?"

"No, you'll need both hands free. You can count down from sixty."

Grayson rolled up his sleeves. "It's hot in here."

"Yes."

He carefully scrubbed his hands exactly as Til had. "I'm not going to have to touch anything I hope."

"No, I'll deliver the baby." Til handed a clean towel to Grayson and together they looked at their semiconscious patient.

"Just you and me, Grayson; how good are you at taking orders?" Til tilted her head to the side, clearly unfazed by the magnitude of the job in front of them.

"Terrible," Grayson replied honestly.

Til grinned, clearly in her element. She appeared to be delighted that he was out of his. "Good to be honest."

Grayson grimaced and looked away as Til started to assess Joan's condition.

"What on earth are you doing?"

"Pelvic exam," Til murmured under her breath as she worked. "Gracious." Til shook her head.

"What's wrong?" Grayson couldn't keep the terror from his voice.

"She's so young." Til shook her head, "I am always saddened when the mother is this young. However, all is in order; her labour has slowed."

Grayson closed his eyes with horror at the thought of what fully dialated might mean.

"I am going to give the baby a little nudge. The head is not pressing properly against the cervix. Once I adjust the head, she should fully dialate and then I can give her ergot to intensify the contractions and get this baby out." Til straightened up to carry out her plan.

"Intensify the pain! You'll kill her!" Grayson sputtered in horror.

"I'm going to need you to help me, though. I need you to lift her just a little." Til ignored his concerns and indicated that he should lift her up off the bed.

Grayson quickly did as instructed.

"I can't give her those drops if I'm holding her up. I don't think I can bear to watch her be in that sort of pain," Grayson sputtered.

"We need her to be semiconscious for what is about to happen next," Til said grimly. "She'll have to work with the pain; however, there is enough in her system to cut the pain in half, so it is at least bearable."

"Bearable!" Grayson gasped. "She sounds like she is dying! And, by the way, what are those drops? I am going to need some," Grayson asked as he gently held the woman up using his chest to support her. Til moved her hands over her abdomen and smiled with satisfaction as the mound under her experienced hands shifted.

"There we are. You are ready little one," Til spoke to the baby and then quickly examined Joan again.

"The drops are chloroform, Grayson, very controversial in childbirth." Til wiped her forehead with her forearm. Til did another pelvic exam. "Perfect! Baby's head is pressing hard on the cervix. That's what we want, a little touch more towards me... that's right. Hold that position."

"Why is it controversial?" Sweat ran down Grayson's back as he held the woman in his arms. "It seems to have relaxed her and helped with the pain. Isn't that a good thing?" Grayson asked in confusion as he held Joan in position.

"Explain that to the masochists running the medical profession. I've tried until I am blue in the face. The men discredit me because I am a woman and they think I'm a brainless fool." Til wiped her forehead on her forearm again; the room was stiflingly hot. She went to retrieve the ergot and as the patient was barely conscious, she injected it. "The reason my clinic is so successful is because I assist women in delivery *with chloroform* and every woman in the land who can afford it pays a hefty price."

"What does that mean?" Grayson wished he was anywhere but here. He soldiered on despite the fear pooling in his stomach.

"If I assist you and you are a 'Lady' or you come from money, I charge accordingly." Til grinned at him.

"Really?" Grayson's eyebrows shot up.

"Really," Til confirmed. "Since I am the only doctor that uses chloroform in childbirth, I can name my price. Conversely, if you are a woman with ten children in a slum, living in over-crowded poverty the service is whatever you can afford, which is often nothing. It's my way of evening out the class system, a system that I despise."

"And you can get away with that?" Grayson's eyes widened.

"Who's going to stop me?" Til shrugged. "As you noticed, I defy most authority."

You mean all!

"A woman doctor, a gynecologist, is unheard of. They watch me for any sign I perform abortions. That's about all they worry about." Til drew her attention back to what was happening with Joan.

"Do you?" Grayson couldn't stop himself from asking.

"If you could stop being a detective for three minutes, it would be a nice change." Til bristled at his tone. "No, I promote *birth control.* I believe, as do many of my colleagues, that if birth control is available to all women we would see the end of abortion. I make sure birth control is available to any woman who asks for it, regardless of who she is or where she comes from and the ladies I treat pay for it. They just don't know it."

"Do the husbands of these women have any say in this?" Grayson tried and failed to take the judgement from his tone.

"No. Not in my clinic." Til bristled as she removed the chloroform mask from Joan's face. "I give contraception to any woman who asks for it. Shouldn't a woman have the choice to go through this or not?" Til indicated to the ordeal the woman was going through on the bed.

Grayson opened his mouth and then clamped it shut.

"Pay attention." Til changed the subject as she studied the girl on the bed. "She's coming around and this contraction is going to be a bad one. Hold her up; we need pressure on the cervix. Are you going to faint?" Til's voice was sharp with worry. "If you faint and drop her, she might tear. You have to hold her up."

"I won't drop her." Grayson's face paled in fear.

"If you faint on me, Grayson, I'll be furious," Til warned him as she kept her eye on Joan.

"I'm not going to faint." He spoke despite the fear tightening his throat.

"See that you don't." Til's eyes narrowed. "All right, love." Til's voice softened. "We're almost done here. You almost have a baby in your arms."

Grayson heart went out to Joan as she trembled in fear and pain in his arms.

"Joan," Til said gently. "When you feel the pain, I need you to push with it. We're nearly there."

"No. I can't do it!" the young woman wept. "I am being ripped apart!"

"I know you're scared." Til spoke to her like she was a little child afraid of the dark. "I know. Hold my hand and lean against Grayson here. We're going to help you and then I'm going to take all the pain away. Come on now, one big push."

"I can't," Joan wept.

Grayson desperately wanted to put the mask back on her face and then pour the entire bottle of chloroform on it.

"I will take all the pain away as soon as it's over. Right now, I need you to push hard against it. Come on, Joan, we're almost done."

The girl writhed in pain and pressed hard against the wall of Grayson's chest. His throat tightened in fear as he helped her lay back to try to alleviate the pain.

Til looked at him sharply. "Keep her upright." She returned her attention to Joan. "You can do it, Joan."

As another pain crashed through the girl in his arms, Grayson wished the room would stop spinning around him. She bucked against the pain. She screamed in anguish. Grayson saw black dots in his peripheral vision.

"Good girl, good girl! The head is born. You did it, you clever girl. The head is born!" Til cheered her on. "We are almost there. Come on now. One big push. Grayson, she's slumping. Help her up."

The room tilted hard. Grayson shook his head to clear it.

The girl screamed as if she was indeed ripping apart. Sweat trickled down Grayson's chest as he struggled to help her up and try to ease her pain as much as possible. He looked down to see how things were progressing. Mistake! The room started to spin; he focused on Til.

Even here, in the bowels of a ship, covered in blood and fluids, she looked cool, calm and completely in control. Til Stone was a gorgeous woman and as she concentrated on the task at hand, no amount of gruesome work could dull her shine. Face glistening with sweat; she wore a mask of professionalism. If this girl was dying, and he suspected that she was, you would never know it from the look on Til's face. She looked as if they were all just about to sit down to tea, as if this wasn't the most horrifying thing she had ever encountered. Granted, what did he know about what Til Stone, or indeed Matilda Bertram had ever encountered? The more he found out, the more he wanted to know.

Finally, the baby was born! Til replaced the chloroform mask on Joan's face, and she gave her two drops and then screwed the top back on the vial. Grayson took the vial from her. His eyes met Til's just as she held up the baby, covered in blood. The front of her apron was soaked. She looked like a warrior on the front line of a battle. Til gave him a nod as if to say he hadn't completely disappointed her. Secure with that knowledge, Grayson fainted dead away.

***

Joan slumped on top of Grayson. The fool had given her too much chloroform.

Til rolled her eyes at him. The man was a giant and the blood and gore of childbirth disarmed him. She shook her head.

No time to think about Grayson. She turned her attention to the baby. Relief washed through Til as the baby started to scream at the top of her lungs. The midwife, at the sound of the baby crying slipped back into the room.

"Glad to see you." Til smiled at Miss O'Hare. "Looks like my assistant wasn't up for the challenge."

"Should I give him some smelling salts?" Miss O'Hare shot a look at Grayson with concern.

"No, no need for him to see the rest of the birth." Til washed the baby and swaddled her in soft, clean blankets.

She placed the newborn on her mother's chest.

Grayson jolted awake.

"You did it, Joan. She is beautiful like her mother." Til's eyes met Grayson's as he continued to hold Joan against him. "Grayson, you can come off the bed now, if you can stand up?"

Grayson's face reddened. He looked completely mortified. "Sorry about that."

"I'll just clean things up here. If you want to go to bed, I'll see myself back to my..."

"Probably best if I take you back." Grayson backed away from the women as Joan started moaning in pain again.

"What is it now?" Grayson swayed as if he would faint again.

"Afterbirth." Til poured a tincture of laudanum on a spoon and pressed it into her mouth. Relief spread across the girl's face. "She's almost done, but not quite. Maybe you should wait in the corridor."

"Perfect." Grayson grabbed onto that suggestion like a man holding onto a life preserver in a storm.

Til grinned at him and shook her head, then turned back to Joan.

"Almost done here," Til said as the door softly closed behind Grayson.

Til didn't leave until she was certain the womb was constricting as it should. She left more laudanum with the midwife and made sure the mother and baby were comfortable. After packing up her tools and supplies, she patted Joan's hand and promised to return to check on her later that day.

Til stepped into the hallway where Grayson was sitting on the floor, asleep. Til placed her hand on his shoulder and he jolted awake.

"Did you faint again?" Til straightened up and held her bag in front of her.

Grayson chuckled. "No, I'm very sorry about that." He got to his feet and held his hand out to carry her bag.

"I'll carry my own bag, thank you. You are a bit of a fragile flower; you might faint and drop it." Til stepped away from him. "You said you have had to beat confessions out of men. I thought you would handle the blood and pain of childbirth easily."

"I never, ever want to see *that* again." Grayson replied honestly. "I can't bear women in pain. There is a reason men are not allowed to participate in childbirth. Speaking on behalf of all men everywhere, that was traumatic." He fell into step beside her.

Til couldn't stop a chuckle as she looked at Grayson's face, grey with the horror of what he had just experienced. He frowned at her which caused her to laugh harder.

"Maybe we would have fewer unwanted pregnancies if men were forced to assist."

"Now, see here," Grayson sputtered.

"Maybe you will think about this when you have a maid in your bedroom serving you breakfast." Til grinned.

Grayson's face flushed with embarrassment.

Til laughed so hard she had to hold her sides.

"I will never live this down. Not being able to see a woman in pain. You'll throw this in my face forever now," Grayson groaned.

"Maybe you didn't beat your wife." Til watched him out of the side of her eye.

"I swear it," Grayson vowed.

"That was a particularily difficult birth," Til conceded.

"She'll be all right?" Grayson's forhead creased in concern.

"She'll be fine. Baby is healthy and strong and so is the mother. The birth slowed down, and she just needed the baby's head positioned and then something to strengthen the contractions. I'll check on her later." Til shot another grin at Grayson and together they made their way to the upper deck.

Grayson stood outside the door to Til's cabin.

"I think we should talk." Til turned to him as she opened the door and indicated he should come in.

Grayson's eyes searched hers as he stood at the doorway.

"Brandy in tea after a difficult birth. That's my oldest tradition. Would you like a cup?" Til waved her hand at the table and chairs indicating he should take a seat. Placing her doctor's bag on the floor, she went to the sideboard.

"Sure." Grayson shut the door behind him and stood near the table.

"It's possible that it might be better if we co-operated a bit..." Til cleared her throat as she poured cold tea and brandy into two teacups and then turned to face him. "You might hear something through telegrams. I would like to be kept abreast of any new developments."

Til joined Grayson at the table, she handed Grayson his cup and then took a seat. He sat down across from her.

Til took a delicate sip of cold tea and brandy.

"Cold tea is terrible. Sorry, do you mind if I help myself to a brandy straight?" Grayson grimaced.

"By all means." Til inclined her head to the sideboard. "Please help yourself."

"Are you well?" Grayson returned to the table with a brandy in a cut glass tumbler.

"I'm fine." Til hesitated, beginning to waver in her distrust for him. He had obviously cared about Joan's pain and had wanted to alleviate it; he would be the same with her. "I've been thinking that it's possible I might have overreacted; slightly." Til's teeth clenched hard. Apologising was foreign and difficult for her.

"Oh?" Grayson's eyebrows shot up.

"Don't make this difficult," Til snapped at him.

"I could have handled things with more delicacy. I am often accused of being a bit tenacious and... well, rather terrifying." Grayson fidgeted with his glass of brandy.

"I too have been accused of tenacity..." Til conceded. "Moving forward, tomorrow, this entire ship will know I'm a doctor and I don't like the look of those three men that were at Malcolm's funeral. They seem to be on the sidelines at all times. If your offer to... uh... look out for me still stands, I would like to take you up on that."

"Of course." Grayson sipped his brandy.

Til watched him for any sign that he was going to hold this against her at a later date; expect something back. The look he gave her over the rim of his brandy glass suggested he was interested in peace between them.

"You'll have to move to first class then. I will need you on hand. I don't want to be waiting around if I am in need of assistance. I'll make the arrangements."

"I will make my own arrangements," Grayson corrected her.

Til bristled. "Fine."

Grayson finished his drink and stood up. "You look exhausted, that was hard work and you did a great job. Good night, Doctor Stone."

He stood awkwardly by the door.

Til got up and slid her fingertip along the curved handle of the teacup. "You did very well. Until you fainted."

He smiled at her. "Again. My apologies."

Til tried not to smile but couldn't wipe the grin from her face.

"I'll move first thing." Grayson opened the door.

"Thank you." Til nodded, picked up her teacup and drained the last of her drink.

As the door shut behind him, Til placed her teacup back down on the table and let her breath out slowly.

After calling for hot water, she washed and redressed in a fresh nightgown.

I have a feeling, Speck, we'll be taking a trip to Brandon when it's time for you to be born. Shannon is the only doctor and midwife I trust.

Til slid into bed. She didn't wake until late the next morning when there was a note from the captain under her door.

'Doctor Stone,

The honour of your presence is requested tonight at eight p.m. for dinner.

Your humble servant,

Captain Obadiah Duval.'

Grayson is a ninny. What harm could there possibly be? A womaniser he claims! Pot calling the kettle black!

Chapter Twenty

Til tossed her hair back over her shoulders. Dining with a captain might be a nice distraction. After opening the door to the maid with breakfast and hot water, she looked out the porthole at the endless Atlantic Ocean. The maid bustled behind her.

"Did you spend the night with Detective Grayson?" She kept her back to the maid and waited for an answer.

"No, madam."

"Did you turn him down or did he turn *you* down?" Til turned to watch the maid's face to see if she was lying.

"I turned him down," the maid said as she went to the corridor to retrieve a bucket of hot water.

"Really?" Til sat down at the table to eat her hot breakfast.

The maid did not reply.

"I'll need some assistance getting dressed." Til changed the subject as she carefully cut the crusts off her toast and nibbled at it. "I have an invitation to dine with the captain tonight."

"Oh." The maid bit her lip. "Are you sure, madam? He's very... well... he is hard to turn down."

"Preposterous. I won't have any sort of trouble; I can assure you." Til sipped her hot tea before it cooled.

The maid shrugged.

"Supper is at eight so please ensure you are here at seven to help me dress." Til slathered honey on her toast.

Time to put Grayson in his place.

He couldn't possibly expect to hand out orders and have her meekly follow along like a lamb. They were creating a fragile peace between them, so the time to make sure he understood how things would work between them was now. She didn't take orders from him. *He would follow her lead.* A precedent had to be set.

As she opened her door to attend the captain's dinner party, Grayson stood on the other side of the door in a suit. Fresh shaven, hair slicked down into submission, she swallowed at the sight of him and then stiffened.

What he looks like doesn't matter.

"What are you doing?" Tone clipped, Til tried to brush past him.

"Saving you from yourself," Grayson said dryly.

"Not necessary." Til bristled.

Grayson took her arm and she pulled it out of his grasp. She swept out of reach and proceeded to the captain's quarters ahead of him.

The room, lit with two chandeliers and candles down the center of the table, looked festive and cheery.

Til stood as far from Grayson as she could. The captain, a very large man, made his way through the crew and passengers to greet them.

"Doctor Stone!" he boomed at her.

Til held out her hand, which was quickly and enthusiastically engulfed by his. He looked at her like a cat looks at a dish of cream.

"I have heard you have already attended a passenger. I wanted to thank you personally." The captain nodded at Grayson. "There is a space for you here."

Til noticed Grayson was being placed half a table away from her. She fought a niggle of concern as the captain leered at her and suddenly, she felt a bit worried that he would expect something in exchange for this lavish meal in front of them.

As the captain led her to a chair beside his, he placed his hand on the small of her back and let it drift lower. Til gasped in outrage.

"I'm not that sort of woman, sir," she hissed out of the corner of her mouth.

"What sort of woman?" His eyes were already bloodshot from drinking. He swayed as he held her chair out. Worry snaked around Til's heart.

He is dead drunk!

He openly stared at the décolletage her gown allowed for. She wished desperately for a shawl, anything to cover up. She tried to catch

Grayson's eye, but he was on the same side of the table and completely ignoring her. He was engaged in lively conversation with a blonde woman to his left.

Til burned in humiliation as the captain leaned into her to speak. His breath was so horrendous she tried and failed to dodge the offensive odour. She scrambled to strike up a conversation with a woman next to her but she was nearly a hundred years old and deaf as a post. Til gave up in frustration.

"So, you are a doctor?" A drip of saliva made its way down the frown line near the captain's lip.

Til shuddered, took a delicate sip of very strong claret, and longed for tea.

"Could I request a cup of tea perhaps? I am finding that claret is a little too much for me at present. I'm pregnant you see." Til hoped the pregnancy would put him off.

It didn't.

Captain Duval ignored her comment. "We could always use a doctor on board. I should hire you, you could be part of my crew." He put his arm around the back of her chair.

"Sir, Captain Duval, I fear there has been a misunderstanding." Til flashed him a cool smile. "I am not interested in any sort of *amorous affair*. I am a grieving widow on my way to Toronto."

"Alone." Captain Duval took a deep sip of claret.

"Alone and *pregnant*, sir. I am unfortunately part of a police investigation. The man that accompanied me here is escorting me." Til shot a frustrated glance at Grayson.

Why isn't he stepping in? He hasn't looked this way once!

Grayson leaned into the delicate, beautiful, blonde woman beside him who tilted her head and smiled at him.

Til squinted as Grayson took the woman's shawl off her narrow shoulders and placed it on the back of the chair. He reached forward and brushed something from her cheekbone.

He is completely ignoring me!

"He doesn't seem to be too concerned for your welfare." Captain Duval indicated that his glass needed to be refilled.

Indeed, Grayson's head was thrown back, he laughed at something the blonde woman was saying. Grayson gave her his rapt attention. Her delicate beauty caused Grayson to look bigger, broader and darker. Til watched as the woman placed her small hand on his heavy forearm. Til tried to catch his eye, he didn't notice.

They made a striking couple. Older women watched Grayson flirt with the beautiful woman and they gave each other knowing glances and spoke behind their fans. Grayson wasn't concerned about Til in the least. She would have to take matters into her own hands and get out of here before the captain disgraced himself and by extension, her. A deep grin pulled at Duval's lips as Til stood up.

"You're ready to *retire* so soon?" He leered at her.

Til shuddered. She had no intention of getting to the bottom of what he believed was retiring. As he reached out to assist her, she sidestepped him.

"I am not feeling well, sir. I will *retire* alone; I'll have supper sent to my room. Good night."

Til took a step back and tried to make her way to the door. She shot a look at Grayson who had no eyes for anyone in the room except the beautiful young woman he was seated next to.

Womaniser!

Til cursed him. He had been right. The captain was disgraceful. The older women at the table had looked at each other with alarm as the captain stood and swayed on his feet. They muttered behind their fans that he was dead drunk. Real worry made the hair on the back of Til's neck stand up.

"I'll escort you to your cabin," Captain Duval slurred.

"That won't be necessary," Til said frostily.

"I insist." Captain Duval stumbled as he walked with Til to the door.

"I came with that man there. He is..."

Grayson had his back to them both.

"He looks like he is having a good time; no need to disturb him." The captain leered at her.

"I insist. I really am fine on my own." Til's voice sounded high in her ears.

"Nonsense." The captain took her by the arm and led her away from the festivities.

Til cursed Grayson as the captain dragged her from the dinner party.

He swayed again and clutched at her to stay upright. Til tried not to gag as his hot, fetid breath washed over her. She tried to stay out of his reach, but even as drunk as he was, she couldn't stay far enough away.

Finally, they stood at her closed cabin door.

"Thank you and good night, sir." Til's tone was ice on iron.

The captain ignored it. "Let's have a night cap."

"I really insist that I am not well. Please sir, I request that you leave me alone now so I can lie down in peace." Til's voice was shrill in her ears.

The captain sighed and Til's knees nearly buckled from the stench.

"I'll help you inside." He staggered and fell forward. His hand cupped her breast as he struggled to pull himself upright.

"Take your hands off me," Til hissed at him.

He pressed her against the closed door of her cabin. "I'm the captain of this ship, my lady. Open the door."

"Absolutely not." Til's heart pounded hard in fear.

"Come now! There is no need for dramatics. Let's have a little drink together and get to know one another. It's been a long week at sea. Open the door; I want to hear all about your fascinating world of being a doctor." The glint in the captain's eye indicated to Til that he would not take no for an answer.

Til knew with certainty that if she opened the door, she would be doomed.

"I will scream," Til warned as Captain Duval gathered her in his arms.

***

Grayson, who was watching the entire episode from a safe distance away, shook his head. He wondered how far to let this go before he stepped in.

He thought about now, but Til was so difficult, she needed a little scare. He had warned her, she had ignored him. Grayson tilted his head in confusion as Til flashed a smile at the captain. For some reason, she was pulling up her skirt! Far enough up that the captain pulled her even tighter into his embrace. Grayson moved down the hall with lightning speed.

Was she drugged?

Til smiled so suggestively that Grayson gasped and stopped.

Maybe she wanted the Captain in her room, and I am interfering?

Grayson's eyes narrowed at the thought.

She is a widow! She should be in mourning and not swooning around with a captain! What kind of woman is this?

Just as Grayson was about to turn and walk away, Til brought her knee up as hard as she could. Without the skirt to soften the blow, Captain Duval dropped to his knees in front of her, moaning in agony, cursing her. Til ignored his howls of pain. She slapped him as hard as she could as he clutched between his legs.

Grayson could not stop a grin from breaking out across his face.

Clearly flustered, she had tears in her eyes as she dropped her key in her haste to open her cabin door.

Finally, Grayson sauntered up between them. He stood between her and the captain as she scrambled for the key on the floor beside him.

"You finally appear." Til fumed at him as she clutched the key in her hand. "Now, when the crisis has been averted!"

"You said you could handle it!" A kick of guilt bothered him. He shouldn't have waited and let her be terrified by a drunken old captain. Grayson reached for her key. Til snatched it away. "I was just down the hall and about to step in. I wasn't going to let anything happen. When you lifted your skirt, I thought maybe I was intruding."

"You thought I wanted... him!" Til howled. She tried to press the key into the lock of the door. Hands shaking, she couldn't manage.

Grayson took the key from her hand and unlocked her door.

Til preceded him into the room. "Get in here." Til pointed into her cabin. "You are deliberately being difficult. Flirting with a woman at dinner and completely ignoring my plight."

Grayson shut the door behind him. "She was very beautiful." He flashed her an unrepentant grin. "I warned you. You ignored me."

Til's hands clenched to fists at her side.

"If we are going to work together here is how it is going to be." Grayson stood tall.

Til bristled. "I will be the one to establish *any and all* new rules."

"No." Grayson adjusted his stance as he braced for battle.

"What is this word *no* you are throwing around?" Til asked wildly.

"A word you should get used to." Grayson shot her a hard look. "Until the 23rd, which is approximately when this ship is supposed to dock, we are going to conduct ourselves professionally. I want to be perfectly clear; I don't despise you, that's a strong word. You *irritate* me though on levels I didn't know I possessed."

Til's lips thinned to an angry slit.

"I like women," Grayson said simply. "Actually, like isn't right, I love women."

"I noticed." Til's tone frosted with derision.

"But you frustrate me." Grayson sighed.

"Crikey, I am just as fruserated with you!" Til crowed at him.

"I am the lead detective on this case." Grayson crossed the room to speak to her. "Even on this ship, I am on the job. Since you're insisting on meeting Odelia or whoever is going to be on that dock you are an integral part of this investigation. We both want Nora Blackburn returned safely to her family." Grayson took a step closer.

Til held her ground and crossed her arms over her chest. Her chin tilted in defiance.

"We are going to work together until we dock in Toronto. That means you respect me as a police officer. No more prickly comments, no more speaking to me as if I were a dog. If you can't respect me—pretend to."

"I don't know what you are talking about," Til hissed through her teeth.

"You opened the door just now and said 'get in here' as if I were serving class. From now on, you show me some respect or things are going to be very difficult—for you." Grayson towered over her.

"I'm accustomed to being the boss." Til's tone clipped hard with anger.

"Me too." He shot at her. "In this investigation, I *am* the boss. I do not tolerate insubordination from my men; I will *not* tolerate it from you." Grayson's jaw clenched. "So, instead of I'm the boss or you're the boss, I suggest we work hard to be partners. I will respect you and you *will* respect me."

Til opened her mouth and then clamped it shut.

Grayson watched her think about what to say and how to say it.

"Or what?" Til finally hissed through grit teeth.

"Don't test me, woman," Grayson warned. "There's a brig on this ship and I have access to it."

Her eyes narrowed in challenge. Grayson's eyes narrowed right back.

"I mean it," Grayson growled at her. "That's how it's going to go."

"Fine," Til snapped, her fists clenched in anger.

"Try that again, nicely." Grayson took another step forward, forcing her to look up at him.

"Fine." Til scowled but adjusted her tone. There was a hint of frost but less than before.

"Very good." Grayson took a step back. "This is a telegram I am sending to Sol Stein, putting him at your disposal when we dock. He's a good man; I would trust him with my life. If you are nice to me, I will hand you over to Sol."

"I appreciate that." Til spoke stiffly, clearly smarting from the reprimand. "Now, how am I going to escape from Captain Duval's attentions for the rest of the voyage?"

"Not much longer now. Shortly, we will dock in Quebec and go through immigration. The ship that takes us to Toronto is smaller and Captain Duval isn't going to be on board. You'll have a whole new captain to evade." Grayson kept his tone soft, trying to establish a fragile peace between them.

"Are we on the same ship to Toronto then?" Til tucked her hair behind her ear.

"I contacted the constabulary already to make sure we have adjoining cabins." Grayson grinned.

"You did not!" Til gasped.

Grayson threw back his head and laughed at the horrified expression on her face. "I am in the cabin across from you; simmer down. You should get some rest; I'll have some supper sent to you. With any luck, we shouldn't need to see each other until we get to Quebec. I know that would be a nice break *for me*."

"It will give you time to carouse with the blonde woman from the captain's table," Til said waspishly.

"Try that with a different tone," Grayson demanded.

"I have never, ever, in my life had a man treat me like this," Til protested in outrage.

"Well, Til. I suggest you get used to it." Grayson crossed his arms over his chest. "Say it again, different tone."

Til stiffened. "Perhaps you will enjoy getting to know the lady seated at the table with you." Til spoke primly.

"Much better. See? You're learning." Grayson grinned. "She was delightful; I'm supposed to meet with her once I get you sorted out. Good evening, Doctor Stone."

"You realise you'll get a reputation as a womaniser." Til shot at him.

Grayson moved close to Til, towered over her, leaned down so he could speak right into her ear. She tried to move back, she couldn't, pinned between the hard wall of the ship and the solid wall of his chest. His breath was hot on her neck as he dropped his head and whispered in her ear.

"I'll risk it." Grinning at her one last time, he backed away and left her there.

Opening the door, he knelt down and shook the captain who had passed out drunk in the hallway awake.

"All right, soldier, you can't stay here all night; let's get you back to your quarters."

Til leaned against the door frame as Grayson dragged the captain away from her door.

As Grayson left the captain's quarters, the thought of meeting up with young and beautiful Lynne from dinner seemed ridiculous. She had a line up of men after her on this voyage and Grayson had a divorce that wasn't final. He made his way back to his own cabin, alone.

Soon they would go through immigration in Quebec and he worried about the three men who had tailed her on the ship. They had done nothing to her, not even an attempt to attack her.

Why?

Maybe he had been wrong? Grayson frowned at the thought. Those men had an agenda, he was certain. Whatever it was, he needed to be on his toes to deal with his new partner. Who knew what scrapes she would get them both into before they finally docked in Toronto? Grayson couldn't wait to hand her to Sol with his sympathies.

Chapter Twenty-One

Freezing because Cole had all the covers, Shannon woke abruptly. As she curled up against his back to warm up, he woke up and turned over to gather her into his arms.

"Good morning." She pressed her cheek against his chest.

"Good morning, darling. You're freezing." Cole pulled her closer, dragging heavy covers over them both.

"Someone stole all the covers." Shannon burrowed into him.

"Sorry." Cole's arms tightened around her. "Let's stay at home." Cole suggested as he tugged at the strap of her nightgown.

"You say that every day," Shannon giggled as he pressed his lips to her neck and then shoulder.

"Priscilla's 'Hope in Oakland' line of unmentionables for brides is very fetching." Cole's lips returned to her neck. "Makes me forget about work..."

Shannon shivered with delight. "You say *that* every time I wear this." She slid her arms around his neck.

"Are we an old married couple now?" Cole grinned as he pulled her closer.

"We're a very happy old married couple with the *possibility* of a surprise." Shannon kissed him.

Cole pulled his head up. "What surprise?"

Shannon sat up, suddenly serious. "Cole, it's not what we planned and I'm not sure how it will affect things in Canada..." Shannon bit her lip in concern.

"What is it? Has something happened?" Cole's eyebrows knit together with worry.

"Just that we were going to decide *together* when I should plan to get pregnant..." a smile tugged at her lip.

Cole bolted upright in bed, taking her by the upper arms; he blinked as he began to understand what she was saying. "Shannon! Are you pregnant?"

"Just that, I *might* have forgotten to use contraception just once and I seem to be..." Shannon's eyes widened.

"Are you pregnant, Shannon?" Cole's eyes lit up with excitement.

"That's just it." Shannon's eyes clouded with worry. "It seems too early to tell... but I am never late and I am a *few* days late... it might change our plans... I should not have even brought it up. I am likely late due to stress and sadness."

"Maybe not! Maybe you should stay off your feet until you know for sure." Cole's eyes clouded with fear.

"Cole, I am perfectly well, I just wanted you to know it is a possibility." Shannon stroked the side of his face with her hand. "Please don't get your hopes up."

"Too late. They're already up." Cole smiled at her. "You know, if you are pregnant, Til is going to kill me!" Cole warned her.

"You remember the rule!" Shannon reprimanded him as she slid her arms around him. "No talk of *Til* in the marital bed. She is a mood killer. That *topic* is off limits. If I am indeed pregnant, are you pleased?" Shannon grinned.

"Shannon, you know, I want a family with you more than anything." Cole brushed hair from her eyes.

"Even if it derails things with Doctor White?" Shannon tilted her head to the side, giving Cole access to her neck.

Cole kissed her neck in the exact place that made her pulse pound with desire.

"I don't care about Doctor White or wings in hospitals." Cole obliged and kissed along the side of her neck. "Promise me, you will let me know the *minute* you know."

"I shouldn't have told you until I knew for sure... but I am never, ever late even a day, so I think I am quite sure. Do you remember the night I explained all that to you?" Shannon ran her hands over his shoulders.

Cole threw back his head and laughed. "I'll never forget. I kept my notes, no need to go over all that now." He pulled her closer. "You have made me the happiest man in the world, Shannon, and if you are pregnant, that is the best gift of all. I don't care what plans this baby derails, nothing matters but finding out for sure. You think it likely?" Cole's eyes searched hers.

"I think it very likely." Shannon's breath caught with emotion.

Cole and Shannon smiled at each other with excitement.

"Well then, we really are taking the day off. We must celebrate the possibility of this news properly." Cole pulled her closer.

"Have to," Shannon agreed. "I'll have the butler send a telegram to Enid. But, what about my appointment with the couple buying you-know-who's house?"

"Remember, no talk of you-know-who in the marital bed. No need to talk at all really." Cole grinned and kissed her again— a kiss with intent. Shannon shivered with excitement.

***

Shannon checked her watch as she waited on the agent and the lady of the house to arrive. Til's home was in a fashionable and safe part of town. Shannon had dismissed Cole's fears about going on her own. Mrs. Halloway wanted recommendations on which maids should be invited to stay to run the new household. Cole had to meet with agents regarding Malcolm's law firm anyway. As they raced to tie up loose ends, it made sense to save time and get as much done separately as possible.

He handled the men and Shannon would deal with Mrs. Halloway. They had torn apart from each other after breakfast, promising to have an early supper in their formal dining room.

Shannon frowned, hoping their house sold quickly. With the possibility of a baby on the way, she was eager to get to Brandon and get settled before the worst of winter set in. She intended to start her clinic and then start training staff. Of course, Enid was perfectly capable of selling their home if it didn't sell before they left for Canada, but it was an added burden for her. She had started going to medical school and really had almost no time for anything, except maybe Harris, their guard. Shannon thought she saw telltale signs of looks that passed between them when they thought no one was watching. Shannon smiled. She wished Enid every happiness with Harris or whomever. Enid would make a terrific doctor.

Her heart soared with happiness as she walked up the front steps of Til's home with the thought of returning to Oakland and her friends there. No more filthy slums; instead, time would be spent on beautiful Bennett farm with Ada, catching up with Priscilla Hartwell, her dear friend. Purchasing more scandalous lingerie from Priscilla's Hope in Oakland dress shop. She yearned to see Cole's family who had welcomed her with such open arms. She, on occasion, found herself missing even Mrs. Daindridge and Mrs. Carr. Raising a baby in the fresh clean prairie air near Oakland but with a new position in Brandon made Shannon happy and impatient to get out of England.

Shannon ticked through the list of things she needed to pick up on the way home. She wanted to get some of Cole's favourite cognac and a gift for him to mark the occasion. Shannon frowned with frustration. This was all unnecessary anyway. If Mrs. Halloway knew Til, there was no way she would have a maid or butler who didn't work hard and know their job.

Til did pay fairly, so that had to be navigated. Shannon was not about to allow the staff to suffer with insufficient wages. If Mrs. Halloway didn't pay appropriately, Til had instructed Shannon to employ them in Malcolm's house for now and she would sort it when she returned.

Shannon let herself into Til's home. A home Malcolm had bought for her, so she had a place to sleep if she needed to be close to the clinic.

Her breath caught in surprise as she entered the parlour. A woman and two men sat by the fireplace.

"Who are you?" Shannon gasped, her hand flew to her throat.

Alys's eyes gleamed at her with anticipation. "Aunty Alys."

Shannon turned to flee when a man stepped forward and grabbed her.

"Don't hurt her," Alys instructed. "We need her alive and well."

Shannon opened her mouth to scream but one of the men clamped his hand over her mouth with a handkerchief. Recognising the smell of chloroform, Shannon tried not to breathe. She twisted and writhed in his arms to no avail. Within seconds, her lungs burned for air. One deep breath of chloroform and she slumped in his arms.

***

Alys rolled her eyes.

"That was almost too easy." Alys pointed them to the door.

"I hear Matilda uses chloroform in childbirth, I use it for abductions. Fitting, wouldn't you say?" Alys flashed a smile at Shipley Bristol.

He shrugged.

"Carry her to the carriage, my ship is waiting," Alys commanded as she opened the back door.

"After you pay me." Shipley's eyes narrowed at Alys.

"I'll give you half now and half when she's safely on the ship with the rest of the girls." Alys pressed the money into Shipley's hand. Her spine stiffened as she noticed a look between Shipley and his sidekick Brendon.

Crossing the room in moments, Brendon took Alys by the upper arms and dragged her against him. "We could take everything right now. Who would stop us?"

"The rest of the money is on the ship." Alys slid her hand into the pocket of her skirt, wrapped her hand around the derringer and pressed it into Brendon's abdomen. She smirked as his eyes widened. "You're not dealing with an inexperienced shop girl. Let's go before that McDougall shows up. Hurry, my ship leaves this afternoon and we have one more stop to make."

Grudgingly, Shipley picked up Shannon and Alys kept her hand on her gun as they made their way to the carriage.

"To 25 Marrel Street," Alys demanded.

The carriage clipped over the cobblestones. Alys watched working class London through the window of the carriage. Women hanging wash out with toddlers wailing and hanging on their skirts. There were few men on the streets; they were all at the docks or wherever they could find work. Alys shuddered at the sight of the women. To her, this was a fate worse than death. She looked across the carriage at Shannon's perfect coppery blond hair - similar to her own— her flawless skin with the smattering of freckles on her nose; expensive clothes, shiny shoes.

Alys's heart hardened in anger. Matilda had saved Shannon, but she left Alys to be thrown to the wolves. Shannon had worth in Matilda's eyes, but Alys had none. Even as Alys had wept and begged in her darkest moments, Matilda never, ever came. Matilda didn't care. Well. She would care now! Her precious Shannon! She'd pay a king's ransom for her.

As the carriage ground to a halt in front of 25 Marrel Street, Cole and Shannon's beautiful home, copper and crimson leaves fluttered to the ground with a gust of late autumn air. Alys got out of the carriage, slipped down the pavement and pulled a penknife out of her corset. She stabbed the ransom note to their front door, got back in the carriage and headed to the docks to board the Bristol's ship. Twelve girls were already slated to go to Miller in Louisiana and now Shannon. Alys thought about Miller, of how easy he was to manipulate.

"Ask Andy to have *me* bring the girls to you in Louisiana and then we can continue our fun," Alys had suggested.

Miller couldn't drag his eyes away from her décolletage. "I'm married."

"I don't want to be married." Alys threw back her head and laughed. "I bring you two extra girls, you pay me directly. Andy doesn't have to know, and I get a nice holiday in Louisiana. Unless... well, unless you aren't pleased with me?" She had run her fingertip down his cheek as she purred.

"I'm very pleased." Miller had licked his lips with anticipation.

Alys had tossed her hair back and decided that this was all so easy. Really, why hadn't she started all this much sooner? She'd been weak, she'd believed herself to be in love with Andy.

Foolish girl.

She would never make that mistake again.

Alys supervised the twelve young girls and Shannon as they were put in the brig of the Bristol's ship, Aster. Unfortunately, Bluebell, her favourite ship was already gone. She preferred Bluebell because she was much faster.

She paid Shipley and Brendon with the captain looking on. Shipley stayed and Brendon left. Alys handed the captain a forged note from Andy instructing the cargo be redirected to Toronto.

The captain frowned in concern. "It is not customary to have a plan change this late."

Alys smiled at him broadly. "I will make it worth your while, good sir. If you get me to Toronto, I'll split the proceeds with you."

"And be dead the minute I step back onto English soil if this is a trick." Captain Jackson squinted at Alys.

"Why come back?" Alys tilted her head to the side.

"A wife and child." The captain's eyes narrowed.

"Send for them," Alys suggested. "I'll give you five hundred pounds to look the other way. Point this ship to the usual route, Toronto."

"How are you coming by five hundred pounds?" Captain Jackson asked with suspicion.

"Trust me, I'm good for it." Alys smiled.

"You're sure? Five hundred pounds?" Captain Jackson's eye narrowed with suspicion.

"The girls in the brig are worth over one thousand." Alys smirked at him.

"I could take everything right now." Captain Jackson's eyes flickered over her.

"I'm Andy Bristol's woman." Alys swallowed hard hoping he believed her lie. "You have a wife and child still in London. Think it through."

"I heard you are *not* Andy Bristol's woman anymore, I heard Caroline replaced you." He crossed his arms over his chest.

Alys wanted to hiss a reply, she didn't. "How much do you want? To take these girls to Toronto?"

"Half."

"Five hundred is half." Alys pressed her hand to her throat.

Captain Jackson narrowed his dark eyes at her. "What about the woman?"

"I'm asking five thousand." Alys lied smoothly.

Captain Jackson's eyes narrowed. "Then you will give me three thousand, not five hundred." Captain Jackson put his hand out to shake on the deal.

"That's an outrageous amount!" Alys gasped.

"You get nothing if you can't get to Toronto. Who else will you find at this short notice to take a shipment of girls across the Atlantic?"

Alys fumed in fury. No other option, she shook his hand.

"Perfect," Alys said grudgingly.

The captain left her on the deck to reroute his ship.

As Alys felt the ship pull further away from London, further from Andy, she filled her lungs with fresh sea air, and let out a long sigh.

Freedom, in Toronto, new city, and best of all—no man.

For the first time in her life, the thought of being single in a new city made her feel light.

***

Cole could not see around the flowers he had purchased to give to Shannon at supper. He stumbled through the door and handed the flowers to a maid to be put on the dining room table. He pressed his fingertips against the ring box in his pocket. He purchased a gold ring for Shannon, a ruby surrounded by diamonds to celebrate her pregnancy.

"Sid, is Shannon resting?" Cole asked as he checked his reflection in the mirror. He smoothed his hair down and adjusted his tie.

Sid shot him a worried glance as she took the flowers from him. "She hasn't come home yet."

A scullery maid put more wood on the fire and the butler lit the candles.

"She should have been home two hours ago." Cole checked his pocket watch and frowned. "I expected she would have had a rest before supper." Cole's heart started to pound with worry.

"I'm sorry, sir, she hasn't returned." Sid wrung her hands in fear. "Sir, a woman came to the door asking for her. She said she had a piece of jewellery left behind by Doctor McDougall in the flat where she had delivered her sister's baby. She wanted to give her the brooch and thank her for the work that she did... but now Mrs. McDougall has not returned... I am afraid I told her where to find her. I told her about how she was near that area to meet with a Mrs. Holloway... have I done the wrong thing?" Sid's eyes widened in fear.

"Had you seen the woman before?" Terror pooled in the pit of Cole's stomach.

Garret, their butler, appeared in the dining room with a note in his hand, face white with fear.

"What is it?" The blood drained from Cole's face as the butler handed him a note.

Cole read swiftly.

'Dock 318, Warehouse 619, Toronto, £30,000 from the hand of Matilda Bertram. November 2nd, 1906.'

Cole's heart seized in his chest.

Shannon has been abducted!

Cole's breath left him as if he had been kicked in the stomach. "Pack my things." Cole's voice deepened, hoarse with fear. "Instruct Enid and Harris to take over selling Til and Malcolm's property. Have my bags sent to the dock. I'll leave on the next ship to Quebec. Does anyone have any knowledge of who could have taken her?"

Sid collapsed into tears.

Cole turned his attention to her, his jaw clenched in anger. "What did she look like?"

"Sir, I am so sorry." Sid covered her face with her hands. "I am so sorry."

"What did she look like?" Cole repeated, his tone cut through the weeping.

"Pretty, sir, painted," Sid wailed.

"Painted?" Cole's head tilted as if he didn't understand.

"She looked like a... well, a madam, if you know what I mean." Sid tried to speak past the sobs that wracked her.

Cole frowned. "A prostitute?"

"Yes, sir."

Fear twisted Cole's stomach into knots.

"Where are you going now, sir?" Garret the butler trailed after Cole as he tore out the front door to the carriage.

"The police station and then I have to obtain ship manifests. Hurry, there is no time to waste." Have my bags sent straight to the docks."

"Book the fastest ship you can find. Doesn't matter what it costs. Make sure there is enough cash in my bags to purchase a fare to Toronto. I have to send a telegram to the Toronto Police..."

"I'll have her lady's maid pack a bag for Doctor McDougall," Garret suggested.

Cole turned briefly on the pavement. "Thank you, I wouldn't have thought of that." Cole swallowed hard; he rubbed his forehead trying to continue to make decisions while his heart broke apart. "If I can find her and get her back..."

"You'll rip the world apart until you do. Whoever took her doesn't stand a chance. You'll find her," Garret said in his quiet manner.

"Thank you," Cole said as he turned on his heel and scrambled to get into the carriage.

Chapter Twenty-Two

After avoiding the captain for two days, Grayson couldn't wait any longer. He had to check for telegraph messages from Sol.

"Hello, Milo." Grayson entered the telegraph office.

Milo looked up. "Sir, I was on my way to your rooms. I have a telegram for you. It seems urgent sir."

"What is it?" Grayson held his hand out.

Milo handed him the paper and waited.

'Detective Grayson,

Shannon McDougall, abducted in October. Til Stone to provide £30,000 on November 2nd. Dock 318, Warehouse 619, Toronto. I arrive October 29. Save my wife at all costs.

Cole McDougall'

Grayson read the note three times, his stomach sinking with each reading. Til would be furious if he withheld this information from her. There was absolutely nothing Til could do for Shannon and this knowledge would destroy her. He worried that it would put her pregnancy at risk.

He folded the note and asked to send a cable to Sol Stein of the Toronto Constabulary. As the telegraph operator tapped the message, that Shannon McDougall had been abducted and was en route to Toronto, Grayson grit his teeth and hoped to hear from Sol soon. Anything to reveal how the Toronto ring was connected to the London ring. He needed Til to talk and she still didn't trust him enough. He sighed and wondered if Til Stone would ever trust him.

***

Til was tossing and turning in bed when she heard a knock at the door. A young maid, not the usual one, stood at the threshold of her door after midnight. "Please, madam, Detective Grayson has asked for you."

"At this hour of night?" Til frowned

"Yes, madam, he says to tell you a crew member has been injured in a knife fight." The maid's eyes widened with worry.

"Knife fight!" Til's eyebrows knit together.

"He asked if you would come and assist."

"Of course," Til murmured.

Concern niggled at Til's mind. Grayson typically insisted on accompanying her. Neither of them trusted the three men that they both suspected worked for Odelia Shipley Bristol. She shook the worry away; if he was asking for her it was serious, maybe he was busy apprehending the criminals. Grabbing her bag, she quickly followed the maid.

"Why are we going below decks?" Til asked as the hair on the back of her neck stood up.

"They are in the brig, in custody, but one is bleeding badly. If you would follow, please."

Til stopped walking as she sensed she was not safe. Til looked down the corridor, relief swept through her as she recognised Joan's cabin was a few doors down, she could flee there and wait for protection.

"You'll have to have them sent to my cabin." Til took a step back, the man in a green cravat stopped her.

"Where do you think you're going? Detective Grayson has asked for you," he sneered at her.

Trembling with fear and furious at herself for being so stupid, Til stood still and sure enough, the maid slipped away while the other two men who had been at the funeral entered the corridor.

Til took a deep breath. Her eyes darted from the man in the green cravat to the other two men and then started screaming at the top of her lungs.

Chapter Twenty-Three

Grayson spent a long evening sending a telegram to Sol to bring him up to date on where he was and when he expected to arrive in Toronto. He reread the Pitman file hoping they could outsmart Rodd Royce when they went after him in Toronto. He wondered who was working with him. He had no idea, maybe this Shipley Bristol that no one could seem to find.

As he closed his files, his mind drifted to Melinda. Sol had reported nothing about her. Getting tired, Grayson reached for his pocket watch to check the time.

Still missing, he remembered leaving his pocket watch and his vest in Joan's cabin. He had meant to go back for it ever since. Grayson sighed, no time like the present. It was late, but he was certain they would be up with a new baby.

Walking swiftly through the corridor to the stairs that would take him below decks, he tried to ignore the guilt that stung him as he remembered the first week Ella was home. He had worked most of the days and nights, Melinda had been teary and more clingy than usual. Shame burned through him as he remembered being frustrated with her as she wept and asked him to stay home and help her. He had disentangled himself, asking her mother to check on her while he dashed to work.

Grayson wished he had listened to her and taken steps to put her and the baby first. His heart broke as he thought of returning to Toronto and not seeing Ella the minute he arrived. Maybe they should have worked harder to reconcile after the adultery. Maybe divorce was the wrong idea. Grayson shook his head. Melinda had made it clear their life together was over and he agreed.

Just as he stepped foot on the deck of Joan's cabin he heard screaming. Not a woman-in-childbirth screaming. A woman-being-attacked screaming. Grayson broke into sprint towards the sound.

Horror spurred him on as he saw Til being attacked at the end of the corridor.

Her bodice was ripped apart. The man in the green cravat pulled her skirt up, hitting her hard when she screamed again.

Grayson, already at a run, attacked with lightning speed. Taking advantage of the fact the men were all watching Til with hunger in their eyes. He plowed his fist into the nose of the man closest to him. Blood sprayed across Grayson and onto the wall. The second man pulled a knife. Leaping back, Grayson tried and failed to get out of range. He hissed in pain as the tip of the knife sliced across his stomach and then got caught in his shirt. Grayson landed a hard punch to his attacker's jaw and then delivered a powerful jab deep into his kidney. He stumbled and just as Grayson thought he would drop, he lashed out with the knife again. Grayson grabbed the man's hand and slammed it against the wall, hard enough he heard the bones in his wrist break.

One last punch and his second assailant dropped like a stone, gasping for breath. The man with the green cravat turned Til so he was standing behind her and held a knife to her throat.

***

Til's eyes were wide with fear as she watched Grayson approach. Two men down. Blood hot and sticky on her neck; Grayson's eyes met hers. The look in his eyes stopped her heart. The same hard, confident, *reassuring* look that Malcolm had given her before he beat Royce Bristol off of her, Asher Grayson was giving her now. A look that said, 'I will trade my life for yours.'

The night everything changed.

The night that started her towards a new life as Til Stone.

"This is not your fight, mate." The man tried to drag her away from him. "You step away and when I'm done with her, you can take her next."

"Hand her over and I won't kill you." Grayson's voice hardened in warning.

"Can't do that." His breath was ragged in her ear.

"Who hired you?" Grayson lunged at him.

Til gasped as the knife bit deeper into her neck.

Grayson immediately stopped his attack and held his hands up.

Til's heart pounded in fear, her chest tightened.

"What do you want?" Grayson kept his eyes on the man holding Til.

"She's got twenty thousand pounds. We hear ten for Nora and ten for Shannon." The man with the green cravat's breath was hot on her neck.

Horror filled the pit of Til's stomach. She gasped as if someone had kicked her in the stomach.

Shannon!

"Take a step closer, and I cut her."

Til closed her eyes.

"I'm taking her to get the money." His arm tightened iron hard around her.

Til didn't dare speak for fear that moving her neck would cause the knife to press deeper.

"You're not taking Til anywhere." Grayson's jaw clenched.

Suddenly, the knife at her throat clattered to the floor. The man in the green cravat dropped like a stone. Til's eyes flew open and she staggered as Grayson grabbed her before she fell.

"What happened?" Til looked around wildly.

A man in blue and white striped pyjamas stood over the prostrate man, a broken bottle in his hand.

"He hit him from behind." Grayson gathered Til against him. "Thank you, sir," Grayson said to the man in pyjamas.

Til tried to stop trembling in fear against him.

"The missus woke me up and told me to find out what was going on. Is she all right?" His forehead creased in concern.

"I'm not sure." Grayson shifted so he could hold her closer. "Would you ask the crew to have these men put in custody? I would like to attend to her and then, when I am certain she is all right, I will interrogate these men."

"I can do that. Your name, sir?"

"Detective Asher Grayson of the Toronto Constabulary."

"Laurence Wagner." Mr. Wagner nodded and went in search of men to arrest the unconscious men on the floor.

Til's hands shook as she tried to gather the shredded pieces of her bodice together to maintain some semblance of dignity. Her throat ached with unshed tears, and fresh raw fear gnawed at her heart. "Who has Shannon? He nearly... Grayson, he nearly..."

Grayson quickly pulled his bloody shirt down over her shredded bodice. "You are safe now." Grayson's voice sounded low and calm in her ear.

Til took a shuddery breath and pulled back. "What do you know about Shannon?"

Grayson opened his mouth to speak when a door opened and a burly man stepped out of his cabin. "Everything all right, miss?" the big man asked from his doorway. He shot a hard look at Grayson.

"Yes." Til fumbled to put her arms through the sleeves of his shirt.

"You're sure he didn't hurt you?" The huge man stood taller, his eyes narrowed at Grayson.

"He saved me, sir. I am fine now. Thank you for your concern." Til adjusted Grayson's shirt so it would maintain her modesty.

Grayson nodded at the man for his concern. "These men tried to have their way with her. It would help if you would stay and ensure someone places them in custody, I need to assist the lady to her cabin."

"Is he telling the truth, miss?" The man looked hard at Til.

"Yes, sir. He is. He just... he just saved me." Til shuddered as she repeated those words.

"All right, I'll stay with these men and if one comes to, I will make sure he's subdued." The man stood by the three unconscious men on the floor.

"Your neck is bleeding." Grayson led her down the corridor to the stairs.

"Never mind that. He said Shannon! Whoever has Nora has stolen Shannon!" Til's voice escalated with terror.

"Not here, Til, not here," Grayson murmured against her as he helped her up the stairs to her cabin.

"You know something," Til accused him. She stopped and turned to him, her eyes flashed in fury. "You've kept something from me."

Arm hard around her waist; he dragged her up the stairs. "We'll talk in your cabin."

Together they raced to her cabin. Grayson called for hot water, tea and toast before he shut the door and turned to face her.

Til took a deep, shuddery breath, "As soon as my hands stop shaking, I'll stitch the knife wound on your stomach. But you have to tell me..."

Grayson crossed the room and helped her sit on her bed. "Better if you're sitting, Til. This is everything I know. When I finish, if you trust me yet, I want to know everything you know. Someone abducted Shannon early this month."

The blood drained from Til's face. "Who took her?"

"We don't know." Grayson shook his head and clenched his jaw. "She is on a ship to Toronto. Cole confirms that they sold your house to pay for her ransom. The day you go for Nora you will pay to get her back."

"How do you know all this?" Til could hardly form words, she shook from shock.

"Cole sent me a telegram, I got it... recently." Grayson cleared his throat.

Til stood up in outrage. She opened her mouth to blast him. Grayson grabbed her and sat her back down on the bed. "You can scream at me later. Right now, I need to say all of it. Those men must have paid off Milo to give them all the correspondence that was sent to me." Grayson's jaw clenched hard in fury. "When I get my hands on him..."

"Why didn't he send word sooner?" A fist of tears choked her.

Grayson reached forward and took her hand in his. "Listen, Til. He was trying to find the ship she was on. They finally found her on one heading to Louisiana of all places. Once he found the ship, he followed. The ship is bound for Louisiana, but the ransom note says Toronto— Dock 318, Warehouse 619. I wasn't going to tell you because there is nothing you can do until November 2nd. I wanted to protect you and your unborn child."

"You had no business keeping this from me!" Til took her hand from his. She covered her face with both hands as she started to weep with terror.

Shannon paid the price for my past; it should have been me.

Grayson pulled her forward so she could cry against him. He wrapped his arms around her and held her as she shattered.

"I am so sorry, Til." Grayson rocked her like a little girl as he tried to absorb as much of her pain as he could.

A long time later, she stopped crying and became still. Til pulled away and reached for a handkerchief from the bedside table.

"It's a bad cut, you'll need stitches." Til wiped tears from her eyes. She grabbed a second handkerchief and wiped her tears off his chest.

"It's all right." Grayson took the handkerchief from her hand.

A knock at the door interrupted them. A porter brought in tea, toast, and hot water. Til turned from the man to clean her face up. Grayson gave him some money and shut the door behind him.

Til took a deep breath and let it out slowly. "I am terrified. What if Cole can't find her? What if we can't get there in time?"

"I know." Grayson poured her a cup of tea, added sugar and then handed her a plate of toast.

"I can't eat, I'm too upset." Til blew on her tea and then took a tentative sip. "If anything happens to Shannon, Grayson..." Til shook her head. "I can't bear it."

"We are doing all we can. I have already mobilised men in Halifax and Quebec. Their ship has to go through immigration. We'll find her. I promise you that." Grayson placed the plate of toast down on the table.

"What if the ship doesn't go through immigration?" Til gasped in fear. "Do ships that the Bristols own play by the rules?" Til asked wildly, tears gathered in her eyes. She opened her mouth to speak and then closed it. She thought for a few minutes. "It might be a ship that belongs to someone in Louisiana, if they originally meant it to sail there. What does that mean?"

"Here is what we know." Grayson sounded battle hardened and in control.

Til started to calm a little as he recounted the facts.

"You are to meet this kidnapper on November 2nd. There is that date again. It is too much of a coincidence and I don't believe in coincidence. Not in a case like this. I ask you, do you think these events correspond to the events that took place in 1881?"

Til's face crumpled, and she tried to speak through a fist of tears in her throat. "Let me stitch you first; we'll come back to that." She placed her teacup down and rolled up her sleeves.

Grayson ran his hands over her upper arms. "Til, I'm sorry I wasn't there sooner. Other than your neck, were you hurt by those men? Did they... hurt you?" Grayson's eyes dropped to her shredded bodice, covered by his big shirt.

"They were going to." Til met his gaze. "When he put his hands up my skirt..."

Grayson's eyes hardened at her words.

"He wanted the money. Smart, really. Intercept it before I got to Toronto. They were just having some fun first." Til shuddered. "Maybe if I had stayed in London, they would have taken me instead of Shannon. I will never forgive myself. If she pays the price for my past, I will die."

"No, you will not think that. You are almost in Canada. We have the funds to buy her back. Now we need cool heads and a strategy. That is all. A strategy to defeat them." Grayson reached for a fresh handkerchief and wiped her tears away gently.

Til's eyes widened. "What do we do now?"

"I don't know about we," Grayson said grimly. "If you would stitch me up, that would help, and then *I* will interrogate those men."

"But I'll come with you, to the interrogation. I need to hear it firsthand. I'd like to be the one to break their kneecaps." Til's eyes narrowed even as tears spilled from them.

"Break their kneecaps!" Grayson shook his head. "What kind of interrogation do you think we will do?"

"I don't know. Isn't that what you do?" Til's eyebrows arched in surprise.

"No." Grayson frowned.

"Well. We do today." Til's face looked determined in the lamplight.

"I thought you swore an oath; first do no harm," Grayson suggested slyly.

"They aren't my patients." Til moved to her doctor's bag. "Let's get you stitched and then let's get to work." Til's lips thinned in concentration. She poured hot water into a basin and cleaned her neck. She put boracic acid on it and flinched as it stung.

"Are you all right?" Grayson stood near her. Hand under her jaw, he examined the wound once the blood was washed away. Taking the handkerchief from her, he gently removed blood from her collarbone. She stiffened as his hand held her jaw in place so he could survey the damage.

"It's fine." Til's voice sounded hoarse in her own ears. "Just a little flesh wound."

Her heart pounded as Grayson carefully moved her hair away from her neck and checked to be sure she hadn't missed any other injury.

"It looks like more than a flesh wound." His eyes darkened in anger. "If there is another doctor on board, I can take you to him. I think you need stitches."

"Unnecessary." Til looked away from him. "Let me clean up this wound. I'll stitch you up. Then, we need to talk."

"Oh?" Grayson wavered near the bed.

"Yes. Oh." Til put a towel down on the bed, indicating that he should lie down on top of it.

Grayson lay down on her bed, and she surveyed the damage to his skin. She irrigated the wound with warm water and boracic acid.

"I'm worried about infection, so we'll irrigate this twice," she murmured as if speaking to a nurse or Shannon who assisted in operations. Her eyes swept over his torso. Grayson's hard, battle worn body took up a lot of space on her bed. This was not his first knife fight. He had a scar down his right side. A nasty scar on his upper arm.

"What is this from?" She traced her fingertips over the old scar, as if testing to see if it still hurt him.

"Bullet grazed me in a fight on the streets."

"This?" Til pointedly looked at the scar on the other side of his body.

"Sometimes, when I am looking for missing girls, I disguise myself as a homeless man," Grayson said quietly.

"Really?" Til's eyes flickered to his.

"Yes, one night, I was looking for a man who had killed the wife of a friend of mine; he had robbed her at knifepoint. Anyway, he attacked me when I went to question him." Grayson met her gaze briefly and then looked away.

"I am sorry to hear that." Til turned her attention back to the task at hand.

"No. Isold Stein died of infection from the knife wound." Grayson's tone hardened with anger. "Her husband works with me now at the Toronto Constabulary. I trust him with my life. I've assigned him to protect you when you go up against Odelia. He's a good man, one of the best I know."

Til's heart pounded at the thought of how close he would have come to death. She shook that thought away and focused on stitching his current wound.

"After tonight." Til pierced his skin with the needle. "I think it would be foolish of me to ask you to assign another man to protect me. I think it's safe to say we can put our differences aside and start afresh. I am a doctor who has dedicated my life to help underprivileged women and bring birth control to the masses to ease the suffering of my sisters. I realise now you care about women who are stolen and sold into white slavery. We share the same enemy."

"What enemy is that?" Grayson hissed in pain, and then met her eyes. "Odelia?"

"It's bigger than Odelia." Til held his gaze for a moment and then continued to stitch his wound. "Depravity, Detective Grayson, we both despise it and have spent our lives trying to alleviate the effects. I saw your face tonight. When I was in danger." Til's hand stilled in midair. "I saw your very thoughts." Til swallowed a lump in her throat.

Grayson's gaze held hers.

"I haven't seen that since Malcolm. I didn't think you would care so much."

"I told you I would get you to Canada..."

"I think it was more than that," Til whispered.

Grayson cleared his throat and said nothing further. He hissed through his teeth as the needle passed through his skin.

After a moment, she stopped to adjust the wick on the lamp so that the light was as bright as possible.

Til returned to his wound. "I am not in the habit of trusting men, sir, but I am beginning to trust you." Her eyes met his. He didn't look away. She let out a long breath and returned to her work. "I do not know this Mr. Stein."

Grayson remained silent. A sheen of sweat broke out on his forehead as she deftly placed stitches along the wound.

"We're all done here, Grayson." Til's voice sounded small in her ears. "I'll get changed so you can have your shirt back." She slipped behind the dressing screen, pulled off the shredded bodice and redressed into a clean dress before returning. She held his shirt out to him.

He took it from her, heavy muscles in his arms and shoulders moved with the effort of putting it on and not disturbing his wound. She wondered what they would face in Toronto and if he was up for the challenge. She knew what Malcolm had been capable of, but what of this man? What would Odelia try to do to them? How many men did she employ? How many men can he fight in hand to hand combat? He took down two and was prepared to fight a third. The look in his eyes when he fought for her was reassuring. He looked at her as if her life was worth him dying for. Her breath caught, her pulse pounded as she thought about Detective Grayson, prepared to kill the man in the green cravat if necessary. He shocked her. Til never expected to see that look again.

"Are you all right here? If I go to interrogate the three men in custody, will you feel safe on your own?" His eyes searched hers as he buttoned his ruined shirt.

"We will go together." Til bristled. "I want to know what he knows about Shannon. I have to go with you. You might not ask the right question. You might forget something."

"I think I can manage," Grayson said dryly. "I can't have a woman in the room when I interrogate them."

"Before we go, I think you should have all the facts." Til scratched her eyebrow and took a step back, away from him. "I think I need to speak to you about what happened on November 2nd, 1881."

Chapter Twenty- Four

Grayson stood still, his heart pounding with anticipation. The lamp flickered by her, casting a long shadow up the rich oak paneled wall of her cabin. Her amber eyes glittered in the light, as a lock of her coppery blonde hair fell down the front of her shoulder. Impatiently, she tucked her hair behind her ear. Her body trembled as she smoothed her skirt. What she had agreed to speak of was a deep wound. Grayson willed her to speak even as his chest tightened with fear of what she would say.

Who hurt you?

Til swallowed hard and twisted a handkerchief between her long, delicate fingers as she sat on the window seat. Grayson poured them both a drink. Brandy for him and another cup of tea for her. He dragged a chair across the room so he could face her.

Til sat stiff, as she turned to him, murmured her thanks for the tea and took a delicate sip.

He yearned to reach out and touch her; he didn't dare for fear she would break apart.

"My story starts about six months before November 2nd, 1881." Til took another sip. "My mother died in childbirth in the spring. I was helpless as she hemorrhaged. Her blood poured out of her across my hands, I couldn't stop it." Til's shoulders slumped. "The baby lived. His name was James; we called him Jimmy. With her death, something in me broke apart, Grayson." Til traced her fingertip along the gold rim of the teacup handle. "The pain of losing my mother was unbearable."

"I'm sorry, Til." Grayson leaned forward, his eyes soft with sympathy.

"I was the oldest, and I did my best for Jimmy." Til took a deep breath and continued. "The pain in me was so terrible. I was thankful when

I eventually went numb. I would go to bed exhausted and wake up exhausted." Til fussed with the teacup and finally put it down and picked up a handkerchief. "Nothing mattered. I tried hard to keep the baby alive, and I had so little to work with. It crushed me. Hearing him cry from hunger, I... can't..." A tear slid down her cheek, and then another.

"Oh, Til." Grayson's throat tightened as he listened.

"By October my father had drank himself into a stupor." Til dashed at her tears, she struggled for a moment to breathe. "I begged for food from neighbours, for Jimmy." Til covered her face with her hands. "There was nothing left." Her voice broke. "Everyone was starving, and he kept *drinking*. On November 2nd, 1881 he got drunk with a group of men, trying to make enough money at poker to pay the rent."

Grayson's stomach twisted into knots at the scene that flashed into his mind at her words.

Til's face crumpled as she continued. "Winter was just around the corner. The landlord sat at the poker table in the kitchen of our flat." Til's entire body trembled as she spoke.

Grayson swallowed hard, his heart ached to hold her.

"On nights that my father drank, my mother used to send me away to keep me safe." Til scrubbed her hands over her face, wiped her tears, and continued. "I would run to Odelia."

"Odelia Shipley Bristol?" Grayson's voice sounded rough in his own ears.

Til's breath caught, her eyes darkened in pain. "Don't interrogate me." Her voice broke on a sob. "You're not saying anything and when you do speak you sound like a detective... not a..."

"Til. I..." Grayson fumbled for words. "I'm sorry. I'm listening, as a friend. Please forgive me, I... this is hard. I don't know what to say to help...that's why I am saying nothing. Please continue."

Til shuddered and then regained composure. "Odelia's mother and my mother were friends. They protected us by sending us to the other when we were in danger." Til carefully pleated the handkerchief on her lap. "No mother, no alert. My drunk father woke me in the middle of the night. He had..." Til's voice cracked.

Grayson's jaw clenched, his lips thinned as he placed his hand on her forearm.

"He dragged me to the kitchen and into the... light."

Grayson cursed under his breath.

"The landlord, Mr. Carn, ripped my nightgown apart; he looked at me..." Til covered her face with her hands.

Grayson's heart splintered at her words, he ached to hold her and absorb as much of her pain as he could. Trembling, he reached forward and gently placed his hand on her shoulder.

"I was the only girl in the room, with a..." Til wept. "I was in front of the men at the poker table, shocked and confused..."

"Til." Grayson's breath caught.

She looked at Grayson and then away. "I was innocent, you see, only fifteen. Do you believe that I was innocent, a virgin?"

"Of course." Grayson's throat tightened as, helpless, he watched Til suffer as she spoke.

"My father said the landlord would buy me a new dress." Til stopped talking.

Rage thundered through him.

If your father isn't dead, I will kill him myself.

"He said that I would live with the landlord now." Til closed her eyes.

Grayson shook with fury. "Oh my God, what did he do to you?" He could barely force the words past his clenched teeth.

"My father let the landlord... touch me..." Til trembled. "Inappropriately. It was..." Unchecked tears slid down her face and neck. "Monstrous."

Grayson's blood boiled, his body shuddered as he reached for her.

Til got up and moved out of his grasp. She stood in front of the porthole, keeping her back to Grayson; she started to speak again. "I shook with fear in front of them." Til's voice deepened. "They were too drunk to care. They acted as if he was purchasing a horse; the landlord turned me to look at me from every angle." Til pressed her forehead against the glass.

Grayson got up and stood behind her. Close enough to touch her, but he didn't dare. When she looked up, his eyes met hers in the glass.

"He saw blood on my skirt," Til said dully.

Grayson closed his eyes briefly as fury blinded him. "What was the blood from?" His throat tightened, terrified of her answer. "Someone hurt you before this?"

"The customary reason women have blood on their skirts," Til murmured.

Oh, thank God!

Relief winged through him as he realised what she was saying. "I see." Grayson let out a breath he didn't know he had been holding in. He cleared his throat and waited for her to continue.

"He was furious because he expected to take me home… that night… and he didn't want a girl who was… you understand."

"I understand,"Grayson rasped.

"My father screamed at me to get cleaned up. He stood there, eyes bleary from alcohol and said, 'Don't you see I have no choice?'" Til shook as she spoke. "He said, 'Do the right thing, Matilda.' He swayed and stumbled. He wept as he said, 'Do the right thing for your *sisters*'," Til gasped. "A drunk believes and demands everyone do the right thing, but them." Til's jaw tightened, her shoulders tensed as she wrapped her arms around herself.

I wish I had been there that night, I would have stopped this. I would have protected you.

Horror thundered through him as he tried to process the fact that her father had gambled her as if she were a possession he could sell. His heart ached to comfort her; with shaking hands he took the handkerchief from her and gently wiped the tears away.

"I fled from the kitchen and I smashed through the window in the bedroom and I ran, into the night." Til's head bowed.

Don't bow your head in shame; you have nothing to be ashamed of.

"I never went back to my home. I had no choice but to leave them all behind." She covered her face with her hands and wept.

Gutted and heartbroken for her, Grayson gathered his courage. Gently, he pulled Til into his arms. She stiffened as he feared she would. Tenderly, he pressed her face, still covered by her hands, into his shoulder. Til stopped fighting him; she dropped her hands and rested her forehead against his shirt. A shirt torn and covered in blood from defending her from the men in the bowels of the ship now soaked up her tears as she shattered in his arms.

"I'm sorry, Til, I'm so sorry." He trembled as he rubbed his hand up and down her back, trying desperately to comfort her.

She tried to speak past her sobs.

Sadness tore at his chest as he placed his hand against the back of her neck. "Shhhhh, it's all right. We have as long as it takes. Just cry. It's all right." His arms tightened harder around her, trying to lend comfort in the face of her pain.

Eventually, Til stopped weeping. She rested her cheek against his chest for a moment before she pulled back a little. She looked up at him, eyes wet with tears.

"So, you ran." Grayson's heart was in his throat with worry of what happened to her next. His hand shook as he reached out and wiped tears from her cheeks with his fingertips. "Where did you run to?"

"Odelia, but I took a wrong turn." Til bit her lip. "Malcolm was there. My story is not over." Til drew in a shuddery breath, eyes filling with tears again.

"Thank God for Malcolm." Grayson sighed with relief.

Til's eyes swam with tears. "Yes." She created distance between them. Picking up a fresh handkerchief, Til wiped her face and sat down on the window seat. "Do you want the rest of the story?"

"Of course." Grayson sat down across from her and rested his forearms on his thighs.

"It gets worse." Til took a deep breath.

Grayson swallowed bile as it rose in his throat. "Please, continue."

"I ran as fast as I could to Odelia's, but I took a wrong turn into Bristol territory. I was so terrified and distracted; I would never have made that mistake normally." She fidgeted with the handkerchief. "Anyway, once on the streets the Bristols ran, I was caught."

Grayson's heart pounded in dread, he forced the words past grit teeth. "Bobby Bristol?"

Her eyes filled with tears again.

"No," Til whispered, "Royce. Royce Bristol grabbed me and dragged me to the brothel on Bluebell Street."

"Royce!" Grayson's head snapped up. "Royce! All this time, I thought Bobby!"

"No." Blood drained from Til's face. "Royce."

"Rodd Royce is Royce Bristol," Grayson gasped.

Finally! A clue! A link!

Grayson put that thought away. "We'll come back to that. Never mind that now, it doesn't matter now. What happened to you, Til? What happened next?" Grayson's voice softened, his heart pounded with fear that she had suffered at Royce's brutal hands before Malcolm showed up. "What happened in the street between Royce and Malcolm that meant you were finally safe that night?" Grayson threaded her fingers through his. To his surprise, she let him. Her long, fine- boned fingers felt fragile tangled with his.

"His intent was obvious, but Malcolm was there. I had never met Malcolm before so when he sauntered right into Bristol territory, bold as brass, I remember terror filling me, like I was a sponge, and the terror was water. I remember feeling saturated in horror."

"You must have been terrified. Royce is a threat to full-grown men, never mind a girl." Grayson shook his head.

Til nodded. "Royce said in my ear he'd have me when he was done with Malcolm. Anyway, he underestimated Malcolm. It was terrifying, watching two men beat each other nearly to death." She tightened her grip on his hands. "Malcolm prevailed; he beat Royce until he stopped moving. I thought he might have killed him. We left him in the back alley. We ran together. Malcolm took me to Odelia's, and he had to go into hiding that night. He couldn't stay there."

I wish I had been there, I wish I had beaten Royce nearly to death for you. I still will. I will track him down and I will bring him to justice.

"Royce didn't rape you." Grayson let out a long breath of relief.

Til's hands shook and her eyes filled with tears, she continued. "No. I was safe that night. I worried for Malcolm though. The retribution he would face terrified me. There was nothing I could do about that, but when I was finally safe at Odelia's, I don't know how to explain it exactly, but something inside of me broke apart, Grayson." Til took her hands away and tried to stop a sob that tore out of her, by pressing her hands to her mouth.

Pain radiated through Grayson's chest at her words.

"I don't know how else to describe it." She swiped at her tears with the handkerchief. "I couldn't stop crying and I couldn't stop trembling in fear. The whole thing was too much, but Odelia's mother held me and told me I was safe."

"I'm glad you had Odelia's mother." Grayson yearned to hold her as she wept.

"Once she'd heard enough, she sent the police to my home. She was worried about Alys. Especially Alys. We were terrified he would just sell the next girl in line." Til pressed the back of her hand to her lips that trembled as she spoke.

"Did he?" Grayson whispered.

"Grayson, this is the hardest part — I don't know." Til bowed her head before him. "My sisters, my siblings, but especially my sister, Alys still haunts me. I think of them and worry for them. I don't know what happened to them." Til covered her face with her hands. "I must disgust you, running at their expense."

"Please, don't think that. Of course not." Grayson shook his head. He gently tugged her hands away so he could look into her eyes as he spoke. "Never. You have nothing to be ashamed of, Til, you were a child." He quivered with indignation, trying to keep his tone of voice gentle.

Her face crumpled at his words. "Fifteen is not a child in the East End, Grayson." Til's gaze lowered to the floor.

Gathering his courage at the possibility she would rebuff him, Grayson cradled Til's face in his hands, his eyes met hers. "Fifteen is a child, Til. No *girl* should face *any* of those decisions." Grayson stroked Til's face. This time she pressed her forehead into his shoulder, wrapped her arms around his neck and wept again.

Grayson tugged her onto his lap and rocked her like a little girl. "This was not your fault," he said quietly, "none of it."

"It hurts me to speak of it," Til sobbed against him.

"I'm sorry, Til." Helplessness weighed his heart down.

"When I ran, my sisters didn't." Til wept against him. "They were sleeping soundly. They haunt me, Grayson. I don't know what happened to Alys." Til trembled in his arms. "I don't know what happened to Jimmy, either."

Grayson swallowed hard, his arms tightened around Til as she went to pieces.

Chapter Twenty- Five

Til pressed her face against his hard shoulder as the storm within her stilled. His shirt was wet under her cheek from her tears.

"I'm sorry, Til," Grayson said. He continued to rub his hand along her back. "All this time, I thought you were a harpy of the worst sort. Here I find out you aren't. You don't despise men; you are terrified of them." Grayson tucked a lock of hair behind her ear. "The man who should have protected you and cared for you, sold you because of his own weakness. Sadly, in your mind, all men in authority will abuse that authority; it is only a matter of time."

Til took a deep breath. "Right." She closed her eyes for a moment, allowing herself one moment of comfort. In Grayson's arms, a safety and warmth slid over her. For the first time since Malcolm died, her shoulders loosened, she felt comforted and protected.

Suddenly self conscious; Til straightened up and carefully slid off his lap.

"Sorry." She winced. "Your wound, I shouldn't be sitting on you."

Grayson reached for her but she held her hand up.

"We mustn't." Til shook her head, she sat down on the window seat again. "I am a widow, a grieving widow... I am not in the habit of sitting on men I can assure you. I apologise; that was inappropriate."

Grayson dropped his hands to his empty lap. "Of course, whatever you think is best."

"Your shirt is all wet." Til spoke softly.

"I don't care about my shirt." Grayson tugged the soaked fabric away from his shoulder to help it dry.

Til changed the subject. "When you said I am terrified of men, you are right. It hasn't helped that I have spent the last twenty years in impoverished dwellings being reminded of the desperate condition women live in." Til smoothed her hair away from her face, pulling her emotions under control. "I see my mother in them. Endless suffering at the hands of drunk and brutal men."

"Any assurance I give you, that a lot of men will not abuse any authority they have, will fall on deaf ears?" Grayson leaned forward.

"I've seen too much, Grayson." Til shrugged and then lifted her chin.

"You trusted Malcolm?" Grayson picked up his brandy and took a sip.

"It's so shameful to admit this to you." Til shook her head. "You'll call me a harpy, and you would be right. I had rafts of contracts for him to sign in the event that he changed." Til's eyes filled with tears at the words. "He never changed. We were better partners in later years than the beginning. He wanted this baby. He dreamed of a happy family where we would spend our summers at the sea and slow down. His dream terrified me, I don't take days off. I never stop working. I worried my clinic would suffer. I had fundraisers planned that I needed to be at. I had dirt on a judge; I was hoping to add onto the clinic with the money I could coerce out of him."

Grayson tilted his head to the side. "Dirt on a judge?"

"I'm a midwife, I know who has mistresses. I know who has whole families on the side." Til shook her head in disgust.

"How did Malcolm feel about all this?"

"Well, he wanted me to stop with all of it, actually. He wanted to fund my clinic."

"You didn't let him?" Grayson drained his brandy.

"I loved Malcolm." Til bristled.

"As you should have, he sounds like a saint."

"Yes, he was. Here's another terrible thing about me, since we're laying all the cards on the table about my past. I was always wary." Til wrapped her arms around herself. "Always in the back of my mind was an exit strategy, a plan in case he failed me." Til's chest tightened in sadness. "He never did. All those years and contracts." Til shook her head. "It seems ridiculous now. Malcolm loved me in a way I didn't understand. I used it against him." Til's breath caught as she confessed. "I could *always* manipulate him. He always put me first and it pains me to admit that I took advantage of that."

"I saw your skill in the interrogation room at the police station," Grayson said dryly. "You have a real gift, I will give you that. The way you made those men scurry to protect you, I've never seen the like."

"I'll never trust men. The wound is too deep, it will never heal." Til's eyes searched Grayson's eyes for understanding. "I can't."

Grayson put his empty brandy glass on the floor by his chair. "I don't blame you."

"Where were we in my story?" Til took a deep breath and let it out slowly.

"You were with Odelia's mother," Grayson prompted gently.

"Yes. Royce being beaten nearly to death disqualified him as head of the Butcher Family. Bobby would take over, and he needed capital. Odelia, pregnant with his child, wanted to secure herself as his wife. She saw an opportunity with the Blackburns."

"Why would she run with Bobby?" Grayson frowned.

"Money and power. He was her ticket out of poverty and into a world where she would have power. You saw those flats. We crawled out on our hands and knees and sometimes we envied the children who died. Honestly, we did. We wondered if it would be better. No more hunger and sickness. Anyway, we got out and we got jobs with the Blackburn family. Set up by Bobby although I had no idea."

"Really?" Grayson tilted his head to the side as if he were about to interrogate her.

"Really…careful," Til warned him. "You sound like a detective."

"Sorry, please continue." Grayson held his hands up in supplication.

"My mind wasn't devious like Odelia's. When I found out they intended to kidnap Madeline Blackburn, it terrified me. I would have to go up against the Bristols and they were already after Malcolm for what he did to Royce. To keep us safe, I saw an opportunity, and I took it."

Grayson nodded.

"I went to Lady Blackburn and asked for protection money. She laughed in my face. So, I went to Lord Blackburn." Til's entire body shook as she spoke. She took another sip of tea and frowned into the cup because it was empty.

Grayson got up, retrieved the decanter, poured brandy in her teacup and then his own empty glass. He set the decanter down within reach. He handed her a fresh handkerchief, sat back down, and waited.

"I walked into his study and I asked Lady Blackburn to leave." Til took a shaky sip.

Grayson's jaw clenched. "I'll never forget it. I told him my whole sordid tale, everything. The night my father sold me to cover the rent and how the Bristols would kill Malcolm and me for interfering in their plot to steal Madeline."

Grayson sat still; he didn't blink or take a sip of brandy.

"He propositioned me." Til's voice hardened in anger.

"I knew it." Grayson grit his teeth.

"I couldn't do it." Til shook her head. "I was facing the streets and certain death *if I was lucky*. But I couldn't let him...do that. I was already so in love with Malcolm I couldn't let another man take what I felt in my heart belonged to Malcolm. Such a silly girl, yes? I should have let him; it would have been easier than what I went through."

Grayson's knuckles whitened on the tumbler of brandy.

"Lord Blackburn was *furious*." Til shook her head. She took a deep breath, let it out slowly. "He tried anyway."

"What did you do?" A muscle jumped out in Grayson's jaw.

"Madeline Blackburn entered the room just as he pounced on me. We were in the library, and she had listened to the entire altercation from behind a bookcase. He stepped away from me and fired me on the spot. His face was purple with embarrassment. I think he was certain he had locked the door, and he hadn't. Anyway, Madeline was an innocent, but she understood what she had walked in on. She told her father I'd saved her and that they owed me payment for saving her reputation if not her life. He said I was worthless, an insubordinate servant. That's what all the gentry say if they want to get rid of someone. He said I didn't know my place." Til's tone of voice hardened. "He was right about that, I refused to *ever* know my place. Then or now. However, his dismissal of me upset Madeline."

Til's eyes met Grayson's. "I left his study; I went to my room to pack up to go. I knew I was dead. I was just leaving the room when Madeline Blackburn stood in the hallway. She looked up and down the hall and then slipped into my room. Quietly, she handed me enough money and jewellery to start a new life in a new town. It was her own jewellery, Grayson. I couldn't believe what she gave me." Til shook her head, still surprised. "She was getting married to Lord Harper and did not need to worry about money another day in her life. I will *never* forget the weight of the purse as she thanked me for saving her life, her virtue and her engagement. Her eyes were full of tears as she apologised for her parents sacking me. She said she couldn't wait to get away from them. That was the last time I saw her.

"She told me she was moving to Canada with Lord Harper, so I wrote to her and she wrote back to me. We've stayed in touch all these years. In 1904, I heard from her again, she needed someone to assist her in her pregnancy. They arrested me that year. I would have gone; I owed everything to Lady Madeline Harper. One piece of jewellery alone paid for the private tutors which taught Malcolm and me. It was enough to start at the London Royal Free Hospital School of Medicine for Women, where I went, and university for him.

"Anyway, I tangled with another 'Lady' years later, and the fall out was extensive. I needed Shannon out of England, so I sent her to Madeline and interrupted her study... it was worth it. She was safe there. Well, sort of. I didn't like that she was coming back with a man. I prepared to hate Cole McDougall, turned out I couldn't. He loves her, the way Malcolm loved me, completely."

Til took a long, deep sip of brandy and coughed a little and then took another sip.

"I'm glad I was wrong. That you didn't have to go with him," Grayson said delicately. "Why not just tell me though?"

"I wanted to see how you would treat a prostitute." Til's gaze met his gaze square on, watching his reaction carefully. "I wondered how much worth you would place on me if I wasn't pure." Til lifted her chin in defiance. "It was a test. I wanted to know if I could trust you to go after the person killing those poor girls and branding them if you think women who compromise in that way are worthless."

"Did I pass?" Grayson didn't drop his gaze.

"Yes," Til said.

"Then what happened?" Grayson prodded gently.

"So, as I ran to another town to be schooled, I decided right there I would have to take care of myself. I refused to be known as my previous name. I couldn't be. The Bristols were after me. My father called me Matilda and I would *not* answer to that name anymore. It brings back all those memories of being in the kitchen, being sold to the landlord. I refused to be Bertram." Til shuddered at the name. "I would now belong to no one, only myself. So, that night in a cramped little room, in the deepest darkness, I became Til Stone. Til because my mother called me Til, and Stone because once I fell apart it was hard to feel anymore. I was like stone and if I would survive, and stay out of the slums, I would have to be as hard as a stone. Emotion was a luxury I could no longer afford." Til straightened up.

"I worked hard, very hard, to get my education. A woman's group heard of me, and once they saw my marks, they paid for my education. I paid them back, every penny, with interest. They took a chance on me and I told them they would not regret it. Every year, I have paid a student grant that puts one girl through medical school to be a doctor. I do it under the name of Lady Madeline Harper. I can't thank her enough. Enid, you met her in my clinic, was a victim of white slavery. She was sold to a brothel in Oakland, Manitoba. Shannon met her when she was in Canada. This year she is going to medical school with money from the foundation I run under Lady Harper's name."

Til stood up, went to the porthole and looked out to sea.

"Til Stone, I'm not sure I have ever had the privilege of meeting such a selfless woman in my life," Grayson said to her back.

"Oh, don't be fooled." Til turned back to look at him. "I am selfish. Crikey, Grayson, you have no idea." Til clenched her jaw, laying all her faults out for him. "If I need something to further my cause, I *take it.* However, that being said, I have a weakness. I have a great fear." Til hesitated to share more of her vulnerability with him. She moved to the lamp as it flickered. She turned the wick down to soak up more oil which made the room darker. "Can I tell you my greatest fear?" Til finally turned to face him, to look him in the eye. "Can I trust you with that?"

"Of course." Grayson's voice rasped.

"My greatest fear in life is poverty. Being poor and back in a slum. I would rather die. I have worked twelve hours a day for twenty years and built this great fortune and it is *never enough*. I cannot give back enough, and I couldn't find any of my siblings, only Shannon. Martha's daughter." Til stared at the flickering flame as she wrapped her arms around herself. "I looked, so help me. I looked high and low, but the streets swallowed them up. I couldn't find them. It is as though they were scattered to the wind."

"You did your best with what you had. I think you should be very proud of the life you have built," Grayson suggested gently.

"You don't really know me at all." Til straightened up.

"I know enough." His eyes were intense as she met his gaze again and this time she didn't look away.

For a moment, silence settled over them. Til watched him.

"I don't want to sound like an interrogator and if you have spoken enough for tonight, I understand. I will leave you to sleep," Grayson said gently.

"Just say it; what do you want to know?" Til lifted her chin.

"Royce Bristol, he's Odelia's brother-in-law. Right?" Grayson rubbed the stubble on his chin as he thought.

"Yes. I am sorry." The blood drained out of Til's face. "I should have told you everything before. I always thought Royce was still in England. I assumed that it was Odelia's son, Shipley Bristol, in Toronto!"

Grayson waved her apology away. "Rodd Royce, he calls himself now. If it's the same man, and it must be, he's been a gunman for Eli Pitman. Eli had been trafficking girls for years until we caught him." Grayson shook his head. "I have all the documents in my cabin. I'll show you everything and maybe you will see something I've missed."

"Who is Eli?" Til asked.

"Eli Pitman was the biggest crime boss in Toronto. Royce worked for Eli. Cora, Sol's wife, and Sol found enough evidence on Eli to have him convicted of murder and sentenced to death two years ago. They incarcerated Royce for two years hard labour. Anyway, he's out now and the girls with the brands showed up shortly *after* they released him."

"When Odelia's husband died and she needed another man to operate under, those two events coincided... is that what you are saying?" Til's entire body braced for battle.

"I think that is the best guess. I take it there is no equality in the streets?" Grayson moved closer to her. Til did not move away.

"I told you about that in the examination room. There is none. Worse than none." Til shook her head. "Odelia is in Toronto ready to prostitute herself to Royce, obviously. She wants to keep running her white slavery ring, but she'll need muscle."

"Who is her contact in England?" Grayson's eyes lit up as he waited for the answer.

"I don't know. I presume whoever is running the Bristols now. It might be his woman?" Til blinked.

"All right, but someone who hates you. Who hates you that much?"

"I don't know." Til crossed her arms over her chest. "I clawed my way to the top over anyone who tried to stand in my way." Til's eyes narrowed, watching his for judgement. She was surprised to see nothing but respect in his eyes. "So, quite honestly, it could be many people. From maids to ladies, not to mention men who foolishly thought they could buy me off to perform illegal abortions. If we have to go through my list of enemies..." Til shook her head. "It'll be a long night."

"Those three men in custody might know. It's time for you to go to bed, and I will interrogate them." Grayson squared his shoulders.

"Not so fast." Til placed her hand on his forearm to stop him from leaving. "It's your turn. What caused you to feel so strongly about missing girls? What caused you to ruin your marriage and chase after Nora Blackburn?"

Chapter Twenty-Six

"It's only fair; I've laid my past bare and confessed my deepest failings to you. It's your turn, Grayson. I want to know, what happened?" Til tilted her head to the side.

Grayson sighed. "It's a long story." He went to the dressing table and poured himself a glass of water.

"We have all night." Til returned to her seat and gave him her rapt attention.

"I have an interrogation to do." Grayson hesitated by the door.

Til frowned as she looked up to him.

"We're doing that together," Til said firmly. Her heart pounded at the thought of facing the men who had attacked her. "Sit down. What is your story?"

Grayson sighed. "I was twelve when my sister was stolen on her way home from school and we never saw her again."

"Oh no," Til gasped.

"I remember my mother screaming and crying. My father nearly went mad. He went to the police trying to get them to search for her. They searched but seemed disinterested. I was only twelve, so my memory isn't very good. Girls getting stolen in a city like Toronto is not unheard of. My father searched for years. My mother became delicate. She couldn't manage after that. It destroyed my family completely."

"I'm so sorry." Til's eyes filled with tears for him.

"My mother couldn't handle anything. Finally, my father moved out of their room and then out of our house. He found another woman, and that destroyed her. She died shortly after; I think it broke her heart and she gave up."

"Did you ever find your sister?" Til placed her hand on his forearm.

"No, my wife— former wife I should clarify, said I need to stop looking. I can't seem to." Grayson scratched his forehead and took another sip. "I started the department that searches for stolen girls. For obvious reasons, white slavery is particularly horrifying to me. When the Blackburns hired me to find Nora Blackburn, I needed a distraction. England seemed like far enough away."

"What happened between you and your wife?" Til pressed him for an answer.

"I am a very driven person." Grayson evaded the question.

"I noticed," Til said dryly.

"Too intense and I work long hours. My wife wanted me to choose between work and her. I couldn't stop working." Grayson sipped his water.

"You're still searching for your sister." Til took her hand back.

"Yes. I am still searching for her. I keep fighting against the slavers in a system that supports them. You know what that's like." Grayson's jaw clenched hard in anger. "The slavers get reduced sentencing. The chastity of the girl should have no bearing on the sentencing. *No woman* should be stolen and sold and transported no matter *what* her background. The law fails these women completely. Having different sentencing based on the chastity of the girl, ends up putting the girl on trial. I've seen it, it's deplorable. The lawyers attack what they wear, where they walk, as if they are to blame for being taken and sold."

"The law fails all women completely, stolen or not." Til's eyes hardened with anger. "I'm sorry about your sister."

"Me too. I will never stop looking for her. I wish I knew she was dead because then I would know she wasn't suffering. That is the hardest thing. Not knowing and women are so vulnerable, it kills me to think of her and not know if she is safe or what happened." Grayson scrubbed his hands over his face. "I see her face sometimes, it's awful. When I go after another missing girl or in this case many missing girls, I see her. I see her smile before she takes a lick of ice cream or laughing when she is on a swing in the park. My good memories of her, I see them, and I am gutted that someone cut that short and got away with it."

Sorrow tightened Til's throat, she yearned to reach for him, to offer him comfort as he had comforted her. Heavy guilt washed through her at the thought, chained her down and tied her hands. She couldn't allow herself to touch him, instead she said, "I'm very sorry."

"I'm sorry about what happened to you, too." Grayson's eyes flicked to her neck.

"Well, Grayson, it looks as though we are both perpetually looking for our siblings, and now Shannon." Til's eyes filled with tears at her name. Grayson took her hand in his. "It's the worst feeling and the only thing that seems to make it bearable is work. So, let's get to work. We have an interrogation to do."

"You aren't going." Grayson's tone indicated he was prepared to battle if she disagreed.

"Grayson, I know you wouldn't have chosen me; you would prefer some big burly Icelandic man but until you are back with your precious Sol Stein as a partner, I'm all you've got. So, like it or not, I'm going." Til dried her eyes and tilted her chin. "You can follow my lead." She got up and went to the door.

Following her, Grayson clenched his teeth and reached around her to hold the door open for her.

"It will be ugly. What I will do to those men if I suspect they are lying." Grayson's tone deepened as he spoke.

Til turned to face him. He was closer than she thought; she bumped into him and this time didn't move away immediately. Til's breath caught as Grayson moved even nearer to her. Her eyes flicked over him, the breadth of his shoulders, the power evident in his body. His willingness to defend, and protect her, obvious in his stance.

"I think you'll find that I am not delicate like your mother, or needy like your former wife. I told you, they don't have a category for me because, I think that night I fell apart, I could have gone two ways. Delicate or hard." Til's eyes hardened in the lamp light. "I chose hard."

Til's breath caught as Grayson gently brushed a piece of hair away from her eye with his fingertips. He moved closer and stroked her face gently. "You shouldn't have had to choose. That is the greatest tragedy, Til. You should never, ever have had to choose."

Her heart hammered as Grayson's fingertips moved along her cheekbone, as if he could erase the bruise blooming there. "I'm not comfortable... with this..." Til whispered. She swallowed hard.

Grayson dropped his hand and immediately loss hollowed out her heart. Stiffening her spine, she took a step back. Her heart, gutted by the loss of Malcolm, craved the comfort he offered.

"My apologies, I won't touch you again." Grayson's voice, like an axe dragging through gravel, darkened, edged with embarrassment.

Grayson's care and concern unravelled her. She prepared to hate him, keep him at arm's length and keep the icy wall of fury and fear wrapped tight around her. It was difficult to do, as he kept her safe and kept breaking through her defenses with gentle, tender kindness.

Together they made their way to the jail cells in the bowels of the ship so they could interrogate the men. Grayson hesitated before opening the door into the jail. Til bit her lip as he turned to her.

"I can go in first," he offered. "You can listen at the door and if you want to ask something you can knock."

"We're partners, Grayson." Til held her head high. "Let me ask them some questions; it's my niece that's missing."

"Are you sure you are up for this? You *are* pregnant and forty," Grayson asked cautiously.

"Why does everyone keep saying that as if I'm some sort of fossil?" Til hissed at him. In an instant, they were back to sparring, safe, on familiar ground.

"Til, pregnant and forty *is* a fossil," Grayson said so deadpan serious it took Til a moment to realise he was teasing her.

Amidst all the horror, a smile tugged at Til's lip as he held up his hands to ward off an attack. "Let's sort this out," Til snapped at him even as her eyes gleamed in anticipation.

Chapter Twenty-Seven

Shannon woke up with a headache and a dry mouth. Recognising the after effects of chloroform, she rubbed her temple as her eyes slowly focused in the dim light. Moaning from across the room caused her to sit up quickly. Closing her eyes from the pain that pounded in her head, she laid back down until the pain subsided. A young girl, dirty, eyes wide with fear, came to her side.

"This will help, miss." She handed her a dipper of water.

Shannon smelled it before taking a long drink.

"Thank you." Shannon sat up slowly this time and ran a hand over the back of her neck. "What is going on?"

Some girls wept, others clung helplessly to each other and others whimpered softly.

Shannon strained her eyes to see in the gloom. Twelve girls looked back at her.

"What is your name?" Shannon whispered to the girl with the dipper.

"Belle."

"What happened?" Worry gnawed at Shannon.

"We were stolen off the streets and put in this ship." Belle's hand trembled on the dipper as she went back to the pail and brought Shannon more water.

"Who stole you?" Shannon drank the water gratefully.

"We don't know." Belle bit her lip. "We're scared."

"They had a kitten and said if I came with them, they would take me home and I could keep the kitten," a young girl with blonde hair and blue eyes whispered.

Anger roared through Shannon at the thought. "What is your name?"

"Anna."

"Anna is the youngest. They had different tricks for us," Belle said bitterly.

"I want my mother." Anna broke down in tears.

"I'm going to do everything I can to try to work this out." Shannon's heart went out to Anna.

"They gave me ice cream," the girl holding onto Anna said to Shannon.

"What's your name, darling?" Shannon pressed her hand to her heart.

"Olive."

"They are both the youngest. They're only thirteen." Belle's face crumpled.

Shannon's blood boiled as she thought of the innocence that had already been stripped away from them. Her hands shook as she reached out to the girls. They scrambled across the cell and shuddered against her.

"Have you heard where they are taking us?" Shannon's chest tightened in fear as she directed that comment to Belle.

"I keep listening as close to the door as I can. I'm Cissy, I'm the oldest." Cissy stood up and held her hand out to Shannon formally.

Shannon shook her hand. "Cissy, how old are you?"

"I'm sixteen, miss." Her grasp was firm.

"We don't know anything." Belle shook her head, tears filled her eyes.

The pit of Shannon's stomach fell as she looked over the twelve stolen girls.

Shannon disentangled herself from Anna and Olive and stood up to start assessing the health of the girls when a door opened at the end of the room.

Alys, the woman who had called herself Auntie Alys in Til's house, entered and stood against the bars of their cell. Tall, whip thin, with glittery green eyes. Coldness emanated from her.

A chill sliced through Shannon as her Aunt Alys's eyes landed on her. The girls whimpered in fear.

"You, come with me." Alys pointed at Shannon, produced a key from the pocket of her skirt and opened the door to the hold.

Shannon's heart pounded as she followed her up two sets of stairs to a cabin.

Alys opened the door and pointed at her to enter the room.

"What is going on?" Shannon jumped with fear as the door slammed shut.

"How much is Matilda Bertram worth?" Alys cut straight to the point.

"What?" Shannon rubbed her temples, trying to ease the pain throbbing there.

"You were selling her house for her. You are her partner at the clinic. What is she worth? How much money has she got?" Alys demanded.

"I am not sure of the total value." Shannon's eyes moved from Alys to the man in the corner wondering who presented the biggest threat.

"How much did you sell that house for? The one you were showing?" Alys's tone sharpened.

"I would have to check the paperwork; I handled many transactions for Til after she left," Shannon answered cautiously.

Alys slapped Shannon hard, her head already reeling from the chloroform, split apart from pain.

"How much?" she shrieked in Shannon's face.

Shannon wiped blood from the corner of her mouth. The man stirred and stood up. Gritting her teeth, Shannon, with great difficulty, drew herself to her full height. She remained silent.

"Talk, or I'll leave you here with him and he can get the number out of you. I guarantee, he'll enjoy it," Alys hissed at her.

There was a hint of madness in the green eyes that searched hers.

"I sold that house for twenty-eight thousand pounds."

"I told you she had enough," Alys said to the man in the corner of the room.

He moved closer to Shannon.

She shivered as his eyes swept over her.

"Good." He left the room.

Shannon took a deep breath to try to calm her pulse as the door shut behind him.

"Why, of all of us, did she save you?" Alys's lips twisted with bitterness.

"Us?" Shannon's brow furrowed in confusion.

Alys reached her hand out.

Shannon flinched as Alys stroked the side of her face. "Gorgeous. You're perfect."

Shannon trembled in fear as Alys caressed the side of her face again and then dropped her hand.

"Why are you doing this?" Shannon spoke past the terror that fisted in her throat. "I could hand you that money. I'll pay for the girls and I'll give you whatever you want. I have access to all of Til's money. There is no need to resort to kidnapping."

"It's not that simple." Alys shook her head.

"It *can* be that simple. What are the girls worth?" Shannon pleaded with Alys, "I can have the money deposited in a bank. One telegram is all it would take. How much do you need to walk away from this and start a new life?" Shannon tried and failed to keep the desperation out of her voice.

"When Matilda ran, we were scattered." Alys's eyes went vacant as if she recalled a distant memory. She shook her head, eyes darkening with pain. "She owes me for Jimmy."

"Who is Jimmy?" Cold dread washed over Shannon as she looked at the woman closer.

"My baby." Alys blinked and looked away.

"Your son?" Shannon's breath caught.

"My baby brother, who died in my arms. I feel the loss of him still. I will never forget holding his cold body." Alys's eyes slid shut. "Died because Matilda ran and left us to the workhouse. She is a selfish..." Alys's eyes snapped open, she stopped speaking abruptly.

"I'm sure there's an explanation for why Matilda ran." Shannon spoke softly. "I know there is. She said something about being owned. She would never speak of it."

"Owned." Alys tossed her head and scoffed. "Well, now I *own* you. The only person she came back for." Alys's eyes hardened to green flint. "I'll take her money and then kill you in front of her. It would be perfect justice. To see her pain as she watches you die... and then she'll be next."

Shannon gasped, "This is madness! We'll give you whatever you want..."

Alys's eyes darkened with pain. "In the streets it's an eye for eye. My Jimmy died, so Matilda's Shannon must pay the price. But... she will pay me first."

"You will never get away with this. You don't know who you are dealing with." Shannon's heart lodged in her throat.

"Everything that I love, *everything* I hoped for has been stripped from me; it started November 2nd, 1881 when she ran. She is the *root* of it. Just like a weed... to get rid of it, you must get to the root and pull it out, destroy it. I know she loves you as much as I loved Jimmy. It's perfect justice," Alys whispered.

"This is absolute madness." Shannon's eyes widened as she took a step back.

"No." Alys tilted her head to the side. "It is street justice. The only justice that matters. I lived on those streets my whole life. Bought and sold, clawed my way to the top and now... now *everyone* pays for what happened to me."

Shannon swallowed hard. "I have enough money to set you up and you can live anywhere, away from this life of crime, away from everything that hurts you." Shannon repeated her offer gently. She took a tentative step forward, desperate to draw Alys out. To understand her, in an attempt to stay alive and get the twelve girls in the brig of the ship safely back to their parents, Shannon kept her voice calm, low and gentle. Her professional voice, the voice she used with women suffering with tremendous pain.

Alys shook her head. "No. It's not enough. It's not just money. Matilda must pay. I killed Malcolm, I will kill you... but I want *her*."

"You killed Malcolm." Shannon reached out to grab the back of a chair to steady herself.

"Easy." Alys wrapped her arms around herself. "Derringers are so easy to hide. A man can be dropped like a rock in the street." Alys shrugged. "No one ever suspects a woman."

"Why did you kill Malcolm?" Shannon's heart pounded in horror.

"Because Matilda Bertram loved him. Everything Matilda loves must die until I can take her money and kill her." Alys blinked again. She reached out to stroke Shannon's cheek. "She left me."

Shannon swallowed hard.

"You look like Martha. She was beautiful, delicate, just like you." Alys's head tilted to the side as she looked at Shannon.

Shannon's pulse beat faster. "Why would you want to hurt Martha's daughter?" Shannon pounced on that line of reasoning.

Alys moved closer and whispered in her ear. "I want peace in my heart. As long as Til has you to love, there is no peace."

"Auntie Alys, you should think about letting me give you the money." She forced herself to speak softly, like a little girl. Shannon tamped down the raw pain of knowing this woman had stolen Malcolm's life. Her heart twisted as she tried to negotiate with Malcolm's killer.

"Don't call me that." Alys's head snapped up, her eyes hardened. "You mean nothing to me." Shannon sat very still as Alys turned on her heel and opened the door.

"Shipley, take her back. I'm done with her for now." Alys left her to Shipley and another man.

Shannon couldn't stop herself from trembling in fear as the men took her by the upper arm and dragged her back to the brig in the bottom of the ship.

Chapter Twenty-Eight

Til entered the jail cell, her eyes swept over three men shackled to the bars behind them. Head bleeding, the big man with the green cravat looked up at her like a wolf about to devour a lamb. She didn't allow herself to shiver; she refused to give him the satisfaction of knowing he had terrified her.

Until that moment when the men attacked her, she hadn't realised how alone and vulnerable she was on this ship. In all areas of life. First the captain and now this lot. Yes, Grayson had intervened but what if he hadn't forgotten his pocket watch at Joan's? What if no one had come to her rescue? A curl of fear coiled through Til as she shot a look at Grayson.

He met her gaze and held it. Standing straight, braced for battle, he exuded confidence.

She straightened and addressed the man in the green cravat.

"What is your name and where are you from?" Til demanded.

Grayson moved closer but didn't intervene.

The man spat at her, refusing to speak.

Til inclined her head at Grayson and took a step back.

Grayson dragged him to his feet. "Talk or I beat the life out of you." Grayson shook him as if an answer would fall out.

The man sneered at Til.

Til took a step back and nodded at Grayson.

Grayson dropped him with one strong fist in the jaw, then pulled him up and smashed him into the bars of the cell. "The lady asked you a question. Talk or I'll ask her to leave and I will interrogate you—my way."

"Grant Brooks." The man ignored Grayson and kept his eye on Til.

"Who do you work for?" Til stepped closer, cautious to keep Grayson's shoulder between her and Brooks.

"The Bristol Butchers. Royce sends his regards." Brooks grinned at her. "Just giving you a little taste of what you can expect, then this one showed up." Brooks nodded at Grayson.

"Why now?" Til shuddered at the name Royce Bristol.

"No Bobby, no protection." Brooks spit blood at the floor by her foot.

Til refused to step back. She gulped down her terror at the words 'no Bobby, no protection'. Dreading the answer, she forced herself to ask, "Who abducted Shannon?"

"Don't know." Brooks tried to struggle out of Grayson's grip. "The telegram said you had enough for both Nora and Shannon. Why should Royce get that money? He's done nothing for it." He leered at her. "You felt good... when Royce takes you..."

"Beat him," Til commanded Grayson.

Grayson complied, driving his fist into Brooks's mouth, hard enough to knock out another tooth. Brooks slid down the bars and collapsed to a heap on the floor.

"I'm in irons!" he spit out his tooth and glared up at Grayson.

"Who stole Shannon?" Til demanded, clenching her hands into fists, wishing she could hit him herself. She didn't dare as a curl of tightening pain in her lower back caused her concern.

"I don't know." Brooks dragged himself to his feet and then lunged at her.

Grayson stepped between Brooks and Til, intercepting him.

This bully wants to see terror in my eyes. Brooks is like Royce, he's like all of them.

Grayson hit Brooks so hard, Til winced as she heard a crunch. She grimaced as blood spattered over Grayson and past him to land on her face.

Til narrowed her eyes at Brooks, took a step forward, still behind Grayson's shoulder, letting his body protect hers in case Brooks got out of Grayson's grasp.

"Who is the head of the Bristol Butchers in London now that Bobby is dead?" Til watched Brooks carefully, looking for evidence he was lying.

"Andy Bristol." Flecks of blood landed on her face as he spoke.

"And who is Andy's woman?" Til demanded.

"Alys Bertram *was* his woman." Grant's lip curled as he spoke.

Til reeled at the name. Memories of Alys bloomed in her head. Thoughts of what might have happened to her without Til's protection devastated her. Heart pounding, she pushed the guilt that winged through her at the name Alys aside, as she hung on to the bars of the jail cell to stay upright. "What do you mean was?" Til rallied as she forced the sentence past the tight fist of horror in her throat. A sliver of pain snaked around her womb, frightening her on another level.

Grayson tightened the chains holding Brooks to the wall.

"Too old." Brooks taunted her. "New girl is young."

Pressing her knuckles into her lower back, Til tried to ease the intensifying aching pain. "You mean Alys was with the head of the Butchers?"

"Was."

"She has Shannon?" Helplessness flooded through her, there was nothing they could do but wait to dock. "Where will they go through immigration?" Til demanded, still holding onto the bars as her knees weakened with fear of what Alys was capable of doing to Shannon. Of all the people from Til's past, no one could have hated her as much as her sister Alys. If Til's fears were correct, Alys would have had the worst possible life imaginable.

"Immigration?" Grant crowed. "They aren't bringing tea and cakes across. They don't go to immigration."

"What is Royce Bristol's address? Where does he live?" Til shook her head to clear it. Her mind battled to form a sentence.

What will Alys do to Shannon? Would she kill her as revenge?

Til shuddered, her blood ran cold at the thought.

"Don't know." Brooks's face paled as Grayson turned his attention from Til to him. "Honest." Brooks tried to pull away from him.

"Detective Grayson." Til wiped at the blood on her face as she spoke. "Beat him until he gives us an address. I'll give evidence that you had to protect me from assault."

"I don't know it!" Brooks screamed in protest.

"Start with his kneecaps!" Til demanded. Her eyes narrowed at Brooks. She opened the jail cell. "Detective Grayson is a gentleman and he won't beat a confession out of you if I am in the cell. He's old-fashioned that way." Til tilted her head to the side. "I suggest you speak, or I leave."

"Bleeker something, in Toronto." Brooks gasped in fear as Grayson pulled his arm back.

"Eli Pitman's old apartment?" Grayson growled as he held him against the bars by his throat.

"I don't know. I heard Bleeker Street." Brooks looked wildly from Grayson to Til. "He took over Pitman's ring and his old lady."

"He has Adeline?" Grayson's face twisted as he hit Brooks hard enough to break his jaw.

Brooks's head snapped back and forth. "No, Mira something."

"Mirabel?" Grayson gasped. "You're sure?"

"Yeah."

Grayson dropped Brooks to the floor and turned so his gaze locked with Til's.

"Did Royce order Alys to take Shannon?" Til stood over Brooks and demanded an answer. "Speak or he hits you again. What do you know about Shannon?"

"I don't know nothing." Brooks lunged for her but the chains holding him to the bars behind him made it impossible.

The dull ache in Til's lower back troubled her. She wanted to stay until the end of this interrogation, her body demanded to lie down. Til despised the new limitations this pregnancy placed on her.

"Royce has a message for you." Brooks narrowed his eyes and lifted his chin defiantly. His eyes lit up as he spoke to Til. "He says you're nothing, Matilda Bertram from Ann Street. He can't wait to see you and remind you of where you came from." Brooks shot a terrified look at Grayson. "A worthless little girl from a slum."

Til stepped back as Grayson grabbed Brooks, dragged him to his feet and hit him so hard he passed out.

Taking Til by the upper arms, Grayson whispered against her ear. "That's enough. I can tell you're in pain. Let's get you back to your cabin and I'll deal with the rest of them later. I can't get anything out of him now."

Mortified at her fragility, she leaned into him as he closed the door behind them and supported her as they walked into the corridor. The pain in her lower back caused her to sweat with a different worry.

"What's wrong?" Grayson turned to her. "Is your back sore? Did you twist it in the struggle?"

"Cramping pain." Til's eyes flashed with fear. The ship heaved, and he braced them both.

Grayson's face paled.

"Grayson." Til slid down him as her body betrayed her.

He caught her, put his arm around her waist and pulled her against him.

"I'm not feeling well." She heard the tinge of hysteria in her voice.

"I told you an interrogation room was no place for a lady." Grayson growled into her ear.

"When a lady shows up, we'll let her know." Til pressed her hands against her abdomen and gasped in worry and pain.

"Don't listen to a word he says. What happened to you never should have. You are a lady in every sense of the word." Grayson held her up with an arm of iron.

Til straightened up and gasped as the ache intensified.

"Can you walk?" His arm tightened around her.

"Yes." Sweat broke out on Til's forehead.

"I'll take that as a no." Grayson half carried, half dragged her up to the top deck. Despite her protest, he picked her up and carried her the rest of the way.

"Please, Speck, please don't do this. Please." Til pleaded with her body to stop cramping.

Laying her on the bed; Grayson tore into her doctor's bag looking for calcium carbonate and laudanum. His hands fumbled as he poured a spoonful of calcium carbonate and offered it to her. She bolted it down and lay on the bed.

"Let me help you with your corset." Grayson knew his way around a woman's clothes. She bit back a comment about him being a rake. A snide snipe like that wouldn't help anyone.

He maintained her dignity as he unlaced her corset. In a chemise, she curled onto her side. He put a pillow between her knees and pulled a light blanket over her.

"Would you find the midwife, Miss O'Hare, the one who assisted Joan?" Til swallowed a hard knot of salty tears. "I think I need someone to examine me, I think I'm losing little Speck." Til's breath caught on a sob. "First Malcolm, next Shannon, and now this child. I haven't even been allowed time to properly grieve for Malcolm and now this child is going to die!"

Til put her face in the pillow and took a deep breath to stop the tears.

"Til, we'll do everything we can. I'll be back with the midwife. Just take deep breaths." Grayson's tone of voice was low with fear.

"I'm terrified, Grayson." Til's face crumpled in fear as she took the pillow away from her face and looked up at him. "I lost two babies before this one."

***

The blood drained from Grayson's face. "I'll get the midwife," he repeated.

Til reached out and took hold of his wrist. "Please, don't leave me... yet."

Grayson hesitated. A woman like Til didn't ask for help.

Ever.

Telegrams to send, an interrogation of the two men pending, Grayson paused and thought about how to leave her and get back to work.

He checked his pocket watch.

"Never mind." Til's eyes met his as he looked up from checking the time. Her face fell and Grayson wanted to curse himself.

"Never mind," Til repeated as she wiped her tears on the pillow. "Please send the midwife and don't let me delay you." Til pulled the pillow tight against her chest. "You have work to do. I understand."

Grayson saw defeat in her eye. This potential miscarriage defeated a woman who had defied all the odds and dragged herself out of the tenements. Grayson's heart ached as her shoulders slumped. Out of his depth, Grayson wondered how to stay and help a woman facing miscarriage and the grieving that would follow. His father had run from his mother; he had run from Melinda. Grayson didn't know how to comfort a woman. He had never learned it.

As Grayson gripped the door knob and prepared to flee to work, to what he knew, he realised with a flash of clarity, he was facing a long, lonely life. Grayson knew with certainty, if he walked away from her now, at her most vulnerable, there would be no walking back in. Not with a woman like Til Stone. She had a look in her eye that said she would survive no matter what. That included walking away from a man who wasn't strong enough to stay and help her through this.

Sitting with a woman who wept made Grayson uneasy.

Gritting his teeth, he opened the door and looked back one last time to see Til rock from the pain. Not just the physical pain, the fears of facing the unknown alone. The same look Melinda had given him when she held newborn Ella in her arms and was unsure of how to feed her. He'd sent for her mother and went to work. Because that is what men did. They worked and women dealt with all the emotional parts of life. Everyone understood men were not cut out for that. That's how the world worked. Grayson sighed from deep in his soul. Maybe that is how the world worked, but it wasn't how it would work between him and Til. Bracing himself for what was to come, he called for a porter.

"Please find the midwife, Moira O'Hare." Grayson slipped money into the porter's hand to make it clear he needed him to hurry. "Have hot water and fresh towels brought here, quickly."

Grayson took a deep breath and turned back to Til.

Partners handle things together.

He closed the door and picked up a chair, then set it down by the bed.

Startled, Til peered up at him through tears.

"With your permission, Til. I would like to stay and see this through." Grayson hovered, waiting for Til to invite him to sit.

"Thank you." Til swallowed hard.

The depth of her fear ran deeper than he thought.

Grayson sat down, reached forward, and put his hand on her shaking shoulder.

"I'm out of handkerchiefs." He rubbed her upper arm. "I called for some towels so, maybe we can use that."

Til nodded. "Right."

She didn't protest as he stroked her cheek with his shirt sleeve, to wipe away her tears and Grant's blood spatter as best as he could.

"You have work to do." Her breath caught on a sob as she tried to be tough.

Grayson smiled at her. "You're giving me an out." He adjusted the covers over her shoulder.

"Yes." She glanced up at him and didn't look away.

"The work can wait." Grayson stroked her cheek with his fingertips.

Til blinked in surprise.

"Are you warm enough? Is the tincture or whatever you took, is it working?" He left his hand on her upper arm to provide support.

"Yes," Til said. "The cramping is lessening. I think I did too much and maybe the fear from what the men were about to do..."

"I'm glad the pain is stopping." Grayson stroked her face. His eyes traveled down the length of her and then his eyes met hers. "Whatever happens here today, I'll stay if you want that."

"You can't stay if I lose this baby, it will be terrible." Til covered her mouth with her hand. "You'll be fainting all over the place."

"I know," Grayson whispered as a smile tugged at his lip. He took his hand in hers. "I'll stay."

"If it is a miscarriage." Til's voice twinged with panic.

"It isn't." Grayson threaded his fingers through hers. "Til, it is not."

"You don't know," she sobbed.

Grayson's heart broke for her. "If it is, then I'll stay, and I'll try to faint without getting in the way."

Til stopped crying.

Encouraged that possibly she needed to laugh at him, he soldiered on. "I'm not good at any of this. I am just telling you now, I am out of my depth, but I remember one drip of chloroform every sixty seconds."

His eyes met hers and held her gaze.

"That's right." Til nodded. "One drip every sixty seconds. Good you remembered that."

"Save your strength, Til." Grayson held her hands hard in his.

"Grayson, you should know." Til's eyes filled with fresh tears. "No one is good at this."

"Well, I'm particularly terrible," Grayson said gruffly. "However, whatever happens, we'll deal with it together."

"I'm not sure how to thank you..."

A knock at the door interrupted Til's sentence.

"It's the midwife," a woman called from behind the door.

"Come in," Grayson called back.

"You can leave now, sir," Miss O'Hare said as she bustled around the room. "Let's see how mother and baby are doing."

"Sorry Miss O'Hare; I know this is highly unusual, I think Til wants me to stay." Grayson smoothed the hair back from Til's face.

"Are you certain?" Miss O'Hare asked, her eyes darted wildly between Til and Grayson.

Til's eyes met his.

Grayson leaned in closer.

"Yes." Til tightened her grip on his hands. "We're partners, he's staying."

Chapter Twenty-Nine

As a storm battered the ship, Shannon awakened to moaning from a girl near her. Scrambling to her feet, she yearned for light.

She stumbled twice in her haste to get closer to the girl moaning in pain. Warm vomit washed over her hands as she reached out for her.

"I'm so sorry, miss. I'm sorry." The girl wept as the ship heaved and tossed.

Shannon recognised the voice as Belle.

"You're seasick, love. It's awful, I know." Shannon murmured as she swept Belle's hair back off her face and handed her a ripped piece of petticoat.

They huddled together as the storm tossed the ship, rocking it back and forth.

"Are we going to die?" Belle wept against her.

"No, it's just a storm," Shannon said quietly to the girls in the prison with her.

"I'm not feeling very well."

"As soon as this storm passes, it will get better." Shannon strained her eyes to see in the gloom. "I'm freezing." Belle shivered against Shannon who pressed her hand to Belle's forehead.

"How long have you had a fever?" Shannon asked as her stomach rolled, from seasickness or the ever-increasing possibility she was pregnant. She had lost track of days because of being chloroformed and being kept in the bowels of a ship with little natural light. Shannon began to believe her early morning nausea was more than seasickness. Shannon put that thought aside as she turned her attention back to Belle.

"It just started, miss."

"All right, you need to drink lots of water. Girls, everyone take a sip of water because when Belle drinks from the dipper, no one else can use it. Until I know what the cause of her fever is, she might be contagious."

Shannon yearned for her doctor's bag. The grim memory of the last time she had been on a ship to Canada hit her hard, she'd been expecting that time too.

"Hopefully, they'll bring us fresh water in the morning and food." Shannon adjusted herself so Belle could lay her head on her lap. "How old are you, Belle?"

"Fifteen."

A curl of horror slid around her heart at the young women whose lives were subjected to untold suffering if she could not negotiate them off the ship.

"Ladies, we all just need to survive tonight, and I will think of something in the morning."

Not one of you will be sold. I guarantee it.

"What will you do?" Cissy trembled in fear beside her.

"I don't know yet. I'll think of something." Shannon reached out and took the girl's hand in her own.

She swallowed a lump in her throat as Cissy lay her head down on Shannon's shoulder.

"I'm afraid."

"I am too." Shannon stroked Cissy's hair.

I am pregnant and I am terrified I will get sick and lose this baby. Or Cole and Til will never find me.

"What will happen to us in Canada?" A young voice whimpered in the dark.

"I am uncertain." Shannon stroked Belle's hair back from her face. "I know we are all in this together and I will do everything in my power to keep you all safe."

At Shannon's promise, the girls calmed down as the night wore on. Shannon made sure Belle drank enough water.

Despair dragged through Shannon as she thought about the fate of these girls if the Toronto Constabulary didn't intervene. Detective Grayson seemed to be honourable, but were his men? Would they look the other way? Were they corrupt like the London police?

First thing the next morning, Shannon struggled with morning sickness that was compounded by the heaving of the ship. Shipley and one of their guards threw the door open and entered the cell with a bucket of water and bread. As the lamplight flooded the cell, Belle moaned as the light hit her eyes.

Quickly, as Shannon fought nausea, she examined Belle for scarlet fever.

No rash.

"You need to let Alys know some of these girls are sick. Belle has scarlet fever and if you don't get us into proper living conditions and give me supplies to treat her, she will die. I suspect these other two girls have dysentery. If that is the case, I warn you, the entire crew is in danger. Scarlet fever is deadly. I need a doctor's bag if you want these girls to live to see Canada." Shannon narrowed her eyes at him.

The girls howled in fear.

"You're lying." Shipley put the bucket down in the cell and turned to leave them.

"Move us into clean quarters immediately." Shannon raised her voice over top of the girls. "Each girl needs her own water and I need vinegars and salts at the very least. I need a doctor's bag before I come down with it too. If the rest of the crew has been drinking from the same water source, we're all in trouble," Shannon barked orders at Shipley through the bars. "If you plan on selling these girls, dead ones will cut into your profit margin. I suggest you hurry."

Shipley turned on his heel and left them.

Shannon slumped against the bars, desperate to have proper facilities and medicines to assist Belle. She allowed herself a moment of self-pity before bracing herself for the work at hand and turning her attention back to the girls.

"If I can get us out of this jail cell, I might hear plans or find out information so I can negotiate," Shannon whispered to the girls. "It will look suspicious if we all pretend to be sick, just the youngest girls, please. I need you to pretend to be sick."

Twelve pairs of wide eyes blinked back at her in the prison's gloom.

"They will sell us?" Cissy's voice croaked in fear.

"I won't let them." Shannon tried to calm them down. "I will negotiate with our captors. I will buy you. I don't know how but that is my plan. We have to get out of here though, so you pretend to be sick, can you do that?"

Two girls wept openly. Shannon's heart broke as she heard their sobs.

"I know you're scared, but we will get out of here. Alive. When he comes back, the youngest two girls need to be clutching your stomachs and moaning. If you can make yourselves vomit that would help. Whatever you can do, the rest of you show symptoms over the next few days. Let's keep our kidnappers distracted. Moan and cry and carry on. Who are the youngest? We start youngest to oldest."

The girls held onto each other, more cried with fear.

"I don't want you to be afraid," Shannon reached out and held their hands. Her voice shook with emotion as she tried to calm them. "When they take me out of here to attend to the younger girls, I will come back for you, no matter what. Girls, look at me. I promise to come back for you no matter how long and no matter what happens."

Weeping, the oldest, Cissy, trembled as she spoke. "We'll do it."

Alys opened the door and stalked over to stand at the bars of the cell. Shannon went to speak to her.

"Dysentery, a terrible case. This girl, Belle, I think has scarlet fever. I won't know for sure for a few more hours. Two of the girls are already sick. We need to move them, and I need a doctor's bag, fresh water, salt, and vinegar. Immediately." Shannon held onto the bars.

Alys's face flamed in fury. "You're lying."

A wave of morning sickness brought Shannon to her knees. She couldn't stop herself from vomiting. Two of the youngest girls vomited once she started.

Alys, disgusted, picked up her skirts and took a step back.

"I need a doctor's bag," Shannon repeated as she wiped her mouth on her skirt.

"Absolutely not," Alys hissed.

"Suit yourself. These girls won't live to see Canada if you don't let me treat them. How much are they worth to you?" Shannon stayed kneeling on the floor as another wave of nausea crashed over her.

Alys's lips thinned in anger. She turned on her heel and left the brig.

Shannon sat down with her back against the bars. She closed her eyes and wiped perspiration from her forehead.

"Are you all right, miss?" Cissy asked timidly.

"I'm pregnant, Cissy. This is just morning sickness. I am just fine. Thank you, though," Shannon smiled weakly.

"Oh! But do you want to be pregnant?" Cissy bit her lip.

"I do, very much." Shannon fought tears at the thought of losing her baby in the brig of a ship.

"Does the father know?" Cissy placed her hand on Shannon's shoulder.

"I told him, before I was abducted, that I thought it was possible." Shannon's heart glowed with the memory.

"Will he be happy, do you think?" Cissy tilted her head to the side.

Shannon took a deep breath and rocked back on her heels. "He will be elated." She smiled at Cissy. "That's why we have to stay strong and stay alive. We must get out of here and I'm not leaving here without you."

"You said you think we will die, though?" Cissy's voice shook with fear.

"No." Shannon took her hand in hers. "Absolutely not. That's just to get us out of here," Shannon whispered. "She'll come back, I'm certain."

Shannon tried to sound more confident than she felt. There was a madness in Alys's eyes that indicated she was past reason. Losing Jimmy had deranged her and whatever recent event happened to push her to this point; it was very possible that Shannon was dealing with an incurable.

Shannon moved closer to Belle and felt her forehead. Hotter. Taking a deep breath, Shannon reached for the girls.

Moments later, Shipley returned and opened the door.

"The sickest are to come up and you'll treat them." He dragged Shannon up off the floor. Roughly, he pulled her through the door of the cell.

Shannon struggled against him. "Let me help her. She's contagious...."

Shipley dropped her arm.

Shannon kept her eyes lowered as she helped Belle to her feet. She bit back angry words as he roughly pushed them through the door of the cell. The remaining girls clung together as Anna, Olive, and Shannon with Belle in her arms followed Shipley out of the cell and up the stairs.

Shannon nearly wept with relief as she spied medical supplies and fresh water. The cabin allowed access to bright light and some fresh air. She blinked as her eyes adjusted. Immediately, she set to work trying to take Belle's fever down as the door slammed shut.

Shannon leaped across the room and pressed her ear against the door, hoping to hear something.

Nothing.

She turned back to Belle and the other two girls. She immediately mixed salts with water and helped Belle drink it so she wouldn't dehydrate.

Little Anna with her white blonde hair and big blue eyes held onto Belle's hand. Olive offered comfort by stroking Belle's hair back from her forehead.

Shannon swallowed a hard fist of salty tears, watching these girls try in whatever way they could to lend comfort to Belle. She vowed that if she ever got off this ship, she would drag Alys to the gallows herself and watch her hang and not feel a hint of remorse.

Chapter Thirty

Til laid in bed for an entire day. Every time she tried to sit up, the cramping started. Grayson wrung his hands and tried to keep her comfortable. Finally, she sent Grayson out of the room to find supper and give her a moment of peace.

He knocked on her door later that evening. After six hours of no cramping, Til allowed herself to be cautiously optimistic.

"How's the patient?" Face white with fear for her answer, Grayson held a tray of food by her bed.

"Irritated," Til growled from the bed. "I can't continue like this. I can't lay in a bed until this baby is born."

"Don't panic yet. The midwife just says you had too much bad news, and the worry caused an episode." Grayson put the tray down near her.

"That's what is so frustrating," Til huffed. "I despise weakness of any sort, especially my own."

Grayson nodded in agreement. "I understand."

"How could you possibly?" Til snapped. "You're built like a steam engine; you've never been weak a day in your life."

"I fainted assisting Joan." Grayson grinned as he corrected her.

"That's true," Til relented and grinned back.

"Anyway." Grayson adjusted a pillow behind her so she could sit up to eat. "Just an update; we dock at immigration tomorrow. I hope that won't be too taxing for you."

Til harrumphed, "Taxing! I hate this. It is humiliating."

"You're pregnant." Grayson shrugged. He poured tea into a teacup and added the exact amount of milk she liked. "Not weak, *pregnant.* Anyway, we have to leave this ship, go through immigration and then get on a smaller ship. I have already alerted every port of immigration that Alys is en route to Toronto. However, as Brooks pointed out, she's not going through immigration, so we know she is on a privately-owned vessel, a ship that is small enough to get through the Saint Lawrence Seaway." Grayson shook his head. "That's the bad news. This isn't their first abduction and as far as I can see, they will slip into the Toronto area with no paperwork. Until she contacts you or you meet her on November 2nd, there isn't much we can do."

Til's eyes flashed with anger. "That is disturbing."

"I know, that is the bad news. However, this is every piece of information we have on Eli Pitman's old ring." Grayson handed her a folder. He'd brought it in under the tray. "Sol is keeping an eye on Royce; this file is the list of girls stolen from England, shipped from the Bristols to Eli Pitman and Rodd Royce." Grayson handed Til a picture of Rodd Royce.

Til's hands shook as icy cold fear settled in her heart just looking at a photo of Royce Bristol.

Grayson reached out and placed his hand on hers.

"You're meeting with Odelia, not him. I guarantee Royce Bristol will *not* lay a hand on you. When we get to Toronto, there will be a team of men to protect you, and I will be the first in line," he promised.

Til took a deep breath and didn't let it out until her heart stopped pounding with fear. She reached for the file and traced her fingertips over the names on the ledger. "All these girls at the mercy of the Bristols." Til's eyes filled with tears. "After that night in the flat, I know what this feels like. This breaks my heart." Til's breath caught. She rested her hand on her abdomen. "How do we protect these girls?"

"No choice but to wait for them to contact you. My men will do surveillance; we'll try to find out where they are." Grayson pulled out another file. "This is every piece of property we suspect..."

A knock at the door interrupted them.

Grayson got up to answer. A maid handed him two pieces of paper.

"What is it?" Til's lips were white with fear.

"A telegram from Toronto..." Grayson read it swiftly.

"Is it about Shannon maybe?" Til tried to get out of bed.

"I'm sorry." Grayson put his hand on her shoulder and gently pressed her back down onto the bed.

Til slumped back against the pillows.

"It's from Sol Stein. He confirmed that Rodd Royce lives in Eli's penthouse on Bleeker, Brooks is telling the truth. Royce has taken over as the head of Eli's men." Grayson searched through the file.

"Or, he's sentimental." Til read the telegram and placed it on top of Royce's picture.

Grayson smirked. "Yes, crime bosses are known for being nostalgic."

"Well, if he's a crime boss and we're dealing with Alys, who is desperate by the sounds of it, it's time to take control." Til grit her teeth and snapped the file closed.

"Oh?" Grayson's eyebrows shot up.

"Up to this point, we have been dancing to Odelia and Royce's tune, with Alys behind the whole thing. That stops right now." Til's eyes narrowed, her lips thinned in anger. "Is your constabulary corrupt? Can we trust your men?"

"My men are straight." Grayson straightened up.

"You're sure?" Til adjusted the pillow at her back so she could sit up straighter.

"Positive." Grayson braced himself.

"Then, I have an idea." Til leaned forward. "I want to meet Royce on my terms."

The blood drained from Grayson's face. "Absolutely not."

"What do you know about that Mira girl?" Til ignored his concern.

"Mirabel Salter was Eli's mistress, pregnant at the time of Eli's incarceration. She gave birth to a son, Tommy Salter. She lived at Hope House until things became difficult between her and Adeline." Grayson rattled off the details of Mirabel's past as if he was writing a crime report.

"Why?" Til tilted her head.

"Adeline was Eli's wife. She is the president of Hope House."

"And yet she let her stay there?" Til's eyebrows raised.

"Adeline is a very good woman. Anyway, once she remarried Judge Martin, things changed. Cora, Sol's wife, believes that Mirabel became very jealous. Adeline was living the high life. By high life, I mean very high. Cora ensured that Adeline received half of Eli's fortune."

"Half!" Til gasped. "Unheard of! Grayson, I want to meet these women, badly."

"Believe me; they want to meet you too." Grayson grinned. "Anyway, Cora is a genius. She manipulated the entire Canadian Court, including me I might add, to ensure her client got half. I still shake my head at her brilliance. She is amazing."

"You sound like you might try to run off with her." Til reprimanded him.

"Oh, no. Sol would kill me and not think twice," Grayson said cheerfully.

"Adeline and Judge Martin live in a stunning mansion at the end of Sol and Cora's street. They are just coming home from a honeymoon in Paris. I think it was all too much for Mirabel; she works in a laundry. She took her son and moved in with the women she works with. I guess the women at Hope House sort of shared a sigh of relief. Cora worried that Royce might come for her and she fears Royce."

"As she should." Til shuddered.

"They would not ask her to leave; she has a one-year-old son. It would have been wrong. However, she left."

"Would you ask Sol to investigate further? If she's living with Royce in Eli's old penthouse, where is her son?" Til tilted her head to the side.

Grayson frowned. "I assumed with her?"

"Men like Royce aren't in the habit of raising other men's children." Til picked up her teacup. "She's left that son somewhere. Have your men find him and we'll use him as leverage."

"Til!" Grayson gasped. "You wouldn't..."

"I will do what it takes." Til's determined eyes clamped on Grayson's. "We need Tommy Salter in our custody. Immediately."

Grayson stood up and shook his head. "I hate this. This isn't right."

"Today." Til sipped at her hot tea and then returned the cup to the tray. She picked at the plate.

"Some would say you are unconscionable." Grayson shook his head.

"Grayson, I don't care two figs what anyone says. I do the job." Til shrugged. "I need something to use as leverage for the weakest link. If Mirabel is driven by jealousy and emotion, she's weak."

"This is her *child*. We're talking about *taking a woman's child*." Grayson shook his head.

Til rolled her eyes. "No. We aren't." Til challenged him. "If that son is with her, and I doubt he is, then we need a new plan. If she had to give him up, we'll take him, keep him happy and well, and use him as leverage. Grayson, I'm surprised you haven't thought of this already. Please find out. Also, let Cora know I look forward to meeting her. She sounds fascinating."

"Once they get their hands on you, they'll want to get you to join them in ruling the world," Grayson said dryly.

"One thing at a time, Grayson." Til leaned back into her pillows, thankful that the cramping had stopped. "One thing at a time."

Chapter Thirty-One

Mirabel Salter ran her fingertips over the wound that had changed her life. The scalded skin of her left hand was angry, red, and puckered. Her eyes filled with tears as she thought about the day she got hurt. Dismissed immediately from the laundry after a week of not being able to put her hand in water, there was not enough money to feed her son. She couldn't listen to his cries for food another moment.

Tears filled her eyes as she pressed her hand to her heart. Handing Tommy Salter to an orphanage had broken her. Mirabel resolved to take him back, no matter what it took.

Her eyes hardened as she looked around the familiar penthouse. Memories of the days she spent here as Eli Pitman's lover flooded back to her. Respectability was drab compared to the opulence of this beautiful suite. She shuddered. She was still learning just how high the price was if she lived here with Royce. Hand aching from the pain of the burn, heart shattered from losing Tommy, Mirabel hung her head in grief.

I did what I had to do to feed my son and any future children I have. I had no choice.

Straightening up, she cast those thoughts of shame away. With no intentions of going back to the drudgery at the laundry, Mirabel knew Royce was her ticket to luxury and she would play by his rules to stay here.

On top.

She tossed a skein of flax coloured hair over her left shoulder. She would pay any price, do anything to have enough money to get her son out of the orphanage. He was safe but as soon as she could convince Royce to bring him here, she would. In the meantime, she knew with all her heart, Royce was the only one that would keep her off the streets and provide her with any hope she could get Tommy back. Worst-case scenario, Mirabel hoped to steal enough to get one of her friends from the laundry to raise him.

This Odelia who arrived from London with Nora Blackburn needed to be eliminated. If Royce turned his attention to her, and thought she should run the ring, Mirabel's position was on shaky ground.

Dressing carefully in a red gown cut to show off every physical asset she had, Mirabel had one chance to secure her future. When she met with Royce and Odelia tonight, Odelia needed to realise Mirabel was in a position of power, not Odelia. Carefully, she piled her hair high. A knock at the door startled her.

Opening the door to a telegram boy, she frowned in confusion.

Why is this telegram coming to their private apartment? Why not to Royce's office?

"Thank you," Mirabel murmured as she took the telegram from him.

Addressed to Odelia but sent to Royce's penthouse?

Curious.

The telegram read: Confirming. November 2nd, Dock 318, Warehouse 619, £10,000, for Nora Blackburn. Proof of life for Shannon McDougall required immediately, or no money exchanged. Name of Lady Madeline Harper's daughter. No correct answer. No money— Matilda Bertram.

Shannon? Who is Shannon?

Mirabel frowned and resolved to deal with Shannon, whoever she was, later. A seed of an idea took root in Mirabel's mind.

Mirabel examined the telegram.

What a simple thing to change that one to a four.

Her heart pounded as she thought about what Royce would do if he suspected that Odelia was stealing thirty thousands pounds from him. Searching the drawers in Royce's desk, she found a fine-tipped pen and carefully turned the one to a four. With one tiny crooked line, she sealed the fate of Odelia Shipley Bristol— and her own.

She smiled at the telegram.

Royce killed anyone who stole from him. Mirabel tried to stifle the guilt that pounded through her as she looked at the one little crooked line.

I want Tommy back...

Ignoring the pangs of guilt, she waited to present the altered telegram. In this contest between saving Tommy and letting Odelia live, there was nothing to think about. When there was only ten thousand pounds, Matilda Bertram, would pay the price, not Mirabel.

Draping herself over the chaise lounge, she glimpsed herself in the mirror. She looked like her normal self. Pleased at her appearance, she arranged her skirt to show off her narrow waist and waited for Royce to return.

The sound of Royce bounding up the stairs made Mirabel sit up straight. Opening the door to the penthouse, his eyes lit up as they skimmed over Mirabel.

"Pour me a drink, not much time before Odelia will be here."

Mirabel moved to the sideboard and poured a generous helping of whiskey into a tumbler.

"A telegram arrived." Mirabel forced herself to sound bored.

"From Alys?" Royce's eyebrows raised. "I expected to hear from her by now."

"From Matilda Bertram." Mirabel handed him the whiskey and the telegram.

"Matilda!" Royce's head snapped up.

Mirabel licked her lips as she watched Royce read the telegram.

"Forty thousand pounds! Odelia is stealing thirty thousand pounds." Royce vibrated with rage.

Mirabel's voice shook as she went to Royce and slid her hand across his chest. "What will you do?"

"She won't live to see tomorrow." Royce pulled Mirabel closer. "You'll meet Matilda. You'll take Nora to her and bring me the money, all of it. If you pull that off, you run the ring. If you fail..."

"I won't fail." Mirabel smiled as Royce took the drink from her hand. He took a deep gulp and then pressed his lips to hers. Repulsed by the taste of whiskey on his lips as he kissed her, Mirabel shuddered. She forced her body to respond as she thought about Tommy and resolved to do what it took to get him back.

As Royce tore at her clothes, Mirabel tried to push him away. "She'll be here any minute." Mirabel protested.

Royce's eyes flashed with fury.

Mirabel shivered in dread.

"She can wait," Royce growled as he tore off her gown.

***

"Why Matilda Bertram?" Mirabel's hands shook as she reached for the decanter of whiskey. Desperate to numb her thoughts and pain, Mirabel poured herself a generous helping. Taking a shaky sip, she continued. "Why is it so important that you get your capital from Matilda Bertram?"

"A shared enemy."

"Who are Alys and Shannon?" Mirabel took a deep sip as she tried to put together information about her new rival Alys.

"Alys is Matilda's sister. She says Matilda left her to the wolves or something. I don't know. I don't care. Apparently she's rich and she'll pay anything for Shannon."

"How did this Matilda know to send a telegram here?" Mirabel sat on the edge of the bed; she reached for her dressing gown, her fear of him deepening as he spoke of revenge on an old enemy.

"Alys had three men follow her. If I had to guess, they didn't just follow her and keep their hands to themselves. It looks like Grayson got to Grant Brooks and beat my address out of him."

"Asher Grayson?" Fear tightened Mirabel's stomach into knots. She pulled the robe tight around her like a shield.

"The last cable from Brooks said they were both on the dock and got on the ship together, fighting though. I had the manifest checked. They just cleared immigration and are relocated on a different ship. The three men I sent to keep an eye are listed as prisoners."

Mirabel swallowed hard. "Did Brooks know I am living here?"

"Never mind Brooks." Royce tossed the rest of the whiskey back.

Mirabel's fear drummed through her as his eyes narrowed at her. Whiskey sloshed over the rim of her glass.

"There has been nothing further from Brooks, so I assume he's been arrested and has told them everything. I have something in mind for Detective Grayson." Finished with his tie, he turned to pick up his whiskey. "I can't wait to meet up with him."

"Grayson is a threat." Mirabel's eyes widened in fear. Her mind slid back to the last time Grayson had an altercation with Royce. She had refused to abort Tommy, Eli Pitman's child, and Royce had, at Eli's instruction, attacked her in the street outside the doctor's office. She remembered Grayson intervening and beating Royce mercilessly. Grayson was a straight cop.

Royce shrugged. "I have a plan for him. Get dressed. Odelia will be here any minute."

Royce went to the front door of the penthouse where his bodyguard stood.

"Odelia is stealing from me. This telegram says thirty thousand more than we agreed. Get rid of her."

"Royce's bodyguard, Creston, smiled.

"Stealing!" Creston shook his head. "We can't have that."

"No, we can't." Royce agreed.

Creston's eyes gleamed with anticipation.

Mirabel's heart pounded as she watched Odelia join the men at the top of the stairs. Her face creased in terror as she was handed the falsified telegram.

"I don't understand. Alys told me to ask for ten thousand. I am confused..." she looked wildly from Royce to Creston and then back to Royce.

Mirabel swallowed hard as she listened to the altercation.

Odelia's voice escalated in fear as she begged and then tried to negotiate with Royce.

Mirabel's heart hammered and her stomach twisted with guilt as Royce and Creston shut the door. Soon, the hallway was silent.

Shaking with horror at the events she had put into motion, Mirabel poured more whiskey into the tumbler and gulped it down.

I will do anything to get my son back. Anything.

Chapter Thirty-Two

Alys's eyes flicked over the telegram.

Matilda, asking for proof of life.

Lips thin, Alys squinted as she looked out the porthole over the water. After the storm, sun glittered across the ripples of the sea. The beauty did nothing to stifle the anger raging through her as she thought about Matilda, living in luxury as she scrambled to stay alive on the streets. Memories of humiliation and fear pulsed through her. There was no time to think of that, she needed a clear head; she shook the thoughts away.

Alys swept down the hallway to the room where Shannon was assisting three sick girls. The smell of urine, feces and vomit assaulted her as she opened the door.

"What is going on?" Her eyes landed on Belle, whose head rested on Shannon's lap.

Shannon stroked her hair back from her face.

"I need more supplies." Shannon's tone clipped with outrage. "The storm in the night knocked over the chamber pot. We need to clean up this area. Are there any more sick girls from the brig? If I don't treat them, every girl here will be dead by the end of the week."

Alys's chest tightened in fear at the thought of her investment wasting away in the bowels of the ship. "You know how to treat them?"

"Yes." Shannon didn't even look up.

How dare you disrespect me!

Alys turned on her heel to ask her guards to bring up any sick girls. Once they were all in the room and guards delivered fresh water, Shannon assigned the oldest girls to clean up the room. Shannon immediately started to assess the girls' health by taking their temperatures. Alys's eyes narrowed as she watched Shannon ignore her presence as she worked.

Don't you dare ignore me!

"Come with me." Alys took Shannon by the upper arm.

Shannon looked up in alarm.

Good, Matilda's pet is afraid.

Together, they made their way down a hallway to Alys's room. Hands on her hips, Shannon faced Alys.

Alys slammed the door shut behind them.

"Let me buy these girls." Shannon's eyes narrowed. "I will give you anything you want. I have access to all of Til's money. It's all yours."

"Not enough." Alys whirled to face Shannon. "I want Matilda."

"Why?" Shannon gasped.

Just the sight of Shannon, the one Matilda saved, caused fury to pound through Alys. "She owes me!" Alys hissed at Shannon.

"Let me pay it." Shannon stood tall.

"She owes her life for the one she stole from me!" Alys's icy tone frosted the air between them.

"It doesn't have to be this way. I can pay you whatever you want. What is the price for me and the girls? I can wire the money to you from the ship. You have a telegraph machine it's easy. Once the money is in your account, you can drop us off in Canada, and sail anywhere you want. There's no need to have the law involved. Name your price." Shannon held her hands out.

"It's gone too far." Alys's entire body shuddered as she shook her head. "No. We see this to the end. I need to know the name of Madeline Harper's baby." Alys demanded.

Shannon's head snapped up in surprise.

"Who wants to know?" Hope bloomed in Shannon's eyes.

Slapping Shannon as hard as she could; Alys delighted as the hope in Shannon's eyes was obliterated by a simple act of violence and replaced with fear and fury.

The softness of Shannon's skin against her rough, work- hardened palm sparked a rage inside Alys's heart that burned so bright, it threatened to consume her. Smooth skin—pampered life. The life she could have led if Matilda had stayed or came back to find her. The life that had been torn from Alys, disposed of like rubbish on the street.

"Talk or die." Alys's eyes narrowed to green slits of rage. "I am asking you for a name. If you don't give it, I will have Shipley Bristol beat it out of you. What is the name of Lady Harper's baby?"

Shannon pulled herself up and stood tall.

"No need. I'll do whatever you ask." Shannon ran her hands over her abdomen. "I am pregnant."

"You have that too?" Alys gasped and staggered at the news. "You have all Til's love, her money, a husband and now a baby... you have everything."Alys's face twisted with bitterness as she pounced on Shannon, so close she could see her heart beat hard with fear.

"You can too. I can make that happen..." Shannon pleaded.

"The name!" Alys hissed.

"All right." Shannon held her hands up to ward off a blow. "Madeline Harper's baby daughter's name is Amelia, Amelia Marie Kathleen."

"If you are lying..." Alys grabbed her by the upper arms hard enough to leave bruises.

"I am not. I will protect my child at any cost. Whatever you want, I'll do it." Shannon's breath caught with emotion.

"You really want to buy those twelve girls." Alys sneered at her.

"Yes," Shannon said immediately.

Alys tilted her head. "Why?" Alys roared at her as the rage inside her tore up her throat. "Why do you care about those girls? *Those worthless girls*!"

"All girls have worth, Alys. I care about anyone who is hurting or sick. That is my job." Shannon held her gaze. "I care about you, too."

"Liar." Alys whirled away from her; she dropped her hands and clenched her fists at her side. "You don't care. No one does." Alys despised herself as she heard her own voice catch with emotion.

"I promise you, when you come down with dysentery, and you will, you will be glad you got me more supplies." Shannon didn't back down; didn't take a step back. She braced for attack.

Alys hated Shannon with renewed zeal.

You are privileged and you dare judge me! I had nothing!. I crawled out of nothing with no help from anyone! You will pay for what happened to me. You will both pay. I will watch Matilda's eyes as I make you pay!

Alys breathed in sharply. "How do I know you won't kill those girls to get back at me?"

Shannon jaw dropped open at the accusation. "I am a doctor, I swore an oath. I would never bring harm to anyone! I would never harm twelve innocent girls!"

"So easy for you to be noble." Alys's breath caught with fury. "You stand there, judging me. You don't know where I've come from. Matilda protected you from the hell I endured."

"I do know where you came from, actually," Shannon whispered. "I came from the same place."

Alys slapped her again, with all her strength.

Shannon reeled, and she caught herself with the edge of the table, so she didn't fall to the floor.

"Don't you *dare* compare yourself to me!" Alys's chest tightened, a red veil of rage slid down over her vision, engulfing her in anger.

Shannon held onto the table.

"If you are lying, if you have given me a false name I will kill you." Alys jabbed her finger into Shannon's face.

"What about Martha?" Shannon whispered.

"Don't you speak about Martha," Alys hissed into Shannon's face. "Matilda ran. Like a spoiled child, she ran from the responsibility. She should have kept us all together. She should have protected us like she always did. She ran, and we suffered. *Jimmy died because of her.* Oh, how we suffered." A sob ripped through Alys's soul and escaped through her throat. "I won't stop until she loses everything. Money, you, everything." Blood pounded in Alys's ears. She shook her head to clear her thoughts. "When she dies, I will have peace. I won't have these thoughts anymore. It's perfect justice... perfect justice..." Alys muttered to Shannon and herself.

Shannon opened her mouth to speak and then closed it.

Gripping Shannon by the upper arm, Alys walked her back to the cabin that was a makeshift hospital. She opened the door and shoved her so she stumbled. The girls cleaned up as best as they could. They held onto each other, trembling in fear as Alys's eyes narrowed at them. The youngest one, Anna, sunny blonde hair, big blue eyes, they'd caught her by using a kitten in a carriage. She remembered how her eyes had lit up with excitement when Alys had handed her an orange kitten. Now, she blinked up at her with tears in her eyes.

Alys's vision clouded as she looked at the girl. Her innocence, her beauty, she had everything. No one could save her, just as no one had saved Alys. Adrenaline rushed through her at the thought.

How much money can I get for you?

Alys leaned down, took Anna by the upper arm, and whispered in her ear. "Shannon can't save you."

Anna trembled in fear.

Alys squeezed her narrow upper arm harder, until Anna cried out in pain.

"I am going to kill her," Alys hissed against Anna's ear. "I will sell you to the highest bidder."

Chapter Thirty-Three

Til lay in her bed and watched dust motes dance in the early morning light. Emotional pain dragged at her as she thought about losing Malcolm and Shannon. Tears filled her eyes as the sun streamed in through the window glowing on the wood furnishings in her cabin. Fear for Shannon's life warred with relief that the cramping had stopped; the baby was safe—for now. Taking a deep breath, she thought of how big the baby was now. Til moved her practiced hands over her abdomen. Too soon to feel anything, Til yearned for the day that the baby would move so she could assure herself that all was well.

Who will you look like? What will you do in your life? I promise to do my best, Speck, but I am terrified I will get it wrong.

Her heart broke at the thought of having this baby alone, without Malcolm.

"Your father loved you," she murmured as her hands moved over her womb. "Really loved you. Even though you won't get to meet him, I can tell you he thought the world of you. Already, you have had a great start in life, since you had a father who cared. My heart is broken. I miss him so much sometimes I can hardly breathe."

A knock at the door interrupted her thoughts.

Til crawled out of bed and pulled on a robe. She opened the door to a porter with Grayson standing behind.

He looked grim. "May I step in?"

"Of course." Til stepped aside to let them in.

The porter put her breakfast down on the table and left. Grayson sat down across from her. She fidgeted with the collar of her robe.

"Are you well?" Grayson picked up the teapot and poured the tea into two cups.

"I'm scared," Til answered honestly.

His eyes flicked over her. "Please eat something."

Til tucked unruly hair behind her ear. "I must look like a fright."

"You've been crying." Grayson's eyes softened in sympathy.

"It's hardest in the morning when I wake up. I remember that my husband is dead and my niece is stolen. The pain is fresh then." Til tightened the robe around her.

"I'm sorry."

Til nodded, her eyes filled with tears, she turned from him.

"Anyway, I'd say we both look like frights." Grayson arranged their breakfast on her table. She wiped her eyes on her sleeve. He handed her a teacup and saucer.

Til managed a weak smile.

Grayson looked like he'd been to the front line of a war.

"It looks as though you finished the interrogation without me." Til sat down and sipped her hot tea.

"Yes." Grayson's knuckles were bloody; he hadn't bothered to clean up and he didn't elaborate. He checked his pocket watch, took a sip of tea, and waited for her to eat something.

"I don't think it will stay down." Til sipped the tea and tested her stomach. "We dock tomorrow and I am unsure how this will all work out. I was hoping we would have heard something from Shannon by now."

"I have the name." A muscle jumped in Grayson's jaw.

TIl placed her teacup in the saucer and clasped her shaking hands in front of her on the table. Stomach twisting into knots of fear, she made a simple request. "Read it."

Grayson got up, knelt down in front of her, took her hands in his. Her eyes glittered with tears as she braced herself for the name he would give her.

"The name that came back is Amelia Marie Kathleen." His hands tightened on hers.

Til's breath came out in one long whoosh. "Oh, thank God."

Grayson gathered her to him and held her hard.

Sobs of relief tore out of her as she clung to him. "Thank you. Oh, I was so scared she was dead!"

The muscle of Grayson's shoulder was hard against her face. She shuddered in his arms.

Finally, when she calmed down, she pulled back and wiped her tears from her cheeks. "Thank you, I'm all right now. Sorry, I am being ridiculous. I hate to blame it on my condition, but this baby makes me cry at the drop of a hat."

"No need to apologise." Grayson got up and took his seat across from the breakfast table again. "Sol has reported back a few things, but I think you should eat first."

"Just tell me." Til waved her hand impatiently.

"Someone has murdered Odelia Shipley Bristol." Grayson sipped his tea. "They found her yesterday."

Til's head snapped up as she gasped. "Murdered? What does that mean?"

"Just murdered. I don't know what it means." Grayson shook his head. "I have no idea who would have ordered it."

Til frowned in confusion. "Who will I meet to get Shannon back?"

"I don't know but you will be the first to know when I do. I have men crawling all over Eli's old penthouse and everything he owned." Grayson leaned forward and buttered her toast for her. He handed her a piece. "Eat this before it gets cold."

"I can't bear it." Til waved the food away.

Grayson frowned. "One bite."

Grudgingly, Til took a bite. "It needs jam."

Grayson slathered jam on her toast. "You're like a cross between the world's grouchiest suffragette and a two-year-old," Grayson muttered. He handed her the toast, the way she liked it.

"No crust," Til requested.

"You're not serious." Grayson rolled his eyes and cut off her crusts. "Anyway, they won't quit until they have an answer."

"We have no way of reaching her. What will we do?" Til finished her toast. She got up and paced to the porthole.

"We wait." Grayson spoke grimly.

Til took a deep breath and let it out very slowly. She looked out over the ocean. "You wait. I can't. We have to take control of this. We need to rattle them."

"What do you mean?" Grayson's eyebrows raised in confusion.

"We dock tomorrow." Til turned around to face him. "You take me, in irons, to the constabulary and lock me up."

Grayson rubbed his forehead. "Why?"

Til ignored the question. "Did they find Mirabel's son?"

"Still searching." Grayson stood up. "What then? I take you into the constabulary, in irons, and then?"

"That's all you need to know." Til tossed her hair over her shoulder. "I can't have you fainting on me. This plan needs cunning and cool detachment. We will get Shannon and Nora back. I know how to do it."

"How are you going to do that in irons and locked in a constabulary?" Grayson narrowed his eyes with suspicion.

"Not a real arrest and it gives me an element of surprise." Til's heart lightened at the thought of catching Alys unawares.

"Why would you need an element of surprise? You will not be in harm's way. Your condition is delicate to say the least. You will be protected at all costs." Grayson crossed his arms over his chest.

"Stop sounding so ominous. Lots of women are pregnant and manage perfectly well!" Til reprimanded him.

"They aren't chasing white slavers and murderers across the Atlantic!" Grayson held his hands out.

"That is quite enough of that," Til hissed. "I'm fine if I rest. Anyway, listen, because I'm still devising a plan."

"Scheme?" Grayson leaned forward.

"Plan," Til snapped at him. "I'll let you know when I work it out." Til sat back down and took a sip of tea.

"I don't like this. What are you thinking?" Grayson sat down at the table across from her.

"You'll object." Til arched her eyebrow imperiously. "There is no reason to have a row about it now. We can row about it right before I carry it out."

"I hate this. So, we leave this ship like enemies tomorrow?" Grayson's eyes locked with hers as he conceded to wait to hear the rest of her plan.

"Mortal enemies," Til said softly.

His eyes burned into hers with intensity.

"Only we'll know it's not true." She smiled at him. "We are partners. I didn't think it was possible."

"It was touch and go for certain." Grayson grinned. "At first, I thought you were the worst sort of harpy I had ever come up against and then you spoke and confirmed it."

Til laughed out right.

"I dreaded the thought of trying to keep you alive even though I knew with certainty you would make me into an incurable."

"I may drive you into an incurable state *yet*. The investigation is not complete," Til warned him.

"Too right." Grayson handed her another piece of toast, crust cut off, jam slathered on it. "Don't get used to this treatment. I am only being nice because they stole your niece and you are in a fragile state. What do you call yourself? A forty-year-old pregnant fossil."

Til narrowed her eyes at him and snatched the toast out of his hand.

"All jesting aside, Til." Grayson rolled his eyes as he scraped the crusts to the side of the plate. "I realise you are the strongest woman I have ever had the privilege of knowing and I've known others. Cora, Mrs. King and Adeline are strong women and you are on their level."

"Your first opinion of me was correct." Til fidgeted with her toast. "I am high-handed, opinionated and the most difficult woman you have ever dealt with in your life. I will never change. So, you're stuck with me and tomorrow we leave this ship and I will face the worst sort of past anyone could ever have. I will have to take responsibility for what happened to Alys." Til shuddered.

"That rests with your father." Grayson moved closer to her. "Til Stone, the thought of you going up against Royce, the biggest predator in Toronto's history after Eli Pitman, makes me sick to my stomach." Grayson reached out and brushed a piece of hair away from her eye. "You should get some rest. Tomorrow will be a big day."

Til nodded, her heart pounded with fear of being in Royce's territory. "Sometimes, Grayson, the only way forward, is back."

"I know." His jaw clenched at the thought. "I can't bear the thought of you getting hurt. Royce is a powerful predator and who knows how extensive..."

Til shook her head. "Arrest me. Let's shake them up."

Chapter Thirty-Four

Mirabel Salter stood on the dock and watched as Detective Asher Grayson dragged Matilda Bertram off the ship in irons. Grayson's partner, Sol Stein, stood by and watched everyone on the dock. Mirabel pulled the brim of her hat down so he wouldn't recognise her.

Mirabel's eyes widened as she watched the beautiful woman try to fight out of Detective Grayson's grip. Detective Grayson easily overpowered her. Her head only came up to his broad shoulder. Tiny compared to him, he held her by the upper arm and dragged her to a carriage.

Even from the distance, Mirabel could see they made a striking couple. His tall, dark, powerful body contrasted against her delicate build. Disheveled, a lock of coppery blonde hair had torn free of a pin and cascaded down her back. The late October wind picked up her black skirt, causing it to billow around her. Mirabel's breath caught. Matilda carried herself like a queen. She whirled on Grayson and didn't back down when he towered over her. Mirabel couldn't hear what he said to Matilda, but she erupted, defiantly scowling up at him screaming that he was abusing his authority.

Mirabel bit her lip as Grayson completely ignored her. When he opened the door to the carriage, she tried to break free of him and Grayson simply picked her up and thrust her inside. He slammed the door shut to drown out her accusations of abuse.

Mirabel watched, fascinated, as Sol and Grayson took a moment, exchanged a few words, and then together they escorted Grant Brooks and his two men into another carriage. Mirabel swallowed hard. If Grayson had arrested Matilda, what did that mean? Was she in cahoots with Grant Brooks? Had she somehow seduced him to help her take over Royce's ring?

Mirabel's heart pounded at the thought. She hated surprises; this Matilda or Til being arrested was bad. Matilda knew where Royce lived, she had sent a telegram there. She knew where Mirabel lived… she moved closer to the carriage and watched as Grayson and Stein got in with Til and took her away.

Terrified the money would not show up on a dock for Nora and now Shannon, Mirabel scampered off to report to Royce.

You get rid of one threat and another just pops up. Who is Alys and why did they need to kidnap Shannon? It added too much risk.

Alys would have a fight on her hands; Mirabel had outsmarted Odelia, Alys was next. Mirabel wasn't returning to the laundry on Lester Street.

***

Til tried to take in the sights and sounds of the docks of Toronto before the carriage started to move forward.

"Mirabel was on the dock." Sol shook his head. "Let me out, I'll follow her."

"Thanks." Grayson moved his knees out of the way so Sol could get out of the carriage.

As Sol slipped out, the crowd immediately swallowed him.

"He's a man of few words." Til pulled her attention to the families weeping and hugging each other as they were reunited.

"He despises drama and emotion, so how he puts up with me and my life is a mystery." Grayson shook his head as he looked out the window of the carriage.

A smile tugged at Til's lip. She tried to stop it but couldn't. As the carriage made its way to the constabulary, Til collapsed into laughter.

"I'm glad you find my life so amusing." Grayson frowned at her.

Til held her sides she laughed so hard.

"How long have you been partners?" she asked when she finally calmed down.

Since we fought side by side to get his wife, they were courting then, through a throng of angry men."

"Why were they angry?" Til wiped tears from her eyes from laughing.

"She was being sworn in as Canada and Great Britain's first female lawyer. She had taken the top marks at the bar and they hated her. They tried to stop her, but Sol had me and my men on site. I liked how he handled himself. Sol and Cora were our closest friends."

"Were." Til tilted her head to the side.

"Well, my closest friends still. No longer a couple friend." Grayson turned his attention to the street.

"I see."

Grayson took a deep breath and let it out slowly. "Oh, here we go. The Dominion Women's Enfranchisement Association is here. No wonder Sol leaped out of the carriage as soon as he could."

"Who are they?" Til gasped as a group of women stood outside the constabulary.

"Every man's worst nightmare," Grayson said grimly. He flashed her a quick smile. "I am speaking in jest. They heard you were on your way to Canada, so they are here to welcome you."

"Even though I'm in irons?"

"Most of them have been in irons." Grayson frowned and shook his head. "I hate it. That they have to protest. It's ridiculous. Until I met Cora, I hadn't thought at all about women's rights, ever."

"Ever?"

"It really didn't come up. If any woman in my life thought her rights were being trampled, she never mentioned it." Grayson shot her a look that indicated women in his life were guaranteed to have all their needs met.

Til rolled her eyes at him.

Grayson chuckled. "However, when I met Cora and saw what she was up against to be sworn in as a lawyer, it changed my thinking. I watched her have to manipulate and outsmart a law to get Adeline Pitman, now Martin, a divorce and money. It shocked me, the lack of rights for women in divorce court. You can know it, but until I watched Adeline go through it, I didn't understand how bad things were. It felt like the courts were bare knuckle boxing with her. It was a good day when we got to drag Eli Pitman to jail and hang him. Don't be fooled by Cora, she's pretty, has a delicate look to her, but she is fierce. Fiercer now she has Sol behind her. She doesn't back down from anything. Domestic abuse is what she deals with the most. Wife beaters take one look at him standing behind her and they scatter."

"He's a champion for equal rights too?" Til raised her eyebrows in surprise.

Grayson grinned. "I think he would *love* to have some equality in their relationship. He gave up a lot of his rights when he married her."

"*He* gave up rights?" Til's jaw dropped.

"There was no love, honour and obey in their wedding vows." Grayson adjusted the curtain over the window in the carriage. It was love, honour and *cherish*. They discuss things as a couple and usually because Sol is completely head over heels in love with Cora, whatever Cora wants, Cora gets."

Til grinned. "I can't wait to meet her; sounds like they have a perfect arrangement."

"I thought you might think that." Grayson shook his head. "You're in luck; Cora is right in the front line, leading that battalion of women."

Til's eyes scanned the crowd, she smiled as she picked Cora out. Standing in a black dress against all the white, chestnut hair piled high, green eyes flashing with excitement, Til recognised a kindred spirit when she saw one. This Cora was a warrior. There was a glint in her eye Til had seen in her own. She itched to meet her.

"Ohhhh, I will like her." Til beamed.

"I hope so, because if you don't get along, it will be terrible for everyone. However, I don't know what to hope for because if you do get along, I'm sure, together, you will try to take over the world," Grayson said dryly. "My knuckles will be as bloody as Sol's. You know, Sol and I yearn for a peaceful life. He wanted to be a farmer in Gimli."

"Good heavens, that sounds terrible." Til shuddered.

Grayson laughed. "You even sound like her. It's a pity neither of us know how to say no to beautiful women."

The carriage ground to a halt.

Til sniffed. "No time to be throwing around the word 'beautiful', sir. We are in no condition to be starting into any *courting session*, Detective Grayson. Remember yourself."

Grayson threw back his head and laughed. "Courting session! You make it sound like a criminal investigation and trial."

"It is an investigation of *sorts*." Til's eyes narrowed. "To find all the skeletons in the closet as it were."

"Malcolm must have been an absolute saint to put up with you." Grayson shook his head.

"You keep saying that," Til sniffed.

"I keep thinking it, as I'm cutting off your crusts and serving you your tea the exact way you like it." Grayson rolled his eyes. "When you've had this child, and you are safe, you're making your own toast."

"I think you secretly enjoy it," Til teased him.

"I assure you I do not. When you are not in a delicate state, I expect you to bring me my tea and toast as I like it." Grayson put his hand on the handle of the carriage door.

Til grinned at him. "I can assure you that will never happen. Not in this lifetime or the next."

"All right, Miss. Remember, you are in irons, under arrest and you hate me until we get to the interrogation room and then we'll have a strategy session." Grayson's eyes flicked over her as if expecting her to argue with him.

"All these women know who I am?" Til put her hand on Grayson's arm to stop him from opening the carriage door.

"Advocate for birth control. I'd say they know who you are." Grayson's voice deepened.

"I can't wait to meet them." Til flashed Grayson a smile as he threw open the door of the carriage and dragged her out. For a split second she forgot to fight him. He nudged her to remind her she needed to keep up the act. She screamed insults at him and tried to pull back. He caught her around the waist and half carried her across the pavement to the howl of protest from the women.

Cora fell into step behind them. "Detective Grayson, I am here to represent Til Stone as her legal counsel," she raised her voice so she would be heard.

The door to the constabulary opened. Til screamed at Grayson. "This is police brutality!"

Grayson picked her up and carried her into the interrogation room, Cora followed close behind him. Then the door slammed shut on the prying eyes of the constabulary.

"Til Stone." Cora's brilliant green eyes flashed with excitement. "I've read of your accomplishments. How you battled to the front lines of the women's right's movement! I know what that takes. A pleasure to meet you, finally!" Cora held her hand out.

Grayson took off Til's irons.

"No." Til rubbed her wrists and then took Cora's outstretched hand. "The pleasure is all mine. First woman barrister for Upper Canada and Great Britain. I take my hat off to you." Til beamed at her, secretly wondering if Cora would live up to Grayson's glowing reports.

"Never mind that." Cora waved the compliment away. "You are on the leading edge of the birth control movement. The single most pressing need for women since the dawn of time. What you have done for women is astounding." Cora shook her head. "I can't tell you how much I look forward to watching your career. However, we have a lot of work to do and some new developments." Cora got straight to work. She opened her big brief case and pulled out file after file, map after map, and a pile of telegrams from England.

"Grayson, would you mind getting us some food?" Cora asked.

Grayson looked from Cora to Til and then back to Cora. They attacked the piles of information and sorted things neatly.

"I'm just here to run for your food while you take over my operation?" Grayson protested. "I don't think so."

Cora frowned at him. "Don't be difficult. Til is hungry, and I can't leave. I have to bring her up to date. How do you take your tea?" Cora asked Til.

"Oh, he knows how I like my tea." Til waved her hand to dismiss him.

"You need to bring us both up to date," Grayson huffed as he went to the door and dispatched a constable to bring enough food and tea for the three of them.

"Four," Cora corrected. "Sol should be here any minute."

Grayson muttered something about bossy women which Cora and Til ignored. They had been called much worse. He adjusted the order and turned back into the interrogation room. Til's eyes filled with tears, reading the telegrams from Cole.

"Listen." Cora took Til's hand in her own. "Listen to me. Shannon is here in this city and we know this city. We took down Eli; we *will* take down Royce."

"Sorry. I am gutted by this. Cole must be out of his mind with worry." Til shook her head as she reread the telegrams.

"Very likely. We just need a plan. I brought maps and tax rolls for every piece of property Rodd Royce owns."

Til nodded and gathered the maps for closer examination. "We need to check for property Royce Bristol owns. Rodd Royce is his alias. Also, they didn't go through immigration. Where would they dock the ship if they didn't go through immigration?"

Cora tapped her lip with her finger. "They must have a private dock of some sort, somewhere... I don't know." She shook her head. Picking up a pencil, she scratched down the name 'Royce Bristol'. Her eyes met Til's. "What else do you know?"

"Not much." Til read telegrams from Cole saying he knew Shannon and Alys Bertram were on a ship and that they would arrive in Toronto three days before Til.

"How did they get here before you? As I understand, they left after." Cora tilted her head in confusion.

"Alys is in a better class of ship, and we lost a day of travel in immigration." Til placed the telegrams in a pile near the tax rolls.

A knock on the door and Sol slipped into the room. "Grayson, a moment please?"

"What is it?"

Sol opened the door wider; all three looked up to see a beautiful blonde woman in the doorway holding a baby girl.

"Melinda!" Grayson's head snapped up in surprise.

Chapter Thirty-Five

Til frowned as delicate, beautiful, Melinda collapsed, weeping into Grayson's arms. As she pressed her forehead into his broad shoulder he took the baby girl from her and somehow juggled them both as she sobbed against him.

"I'll see to this and return." Grayson moved Melinda back into the corridor. "I'll be back in a moment. Sol, can you take notes?"

With that he closed the door behind them.

"I should go with him." Cora got to her feet and Sol held his hand out to stop her.

"What's going on?" Til directed her question to Cora.

"Melinda is Grayson's soon-to-be-former wife. Ella is his daughter. He gave her up in the divorce." Cora's face gave nothing away.

He gave up his daughter! Would he have given up a son?

"Why is she back?" Cora asked Sol. "I thought this was final and they were just waiting on the paperwork."

"I'm not sure; there is a bruise on her cheekbone." Sol's mouth thinned with concern. "Looks like Archie the butcher isn't what she thought he was."

"I really should go... she's my friend..." Cora frowned at Sol and moved to the door. Sol stepped in front of her, stopping her from interfering in Grayson's domestic situation.

"She's his wife. He'll figure it out." Sol sighed.

Til remembered Grayson saying Sol despised dramatics.

"Not anymore, Sol." Cora's eyes flashed in fury.

"You said so yourself, the divorce is not final yet," Sol said simply. "I know Grayson and he'll do the honourable thing. They have a daughter together."

Til tried to imagine him giving up his daughter and couldn't.

I expected better from him. Why would he do such a thing?

Cora tidied up the telegrams as they waited.

Grayson re-entered the interrogation room.

"Can Melinda stay with you for a few days until we get this sorted out?"

"Of course," Sol replied.

"Is she all right?" Cora asked quietly.

"Looks like Archie is having a hard time keeping a job." Grayson's lips were thin. He took a key from Sol. "He is moving to Baltimore to work for his uncle. However, his family is quite religious, he doesn't want to show up with a fiancée that has a baby. They will not accept a divorced woman into their family. If she goes, she has to leave Ella with me. If she stays… I'm not sure how things will go if she stays." Grayson took a deep breath and let it out slowly. "They have been fighting; she has a bruise on her cheekbone. She wondered if she could stay with me."

"That would end your divorce proceedings!" Cora gasped. "Is she back for good? Will you take her back?"

"I would prefer if she didn't stay with me." Til noticed Grayson avoided answering the question.

"Are you sure it wouldn't be an imposition if she stays with you both?" Grayson asked Sol and Cora.

"Of course not. I'll send notice to our staff to expect her right away." Cora left the room.

"Let's get back to work, shall we." Grayson shot a look at Til.

Til mutinously met his gaze and then dropped her eyes to the table. She tidied up piles of paper that didn't need to be tidied up.

Why did you give up your daughter? How could you do that? Does she have no worth in your eyes? Just as my father I had no worth? I trusted you on that ship, now I feel like I don't even know you. I was wrong.

"Odelia Shipley Bristol was murdered a couple of days ago, as you know." Sol took control of the room. "Alys Bertram and Shannon McDougall are in Toronto. They didn't go through immigration, so it's anyone's guess where they are now. Maybe the penthouse on Bleeker? It's a long shot."

Til's heart pounded as she spoke to Sol. "I can go to the penthouse on Bleeker tonight and take them off guard. They think I am in custody."

"This was the plan you spoke of on the ship?" Grayson's stance widened. "Absolutely not! You have no idea what you are walking in on."

"I'm not giving up Shannon without a fight," Til said bitterly.

Like you gave up your daughter.

Grayson frowned in confusion.

Til turned her attention to Sol. "Would you offer your protection if I go to Bleeker?"

"This is my investigation and it is my final decision," Grayson growled at Til. "Your safety is my first priority."

Til lifted her chin and faced Grayson across the desks and the maps. "Shannon is my first priority. I'm not waiting a week. We go tonight."

"You are *not* going to Royce Bristol's apartment tonight." Grayson pointed a finger at her.

"I have to. I go to that dock, I'm as good as dead." Til shot back at him.

Sol nodded his agreement. Grayson frowned at Sol and straightened up.

"We stay with the plan." A muscle in Grayson's jaw jumped as he spoke and then clenched his teeth.

Pacing in fury and fear, Til whirled on him.

"How dare you?" she hissed.

"I am the detective in charge of this case. You will do as you are told," Grayson warned her.

Til's mouth opened and then shut.

Sol shifted in his seat. Cora re-entered the room and sat down beside Sol.

"I am the lead on this," Grayson reminded everyone in the room.

Til's eyes narrowed to slits. She stood in front of him, hands on hips. She couldn't go up against Royce without him. He knew it. He had the upper hand. Hot anger seethed through her.

"If she could turn Mirabel, we could bring all this to a close much quicker," Sol suggested calmly. "We could attack tonight. It's not a bad plan. Alys could hide forever in this city. We get into that apartment; there might be correspondence from Alys to Royce. Who knows what we'll find!"

"I disagree." Cora stood up to interject. "I know you want to take them by surprise, but think of what you might step in on."

Til drew herself up to her full height. "I don't care."

"You might," Cora countered. "When I went after Eli Pitman, I saw him shoot a man and sell thirteen girls. I still remember. It has scarred me for life. I wake up at night thinking of it. I worry for you if you see something like that. Will you be able to cope?"

"I am from an East End slum, I'll manage," Til said dryly. "However, if something happens to Shannon that I could prevent, that will destroy me." Til's tone hardened as her eyes clashed with Cora's. "I can't live with that."

Cora held her hands up. "I just thought I would mention it. It's traumatic."

Til shook her head. "It's traumatic either way," Til asserted. "I say we go tonight."

"But we *know* she wants to confront you November 2nd. That is the date." Grayson's lips thinned, his cold gaze swept over all of them.

"But if we go in and get Royce out of the way tonight, we face only one predator on November 2nd, not two," Til snapped at Grayson. "If there is a chance I might get Shannon back sooner, I have to take it. Sol, I ask you again, would you come with me if Grayson refuses?"

"I answer to Detective Grayson, he's my boss." Sol crossed his arms over his chest.

Til threw her hands up in the air. "So. You just have the final say and there is nothing anyone can do? Is that how it is? Am I reduced to waiting for permission from *you* to save Shannon? Is that how it is going to work now that we are on land?" Til's voice cracked from fear and fury.

Grayson scrubbed his hands over his face. "Til, please. We'll find a solution."

Til's nails bit into her palms as she took another tactic. "You said Mirabel has a son. Where is he?" Til whirled on Cora.

"Mrs. King is bringing him this afternoon."

Til heard warning in Cora's voice.

"I'll need a gun," Til said to Grayson.

Cora looked up in alarm.

"We are not arming civilians with guns!" Grayson exploded.

"Sol." Til turned her back on Grayson. "I will need a gun. Nothing too big. Something I can use at short range. Who is Detective Grayson's boss? I'll go over his head."

A knock at the door interrupted their argument.

Sol looked at Grayson.

Grayson groaned.

"Don't remove my element of surprise," Til warned him.

Grayson grit his teeth and moved to the door to open it. "Sol, get her a derringer. I better show her how to use it."

Grayson opened the door to an older woman with steel coloured grey hair and a baby in her arms.

"Mrs. King and Tommy!" Cora smiled at her and indicated she enter the room and take Grayson's chair. Mrs. King took a seat as the coach driver followed behind her with a bassinet, and a small suitcase.

"How are you?" Cora reached for the baby.

"I'm fine," Mrs. King said as she handed the baby to Cora. "But, Tommy is very sick. I picked him up at the orphanage just an hour ago. Appalling place."

Til moved to Cora and immediately placed her hand on Tommy's forehead.

"He has a fever," Til murmured. "I will examine him."

Cora handed Til the child.

"I'll need my bag while you go and fetch me a gun," Til commanded Grayson.

"I'll be back shortly." Grayson bolted from the room.

"He's been sick on and off for weeks apparently." Mrs. King's lips pursed together in disapproval. "While I wanted to object to taking a child to use as leverage, it seems it may save his life."

Til ignored Mrs. King's judgements as she unwrapped his thin blanket to do an examination. She pressed her ear to his heart and hoped Grayson was quick with her medical bag.

"Poor little darling." Til wrapped him back up against the chill.

"There is a bottle of milk here." Mrs. King rummaged in the carpet bag.

"I'll see if there is any fresh milk I can warm up." Cora took the bottle from Mrs. King and quickly left the room.

Grayson returned with three doctor's bags. "I wasn't sure which one."

Close on his heels with a bottle, Cora closed the door behind them.

Til handed the baby to Grayson to free her to pull a box of vials out of her bag. She laced his milk with actinilid and added sugar. There was no need of the sugar to mask the taste of the actinilid; he was so hungry he drained the bottle in minutes.

"Goodness. He's starving!" Cora's eyes were hard with fury. "I'll refill the bottle."

Cora raced to refill the bottle with milk.

Til wrapped him securely in a blanket as he wept.

"Mrs. King, are there fresh napkins, clothing and blankets in that case? He needs a bath and another bottle and fresh clothes to change into."

Cora was back in record time. She stood near Til and pressed her hand against his forehead.

"Poor little darling." Cora caressed his cheek.

Til shook her head. "I hate this, I see far too much of this."

"It doesn't matter how many social programmes." Cora shook her head and handed Til the bottle. Little Tommy Salter drank the milk as if he had never seen food before.

"If you don't educate women, you will only *ever* have social programmes," Til finished her sentence. She pursed her mouth in fury. Their eyes met over the head of the baby. "Mirabel would make half what a man makes at the same job. She'd barely be able to put food in her own mouth never mind the child's."

Cora's eyes hardened with equal fury. "I feel helpless when I see this."

Once fed and his fever under control, Tommy was changed into fresh nappies and clean clothes. "I'll bathe him at home. I don't want him to catch a chill," Cora said.

"That is a good idea." Til gathered Tommy into her arms and swayed back and forth until he fell asleep. She sat back down on a chair as Tommy slept like a heavy weight against Til's shoulder.

"If you were in my place, would you go tonight?" Til's gaze met Cora's and held it.

"This girl is like a daughter to you?" Cora asked.

"Yes," Til confirmed patting Tommy's back.

"It's a terrible thing, to go up against a predator like that." Cora took a deep breath and let it out slowly.

"How many girls did you protect by going that night? You stopped the ring for two years. How many lives did you save?" Til met her gaze and didn't look away.

"I don't know. But, honestly, it's ugly, what these men are doing. Maybe you are strong enough." Cora crossed her arms over her chest.

"There is no maybe about it. They have Shannon and I will stop at nothing to get her back. I don't have a choice." Til pressed her lips together, finally she spoke. "Shannon is everything to me."

"Well, they expect you to be in jail." Cora sided with Til. "As you said, you would have an element of surprise. You should take it. You're right. I know Mirabel; she's a mother and she'll do anything for this child. She must have been completely out of options to leave him at an orphanage as sick as he is. To run to Rodd Royce is… well, she's desperate. "

"Royce is a terrible man." Til shuddered.

"Yes, he is. You're like me though; you've been up against terrible men before. The more terrible the man, the more we need a strategy." Cora patted Tommy's back as he snuggled into Til's neck.

Til's heart strings pulled as he sighed against her neck. Tears stung behind her eyes as his breath caught.

Cora's eyes softened in sympathy as she watched Tommy.

"The poor darling is starved for love and attention." Cora shook her head and then met Til's gaze. "Back to Royce, I remember when I came up against Eli, I had to let him think he was in complete control. He made a fatal mistake, thinking he had the upper hand. He thought I was a stupid and emotional woman. I played that role as much as possible to trap him. When you go up against Royce, you have to make sure he thinks he has total control over you. What does he think about you or women, and how can you use it to outsmart him?"

Til took a deep breath. "He thinks all women from the East End are worthless. The best way to be worthless is to go in there dressed as a prostitute. Do you have access to clothing like that?"

"I do. Scads of it at Hope House. I will get you a dress," Cora promised.

"I can't let Grayson see me in the sort of dress a prostitute would wear; he would have fifty fits." Til moved to lay Tommy down in the bassinet Mrs. King had brought. The minute she let go of him he woke up, terrified.

"Goodness, he's afraid he's being left alone." Til shook her head and reached for him again. As Tommy snuggled back into her embrace, memories of Jimmy made Til's throat tighten with sorrow. She patted his back and pulled the blanket tighter around him. She drew her attention back to the matter at hand. "We'll have to hide it. If you could find me something to cover me until it's too late for Grayson to force me to redress, that would be helpful."

"I'll go right now and get that for you," Cora said softly. "I was going to take Tommy to the nursery in Hope House, but I dare say, he isn't going to leave you."

"It feels good." Til hugged him against her tightly. "All these years, I never took time to hold the babies; I handed them to their mothers, cleaned up, and moved on. I've never really held a child like this since my brother Jimmy." Despite her best efforts to leave the past in the past, tears filled Til's eyes.

Jimmy was this age when I fled. He felt like this in my arms. What happened to Jimmy?

"All that feels so long ago, and yet it still makes my heart ache. He was the youngest... I never found him." Her voice faded away. "I never found any of them."

"I can't imagine that pain." Cora's eyes softened in sympathy. "When I went up against Eli; he had a boat load of girls. Sol and I watched them be sold. It haunts me still. The girls we couldn't protect." Cora jaw tightened. "A wise friend once said let the injustice spur you on. So, I will say it to you. Sometimes, we have to confront the past to rebuild the future."

"Thank you, I so badly want to believe that." Til pressed her lips against Tommy's temple. "That is very kind of you to say. Your wise friend is right."

Quiet filled the room as the women listened to Tommy breathe.

Til shifted him a little. "He smells good."

"That's how they trap you." Cora smiled at Til. "Can I make the silliest confession? Sometimes, I just smell Silas's night shirt and remember all the late-night feedings when it was just us. I would fall in love with him more every night."

Til smiled.

"Now, he's getting big! I look at those tiny little shirts and wonder how he ever fit into them. When I want to remember those nights, I have shirts I will never part with, I sneak into the closet and smell to my heart's content." Cora chuckled. "Sol laughs at me and wants another baby, but I know my body isn't ready."

"I can help you with that," Til offered.

"Why do you think I was the first woman in the room?" Cora grinned. "Trying to get access to contraception in Toronto is like pulling hen's teeth. So difficult. Do you happen to have..." Cora glanced at the door in case someone was hovering and listening.

"I brought boxes of it." Til's eyes crinkled at the corners. "I marked the boxes as knitting supplies. I'll trade you a prostitute gown for contraception."

"Done." Cora laughed. "We sound so wicked!"

Til smiled. "I've never worried about what people think of me."

"Me either." Cora shrugged. "You can't in our line of work; you'd never get anything done."

Cora pressed her hand against Tommy's back. "You're good with him."

"In all honesty, Cora. I'm terrified of having a child." Til hugged him tighter.

"You're pregnant!" Cora gasped.

"I know. Pregnant and forty," Til groaned. "Please, I've heard it all. No need to..."

"No! I wasn't going to say that!" Cora's eyes softened. "To lose your husband; in a new land and facing this; it's too much for anyone."

"How hard is it?" Til cut straight to the point, as one professional woman to another. "Do you regret having a child? You have a profession and so much to juggle."

"Oh, it's not like that. I would never regret having a child." Cora shook her head. "He's my heart. I worried too, about the impact on my work. It was scary to think of the responsibility and it's not really something you can hire done."

Til's heart sunk at the thought of not being able to hire the work done.

"You know, feeding and that sort of thing. Don't get me wrong, I have a team of servants so I can do both, but it is very hard to leave him. It's so hard."

Til's brows knit together in confusion.

"We're used to climbing ladders. Do this exam, learn this skill, apply and move up. Always, strategising —what is the next move, the next hurtle to jump closer to the goal. Of course, the ultimate goal is your own practice, or clinic. Right?"

Til nodded in agreement.

"Being a mother is so hard, there is no ladder. No way to gauge success. I find myself wishing for a chart I can tick off. You always feel like you aren't enough. Work is now one part of life, not the whole part. Marriage, that's another part, but the babies. Well, the babies are the joy, sparkle and zest of life!"

"Zest?" Til's eyebrows shot up. "That's a little high flown don't you think?"

"Maybe," Cora conceded. "I just think they bring all the enthusiasm and spirit to life. You are going to be a lovely mother. Yes, this baby will change your life, but it will make it worth living all the more."

"I don't know how work is one part..." Til sputtered, she frowned at Cora. "I am not sure I follow you."

"But marriage..."

"Marriage had to fit around work." Til clenched her teeth, braced herself for judgement in Cora's eyes.

Cora tilted her head to the side. Til saw a softening there, no judgement.

"Everything came second to work, Cora." In the absence of judgement, Til confessed. "It was the only way to be sure I would be safe, never in poverty again. What you're describing, well, that's completely foreign to me. Marriage didn't spur me on, babies didn't give me purpose. My whole life, I have worked..."

"Why? Why work so hard, for so long? What was behind it?" Cora leaned in to listen.

Cora's gentle tone slid past the wall of ice around Til's heart, probing deep into the emotions hiding there. Exposing them, finally laying them bare. The truth about Til surfaced in her soul.

Til's mouth dropped open, tears filled her eyes. "Gracious, Cora," Til gasped as realisation dawned in her. "Fear."

Tears spilled down Til's cheeks as Cora put her arms around Til.

"It's all right."

"It's not all right." Til's voice roughened in pain. "Every motivation, every minute of my life since November 2nd, 1881 has been tainted by fear and it has been a cruel master."

"What happened that day?" Cora tightened her arms around Til. "Tell me."

"My father sold me to the landlord to pay the rent. He lost me in a poker game." Til rattled off the painful experience as if she was ordering milk for her tea. "Since then..."

"Since then, you expect every man to do the same thing. Put their needs ahead of yours. Use you to pay for their mistakes," Cora finished her sentence.

Til gasped at the accuracy of the statement. So clear and true. She pulled back and was surprised to see sympathy in Cora's eyes.

"Yes," Til said simply.

"What happened to you is a crime, a crime I wish I could prosecute." Cora rubbed Til's arms. "There are very good men in this world. They are not all like that."

Til nodded. "I'm slowly learning that, but it is so hard to trust. I worried about my niece with her husband." Til wiped her eyes with Tommy's blanket. "All the time I was harping on her to be careful about giving her heart to a man; little did I know, it would be my past that would ultimately destroy her. I can't believe it. I should have taken more precautions when Bobby was gunned down in the streets, I should have..."

"There is no need to beat yourself up." Cora shook her head. "We need cool heads and a plan. That's all we need right now."

Til's heart clouded with worry. "If you were Alys Bertram, where would you take Shannon?" Til asked quietly so as not to disturb the baby.

"Don't think about Royce or Alys." Cora's eyes met Til's, she held her gaze.

"What do you mean?" Til's muscles tightened in her neck as she heard those names together.

"You go after Mirabel. That's your target. She's the weak link. She has nothing to lose and everything to gain by cooperating with you. When you present yourself as a worthless prostitute to Royce, it will work against Mirabel too."

Til's eyes gleamed with anticipation as she lay Tommy Salter down in his basket.

"Press down on his chest as soon as you lay him down, just like this... it settles him," Cora suggested.

Til did as she instructed and sure enough Tommy settled. "I don't have the first clue."

"You'll learn, and I'll help you any way I can. This is the unwritten code of women, Til. We're up against the impossible, so we hang onto each other and try to navigate motherhood as best we can." Cora patted Til's shoulder.

"Today, you don't have to think about motherhood. Just get through this crisis. Back to Mirabel. She needs to think you have no options, like her. If by some chance she sees you interact with Grayson, he has to treat you as if you are worthless in front of her. You have to be *on her level*. Take down Mirabel, the rest will fall into place." Cora's voice hardened with intensity. "This is a game and you need Mirabel to be your partner. She needs her son; she needs money and a new life out of here. She'll take it wherever she can get it."

"You *are* brilliant," Til breathed. She recognised the same fierce determination in Cora that burned in her. Amidst all the horror she was facing, it was clear Cora was fast becoming a friend. Her first real friend. Her equal in every way. Cora could show her ways to live and love that were foreign to her. Shannon, as her niece, was a friend but not like this. Her heart shed a layer of ice as she reached out to Cora and held onto her as if she were a life preserver in a storm.

Cora hugged her back to offer comfort. "Take down Mirabel. Then you can't fail."

"Right." Til shivered, because going after Mirabel meant going up against Royce. "Mirabel."

Chapter Thirty-Six

Later that same night, when Tommy Salter was safely tucked into Cora and Sol's nursery on Cherry Street, Til waited in the interrogation room. She tapped her fingertips on the gleaming oak table hoping Cora wasn't delayed. The lamplight glowed over paneling along the walls. Til decided she hated the dull colour of green on the walls, it did nothing to accent the wood. A warm caramel colour would have been better, although this room was for confessions, not tea and crumpets.

Just after midnight, Cora slipped into the interrogation room and opened the bag of clothes. "Quick, before the men get here. Get changed." Cora's eyes darted around until the door was firmly shut.

"Blimey." Til's hands shook. "I'm a nervous wreck."

Cora helped her pull off respectability and pull on a dress a strumpet would wear.

Once they were done, Cora stood back. "You'll look more like a prostitute if you let your hair down." Cora's eyes swept over Til.

"Thank you for bringing this." Til pulled the long coat over her scandalous attire and buttoned it.

"Do you need anything else?" Cora asked as she packed Til's good clothes away.

"Make sure Tommy has more actenilid; he is teething and it will relieve his pain and keep his fever down." Til smoothed the skirt down so the torn lace on the bottom of her dress wouldn't show.

"I will." Cora moved to the door. "Good luck tonight. Remember, Til. If you can't go through with it; if you can't face Royce, there is no shame in that."

"He has my niece." Til's heart pounded in her throat at the thought.

"I know." Cora's eyes softened in sympathy. "Be careful, stay safe."

Til nodded and braced herself as Cora left the interrogation room and the men came in.

Tension filled the room as Grayson, Sol, and Constable Collins and Haggerty joined Til a little after one in the morning.

"You changed your clothes?" Grayson closed the door behind the last man that entered.

"Cora was worried I would be cold. She brought me a change of clothes and a coat," Til lied smoothly.

"Good," Grayson said distractedly as he paced around the room and checked his pocket watch.

Sol handed him his rifle.

Grayson loaded a derringer with bullets and placed it on the table, barrel pointing away from Til. He adjusted a strap on a holster designed to fit inside her boot.

"If Royce Bristol puts a hand on you, I want you to put this in his ribs and pull the trigger." A muscle jumped out in Grayson's jaw.

Til's stomach twisted with guilt as she looked at the gun on the table in front of her. Having sworn an oath to heal, not harm, her conscience accused her of being false to her vow. Palms slick with the sweat of trepidation, she reached out to pick up the gun and then pulled her hand back.

"You're not up for this," Grayson growled at Til.

"I am. I am not going to wait until we're all standing on a dock like a bunch of fish in a barrel. We have to take Royce by surprise. It's now or never." Til shot back at Grayson.

"For the record, I don't know when we started arming women with weapons and expecting them to take down white slavers. It's lunacy," Grayson muttered under his breath.

"Is he always like this?" Til asked Sol. A trickle of sweat slid down her back. With the heavy coat over her dress and the added warmth of being pregnant, Til felt like she was boiling alive.

"He's emotional." Sol grinned at Grayson as if this was a common joke between them.

Grayson's granite like expression showed no evidence of being amused.

Til wiped her palms on her coat, and then silently commanded herself to reach out and pick up the derringer. The weight of it surprised her. She balanced it as if it were a tool she was about to use in surgery.

Grayson knelt down in front of her to attach the holster to her ankle.

Nervous that he would see evidence of her prostitute's attire, she carefully pulled her skirt up, making sure the lace stayed hidden from his sight.

He hesitated and dropped the holster as she exposed her ankle to him. Scrambling to pick it up, taking a deep breath, he attached the holster to the inside of her boot around her ankle.

"Does that feel secure?" Grayson's voice sounded strangled.

Til slid the little gun into the holster and then unconsciously pressed her hand against a small knife she had sewn into her corset.

"It feels secure." She tugged at it to ensure it didn't loosen.

He looked up at her from his position on the floor at her feet. "Are you ready?"

"Ready." Til stood. The rest of the men stood with her.

"Before we leave, I need a moment with Doctor Stone." Grayson stood up as he addressed the men in the room. "If you would just wait one moment, we'll be right with you."

The men filed out of the interrogation room. Grayson shut the door behind them and leaned his back against the door.

"Til, you need to think about the possibility that you will have to use that gun on Alys if she is in the penthouse tonight." Grayson's eyes burned with intensity. "I am convinced that she shot Malcolm. If she can do that, she will kill Shannon and you without a thought. Your greatest enemy, and the link to your past, is Alys." Grayson crossed his arms over his chest. "You have to be mentally prepared to kill her in self defence."

Til lifted her chin defiantly. "I can do it, I will think of my child being raised without a father and I will pull the trigger and not think twice."

"Be very careful because we don't know what has happened to Alys or what she has seen or been through. She's been part of the Bristol Butcher gang since she was fourteen years old."

Til stood up and straightened her shoulders.

"She is, at best, a damaged woman." Grayson pressed on relentlessly. "At no point can you treat her as if she has a conscience," Grayson said ominously. "Anyone who is part of a gang like that would have been completely desensitised to violence."

"Well then she has met her match." Til's jaw tightened as she spoke. "We come from the same streets and we have seen horrors no one should see. I will protect Shannon with everything I've got. If it comes down to Shannon or Alys, I will do what I have to do." Til lifted her chin.

"Listen to me." Grayson stood near her, towering over her. "Do you really think you are prepared to drop her if you get a chance?" Grayson repeated. "You are a doctor. Sworn to heal."

A flash of pain darkened Til's eyes. "I am an aunt and mother first." Til's teeth clenched together. "I will take down Royce, Alys and anyone else who tries to stand in my way."

"You cannot be driven by emotion. There is nothing more dangerous than that." Grayson crossed his arms over his chest.

"A woman driven by emotion?" Til looked at him squarely.

"Anyone driven by emotion." Grayson held her gaze steadily. "You need a clear head."

Til took a deep breath to steady her nerves. "I am ready."

"Right. Is there anything else you are concerned about? I should know it now before we go." Grayson placed his hand on the door handle of the interrogation room. He waited for her answer.

"About Mirabel and Alys." Til touched the knife in her corset again, to be sure it was there and ready. "I spoke to Cora and she had a suggestion. A very good one. I had not thought of this but she mentioned that if Mirabel sees us together, you have to treat me like a worthless prostitute."

Grayson frowned. "What?"

"You've done it before," Til reminded him.

"I've apologised for that at length," Grayson protested.

"Grayson, you will be apologising for that for the rest of your life," Til snapped at him.

"How do you mean, treat you like a prostitute?" Grayson tensed at the suggestion.

"Treat me as if I have no rights, proposition me in front of her. Be like a white slaver. I'm sure you can do it, you've seen enough of it." Til took a deep breath. "I need Mirabel to be my partner. We need her to think that we are on the same level. She needs to think that I'm your prisoner. You're going to say that both of us are under arrest, that you used me to get to Royce. You have evidence that links me to Nora's disappearance, and then I'm going to seduce you into making a deal for Mirabel and me."

"Seduce?" Grayson's eyes widened.

"It's the only currency she understands." Til's eyes hardened.

"You think she'll be fooled by that?" Grayson asked. "She is desperate." Til stood by him at the door.

"She might see right through it," Grayson warned.

"Grayson." Til threw her hands up in the air. "She is a terrified, desperate woman. We need to manipulate that. When I assisted Joan, if I'd gone in there sounding like a toff, they wouldn't trust me. The women of the slums, my mother and countless other women that I grew up with, felt worthless, Grayson. Mirabel has to believe I feel the same way about myself. If I offer myself in the same manner in exchange for a deal, we're essentially on the same level."

"Have you spent your entire life manipulating people to get what you want?" Grayson asked bluntly.

"Of course!" Til blinked. "I have had to manipulate to survive. If you throw in a few fundraisers where I knew things I shouldn't and used it to my advantage, then yes, I tend to rely on manipulation quite a lot."

"You're unbelievable," Grayson gasped in surprise.

"Thank you!" Til deliberately misunderstood him.

Grayson shook his head. "I hate it, but I'll do it. I can't believe this entire case rests on the back of Mirabel Salter of all people."

"You just never know who is going to crop up." Til shrugged.

Grayson fiddled with the handle.

"Everything sorted then?" Til asked, concerned that they had kept the men waiting too long.

Turning to face her, he gently took her by the upper arms and looked deep into her eyes. "Before we go, I need to be sure of one last thing."

"What?" Til's heart pounded with worry he would try to stop her from going after Shannon.

"I know how you feel about protecting Shannon, but if it is between your life and Alys's, can you kill her?" Grayson's eyes searched hers for the truth. "Are you ready to do what you have to do to protect yourself? If you aren't, I'm not letting you go."

"I'm ready." Til's jaw clenched hard. "Let's go."

Chapter Thirty-Seven

Shannon's heart fell to her feet as she woke up in the brig to the sound of whimpering. Alys had terminated any further medical treatment for the girls. Shannon strained to see who was crying. Lamp light poured into the cell as Alys swung open the door and her henchman, Shipley Bristol, came straight to Shannon.

Icy fear twisted her stomach into knots as Shipley dragged her hands together while Alys clamped irons on her wrists.

Shannon watched in horror as every girl in the brig was ruthlessly pulled apart and chained in the cell.

Shipley and Alys's movements were jerky with anger.

Something has changed.

Once everyone was chained around the jail, wordlessly, Shipley and Alys left them with no light, no knowledge about why they were suddenly chained this securely.

The girls wept and called for their mothers. Shannon worried they would cause their kidnappers to return and silence them with force. Heart breaking for them, Shannon tried to reach them the only way she could. With her voice.

"Girls, I want you to remain calm." Shannon's chest tightened in fear. "I know you are terrified, I am too. But, right now, we have each other. Before I left England, my aunt and a detective were working to find the people who have stolen us. My husband is also looking for me. When Alys took me upstairs, she asked me for a name. That proves the people looking for me know I am alive."

The girls wept, but softer now.

"They will find us. Detective Grayson is very good at his job."

I hope!

"When they find me, they *will* find you." Shannon spoke confidently as her stomach churned. "If we get separated, I will never stop looking for you. I want you to tell me your full names and where you come from. That way we can buy your tickets back home and let your parents know you are all on your way."

Thankfully the darkness in the cell hid the tears in Shannon's eyes as the girls told her their names and addresses, all in London.

These girls are so young!

Resolve to seek justice for what the girls had endured to this point caused Shannon to sit up straighter.

Hours later, having wept themselves into exhaustion, the girls fell asleep. Shannon braced herself as the door was flung open; they were shaken awake, and dragged in irons, into a row.

Screaming and crying, Anna reached for Shannon and was brutally shoved away from her. Anna slipped and as Shipley grabbed her and dragged her up off the floor, Shannon couldn't stop herself from bolting across the room and grabbing his arm before he could hit her.

Shipley dropped Anna and turned on Shannon.

"She's thirteen years old. She stumbled. Don't hit her," Shannon gasped. "Please. She's a little girl and she is terrified. Please don't..."

"Shut up," he hissed as he backhanded Shannon so hard she reeled and dropped to the floor.

Terrified he would kick her if she stayed down; she tried and failed to struggle to her feet.

"I will buy these girls for twice the price you can get on the street," Shannon begged from the floor. "I will send a cable and have the money to you within twenty-four hours. Please."

Shannon tried to curl into a protective ball around her unborn child as he stomped over to her. The hard nails in his boots made her mouth dry with fear; boots like that would do untold damage, enough to lose her baby.

"Please, please don't hurt me. Listen, I'll pay you double the ransom for me and double for the girls..." Shannon begged as he crouched down to drag her to her feet so he could hit her again.

"Shipley," Alys called out from the stairway. "There is no time for that. We have to go."

Shipley shoved Shannon to the back of the row of girls. A guard shackled her to Anna and they were led like cattle out of the brig.

Silvery moonlight exposed the level of suffering the girls had endured. Haggard, filthy, and sick, the girls wept as they were dragged forward. They stumbled and were quick to try to hold each other up as they were forced to march across a gangway and down the dock onto the shore of a massive lake. Shannon's jaw clenched in anger as the men on the dock looked the girls over like animals at auction. She felt unsteady on her legs as they were herded into the forest towards a clearing. Shannon's pulse raced as she realized she and the girls were caught between Royce's men on the shore and the captain and crew on the dock. These were men who knew no honour. Alys had been foolish to trust any of them. Ice cold fear caused Shannon's breath to catch.

A tall, thin man walked toward them and greeted Alys. The entire group stopped as they spoke.

"Creston." Alys smiled as she greeted him. "Twelve girls as Royce requested."

"Royce will be pleased." Creston's cold eyes met Shannon's briefly. "They look good."

Acid pooled in Shannon's stomach as Creston's icy gaze flicked over her again.

"This is Shannon?" Creston took a step toward Shannon and she tried to take a step back. Her irons kept her shackled to Anna in front of her. She shuddered as he moved closer.

"Yes." Alys stiffened.

Shannon's pulse pounded as Creston stood near her.

"What is her price?" he asked Alys.

Shannon shuddered.

"She's not for sale. I have asked for a ransom." Alys's eyes narrowed.

"Royce has agreed to that?" Creston reached forward and trailed his hard fingertips down Shannon's cheek.

"Yes," Alys said tightly.

"Pity." Creston ran his fingertips down Shannon's throat.

Shannon shook in horror as he tugged at the opening of her blouse. Eyes wide in fear, Shannon looked around at anyone who might step in.

Her eyes met Captain Jackson's. He smirked at her as if interested to see how far Creston would go.

Emboldened by Creston's behavior, the men on the dock whispered among themselves. Shannon realised with sudden terror that Creston and Shipley were outnumbered by Captain Jackson and his men. Captain

Jackson's eyes slid over Anna. Shannon wanted to shield her from his gaze but knew with certainty if Captain Jackson wanted Anna, there wasn't a thing she could do about it. Shannon noticed them shift and whisper to each other on the dock.

Alys turned to speak to the Captain and crew.

"The girls are sold tomorrow; you'll have your payment in full."

Alys sounds shrill, she's terrified. If Captain Jackson and his men try to take the girls, there is nothing Alys can do to stop them.

Captain Jackson and his men grinned like wolves.

The hair on Shannon's neck stood up as she heard Crane murmur to Jackson. "There's only two men."

As Creston ran his fingertips along Shannon's collar bone, she swallowed a hard knot of fear. She mentally braced herself for what he might do next. From the direction of the dock, she heard the very discreet click of a hammer being pulled back on a pistol.

Creston dropped his hand as surprise flashed in his eyes.

Immediately, Shannon dropped to the ground and covered Anna with her body just as the first shots rang out. She shrieked at the girls to stay down as gun battle broke out between the men.

Screaming and weeping, the girls scrambled to try to find protection, their irons holding them in place so they were exposed to the gunfire around them. Men ran for cover, shots rang out and finally, when the battle was over, Shannon raised her head cautiously. Captain Jackson and his men had underestimated the deadliness of Shipley Bristol and Creston, this new man, who worked for Royce. Gun smoke slowly dissipated as Shipley and Creston holstered their weapons and turned their attention to Alys. Shipley pressed his hand to his arm.

Heart pounding with fear, Shannon noticed the blood dripping from a bullet wound and for one brief moment of hope, thought maybe he would need her to stitch up his arm and she could plead for him to save them.

"Anyone who steals from Royce dies," Creston said simply.

Shannon's heart plummeted with disappointment. Her hope fled as she heard that statement.

Creston darted his gaze between Alys and Shipley, "If you had plans to double cross him, my face is the last face you'll see."

Shannon's swallowed down her terror as they were dragged to their feet and marched forward towards a large cabin in the clearing. Anna stumbled and the irons that held them together sliced Shannon's wrists to ribbons. She gritted her teeth from the pain in her face and hands as she tried to hold Anna up. Shannon tried and failed to blink back tears at the thought of the girls being sold tomorrow.

Even if they are by some miracle saved, how will they recover from this ordeal?

Shannon turned her attention to the landscape around her with the hope that if the chains were removed, maybe they could run into the woods to escape.

Towering pine trees reminded Shannon of ancient pikes in a prison. There was no escape here. She wasn't dragging twelve girls anywhere.

Her heart fell as the door to the cabin was dragged open and they were unchained one by one and marched down into the cellar.

Shannon was the last one. The girls' muffled weeping from the cellar broke her heart. Shipley took her irons off, marched her down the stairs. Shannon waited for him to drop the cellar door down on them, leaving them alone, and then quickly scrambled up the stairs to hear.

"Matilda Bertram or Doctor Til Stone is under arrest," Creston said.

"What!" Alys gasped.

The sound of boots walking across the floor and a door slamming frustrated Shannon as she realised they had taken their conversation outside. Straining her ears, Shannon couldn't hear anything but the soft whimpering of the girls who now knew they were one step closer to being sold.

Gutted by the news Til was in irons, praying Cole had worked out what ship she was on, she turned to face the girls.

"What is it?" Belle reached for her, shaking with emotional strain.

"Everything is going to be all right," Shannon lied.

Anna scampered across the cellar and curled up against Shannon.

"I'm scared." Anna buried her face in Shannon's skirt.

Shannon fought back sobs as she put her arms around Anna and held her tightly. "I know darling, I know. Me too."

Chapter Thirty-Eight

Til forced her feet to move forward as Grayson opened the door to the lobby of Royce's apartment for her. One constable stayed on the street but Haggerty went up the stairs ahead of her. Sol hovered just a few feet behind her and Grayson. Til's stomach clenched with dread as she pulled the derringer out of her boot. Taking a deep breath, she followed him through the lobby and up the stairs to the penthouse suite. Eerie silence met them on every floor. They braced themselves, expecting an attack; none came.

Either he isn't here or the army of men to protect him is in the penthouse with him.

Heart in her throat, Til held the derringer in a death grip as they stood in front of Royce Bristol's door.

Which woman is behind this door?

Sol and Grayson moved down the hall to keep an eye on Til as she knocked on the door. After pounding on the door for a few moments, Grayson came to her side.

"Step aside." Grayson physically moved her further back and then broke the door down with his shoulder.

A trickle of nervous sweat slid down her back as she peered around him into the dark apartment. Grayson and Sol swept through the rooms.

"No one is here," Grayson confirmed as he drove his pistol back into his holster.

Til's shoulders slumped in disappointment and defeat. "Where could he be?"

Bending down, she lifted her skirt and put the derringer back in the holster at her ankle. She worried the gun would go off by accident.

"We'll keep looking, and now we're here, we search for clues." Grayson moved to a desk in front of a massive window that overlooked the docks. He lit the wick on the coal oil lamp to illuminate the papers strewn across the desk.

Together, they pounced on the telegrams. She found her original telegram to Royce. She turned the wick up, so she had better light to read it.

Someone has changed the one to a four.

The tiny crooked mark was so perfect, only the one who sent the telegram and knew what it *should* say, would see it.

"Grayson," Til gasped. "The original telegram said ten thousand pounds. Someone has changed this to forty thousand." Til handed Grayson the telegram.

He held it to the light and read it.

"Odelia's dead because this telegram makes it look like she was going to steal thirty thousand pounds?" Grayson's eyebrows raised.

"Who is threatened by Odelia?" Til took the telegram back and reread it.

"Who do you think?" Grayson kept searching through paperwork on the desk.

"The woman in his bed when we find him is threatened by another woman running the ring," Til said ominously.

"Why?" Grayson tilted his head. "Wouldn't a woman prefer not to be part of criminal behaviour?"

"The criminal behaviour is paying their way. Women like Mirabel and Alys only know one currency." Til inclined her head toward the bed in the adjoining room. "I'm presuming Alys coming to Canada wasn't part of the original plan. Either she had Odelia killed because she wanted her job or Mirabel panicked, terrified Odelia would take over her... uh... relationship with Royce." Til shuddered as she spoke the words.

"I see." Grayson frowned as he sifted through more notes on the desk. "This is a telegram from Alys to Royce." Grayson read it to Til. "Meet me at the dock, October 29. 2:30 am. Bring Nora."

"That's tomorrow night," Til breathed. "They are getting ready. But, where are they now?"

"Let's keep looking." Grayson arranged notes, ledgers and telegrams into neat piles. "What concerns me, Til, is every time we have read about a dock where they are meeting it is specific. They detail dock and warehouse. This one doesn't list it."

"Maybe it's just assumed?" Til examined the note again in case they listed the dock and the warehouse on the back of the telegram.

"Or it's a different dock." A muscle jumped in Grayson's jaw. "I'll ask Cora to dig deeper. There might be other land that Royce Bristol owns. I'll have her check tax rolls as soon as possible."

"Thank you." Til rubbed her eyebrow to relieve tension there. "There might be another note that explains things."

Once they read the last paper on the desk, Til took a deep breath and let it out slowly. "There is nothing here. No addresses, no more telegrams that indicate anything."

Til cursed under her breath.

"There is one bill for food delivery to a brothel near the docks." Grayson flattened the paper so he could read the address.

"How many brothels does Royce run?" Til squinted to see the paper.

"Two," Sol answered from the doorway.

"The address of this brothel is near Bathurst Street." Grayson handed her the invoice. "That's where his offices are."

Til examined the bill. "This is a big delivery of food. Maybe enough to feed the girls before they sell them? Is it possible they have moved there for now?"

"Possible." Grayson took the note and added it to the falsified telegram as evidence. "Let's go. You were right, Til, there is no time to waste."

"Do we need more men?" Sol asked.

"There is no time." Grayson double checked the bullets in the chamber of his gun. "It's late. Best we don't make a big raid out of this. Just slip in and apprehend him. We can't risk alerting Alys or Mirabel. Fourteen innocent lives are at stake here."

"Right." Sol nodded. "Let's go."

***

As the carriage pulled away from Royce's penthouse and took them to the roughest streets of Toronto and the Bathurst brothel, Til shivered from cold.

Grayson reached forward and took her chilly hands in his. "Your hands are freezing." He rubbed her hands together to warm them.

"I'm all right." Til bit her lip.

"We're going to just enter and pretend to be customers." Grayson held her hands hard in his. "I'll follow you."

"Right." She nodded, trying not to weep with frustration that Shannon wasn't in the penthouse and there was no guarantee she would be in the brothel. For all they knew, she was dead.

"You can back out." Grayson leaned forward. "You don't have to do this."

"What if we're too late and she's dead?" Til ignored his offer. A tear escaped despite her iron-hard determination to keep a stiff upper lip. "What will we do then? How will I..."

"Hey." Grayson squeezed Til's hands in support. "Listen. She's worth too much. They will have done everything to keep her alive and well. Ten thousand pounds, it's a king's ransom. I bet they are handing her hot soup right this minute to keep her strength up."

Til shook her head, tears glittering in her eyes. "Hot soup?"

"I know Shannon is alive and I know we will find her." Grayson wiped Til's tears with his shirtsleeve. "Sorry, no handkerchiefs."

"We're a disaster." Til gulped down raw pain that tightened her throat.

"Well, we're the disaster about to blow this case open and arrest some terrible men." Grayson stroked her face with his fingertips. "I'm right here with you."

Til straightened at his words of encouragement. "You're right. Sorry, I fell apart. I'm sorted now. Gutted, but sorted." Til sat up taller.

"It's better if they don't know the police are helping you." Grayson leaned back. "If someone touches you or tries to drag you off into a room, if I intervene... I'm well known on these streets... I need to stay out of sight."

"I get it." Til's mouth went dry with fear. "You can't intervene."

"I can, but I *won't* unless you scream my name. You scream for me, I'll come to your side. No matter what." Even in the gloom, Til could see Grayson's gaze burned with intensity. "I hope Cora is right and Royce will confess because he thinks you are a worthless girl from the East End."

"Those women are less than worthless in his eyes." Til shuddered.

"Which is not true. They are not worthless." Grayson reached forward and brushed a stray hair from her eye. "If you scream for me, I'll be right there."

The carriage stopped in front of a brothel. Til's eyes narrowed as she watched two men brawling in the street.

"We're here, Til. I promise, when this is all over..." Grayson turned her face to look at him as Sol whipped the door open and interrupted him.

"Two men around the back; I'll stay in the front and you follow Doctor Stone. Sound right?" Sol didn't waste words.

"Yes." Grayson agreed.

"You were saying?" Til asked as he slipped out of the carriage.

"No time now." He held his hand out to assist her.

Til placed her hands in his and stepped out of the carriage onto the street.

Grayson's eyes widened as she pulled her heavy coat off and tossed it into the carriage. Revealing the low-cut dress beneath, she pulled the skirt up to the middle of her thigh to reveal striped stockings.

Grayson's eyes widened. "What are you doing? Where did you get that?"

Til ignored him as she pulled pins out of her hair and tossed them on top of the discarded coat.

"Til," Grayson breathed. His eyes smoldered as they swept over her. The rest of the men shot a look at her before they met Grayson's angry eyes and moved on.

Til pulled her hair to one side.

"If he's distracted, I have an advantage." Til bent forward and double checked that her derringer was in her boot.

"Distracted!" Grayson's jaw dropped. "You're distracting all of us!"

"Not so bad for a forty-year-old pregnant fossil," she said dryly as she straightened up.

"Did you know all along... we'd be doing this?" Grayson couldn't tear his gaze from her décolletage.

"We're dealing with a white slaver."

His head snapped up and his eyes met hers. "Sorry. I got distracted." He shook his head. "This is all... very... distracting. I already said that."

"I knew all along I would be confronting Royce Bristol." Til brought them back to the matter at hand. "I go to him looking like a respectable lady, I'll get nowhere. I was certain you wouldn't let me flounce around a police station in this."

"Too bloody right." Grayson cleared his throat.

"You agreed with me that prostitutes have no human value for him. He thinks they are subhuman. I go in as a prostitute, he'll say anything. He won't know I'll use it against him. Don't you go around as a homeless man to gather information?"

"But, I'm a man... it's different." Grayson choked on the words.

"I don't know why." Til adjusted her stocking.

Grayson swallowed hard. "You are a vulnerable woman."

"No, I'm not. You're going to keep me alive. I have no doubt. Anyway, let's get this over with." Til straightened up, nerves causing her stomach to tighten in fear.

Grayson dragged his eyes from her thigh to her décolletage, where his gaze lingered, to her eyes. He cleared his throat and together they moved to the front door of the brothel.

Til took a deep breath and then slipped into the crowd of men and women who were drunk and pawing at each other. She slid past hands that grabbed out for her. One man tried to drag her onto his lap. She leaped out of his grasp, but bumped into a gigantic man.

He looked her over and his eyes gleamed at her in anticipation. Seconds later, just as her pulse raced in fear that this man would grab her and detain her, Sol appeared by her side. Putting his big body between Til and the man before he could lunge at her, Til breathed a sigh of relief.

Frustrated, the big man swung a punch at Sol who dodged it and dropped him with one solid punch to the jaw. Til gasped, the floor shook as he landed.

Sol grabbed her and helped her avoid being pulled onto various men's laps on her way to the stairs.

Til heard heavy boots on the stairs behind them. She didn't need to look behind her to know it was Grayson. The three of them convened at the top of the stairs.

"You'll want to stay within earshot of Til. There is another floor, I'll take it." Sol left them.

Grayson and Til split up and searched every room until she was standing at the last room on the floor. Acid churned in Til's stomach as she stood at the threshold of a room that might contain Royce Bristol.

I'll have you when I'm done with him.

Til straightened up, placed her hand on the doorknob, and braced herself to deal with this threat from her past once for all time.

The only way forward, is back.

Shaking with terror, Til took a deep breath and opened the door.

Chapter Thirty-Nine

Til blinked as she stepped into the room and her eyes adjusted to the poor light. A man and woman slept in bed.

Good. Element of surprise.

Til crept to Royce's side of the bed and quietly picked up the gun that rested on the bedside table. She braced herself as he opened his eyes. She leaped back, out of his grasp as he sat up.

"You asked for me, Royce Bristol." Til kept his gun in her hand pointed straight at his heart. "Here I am."

"Who... what?" Royce sat up in bed.

Blimey, he's bigger now!

Til's hand shook as she kept the gun on him. Mirabel sat up and rubbed her eyes beside him. The light from the hallway filtered in so she could see the flimsy nightgown Mirabel wore.

"You have something I need; I have something you want." Til shifted on her feet. The hand gun was heavier than she expected and she had to use both hands to hold the gun steady.

Hands up, eyes narrow, Royce slid out of bed.

"Don't move." Til desperately wanted to take a big step back, but didn't dare show him any weakness.

Mirabel quickly scrambled on her bedside table for her gun.

Til didn't acknowledge Mirabel as she turned a derringer on Til.

Royce smiled like a wolf about to devour a lamb.

"No need." Royce gestured to Mirabel. "She won't kill me. I've got Shannon and I know who killed Malcolm."

Mirabel frowned but put the gun back on the nightstand.

Royce took another step towards Til.

"You said after you killed Malcolm, it was my turn. So, here I am. Matilda Bertram. Fresh from the slums, and if you take another step closer, I will kill you." Til grit her teeth to stop them from chattering in fear.

"Kill me, you'll never find Shannon," Royce scoffed.

"What do you want, Royce? Am I to trade my life for Shannon's?" Til's hands trembled.

"I want money." Royce lunged for her; she leaped out of his grasp.

"Why did you kill Malcolm?" Til gulped down panic.

"How would I kill Malcolm all the way from Canada?" Royce took another step.

"You ordered Odelia to do it." Til pulled the hammer of the gun back.

The weight of the gun dragged at her arms.

"No." Royce shook his head. His eyes lit up as he looked at her breasts, straining against the tattered bodice. Her heart shuddered in fear as his eyes travelled over her. "Odelia was useless. I don't know why Alys insisted she come here. She stole from me and paid the price."

"That's not what I heard." Til stood straight, hoping he wouldn't see her body tremble in terror. "I heard Alys took Shannon to raise enough capital to take over everything. She will run this ring."

Royce sneered, "A woman can't run a ring."

"Don't be so sure." Til lifted her chin as she baited him. "If not Odelia, then I believe Alys killed Malcolm on your orders." Til's voice cracked with emotion.

Royce shrugged.

"Or maybe she didn't." Til tilted her head to the side. "You have a hard time getting women to listen to you, if I remember correctly."

Royce grabbed for her; she nimbly stepped out of range.

"The fact is, Royce, as I understand it from Alys, my *sister*, Alys intends to take over your entire operation. Guess who will help her?" Til smiled despite the horror that galloped through her chest.

"She killed Malcolm, *you* won't help her!" Royce roared at Til as he lunged for her again.

Til tried to move quicker than him, his fingertips brushed her skirt.

"You don't finish what you start." Til's breath sounded ragged. "She knows that as well as I do," Til taunted him. Her hand was slicked with sweat as she gripped his gun and kept it level with his heart. "You don't have what it takes to be a crime boss. You didn't in 1881 when Malcolm beat you to a bloody pulp in a back alley and you don't now. Alys knows it, I know it. The only person who seems confused is you."

As Royce pounced on her, Til pulled the trigger.

Missed!

Terrified, Til tried to leap away from him but Royce knocked his gun from her hand, grabbed her and dragged her to the floor.

"We had a deal, Alys and me," Royce hissed at her as he ripped the front of her bodice apart. "She killed him quick. Nice bullet to the kidney in the street. I didn't promise to kill you quick, Matilda. I intend to take my time."

Til's pulse raced with fear as she tried to pull her leg up to get the derringer out of her holster. She couldn't reach it. Panic roared through her as she tried to stop him from ripping her clothes off. She twisted from his grasp and finally grabbed the derringer from her holster and pressed it into his ribs.

Surprise flashed across his face as he held his hands up.

"I'm here to offer you triple what Alys offered if you retrieve Shannon for me, tonight. There is an account in the Toronto bank with thirty thousand dollars ready to transfer. Why split the profit with Alys? You don't owe Alys anything and neither do I. You think she came all the way from England to work under your authority? Never. She's here to destroy you and run her own ring, and why wouldn't she? Alys doesn't need a man, she's brutal enough. As you said, a bullet to the kidney takes care of most problems and we don't need a man to do that," Til rasped. "Alys has already turned on you. Someone will get thirty thousand for Shannon, why not you?" She pressed the muzzle deeper into his side.

"Shut up." Royce held his hands up higher. His eyes squinted as he looked down at her.

"If I betray you, I'm dead in what, twelve hours?" Til tried to reason with him. "Take me to Shannon, you get your money."

Royce, with lightning speed knocked the gun from Til's hand, dragged her hands over her head and spoke directly in her ear.

"I'll take everything," he said as he pressed her wrists into the floorboards. "I thought I would have to wait until we swapped for Nora."

He let go of her arm so he could drag her skirt up. Til tried to hit him. She hurt her hand, and he didn't feel it.

Where is Grayson?

"Mirabel. Help me!" Til screamed at her.

"Scream all you want," Royce grunted in her ear. "I like it."

Mirabel stood over Royce and Til, pointing a gun at Til with shaking hands.

Til scrambled to free the knife from her ruined corset.

"Mirabel." Til tried to make eye contact with her as Royce tore at her skirt. "I have your son."

Mirabel's eyes flew open as she gasped.

"I will give you ten thousand pounds and your *son* if you put that gun on Royce instead of me," Til pleaded with her.

Royce slapped Til so hard she saw stars and tasted blood.

"Shut up." Royce tore the front of her chemise with one rip.

Terrified, Til twisted as she tried to keep eye contact with Mirabel.

"Mirabel, ten thousand pounds and Tommy," Til begged as she gripped the knife in her hand and kept it hidden in the fold of her skirt.

Royce backhanded her again; black dots danced in her peripheral vision. "She's not taking ten thousand pounds from you and she knows it. She'd be dead by the time she left this room."

Mirabel Salter's hands shook on the gun.

Til fought to keep her gaze and repeated one more time. "I have your son."

Mirabel placed the muzzle of the gun against Royce Bristol's temple and pulled the hammer back.

"Take your hands off her," she whispered.

Royce's hands stilled.

"Put that gun down. Creston will have you face down in a river if you even think about..." Royce sputtered.

"Ten thousand pounds and you can run. Anywhere you want." Til gasped for breath as she spoke over top of Royce. "You can take Tommy and move anywhere..." Til struggled against the solid, bulky weight of Royce.

Til gasped as Royce hit Mirabel so hard she went flying across the room, knocking the gun from her hand.

With his torso exposed, Til drove the knife into Royce's side as he reached for Mirabel. Hard enough and deep enough to wound him. She held onto the knife as he roared in pain. He scrambled away from her, pressing his hand to his side. She crawled away from him.

The knife wound did nothing to stop him. He lunged after her and grabbed Til again. As he tried to take the knife from her, Til stabbed him, higher this time. Royce hit her so hard she tasted the iron metal of blood in her mouth again.

Til screamed for Grayson and then the room went silent as a crack of gunshot stunned her.

Royce dropped on top of Til.

Shrieking and clawing at him, Til tried and couldn't push him off of her.

Grayson flew into the room and pounced on Royce, dragging him off of Til. Royce dropped beside her, dead. Til shuddered and scrambled to put as much distance between them as she could. Grayson pressed his fingers against his throat, checking for a pulse.

"He's dead."

Mirabel, shaking with fear, tears streaming down her face, stood in the middle of the room with a gun smoking in her hands.

"Mirabel, you are under arrest." Grayson tugged the gun from her hands, dragged her arms behind her, and secured her wrists with irons.

"She's all right?" Sol asked Grayson.

"She's under arrest, she doesn't matter." Grayson growled at Sol, "Search these entire premises for Nora."

"We found her," Sol said. "She's on the way back to the constabulary; we've already called for a doctor."

"Is Nora all right?" Til's hands shook as she tried to pull her shredded chemise back together.

"I guess you don't have to come up with the money for her. How convenient." Grayson snapped at Til.

Sol looked from Grayson to Til in confusion.

Til held her arm across her chest to try to maintain some semblance of modesty. "We had a deal, Grayson. I find Royce and you help me find Shannon."

"I don't do deals with prostitutes," Grayson growled at Til, playing along with their agreed plan. "I got what I want. A confession from Royce. Now, you and Mirabel are off to jail."

Mirabel gasped in horror.

"I have to find Shannon," Til begged.

"I know where Shannon is," Mirabel said breathlessly.

"Where?" Grayson turned to address Mirabel.

Til, hurt and shaking, pulled herself to her feet. She wiped at blood from her split lip.

"You and I need to talk." Mirabel spoke only to Til.

"Of course." Til moved toward her.

"Not in front of him." Mirabel inclined her head at Grayson

"You're both under arrest." Grayson spoke to Mirabel. "Neither of you are in any position to do deals."

"What if I gave you something you want, in exchange for a deal for Mirabel." Til turned around to face Grayson, putting herself between them.

Grayson dismissed the rest of the men from the room, closed the door, and faced Til.

"There is nothing you have that I want," Grayson growled.

"Please." Til turned her back to Mirabel and let her ruined chemise fall open.

Grayson's eyes lit with desire. Til saw it and hoped Mirabel saw it too.

Mirabel's breath caught behind her.

Til stepped closer to Grayson. "I am begging you, sir. This is my niece. This is Shannon's life. Whatever you think of me, I am innocent until proven guilty. Please, Detective Grayson." Til placed her hands on the hard plane of his chest. "Please, make a deal for Shannon's life. I don't care what happens to me; you can charge me with whatever you can dream up tomorrow, but let me find my niece tonight."

"I can't give her a deal." His eyes narrowed. "You're both going to jail for your involvement with Royce Bristol and his organisation. Mirabel Salter is the only one who gained from changing a one to a four on a telegram from Alys to Royce. No one else would have done it. I have to take her in and charge her with conspiracy to commit murder. I *have* to."

"That evidence is circumstantial. Could have been anyone and you know it," Til pleaded. Her eyes filled with tears. "Drop the charges against Mirabel if she cooperates and tells us where Shannon is."

"Who do you think you are?" Grayson shook his head. "She's guilty of killing Odelia, I can prove it."

Mirabel sobbed in fear.

"Odelia was part of the Bristol Butchers. Please, I am begging you not to risk Shannon's life to prosecute a woman who was a *white slaver*. Please listen to your conscience."

Grayson's jaw clenched. "A prostitute talking about conscience. That's a new one. I give you that. What do you have that I want?"

Standing in front of him, Til slid the ruined chemise down over her shoulders. She traced her hands over his shoulders and down the front of his chest. "There must be something I have that you are interested in."

"No." Grayson's eyes narrowed.

Til, standing on tiptoe pressed her body against his. Twining her hands in his hair, she pulled his head down to kiss him.

Taking Til by the upper arms, Grayson pinned her to the wall. "Anything I want from you," Grayson roughly pulled her skirt up. "I can take any time."

"Don't!" Mirabel cried. "Please!"

"You need those hostages returned." Til ignored Mirabel. "Twelve girls and Shannon. How will it look if you retrieve them tonight? What sort of *promotion* would you get?"

Grayson stopped.

"If I get the location from Mirabel and those girls are there, I promise to finish what I started here. You drop the charges." Til begged breathlessly.

"I could take you right here." Grayson pressed his knee between hers, pinned her harder against the wall, and flung the ruined chemise across the room.

Mirabel flinched.

"What would your men say?" Til looked down at the floor in a show of submission.

Grayson finally pulled back, his breath ragged as he spoke. "I drop the charges against Mirabel, and you finish what you started here?"

"Yes." Til's knees buckled, she tried to stand straight.

"You give me your word?" he demanded.

"I give you my word." Til spoke letting her head drop down. "If you would be so kind, please let us dress before we leave here. I don't like the way your men are looking at us."

"You're a worthless prostitute." Grayson roughly took off their shackles and turned on his heel as he opened the door to leave. "Why do you care how men look at you? I warn you." He pointed a finger at Til. "If this is a trick, if you try to run, I will hunt you down like the dog that you are. I will have my payment. In full."

Til trembled as she moved closer to Mirabel. The door slammed shut behind him.

Mirabel burst into tears.

Til shuddered as she tried to gather her composure. Grayson's hands on her, even if it was a show for Mirabel to manipulate her into taking them to Shannon, was still Grayson's hands on her. She pressed her fingertips to the lips he bruised as he had kissed her. Her hands shook as she tried to find anything to cover herself with.

"I am so terrified of him." Mirabel wept. "He's... he's just awful. He must have changed from all his years chasing slavers." She met Til's eyes.

"We need to find Shannon before he changes his mind, or the deal is off." Til spoke harsher than she intended to. Immediately she softened her tone.

"I can lead you to Alys and Shannon. You said ten thousand pounds and my son? You will make sure he drops the charges? You'll do what it... um... takes?" Mirabel kept her gaze level with Til's.

Til moved to Mirabel and looked her in the eye. "It's a deal."

Chapter Forty

Til peeled off the rest of her ruined gown.

Mirabel went to her closet and found respectable clothes for Til and herself.

Mirabel's eyes were wide with fear as she handed Til a plain black skirt and white shirtwaist.

"Why did you offer that? Your body for a lesser sentence for me?"

"How do you think I clawed my way out of the slums of the East End?" Til lied smoothly. "Not my first time using my body to get what I want. I hope it's my last. Do you know where Shannon is? I don't want to wait until November 2nd. I want her back now. Tonight. They might torture her. I'll do anything, *anything*, to get her. I can't wait for the police. They'll never find Alys."

Mirabel took a deep breath. "How can I trust you?"

"I came from the slums where women are worth nothing," Til said bitterly. "My father sold me for the price of the rent for the winter. I suspect we came from the same place, and the world we live in isn't so different. We're the same, you and I. No options but the worst ones."

Mirabel's head snapped up.

"I worked hard to be a doctor, but that feeling of worthlessness is always there, just under the surface. Men like Grayson see the reality of me. What I did to get there and they exploit it." Til's eyes filled with tears as she spoke the truth to Mirabel Salter. Her breath caught, and she stopped speaking for a moment. "Sorry. It's hard to speak about. Harder is the life they reduced me to after. The only way to claw yourself out is with money."

Mirabel looked up at Til as tears gathered in her eyes.

"You did the same thing, didn't you? You had to give Tommy to an orphanage because you couldn't afford to feed him or buy him the medicine he needs. You went to Royce's bed to keep him and yourself alive so you wouldn't starve on the streets. What I'm doing for Shannon is no different."

Tears spilled down Mirabel's cheeks. "How did you know about that?"

"I've engaged Cora Stein as my lawyer. When she found out Tommy wasn't with you, she found him and took him. Tommy was starving and had a fever," Til softened her tone. "He is warm, well fed and Cora has moved him into her own home. They have us lumped together, Mirabel. Cora intends to represent you too. And Tommy, he will be just fine."

Mirabel collapsed in sobs on the bed again.

"Here now." Til went to her and put her arms around her.

"Listen. I know. I know what it's like to have nothing. If you could have made a proper wage you would have raised your son and never had a thing to do with Royce Bristol. I am a woman who's come from the same place as you, Mirabel. If I had options, I wouldn't have offered... what I offered."

Mirabel wept harder, Til drew her closer.

"I give you my word; I will give you ten thousand pounds, your son and the charges will be dropped." Til squeezed her arms around her. "Enough to start afresh anywhere. You can trust me; tell me where Shannon is."

Mirabel swallowed hard.

Til pulled up her skirt and pulled out a pouch of money. She counted off five thousand pounds and held it out. "Where is my niece?"

Mirabel looked into Til's eyes.

"They are to meet at the dock tomorrow night." Mirabel's voice shook.

"Yes. I read that telegram but there was no dock number listed." Til bit her lip impatiently.

"Not the docks at Bathurst Street," Mirabel whispered.

A dark dread pulled at Til's heart as she waited for Mirabel to speak.

Mirabel gritted her teeth and shook her head in fear.

"All right, then I expect we'll both get processed at the constabulary." Til's jaw clenched in frustration, tears filled her eyes.

"No. No," Mirabel cried out. "I will tell you what I know."

Til waited for Mirabel to gather her thoughts.

"Royce has a piece of waterfront property that looks like a farm. It isn't." Her voice faltered. "There is a dock there; Alys has been shipping girls to that dock for the last few months. Since Royce got out."

Til caught her breath as she waited for Mirabel to continue.

"Where is it?" Til tried and failed to remain patient.

"I can draw you a map. There is only one road to it." Mirabel wiped tears from her eyes.

"No. You'll take us there." Til stood up and went to the door. "We're ready."

Grayson bounded into the room.

"They are being held at a piece of property outside of the city," Til said to Grayson.

"How many men are guarding the premises?" Grayson asked Mirabel.

"I know Creston is there, but I don't know how many men Alys will have with her."

"What is the layout?" Grayson demanded.

"There is a cabin and a dock. Not much else." Mirabel's eyes widened.

"Trees?"

"Yes, very wooded."

"Are these necessary?" Til frowned at Grayson as Sol shackled her.

"Shut up," Grayson growled at Til. "I'll take them off when you go to confront Alys." Grayson gathered Mirabel's wrists together in front of her.

Til glared at him.

"I've had enough of your lies and your tricks," Grayson said to Til as he pulled her down the stairs.

Together, Mirabel and Til sat side by side in the back of a carriage. Mirabel trembled beside Til.

Good, she believes this.

"Let's go." Grayson slapped his hand against the side of the carriage, and it jolted to a start.

No one spoke as they slipped down the dark streets of Toronto. Mirabel gave instructions as they left the city boundaries.

"There is a road with an old pile of logs on the left side. At that pile of logs, we turn left." Mirabel's face paled in the moonlight.

"All right." Grayson knocked on the roof of the carriage, then got out to speak to the driver.

Mirabel leaned against Til. "I don't know how many men are guarding the women."

"We'll work it out. You're all I've got," Til whispered to her.

Mirabel shuddered. "Creston is terrifying. Royce ordered Odelia's killing but Creston carried it out. I'm terrified of him."

Til held Mirabel's hand, their irons clinked together. They jumped apart as Grayson pulled the carriage door open and got back in.

The surrounding woods were hard to discern in the darkness before dawn. The road became rougher the further they travelled from the city. Til took a deep breath and let it out slowly.

"Are you scared?" Mirabel whispered.

"Yes, if anything happens to Shannon, I don't know what I'll do." Til's breath caught on a sob.

Mirabel nodded. She pressed her arm against Til's as a show of support.

Grayson cleared his throat.

"We'll get her back." Mirabel reached out and took Til's hand in her own. "We will."

Til squeezed back and hoped she was right.

Chapter Forty-One

Heart pounding with fear, Alys paced over to the trapdoor that led to the cellar. Mentally, she calculated the money going to Royce and the ransom money no longer available now that Matilda was in custody.

What am I going to do? Royce is expecting his money on November 3rd.

Alys pulled open the trapdoor and called to Shannon to come up. Shannon blinked in the light and slowly dragged herself up the stairs.

"Come with me," Alys demanded.

"I'm not leaving these girls." Shannon winced as the trapdoor slammed behind her.

"Come on." Alys pointed her gun at Shannon. "Back to the ship or I leave you to Creston."

The blood drained from Shannon's face. "You wouldn't."

"He's quite taken with you." Alys pressed the gun into her side harder.

"How could you?" Shannon's eyes narrowed.

"Easy. I think about how Matilda left me to the wolves. You had everything handed to you on a silver platter. It becomes simple. I turn a blind eye." Alys shrugged.

"I'm pregnant." Shannon shook against her.

Alys nudged her forward with her gun. "There is a telegraph machine on the ship. You will wire your ransom money to Royce's bank account." Alys pushed Shannon out the door and across the grass to the dock.

"How?" Shannon frowned in confusion. "I don't know the telegraph code. They shot the telegraph operator!"

"There's a book of code by the machine. You're a clever girl, you'll work it out." Alys pushed her ahead. "Let's go."

***

Dawn broke as the carriage ground to a halt. They could hear the other carriage with the rest of Grayson's men behind them in the darkness.

"We should walk the rest of the way in," Mirabel suggested to Til.

"We need a distraction." Til scowled at Grayson as he took their irons off, keeping up the appearance that she was a prisoner.

Rubbing her wrists, she thought about the best way to distract the men who were guarding the girls. Together with Mirabel, Til crawled out of the carriage into the dense Ontario woods.

"What if we take three horses with us, we'll say the reins broke. They would have to gather them right?" Til suggested.

Mirabel nodded. "That might work."

Grayson and Sol broke clasps, letting harness drag to the ground behind the horses. Til and Mirabel took the reins.

"We'll walk them in and then run them through the clearing to see who comes out to investigate." Mirabel suggested. "That should give us an idea of how many men are in there."

"Right." Til's heart hammered as the horses stamped near her. Picking up on her nerves, they tossed their heads. The reins tugged at her hands as she tried to subdue them.

On Bristol land once more, but this time the threat was from a woman not a man. Til gulped down her fear as they led three horses toward the cabin. She was thankful that the pine trees allowed them to get close without being seen. She took a deep breath. The smell of lake water, moss and pine trees filled her lungs as she tried to remain calm.

Til and Mirabel struggled to keep their horses under control, but as they dragged the three away from the remaining one at the carriage, the horses didn't want to be separated. They tossed their heads and whinnied and neighed at one another, creating a racket. Once the cabin was in view, Til let go of one horse and immediately the horse bolted away from them. The other two horses whinnied as they watched the third horse run.

Til and Mirabel struggled to keep their horses under control as a man stumbled out of the cabin.

"Don't let your horse go yet. Who is that?" Til murmured as her horse pulled and pawed, trying to get away from her.

"Creston." Mirabel tried to subdue her horse as it snorted, pulling against the reins.

"Only one man?" Til whispered.

"There has to be more than one man." Fear laced Mirabel's voice.

"Let yours go," Til whispered to Mirabel. "See if anyone else comes out."

Mirabel complied. The horse Mirabel had been holding bolted to the clearing.

The final horse Til held onto went wild as the other two horses took off, leaving him behind. He dragged Til forward three feet, tossed his head and neighed for the other horses.

Both women tried to hold the last horse back as he pulled and stamped, his whinnying becoming more frantic.

"I only see two men," Til gasped as she tried to drag the horse under control.

"I see Creston and I don't know who the other one is." Mirabel's eyes widened in fear.

"The other is Shipley Bristol." Til bit her lip in fear as the horse she was trying to subdue bolted and she had no choice but to drop the rein.

Both women watched as the men lured the horses with oats to calm them.

Til swallowed hard. "It's up to you."

"Right." Mirabel straightened up.

"Tell the men they sent you early to bring the girls to Royce, the horses got away and you need them to fetch the carriage."

Mirabel nodded.

"Once you lead the men from the clearing, you show me with your fingers, rub them along the side of your face, if there are any men left in the cabin." Til instructed.

"Right." Mirabel agreed.

"Thank you." Til followed behind Mirabel as she scrambled through the underbrush towards the cabin.

Her heart in her throat, Til watched as the man called Creston gathered the horses with a pail of oats. Together, he and Mirabel walked by and Til watched as she rubbed the side of her face with one finger.

***

Grayson's stomach rolled as he watched Mirabel lead one man and three horses toward them. Til's plan had worked. Mirabel led a man he was certain was Creston, the gunman his men had been following for weeks, straight into Sol's fists. Grayson kept his eye on Til's white shirtwaist, crisp against the changing leaves. She walked with such purpose, her black skirt billowed around her; she didn't seem to notice as copper bushes clung at her. Grayson scrambled to keep Til in his sight as she entered the clearing.

Til knocked on the door and then hid behind the woodpile.

No one came to the door. Grayson held his breath to steady his hands as a man crept around the back of the cabin with his gun drawn. Grayson held his rifle steady, put the man in his sights. He breathed out slowly, three short breaths. He waited for a clear shot.

***

Horrified, Til gasped in fear as Shipley Bristol came around the side of the cabin with his gun drawn. Holding her hands up, she tried to take a step back so he wouldn't shoot her.

"Matilda Bertram..." Shipley moved closer. "Royce has been waiting a long time for you."

"Where is he?"

"On his way tomorrow, but maybe I should show you what to expect..."

A bloom of blood exploded in his chest and Shipley dropped to the ground in front of her.

Til gasped as the crack of the rifle shot followed a second later.

Grayson!

Til pressed her hand to her heart, hoping to calm her pulse. She stepped back, away from the dead man and silently thanked Grayson.

Hands shaking, she wiped sweat from her forehead with her forearm. Til moved to the front door of the cabin and opened it a crack. Her eyes swept around the kitchen as she heard muffled screaming.

She saw a brass ring on a trap door and pounced on it.

Til struggled to drag the trapdoor up. She gasped in horror as twelve young women blinked and cried out in fear.

"Shannon, are you there, Shannon?" Til couldn't keep the hysteria out of her voice.

"They took her. We heard gunshots." One young woman with blonde hair and blue eyes wept into her skirt.

Til knew this look of despair, her heart went out to the child.

"She's dead." One girl stepped forward and wiped tears from her face.

Til dropped to her knees at the entrance of the cellar.

"Please stay here, where you are safe." Til could barely force the words past the knot in her throat. "I'll leave the trapdoor open; don't leave until the police come for you. They will be here in minutes. You are safe. You are all going home."

Til scrambled for the door and stopped for a moment, wondering where Alys would have left Shannon's body.

Shannon is dead. Alys has killed her. She took Malcolm, and she took Shannon. How will I go on?

Chapter Forty-Two

"What was that?" Alys's voice was tinged with fear.

"Sounds like a horse." Shannon's eyebrows drew together in confusion. "Is Royce early?"

Shannon's hands fumbled as she tried to work out how to run the telegraph machine to buy her freedom.

"Come with me." Alys pressed her gun into Shannon's side. Dragging her out of the ship and onto the dock, she saw horses stampeding through the clearing and they both saw Shipley drop from a gun-shot wound.

"Back on the ship," Alys's shrieked.

"Is this a rival gang? The ship is the next place they'll look," Shannon rasped.

Panicking, Alys pressed Shannon forward down the dock and to a narrow trail just past the dock.

Alys shuddered as a woman walked towards them.

"Matilda," Alys breathed as if she never expected her to find her. "Come on." Alys pressed the gun against Shannon's side. "Down this path."

Shannon scampered down the path ahead of Alys until they reached another clearing.

"Down, on your knees." Alys instructed Shannon.

"You wouldn't." Shannon begged. "I am pregnant."

Alys pulled back the hammer on the derringer, "I'm not asking again." Alys pressed the muzzle of the derringer against Shannon's temple as she braced herself to face her greatest enemy, Matilda Bertram.

***

Til, her own derringer in hand, noticed a flicker of movement out of the corner of her eye.

Taking a deep breath to steady her nerves, she walked swiftly down a narrow path. Her breath caught as she took in the scene. A peaceful meadow surrounded by majestic pine trees set the stage for terror.

Alys held Shannon in front of her as a shield. Til's eyes swept over Shannon, no obvious injury. Til let out a deep breath of relief. Shannon was alive, manacled, doing her level best to stay strong, stay courageous, as Til faced off with her sister.

Every muscle in Til's body tensed as she held Alys's gaze.

"This is all your fault," Alys cried out. "Don't come closer or she dies."

Sweat slicked Til's hands as she gripped her revolver. "Alys. It doesn't have to be like this. I will give you whatever you want." Til tried to keep her voice calm.

"Everything that happened. Everything. It's your fault." Alys jumped at a sound behind Til. "You ran, you didn't protect me." Alys wept as her hand shook on the gun.

"I know." Til wept with her. "I was utterly wrong, and I am here to tell you I am sorry. I should have saved you. I should have saved all of you."

"Don't lie!" Alys screamed at her. "Don't lie. You ran because you cared more about yourself than us. You always put yourself first."

"What happened that night?" Til wiped tears from her eyes. Trying to keep Alys talking while her heart broke at what she would say.

"You don't care!" Alys shrieked in anguish.

Til tramped down guilt that roared through her at Alys's words.

"I care." Til took two steps forward. Her voice gentle, she tried to draw Alys out. "What happened to you that night? It has haunted me since November 2nd, 1881." Til braced herself for an answer, an answer that terrified her to her core.

Were you sold to Mr. Carn that night?

It was the unknown she couldn't reconcile. Bad as it was, it had to be said. Til braced herself to hear a tale of rape and devastation.

"The police came and took us away," Alys said bitterly. "They split us up; they put us in orphanages except for me. Me and Jimmy. I wouldn't let go of him, they tried to force me. I loved him when you didn't."

A burst of breath gushed from Til as the knowledge that as bad as an orphanage and workhouse was, Alys had been safe.

"Oh, thank God." Til sucked air past her tight throat. "I thought all these years it was worse than that." Til covered her face in her hands. "Oh, Alys, what a relief."

"What is worse than a workhouse where you watch your baby brother die in your arms? What is worse than that?" Alys howled in pain.

Til dropped her hands.

"Jimmy died?" Til asked, eyes wide, tears spilling down her cheeks.

"Jimmy died because you didn't care," Alys screamed at her. "I lost Jimmy so you will lose Shannon. That way you will know how much I hurt. I still hurt."

"Let Shannon go and kill me instead." Til, with a show of faith, tossed her gun across the clearing.

Shannon's eyes widened in panic.

"Please. Let her go. We'll settle this between us, Alys. This has nothing to do with Martha's child." Til held her hands out in supplication.

"Stop calling her Martha's child," Alys swore at her. "Stop pretending you care. You're vicious..."

"This is between you and me." Til kept her tone soft. "Put the gun on me; let Shannon go. I'm pregnant, Alys. You kill me, you kill my child with me. Shannon can stay out of this. This is street justice and I remember it well. No mercy, right?"

Alys, her hatred for Til so clear, so big, it was like a presence between them, thrust Shannon away. Shannon stumbled past Til.

Til kept her gaze steady on Alys. The gun in Alys's hands shook as Til took a step forward and put her body between Alys and Shannon.

"We can resolve this without violence," Shannon said to both of them. "We can pay to set you up in a new life. Anywhere."

"No. We can't," Til said. Her gaze locked with Alys's. "We have to play by Alys's rules and someone has to die. Right Alys?"

Alys ignored Shannon's plea.

"Before you kill me, I want to tell you what happened, Alys. I want you to hear it." Til kept her hands up. "Shannon, I would rather you left and didn't overhear this."

Shannon hesitated and then moved away.

Alys's eyes narrowed to slits. Til took one step closer. Alys closed the gap between them, placing the muzzle of the gun right between Til's eyes.

Til swallowed hard.

"You left us." Alys's jaw clenched, tears filled her eyes. She pressed the derringer harder into her skin. "You left us to the wolves."

"I ran because our father sold me to Mr. Carn." Til's breath caught with terror as she held Alys's gaze. "He dragged me from my bed and said I would go with Mr. Carn to pay the rent for the winter."

Alys gasped in horror, "What?"

"He gambled and lost," Til rasped. "Do you remember Mr. Carn?" Til tried and failed to take the emotion out of her voice. "Fifty years old, huge belly from drink and he was going to take me home that night. My innocence for the price of a flat for the winter. That's all I was worth to our father."

Alys's jaw dropped, the derringer pressed harder into Til's forehead. "What happened then?"

"There was blood on my skirt, Alys." Til's jaw tightened. "I was bleeding and he was furious. He envisioned taking me that night and the sight of that blood put him off. Father said to go and wash myself."

"Oh my God." Alys's face paled in horror. She dropped her arm holding the gun.

Til breathed a tiny sigh of relief.

"I ran past you." Til's breath caught. "I will never forget running by you and wanting to save you and wanting to save myself."

Alys's eyes filled with tears. "I thought of you the most because I feared you would be next. Oh, Alys. The workhouse... terrible... but in Mr. Carn's bed... you must see that would have been worse... I was so afraid you had taken my place." Til broke down. She covered her hand with her mouth until her mouth stopped trembling. "You were such a pretty girl, I was terrified.... but I only knew how to save myself. I broke the window in the bedroom and ran into the night." Til dropped to her knees again in front of Alys. Gutted with emotion, she knelt in front of her. "Believe me, if there had been a way to take you all with me, I would have." Til's anguished sobs filled the clearing. "I was a terrified child, Alys. I was fifteen years old and I ran because I didn't know what else to do."

Alys covered her mouth with her hand. She paced around as Til, wept in front of her.

"I took a wrong turn and ended up in Bristol territory." Til pressed her hand to her heart. "Royce Bristol attacked me, Malcolm came to the rescue."

"You set him up, though." Alys whirled on Til, confusion flashed in her eyes. "Royce was to run the Bristol Butchers... you and Bobby were working together... Royce said Malcolm was hired to take him out of the ..."

"I had never met Malcolm before." Til struggled back to her feet. "I was running to Odelia, like I always did, and I took a wrong turn. One wrong turn and my life changed, just like that." Til swallowed hard. "Royce Bristol was supposed to be head of the Bristols that night. He was knocked unconscious by Malcolm. With that altercation, we both had to leave Bristol territory for good. I had to leave all of you." Tears slid down her cheeks. "I had no choice. I ran to Odelia's, and went into service the next day. If I had shown my face in that place I would have been as good as dead. You know how the Bristols operate. I had no other choice." Til wrapped her arms around herself, trying to stop trembling.

The gun hung at Alys's side. Tears filled her eyes as she spoke. "All this time, I thought you didn't love us."

"I searched for you." Til stepped forward. "I finally had the means to come back and make things right. I only found Martha, so I took Shannon as my own. I would have done that for all of you. I couldn't find the rest of you. It sickened me that Martha was in the same terrible situation as our mother. What can I do Alys? How can I make it up to you?" Til tramped down feelings of fury that Alys had killed Malcolm. Instead, she looked past that to see her as the terrified child in a workhouse holding her dead brother.

Alys covered her face with her hand. "I didn't know. All these years I had no idea."

"I know." Til moved forward and tugged the gun from Alys's hand. She flung it away from her.

Alys pressed her forehead into Til's shoulder.

"You were the only mother I had after Ma passed." Alys wept into Til's shoulder.

"I know." Til tightened her arms around her as police swarmed the clearing silently. "I wish I had woken you all and ran with you into the night, but where? Where would we have all gone?"

Alys sobbed harder.

"I'm sorry." Til stroked Alys's shaking back.

Grayson, irons in hand, stood behind Alys as she wept with her sister.

Finally, Alys quieted and Til stroked her hair back from her face. "Royce blamed you for killing Malcolm. Tell me it isn't true." Til's voice broke on a sob. "Odelia killed him, yes?" Til whispered into her ear. "I have to know, and I need to hear it from you. Did you kill Malcolm?"

Alys's head snapped up. "Til. When Andy replaced me, I had to."

"What do you mean, you had to?" Til's heart splintered in her chest.

"You had to suffer as I had." Alys covered her face with her hands. "I was wrong. Can you forgive me?"

"Alys, it's not just me." Til raged. "You stole a father from his child. I am pregnant. You took away the only loving, protective father Shannon knew!" Til watched her words viciously bite into Alys. "You will have to pay for that."

Alys took a step back from Til, running into the solid wall of Grayson.

"What is going on?" Alys looked around the clearing at all the officers, suddenly realising that they weren't alone.

"Alys Bertram, you are under arrest for the murder of Malcolm Maddox." Grayson took her by the upper arm.

Alys tried and failed to twist away from him.

Grayson slid irons on her as he continued to list her crimes. "The kidnapping of Shannon McDougall, and the procurement of twelve girls for prostitution."

Alys's mouth dropped open. "You tricked me." Her green eyes clashed with Til's amber ones.

"Alys, you killed my husband and stole my niece. I did what I had to do to get Shannon back. I wish things were different." Sadness and loss dragged at Til, her shoulders slumped. "I didn't trick you. I meant what I said. I wish it had all been very different."

"But..." Alys looked wildly from Til to Grayson. "Tell them I made a mistake... please Matilda..." Shackled, Alys tried to twist away from Grayson to reach for Til.

"You killed Malcolm in cold blood. My husband and the father of my child is dead, and you have to answer for that." Til shook as she spoke. "You will answer for that with your life."

Alys wept and begged as Grayson handed Alys to Sol.

Til's heart pounded with loss now instead of fear and dread.

"I was wrong! I..." Alys struggled against the solid wall of Sol's chest as he dragged her from the clearing.

Til covered her face with both hands.

Shannon ran to Til and put her arms around her.

"I'm sorry." Shannon held her hard.

"Are you all right?" Til clung to Shannon. Pulling away, she ran her hands over her to be sure she was unharmed.

"I am." Shannon's eyes filled with tears. "You never should have traded your life for mine. What were you thinking?"

Til shook her head, she couldn't speak.

Shannon held onto Til. "I love you."

"I love you too." Til wept. Her arms tightened on Shannon.

"I have to see to the girls from the cellar. I want to speak to you, but it will have to be later." Shannon pulled away. "They are terrified, and I don't want a male doctor examining them. They are too young. I am so sorry. I have to leave you just now. Are you all right on your own?"

"Of course, but who will be with you?" Til gave her hands one last squeeze.

"Cole came with the reinforcements." Shannon tore her eyes from Til's. She looked down a long path. Til followed her gaze and saw Cole waiting patiently for them to finish speaking before he interrupted.

"Fitting." Til wiped tears from her eyes. "He's a good reinforcement."

Shannon smiled. "I must go to him, he will be frantic."

Til nodded. "Of course."

Til watched Cole run to Shannon, sweep her right off her feet, and kiss her in front of half of the Toronto Constabulary.

Til bit her lip at their obvious love, reminded again that she had been utterly wrong about him.

About so many things.

Finally, Cole put Shannon gently on the ground; together they made their way down the path. Holding branches back so she wouldn't be scratched, Cole held Shannon's hand firmly. Til's heart warmed as she watched them. Cole and Shannon had the sort of love that was like light on a dark day.

Grayson moved forward through the men. "Everyone is safe, Til." Grayson confirmed.

Til turned to look up at him, her face crumpled.

"Good work here today." Grayson reached for her. He pulled her into his arms and held onto her hard.

Tears filled Til's eyes as she pressed her forehead into his hard shoulder. "My sister is going to hang for these crimes."

"Don't think of that just now." Grayson's arms tightened around her. "Shannon is safe, you and your baby are safe, twelve girls are going home. This was the best we could hope for."

"My heart is broken." Til wept. "All these years she thought the worst of me, and she was forced into a life of terror."

Grayson pulled her tight against him and rocked her slightly as if she were a little girl.

"How can I bear this?" Til cried. "How will I ever bear it? This is too much! My heart is broken, Grayson, and it hurts."

"I know." Grayson ran his hand up and down her back.

Til's sobbed against him. "She's my sister, but he was my husband. The father of my child." Anguished sobs ripped up out of her soul. Grayson held her hard against him as she shattered.

***

Shannon walked out of the clearing, her hand warm in Cole's. He stopped her, tears in his eyes as he kissed her.

"I have to know, are we having a baby?" Cole searched her face for answers.

"We are." Shannon, haggard and exhausted, managed a weak smile.

Cole pulled her against him. "You need to rest, I know you want to treat the girls, but Shannon..." Cole warned.

"All is well. No cramping and no problems." Shannon laid her head against his chest. "Those girls cannot face a male doctor. I must go. Please, come with me and help me."

Cole held Shannon tight. "Of course."

Shannon pulled his head down to kiss her.

The sound of Til sobbing interrupted them. Shannon pulled away from Cole to go back and try to comfort Til. Cole put his hand on her arm.

"Wait," Cole said. "Look."

Shannon's eyes softened as she watched Grayson gather Til into his arms and hold her as she wept against him. Shannon smiled a gentle smile at him as he pressed his hand against the back of Til's neck and pulled her closer. Constables came to him to ask for direction, to take the sobbing woman from his arms so he could get on with his work.

"Why are they interrupting?" Shannon frowned.

"He's the lead. The men need permission to take action, so typically a constable would take Til so Grayson could get on with his work." Cole drew her closer to him.

Grayson held his hand up to stop them from interrupting, and shook his head at them. The constables frowned and left them alone. Grayson held onto Til as if she would break without him.

Shannon nodded to Grayson and he nodded back. It was obvious to Shannon that the only man taking Til from the clearing was Detective Grayson.

Matilda Bertram, alias Til Stone, has met her match, in more ways than one.

Shannon couldn't tear her eyes away. Grayson didn't notice. He whispered to Til, adjusting her against his body to lend more comfort.

"What do you think of that?" Shannon's breath caught.

"I will pray for him." Cole grinned down at Shannon.

A smile tugged at Shannon's lip.

"Come on." Cole took her hand to lead her away. "Should I carry you?"

"Carry me?" Shannon's eyebrow arched as she looked up at him.

"Well, you're pregnant and you've been through a terrible ordeal. I can carry you..." Cole's troubled eyes searched hers.

"Cole. I am all right to walk. That is very sweet, but really. I am just fine."

Cole's forehead creased in concern. "If you feel tired, or anything, just let me know."

Shannon's eyes filled with tears at his kindness. "Cole."

"Yes." Cole stopped walking to listen.

"I... I uh..." Shannon tried to speak past the lump of emotion suddenly choking her at the thought of how powerful Cole's love was. Even now she looked down at her filthy, exhausted and emotionally wrung out body, Cole obviously didn't care; he was prepared to put her needs first.

I am a very lucky woman.

"Shannon, what is it? You're crying." Cole gently brushed her tears away with his fingertips.

"I'm just..." Shannon blinked as she tried to gather her thoughts. "I'm overwhelmed with love for you."

Cole smiled as he pulled her into his arms again. "I love you, too."

Eventually, Shannon pressed on his chest to create some distance. "Will Til be all right, do you think?" Shannon bit her lip as she looked up at Cole.

"She's a survivor." Cole kissed Shannon gently.

Shannon nodded and looked back at Grayson holding Til, still.

"They need privacy, darling." Cole took her hand again. "The girls, particularly Anna, are crying for you."

"Right." Shannon squeezed Cole's hand as he led her forward. "Til's in good hands."

Chapter Forty-Three

Til joined Shannon at the wagon as constables assisted the girls, assuring them they were safe, and their friend Shannon was going with them.

"Where are they going to rest?" Til asked Shannon as she stood by her. "This is so horrific. My sister selling girls." She shook her head. "How could anyone?"

"I don't know. She's gone; they took her in a separate carriage. Don't think of it today." Shannon wiped her forehead with her forearm. "Cole is settling the girls."

"He's good at his work," Til acknowledged.

Shannon looked at her and raised her eyebrow.

"It's a thing I'm trying." Til bristled. "I'm trying to find one positive thing in every situation no matter how bad it is. I'm trying to... well... change." Til tucked a stray lock of hair behind her ear, she shot a look at Shannon to see if she would mock her.

"Good." Shannon grinned at her aunt. "That is a very healthy response."

"I'm trying, sometimes I fail." Til grit her teeth.

"It looks like Detective Grayson and you are friends now?" Shannon asked.

"We're professionals, Shannon. He is still married and I am grieving. We had a rocky start, but we have been good partners."

"I see."

"He assisted me on a birth on the way here." Til picked at a thread on her skirt. "All was well until he fainted." Til shook her head. "It set things *back*, I can tell you that."

Shannon howled in laughter. "Fainted?"

"I had to use smelling salts." Til rolled her eyes as she watched him directing men. "He's not as tough as he looks." Til frowned. "A woman suffering unravels him." Til crossed her arms over her chest.

"That is a good thing," Shannon suggested softly.

Til sniffed. "He saved me from being violated by four men - not at the same time mind you. I will give him that."

"I'm glad you were able to work together. It's good to widen your circle of men that you trust."

"Well, trust is a strong word. We have a bit of unfinished business about his daughter... however, now that this is settled, I'm sure we will go our separate ways and it won't matter." Til bristled.

"Til. I missed you." Shannon laughed at Til.

Til shot Shannon a hard look. "Never mind all that and all jesting aside, Shannon. When I heard you were missing my heart stopped in fear."

Shannon's eyes filled with tears. Seeing that, Til's eyes filled too.

"You're crying," Shannon breathed.

"Oh, Shannon, it's this baby. I cry at the drop of a hat. It's a nightmare." Til tried to wipe the tears away as fast as she could.

"Imagine that. My aunty, finally at *forty*, has an emotion!" Shannon chuckled despite what she had just endured. "I wonder if that is how it will be for me? I wonder if my pregnancy will have me crying at the drop of a hat?" Shannon pressed her palms to her abdomen as she shot a wicked grin at Til.

"What are you saying?" Til pressed her hand to her heart.

"Cole and I are expecting a baby in September next year. I think this is the best time to tell you. You'd be all emotional that I'm not dead, you might be happy at the news." Shannon tilted her head to the side.

Til wiped tears from her eyes and swallowed down all the thoughts that sprang to her mind to say.

Your career is over; your life will now change. Are you sure this is what you want?

Til pushed all those fears aside and cradled Shannon's face in her hands. "I'm so thrilled for you, my darling girl. Children are the gift, Shannon. Children are the miracle. I can't wait to be a great-aunty."

"What happened... to you..." Shannon blinked in amazement. "Are you sure?"

"Positive." Til pulled her close. "Let's go. We have catching up to do. I should help with the girls... that would process things quickly and Cole will want..."

"Yes. He will. You're sure... you *are* happy about this baby?" Shannon stopped Til.

Til turned to look at her. "Shannon, this whole experience has been... surreal. I've had to look at a few things differently. I've met people who have changed my perspective."

"Really? I'm happy to hear it," Shannon asked quietly.

"I had to come to terms or accept that what happened in that place was out of my control. I spent my whole life terrified of who would abuse their authority over me next. I took you when Martha died, and I worried about that for you. This constant fear drove me forward and although things looked successful on the surface, deep down the fear stopped me from being complete. What happened to Alys and the rest of my siblings was my *father's* fault, not my own." Til's breath caught. "I had to believe that even if I wasn't a doctor and a surgeon and champion of women's rights every minute of the day, I was still *worth* something."

Til's eyes glittered with tears. "An emptiness inside me has driven me, it is a cruel master. Nothing could fill the void but the truth. What happened to the Bertrams on November 2nd, 1881 was never my fault. It was my father's fault and I'm done answering for it. I'm moving past it."

"Just like that?" Shannon's eyes softened in sympathy.

"No need to draw things out." Til gathered herself up to her full height. "Done and dusted, Shannon. It occurred to me that the thoughts we have at fifteen need to be reevaluated in the harsh light of forty. I will probably have to evaluate these thoughts at fifty and so on. I am a forty-year-old pregnant fossil and I don't have the energy to drag around all this guilt." Til shrugged. "Although, letting all of this guilt and sadness go, I feel like I'm—" Til stopped speaking, suddenly overcome with emotion. Her eyes met Grayson's across the bustle of constables and the coroner who pronounced Shipley Bristol dead. He nodded at her, in his element, thrilled to be working.

She nodded back.

"You feel like what?" Shannon asked softly.

"Shannon." Til's eyes stayed on Grayson as she spoke to Shannon. "I feel as though I am just beginning."

Shannon smiled. "It will be a great beginning, Til. New baby, new country, unless you are going back. What about Grayson?"

"I don't know." Til didn't take her eyes off him. He cut an impressive figure. Tall and broad, rifle over his shoulder, he delegated and ordered men around. His men respected him, they jumped to comply. Til remembered how his body felt against hers in Royce's room and more recently in the clearing. She turned from him. It was too soon. Her heart was too broken with the loss of Malcolm to entertain any thoughts of a shaggy Canadian detective. Til put on a brave face. "His wife and baby daughter came back." Til's shoulders suddenly slumped. "He left his daughter, Shannon, and that has made me see him in a different light. What kind of man leaves his daughter? Would he have left a son?"

Shannon laid her hand on Til's forearm.

"I have enough on my plate just now. A baby on the way without Malcolm. I can't seem to believe he is gone. I keep thinking he's going to show up somehow." Til watched Shannon, her eyes tortured with the pain of loss.

"I know. I think so too." Shannon's eyes filled with tears. "Til, I know you will be a terrific mother."

"Oh, I think you and I both know parenting isn't really my *forte*." Til changed the subject. She tossed her hair back over her shoulder, quick to retreat to her old prickly self as she thought about raising a baby alone, without Malcolm. "Children are the gift, yes, but gracious, I think staff to look after the less pleasant aspects are essential. I expect to *farm out* a lot of that, dear."

Shannon threw back her head and howled with laughter. "Til, you might have changed a few things, but you are the same, and I love you. I really do."

Til turned to Shannon, pulled her back into her arms and held onto her as if she would slip away forever. "I love you so much, Shannon. I am thrilled that you are having a baby and I will be there to help you when your time comes. You can tell Oakland to brace themselves."

"Great heavens, I can't even imagine you in Oakland, Til." Shannon laughed and shook her head.

"Imagine it. I'm coming to assist. No niece of mine will labour without chloroform." Til's eyes hardened in warning. "That is not negotiable."

"Thank you, Til." Shannon grinned, "But what if you are in England?"

"Oh! No! I can't stand the thought of that journey back to England. No. Not now. You are here, in Canada. We are a few days by train apart... I think it makes sense to stay here for now anyway. Once I have the baby, I'll reevaluate." Til shook her head.

"Get some rest. I have to go." Shannon flashed a smile at Til as a wagon drew up next to them. Cole got down to assist Shannon. He helped her up to sit with the twelve rescued girls. The youngest girl, Anna, curled up against her. She held Anna tightly and patted her back. Cole moved behind Shannon so she could lean against his chest instead of the cold wall of the wagon. Til nodded her thanks to him. He nodded back as he smoothed Shannon's hair away from tickling his nose.

"Get some rest," Til repeated to Shannon as the wagon drew them away.

"You too," Shannon called out to her as she snuggled into Cole. She rested her head on his shoulder. He pulled a heavy blanket over her and the young girl in her arms.

Til turned to find Grayson in the crowd. Tired and cold, she was ready for a hot meal and a bed. Grayson moved through men who were dealing with the dead body of Shipley. Til shuddered as she remembered how close he had come to killing her. Finally, Grayson stood by her.

"You're white as a sheet," Grayson murmured in concern.

"Shannon is pregnant." Tears gathered in Til's eyes.

"Happy news," Grayson said cautiously. "Are you feeling well?"

Til shrugged. "I don't know what I am. I can't seem to collect my thoughts." Til's face crumpled with emotional pain.

A carriage rumbled up to them and Grayson pulled open the door and helped Til into the carriage. He told the driver to take them to Stein's house. Grayson crawled in beside her.

"You can sleep on my shoulder if you want," Grayson offered.

"I'm all right." Til rubbed her eyebrow. "Do you have to interrogate all these people today?"

"I am trying something new." Grayson shifted on the bench of the carriage so he could face her.

"Oh?" Til looked into his eyes.

"I've delegated all the interviewing. It's open and shut. The others can handle it. We're going to the Steins. You are going to bed." Grayson adjusted a lap robe over her knees.

"Delegated!" Til gasped.

"I know. It shocked the lads. Anyway. You need to get to bed and I have to deal with Melinda and Ella." Grayson grimaced. "You should get some sleep on the way," Grayson commanded.

As the carriage pulled them towards Toronto, Til shook her head. "I couldn't sleep if I tried."

Conflicting emotions welled up in Til's heart. She turned from Grayson so she could look out the window. Silent tears of relief slid down her face. Tears because Shannon was safe. Her heart warred between wanting Alys to pay and frustration that the one responsible, their father, would never know the havoc he had wrecked. Injustice burned in Til as she remembered his order to do the right thing. As this jumble of emotions cascaded through her, loss hollowed her out. Murderer of Malcolm or not, her sister would pay the ultimate price for her crimes; her father would not. She pressed her forehead against the cool glass of the window in the carriage.

"Hey, that's a lot of crying for the best possible outcome, Til." Grayson put his hand on her shoulder.

Til sat up straight, wiped her eyes and turned to face him.

"Twelve girls saved from prostitution and the streets. *Twelve.*" Grayson repeated. "They are going home to live happy lives because you faced your past including a gang of Bristol Butchers. Nora Blackburn is going home, unscathed. Shannon is safe with Cole. Be proud of what you did here today."

"Thank you. Was it you? Did you shoot Shipley Bristol?" Til asked.

"I did." Grayson tilted his head to the side.

"How do you feel about that?"

"I did my job. Everyone is alive, everyone goes home. That's better than we could have hoped for." Grayson wiped tears from her eyes with his sleeve. "I kept everyone alive, except the bad guys. That's what I'm supposed to do. I would do it again."

"You had Alys in your sights, didn't you? You didn't kill her." Til pulled back a little to gauge his reaction.

"I didn't have Alys in my sights or she would be dead," Grayson answered honestly. "She used Shannon as a shield, and then I couldn't get high enough to get around you. If I could have gotten a clear shot, I would have taken it."

Til shivered. "Instead, she will hang."

Grayson sighed. "As is usual in a situation like this, there is no perfect solution. The least amount of people hurt is about all we can hope for."

Til's heart ached as she thought about those words. "I feel empty and sick."

Grayson's eyes softened with sympathy. "She made a choice. A terrible one. In this world, you pay for those choices."

"Speaking of terrible choices, do you think you could find my father?" Til asked bitterly. "He should be prosecuted."

"I did," Grayson said quietly.

"Where is he?" Til's jaw dropped open.

"He died, Til." Grayson's lips thinned as he spoke. "Stabbed to death in the tenements, no suspects."

Til's breath caught. "Oh. I wish that helped." Til's lips twisted with bitterness. "He should have faced a judge and jury. His failings should be made as public as Alys's will be."

"I hate injustices like that too. I'm sorry, Til, I would have told you sooner, but the time never seemed to present itself." Grayson kept a careful distance. "You should rest, Til. It's all over now."

Til shook her head sadly. "It will never be over in my heart. I will carry this always."

"Maybe. Maybe not." Grayson spoke gently. "Maybe some day you will be able to put it down. It's fresh now, but time has a way of softening things a bit, to make them bearable. You did good work here. You're tough as nails, Til Stone."

Til's throat ached with unshed tears. She nodded and turned her gaze to the window. "I don't know, Grayson. Today I don't feel very tough at all."

Chapter Forty-Four

When the carriage stopped at the Stein's house, cheerful early morning sunlight lit up Cherry Street. Til briefly closed her eyes against the glare of sun as it hit the window of the carriage.

"I asked the constables to have all your things brought to the spare room for you," Grayson said.

"Oh, good." Til tugged at the sleeve of his shirt and wiped her tears. "I'm out of clean handkerchiefs," she apologised.

"Oh, then by all means, use my shirt." Grayson grinned.

"Grayson, you look like a homeless man half the time. No one will notice," Til reprimanded him.

He chuckled and held his hands out to Til; she slid her hands into his. Together they made their way to the house. The butler led them to the dining room where Cora greeted them.

"Please, have breakfast. You must be exhausted." Cora gestured that they should sit.

Exhaustion dragged at Til's arms as she picked up her teacup. She could not make coherent conversation, her back ached, her head pounded.

Cora left for work at Hope House and the maid bustled through, gathering plates and cutlery.

"I'll show you to your room," Grayson offered as Til stood up.

Together, they walked down the hallway to the spare rooms.

Suddenly, as if Melinda had been waiting, the door to the nursery opened. Beautiful Melinda Grayson held sleeping Ella against her shoulder. They made a stunning picture as she stood in a shaft of early morning light. It glowed behind her illuminating her blonde hair, loose around her shoulders. The sun made her body visible under a lacy, gauzy nightgown, and lit up the halo of white blonde wispy hair on Ella's head.

"Could I have a moment, Asher." Melinda ignored Til, and turned her back to both of them. Til's eyes widened. Melinda's lace nightgown was cut low enough to showcase the perfect, smooth skin of her back. Melinda retreated into the nursery, obviously confident Grayson would follow her.

Concern niggled at Til's mind as she thought about this woman, who tolerated a man who beat her, being given sole custody of the perfect baby girl in her arms.

How could Grayson let his daughter go?

Concern turned to anger as Til thought about how Grayson hadn't protected Ella from Melinda's incessant need for Archie.

Grayson looked from Melinda to Til. Seeing the look of confusion in his eyes, she put her hand on his forearm, pulled him down the hallway a few steps and then leaned into him so she could speak low into his ear.

"We solved this crime and we part ways here." Til gritted her teeth. "I'm not chasing any more slavers. You have your perfect partner Sol back. You need to protect your daughter with everything you've got. It is none of my business, but you should go to her and reconcile, you have a child together."

"Til!" Grayson sputtered.

"You tricked me Grayson, I will give you that." Til's eyes darkened in fury.

Grayson frowned with confusion.

"You let her *take your daughter*. I am not sure how you could have done that," Til snapped at him. "Would you have let her take your son?" The words tore out of Til faster than she could stop them.

Grayson's eyes widened in hurt and then flashed in anger.

"I'm tired." Til stepped away from him, gutted that he was not the friend and partner she had thought he was. "I'm so tired I feel sick. I need to lie down. So, please, be a father who does the right thing for his daughter." Til's tone hardened. "Put your daughter first, she's worth it. Don't let her wonder for the rest of her life what her worth is."

Til turned on her heel and went to find the butler to take her to her room.

"Til." Grayson started after her.

"There is nothing more to say." Til shot back at Grayson. She left him at the entrance to the nursery.

The butler led her to her room. Once her luggage was placed in the room, he closed the door behind him.

Finally alone, Til pressed her forehead into the wood of the door. She took a deep breath and let it out very slowly. When she closed her eyes she could see the girls in the cellar. The bloom of blood that exploded on Shipley's white shirt exploded behind her eyelids again. She was grateful to Grayson for all he had done, but her heart hardened as she thought of Ella and the life he had left her to. Til dragged herself to her bed and crawled into it.

She reminded herself as she pulled the covers over her head that Shannon was alive. Nora Blackburn was alive. Twelve stolen girls were in good hands. Til herself had survived. With the threat of Royce and Alys removed, it was time for real life. Til settled into the pillows as exhaustion overcame her. She would settle in Toronto, but Grayson would not be part of her life. Suddenly Til wondered wildly, settle in Toronto and do what? Til, for the first time in her life, wasn't exactly sure where she fit in the world.

I've given so much to the women of the East End, what now?

Chapter Forty-Five

Weak late autumn sunlight filtered in through the drapes in her room. Til awoke slowly; she heard someone bustling around her room. Her head ached as much as her heart.

"Stay in that bed," Shannon commanded as she brought a tray to Til and set it over her lap. "Have some hot tea and some breakfast."

"How are you?" Til sat up, rubbing her eyes. "How long have I slept?"

"A few hours."

Til gratefully sipped tea laced with a generous helping of sugar.

"You are well?" Til asked Shannon.

"I am fine." Shannon adjusted pillows behind Til. "The girls are all well. Everything is settling down."

"That's nice, dear." Til took a bite of toast, testing her stomach. Since she kept the food down, she ate more. She tore into a bowl of porridge as if she had never seen food.

"Are you sure you are well?" Shannon poured more tea into her teacup.

Til put the empty bowl of porridge down and sipped her hot tea. "I feel like I am black inside. I think about Alys and what she did and my heart breaks. It is so bitter to think she did these things. If only she had known. It's like losing her again." Til wiped a tear that escaped. "You are well, the hostages returned, I should be fine! The old me would stand up, dust myself down and go to work. The thought of leaving this bed and facing people or responsibility is overwhelming and I feel like I did when my mother died. Empty, lost and so exhausted."

"Til, you've been through so much!" Shannon exclaimed. "You've lost your sister, again. Your worst fear is confirmed, Jimmy died. You haven't had a minute to grieve for Malcolm. On top of all that, you are pregnant in a new land. If you weren't feeling black inside, I would wonder if you had any feelings at all."

"When you spend your whole life ignoring how bad something is, it's hard to face it alone." Til's voice darkened with sadness.

"You are not alone. You have me, Til, I'm not leaving you until you are well." Shannon took Til's hands in her own.

"What if I never am?" Til responded dully.

"Then we'll drag you to Oakland with us and you can work for me in the wing of the hospital I'm starting." Shannon squeezed Til's hands in hers.

"I am not sure. I've only ever worked for someone when I was with the Blackburns and look at how that turned out." Til frowned.

"You don't have to decide today." Shannon poured more tea in Til's cup. "That's why I will stay."

"You will not," Til reprimanded her. "You have responsibilities to the girls and you have a husband. You should go to Cole. I'm sure he's tired of sharing you with twelve hostages one night and an old weepy aunt the next."

"He understands." Shannon poured herself a fresh cup of tea.

"Shannon, no man is that patient." Til shook her head.

Shannon grinned and settled down on the bed to talk. "We sold or put up for sale everything in London except the clinic which Doctor Cotter is running. I hear from Enid that she is doing a good job. The cottage from Malcolm, we left that for you to decide."

Til's eyes filled with fresh tears. "Oh, Shannon. I can't even think about that! The summer we would have spent at the sea together with our new baby!" Til's voice caught on a sob. "Oh, my... how does anyone live through this pain?" Til gasped.

Shannon reached for Til.

"Gracious! Empty, black feelings rear up and engulf me, with no warning," Til cried.

"It will get better," Shannon murmured as she held Til against her.

"What if it doesn't?"

"It will." Shannon tightened her arms around Til.

"How will I raise this baby without Malcolm? How will I ever do it?" TIl sobbed against Shannon.

"Til Stone, you got out of the East End, became a doctor and then refused to give in until you were a gynecologist. Impossible is a word that has never applied to you." Shannon smoothed Til's hair against her back.

"What if it's a boy and I have to teach him to shave? I don't know how to do that. What if I ruin him with all my suffrage slogans?" Til reached for a handkerchief on her bedside table.

"Til." Shannon smiled as she shook her head. "You're in shock."

Til pulled away to look at Shannon.

"I'm scared," Til whispered. "I'm not up for this. New country, new baby, new everything, but what about my work? If I had that, maybe I could manage, and even as I say it, the thought of leaving this bed is too much." Til pulled a pillow against her lonely body.

"You are grieving. You are normal." Shannon patted her arm. "Every day will get a little easier. These are emotions, and this is new to you I know, but as you work through them, you will heal. You never properly grieved in your life. Eventually, the black will lighten. I know you, Til, you are up to this challenge. Feel these feelings and acknowledge them. It's time to heal."

"I don't think I can cope." Til wept. "It's too much. It starts when my mother died and just compounds from there."

"The Steins are a kind couple and they said you can stay here until you are able to cope. There is no rush." Shannon rubbed Til's upper arm.

"All right." Til wiped her eyes on a handkerchief. "Tell me more about the loose ends you've tied up in England."

"Enid said she would handle any further arrangements if you prefer to sell more property." Shannon smoothed hair back off Til's forehead. "If you return, she said to send her a telegram so she can have staff on site. Enid will deposit the money from the Halloway's, and you can go home as soon as you like, or stay."

Til pulled the pillow against her tighter. "Sell everything but the clinic and the cottage at the sea. Make sure all the doctors and Enid have a key in case they need to get a break from their work. Tell them, they should take regular breaks with their families. They can share it."

"That's a nice idea." Shannon smiled.

"If I return to England, it is the only place with happy memories for me." Til wiped tears from her eyes. "I'd like to keep it. It is comforting to know it is still there if I need it. After all this, I will never set foot in the East End again, Shannon. I am done trying to pay some debt. I owe no one anything. I was an innocent victim."

"That is true. You were innocent." Shannon rubbed Til's back. "I will let Enid know."

Til adjusted the pillow under her head. "When do you leave for Brandon?"

"Cole thinks we should stay with you until you are more settled." Shannon adjusted the covers over Til.

"Shannon, you can't put your life on hold," Til protested.

"It's winter. It is almost November and your baby is due in May, correct?"

"Correct."

"Doctor White has put my internship on hold, Til," Shannon explained. "I am not needed until I am ready. He's been so good."

"Very good of him. I expected him to call it off." Til picked at a thread at the edge of the blanket.

"Me too." Shannon placed the tray near the door for the maid to collect. "We will stay with you until you deliver; then we will spend the summer in Oakland. Cole does not want me working long hours starting a wing of a hospital while I'm pregnant. He will farm with his brothers while I sip tea and invite friends to visit." Shannon shrugged. "I don't know what spoiled women do who are pregnant, and he *is* spoiling me, Til." Shannon blushed as she brushed a stray piece of hair out of her eyes. "I think he would tie my shoes if I let him. He's so overprotective. You know how he is." The excitement in Shannon's eyes was contagious.

"Yes. I know exactly how he is." A glimmer of hope lightened the darkness in Til as she reached for Shannon. "But here is what I suggest. Go. Go to Brandon and get your wing started. You're young and healthy, you can work. Gather nurses, teach them how to fit contraception and assist with chloroform. Break the ice. I can write for some women doctors you can train to run your wing while you have your baby. You can have both, Shannon. You really can. I believe with enough staff, we can have anything.

I am counting on it," Til encouraged her. "Take the summer off if you like; a summer in Oakland sounds lovely."

"I can't wait to have tea with Priscilla after she outfits me with all new scandalous undergarments! Tea on the verandah with Ada Bennett, with lilacs and fresh cinnamon buns. Oh, Til. I am so excited! Also, Hannah, James's wife, is my sister- in- law. I have never had a sister, I think we will be best friends and raise our babies together. Til. I am so thrilled, I feel like I am going home." Shannon's eyes shone with excitement.

"It sounds delightful." Til refused to allow her gloom to touch her niece.

"Join us, Til! Lady Harper said you are welcome to come too. She has a lovely carriage house on the river. However, I know something you don't know." Shannon's eyes gleamed with anticipation. "The women of Toronto have a proposition for you, when you are able. Don't feel overwhelmed. Just know you have options when you are able and up and about."

"What sort of proposition?" Curious, Til's head tilted to the side. The darkness inside of her shifted to grey instead of black at the thought of a proposition involving her new friend Cora.

"I'll let them talk to you." Shannon grinned mischievously. "Cora has invited you to meet with her women. I said I would send a telegram if you were feeling up to it."

"Of course I'll meet with them."

"I have a note here from Grayson." Shannon pulled the note out of her pocket.

Til took the note and read it.

"Dear Til, I didn't want to disturb your rest, so I am writing. I am tying up loose ends in this investigation. When you are well enough to receive visitors, I would like a moment of your time. There are a few things we need to discuss before I close this file, and I want to explain about Ella — Grayson."

Til buried her head in the pillow. "We had a bit of a row."

"You! Having a row with someone?" Shannon mocked Til. "Never!"

"He left his daughter." Til's tone hardened.

"Til, he's a good man. Good enough to keep you alive and you would test the limits of any man. Honestly. So, you better make peace," Shannon warned. "You have to live in the same city and you will share the same friends."

"I don't know why it always seems to settle on me to make peace, Shannon." Til bristled.

"Well, you are grieving and you are sad so I will try to be delicate. You tend to speak your mind before you think," Shannon said cautiously.

"I am making changes, but I can't see myself staying quiet when a tragedy occurs and a young girl ends up being raised by a needy nit-wit and a wife beater." Til huffed. "His daughter should have come first."

"You may remember that you do not know all the facts," Shannon reprimanded her.

Til frowned as she thought about that. "I'll see what he has to say."

"Good. Now, I would like to do an examination and be sure this pregnancy is healthy and when you are well, I will need you to examine me, Til. I wasn't examined in England. Then we'll have a better grasp on when these little ones are due." Shannon beamed with excitement.

"You haven't had an examination yet?" Til sat up straight.

"Not yet. I suspected I was pregnant, told Cole, and then the next day Alys pounced. There was no time."

"How did she get to you?" Til pulled a pillow across her lap.

"I was showing your house to Mrs. Halloway. One of our maids said a woman came to inquire about where I was working that day. She told the maid that I had left a brooch behind at an appointment. She wanted to return it. Anyway, it was Alys. The maid sent Alys to your house, her men chloroformed me and I woke up on a ship sailing west. Again." Shannon shook her head. "Cole tore the city apart; he found me on a ship manifest."

"Til pressed her hand to her heart. "Scared me to death."

"But, here we are," Shannon said brightly. "No need to worry, all is well. I'll check on you before supper, you can check on me, but I'm feeling fit and happy."

"Shannon drew the curtains so Til could rest. Til closed her eyes and was asleep before Shannon left the room.

After a whole day and a night of sleep, Til dragged herself up out of bed. The maid had drawn a bath. Grateful, Til sat on the edge of the tub and swirled her hand through the water to distribute the salts that the maid had added. She peeled off her ugly nightgown and took her time.

"I don't know what will happen next, but I know we will be all right. I'm going to... I don't know what I will do." Til bit her lip. "You are only around nine weeks now, but you should know this about me. I have always had a plan, but I don't have one now. I am sad everyday and I love you already." Til wiped tears from her face. "Speck, before I worked to try to find my worth, I worked to keep myself so busy that I didn't have to deal with how bad I felt. This time, it's different. I am working for fulfillment but you will come before work for me. I promise." With that solemn vow in the air between them, she bathed and got dressed to meet the women of Hope House. A glow of eager excitement burned through the blackness of her grief.

Chapter Forty-Six

Til's mouth fell open in surprise as she looked around the lobby of Hope House. Rich oak panelling and deep ochre walls lit up as the sun poured in onto thick carpeted floors. Huge ferns graced each side of the heavy oak desk. A massive stern-faced guard looked her over and stood up to greet her.

"I'm here to meet with Mrs. Stein." Til stood in front of the desk.

"I'll let them know you are here. Please wait." The guard left her in the lobby.

Other guards stood strategically around the lobby to ensure no men slipped through without authorisation. According to the rules on the desk, no man entered Hope House without written consent from either Mrs. Stein, Mrs. Martin or Mrs. King. Hope House opened its arms to women escaping from domestic abuse, prostitutes hoping for a better life, any girls or women who needed education to stay off or get off the streets. No questions asked, no judgements offered. Any woman or girl willing to work hard was welcome.

The grey dragging at Til began to dissipate as her eyes skimmed over photographs of girls with their pictures taken celebrating recent accomplishments. The ladies who operated Hope House celebrated people. Til loved this approach, and her heart soared as she looked at all the faces that shone back from the pictures. This house presented a choice. A new life for any girl needing one. Not a charity, an education. Til pressed her hand to her heart as she remembered being accepted by the London Royal Free Hospital School of Medicine for Women. Money paid on her behalf to be paid back if she could.

Mrs. Jean King, Mrs. Adeline Martin, and Mrs. Cora Stein entered the lobby, smiled at the guards, and then opened the big doors to the offices. The women holding the door open to Til made a striking picture.

"Please, join us in Cora's office." Mrs. King nodded at Til.

"We're so happy to have you come in and listen to our plans for Hope House. We've been operating together since 1904 and we have had tremendous success." Mrs. King led the discussion. "My job is to oversee the education up to and including grade eight. I hire the teachers."

"Please, call me Adeline." Adeline held her hand out and Til shook it. Her grip was firm. "I deal with secretarial training; I hire educators and make sure any girl who wants to work in that capacity is placed in reputable offices."

"Adeline runs this place and makes sure we have the funds to keep the doors open." Cora smiled warmly at her friend. "My job is to represent these girls legally. I also work for women running from abusive husbands; I represent them in divorce court." Cora smiled at Til as they all sat down to tea.

"This is all very impressive." Til reached for her teacup. "I commend you on this initiative. Women like you assisted me at a young and desperate age. I am thrilled to see these humanitarian efforts continue."

"We were hoping it would impress you because we would like to offer you a position here to promote birth control." Cora couldn't keep the excitement out of her voice. "Also, classes on hygiene and nutrition."

Adeline pulled out the drawings. "These are the proposed changes to the building. This entrance would be for the public. Offices in this area and examination rooms for prostitutes looking for asylum. As you can imagine, we work closely with Asher Grayson, so be sure to take that into consideration when you make this decision."

"I believe you are familiar with his work." Mrs. King tilted her head to the side.

"Yes. Quite." Til stirred sugar in her tea.

"Is this even a possibility for you? Or are you determined to go back to England?" Adeline jumped right to the point. "If you aren't interested, we do not want to detain you. I understand from Cora that you are pregnant, and you've been through a tremendous ordeal. Perhaps this is all too soon, but we thought the faster we could start building you a clinic, the better. We hate to waste time."

"I am not returning to England." Til's eyes swept over the plans. "There is nothing for me there."

"Not even your clinic?" Cora asked Til gently.

"It's in good hands and I need a change." Til looked up at the women offering her this amazing opportunity to work and grow. "Honestly, the thought of the journey back to England is more than I can bear. I have spent my life despising weakness, and here I admit that my body will not handle the journey. I'm exhausted at the thought. I will look for a home starting Monday next week, if I am able. You are right, it has been far too much trauma and sadness; I need to heal. I can't commit to long days, but I can start gathering a team and training them so when my time to give birth comes you will have a fully functioning clinic."

"There is time to rest because this isn't built yet..."Adeline ran her hand over the part of the plan Til would work out of.

"I need very little space to help women one on one. I'll start two hours in the afternoon, every afternoon. That way I can rest. Mornings are the most difficult, but laying in bed for months is not going to help me get through my grief. I'm a worker, I need to work. I also need a place to stay so if you could point me in the direction of a modest place in Toronto..."

My house is empty," Mrs. King interrupted. "You can have the entire third floor. I would be glad of the company. Perhaps it would be better to put off major decisions until you are in a better frame of mind."

A lump of tears clogged Til's throat at the generosity of the women in front of her. "Thank you, that is very kind. Mrs. King, I will not be good company. I didn't have time to really properly grieve for my husband and now I feel raw and heartbroken."

"Never mind that." Mrs. King reached for Til's hand. "I know a woman who needs a mother when I see one. You're not going to an apartment by yourself. You can live with me and we'll get through this together."

Tears gathered in Til's eyes as Mrs. King squeezed her hand. "I... haven't had a mother since I was fifteen years old."

"Then you come today and let me start fussing over you." Mrs. King pressed a handkerchief to her eyes.

"We have room too." Adeline beamed. "If Mrs. King fusses too much, you can shuffle over to my spare room."

"Ah, yes, but you are newlyweds," Mrs. King's eyes twinkled at Adeline. "You need your space. You made Judge Martin jump through a million hoops to acquire your hand. He deserves some undivided attention."

Adeline grinned at Mrs. King. "That is true. The hoops are not put away yet!"

The women laughed together. "He's a darling, don't be too hard on him." Mrs. King reprimanded Adeline.

"Mrs. King, I'll move today." Til smiled.

"Settled!" Mrs. King gathered Til into a tight hug. "I love a full house."

"Shannon has decided that she and Cole are staying with me. I am not so sure," Til warned her.

"Lots of room for all of you," Mrs. King offered. "They can have the fourth floor. I have an obscene amount of room, it's embarrassing, really. I'll have my butler come around for your things."

"Thank you, Mrs. King. I would appreciate that." Til ran her fingertips over the plans in front of her. Where her clinic had given women access to birth control so they could have control over the sizes of their families, it didn't take them out of poverty. Only education would do that. An education that had been generously given to her; now she could return the favour. Til pressed her hand against her womb as if asking the baby what he or she thought. "It is such a great honour to work with you, I appreciate it very much." Til smiled at the women in front of her. "I received assistance during a very critical time in my life, and I am happy to be part of this initiative."

"Good! All settled." Cora beamed with delight. "Besides your own clinic you are welcome to staff as you see fit. There is another feature that might interest you. Please follow me; we have a nursery so we can bring our children to work with us. I have a nanny at home, at night, but during the day, I didn't want to stop breastfeeding so, we had this room redesigned." Cora led the way to the sun-soaked nursery attached to her office. "You can work and check on your child. The girls take turns working in here, it's part of their life skills education."

"You've thought of everything," Til breathed as she looked around the beautiful room. High windows and gleaming wood trim let the sunshine in over a crib with a sleeping baby boy. They had papered the room in a sunny yellow that made the sunshine glow even brighter.

"About that contraception you promised," Cora grinned.

"I can get you contraception today." Til laughed. "I have brought trunks of it. Hopefully, the butler doesn't find it and have me arrested!"

"Cora sighed with relief. "Thank you."

"The spare room will work as a clinic for now." Til ran her hand along the crib. "I can't wait to work here with you all. Thank you for this opportunity."

Chapter Forty-Seven

As Til settled into the third floor at Mrs. King's, she breathed a sigh of relief. The heavy drapery pulled back to let light slant in over gleaming hardwood floors and rich brocaded pillows. Concern niggled at her at the amount of money in her handbag, easy to steal. She counted it and breathed a sigh of relief. All accounted for.

However, she needed to get to a bank today. She needed to make a deposit and she owed Mirabel ten thousand pounds.

Til called for a carriage. "I need to go to the train station, please."

***

Mirabel's heart pounded with fear that Asher Grayson would jump out at her and drag her to jail at any minute.

Mirabel held onto Tommy as if he would disappear if she let him go. The carriage ground to a halt at the train station on Merritt Street. She dragged her few pieces of luggage to the porter and paid for a ticket to Winnipeg. She wasn't sure where to go. Winnipeg seemed far enough, and she could always go further if she chose to.

Mirabel's eyes darted around to see if she was being followed. Sure enough, just as she was about to step on the train, she glimpsed Til out of the corner of her eye.

Mirabel's throat tightened in fear. Unconsciously, she pulled her son closer.

"I'm glad I caught you." Til breathed a sigh of relief.

Tears gathered in Mirabel's eyes. "Is Detective Grayson going to have me arrested for conspiracy to commit murder?"

"Oh, that! Um, no. I'll handle that." Til flashed a conspiratorial smile. "No. I'm here for another reason. Our deal was for ten thousand pounds."

Til handed Mirabel an envelope.

Mirabel opened it and ran her fingertips over the money inside. She gasped as she looked at the bills. Her eyes filled with tears. "Thank you."

"You're welcome." Til reached out and hugged her. "Mirabel, I know about desperation. I know too much about it. Someday, we'll have a world where we have better choices for girls and women, but that day is not today. I wish you all the best."

Mirabel wiped tears from her eyes. "How do I repay you?"

Til shrugged. "It was a business arrangement."

"I never should have gotten involved with Royce." Mirabel pushed the envelope of money down into her handbag and clutched it close to her side.

"Mirabel, you led me to Shannon and Alys. You could have betrayed us, you didn't. Thank you." Til tucked a piece of hair behind her ear, her cheeks reddened from the wind. "I hope you will create a good life with this money. Enjoy your beautiful son."

"Thank you." Mirabel's eyes searched Til's. "I'm sorry about your sister. I understand she pays for her... uh... crimes this week."

"She does." Til nodded. "As much as Alys needs to pay for killing Malcolm, if a place like Hope House had been available to her, she may have made better choices. A girl like Alys faced hard decisions far too early in life."

"I'd say we all did." Mirabel's throat tightened thinking of the decisions she had faced. "We face the most critical decisions at our most inexperienced." Mirabel shook her head. "I'm sorry for all you lost."

"Thank you."

"Thank you for treating Tommy when he was sick. Mrs. King told me you took his fever down and he was in good hands." Mirabel held him tighter against her.

Til waved the thanks away. "Anyone would do it."

"No, Doctor Stone, in my experience, not everyone would." Mirabel's breath caught, her eyes filled with tears. "When I was with Royce and Eli, I learned to trust no one. It feels good to trust again."

Til nodded. "I am working on that myself. Anyway, Nora Blackburn is being returned to England and the rest of the girls we retrieved when Alys was arrested are going home with her. They have assigned two constables to be sure they arrive back in England. This terrible situation has come to a close. It was the best possible outcome."

"What about you?" Mirabel shifted Tommy in her arms.

"I will be here at Hope House. They are designing a clinic for me so I can assist women with family planning and deliver babies and whatever else they need me for." A smile lit up Til's face.

"You'll be perfect for that." Mirabel gave Til a tentative smile, she bit her lip as the whistle on the train blew. "You're sure that the telegram won't show up someday? I am afraid of Detective Grayson."

"Mirabel, you're free. Enjoy it. A deal is a deal. I never go back on my word."

Mirabel let out a long sigh of relief.

"Have a happy life, Mirabel." Til smiled her encouragement.

Mirabel gave her one last hard hug and gathered her few possessions together. Settling into a seat, she looked out at the platform. Til waved to her, Mirabel waved back.

As the train pulled away from the station, Til turned on her heel and walked away.

Mirabel let out a sigh of relief. Pressing her fingertips against the money in her handbag, reassuring herself that it was still there, Mirabel stopped looking back at Toronto. There was nothing for her there any longer. She smiled at her sleeping son and turned in her seat so she was facing west toward her new life. Placing a protective hand on her abdomen, she thought about the new life growing there. She shook the thought away that this baby was Royce's and he was a murderer and a white slaver. This new life inside of her would be given every opportunity to grow and flourish with love and affection. A new life in a new land.

Thank you, Til, I will always remember this kindness. I'm ready for a fresh start.

Chapter Forty-Eight

A fire crackled in the grate of Mrs. King's drawing room. Til leaned back against the brocade pillows on the settee with a hot cup of tea in her hand. Shannon sat across from her. Cole moved to the fireplace and poked around at the coals in the grate.

"We're staying." Cole put more wood on the fire. "Shannon worries for your health and I know if she goes to Oakland and thinks you are unwell, she won't get a moment's peace."

Til took a deep breath and let it out slowly. "Listen. That is kind. However, I have work to do and a house to purchase. I have all the help and support I need. I will spend the winter getting ready for the birth and work as I feel up to it. Go home to Oakland. I see you pining for it."

"What if something happens?" Shannon wrung her hands in worry.

"There are doctors here, my dear, and they will know what to do."

"They don't use chloroform." Shannon bit her lip.

"We can make plans closer to the day." Til sipped her tea. "Go with my blessing."

Shannon and Cole looked at each other across the drawing room.

"It's up to you, Shann. I want you to be healthy and happy." Cole put the poker down.

"If you're sure..." Shannon's gaze met Til's.

She's eager to get started in her new wing, in her new life.

Til's heart filled with excitement for Shannon. "I'm sure, you must go," Til insisted. "Pack your things. You've got a train to catch."

The very next day, same station, different train, Til stood with Shannon and Cole as they were about to board the train to Brandon.

"Are you sure I shouldn't stay? With Alys being..." Shannon offered for the hundredth time.

"Go," Til interrupted firmly.

Cole moved their trunks and then returned to stand by Shannon as they all said goodbye.

"Be very, very happy. Both of you. I mean it." Til bit her lip, worried at the journey ahead of them.

"If it's a girl, we'll call her Matilda," Cole teased.

"You absolutely will not! One Til in a family is enough, I think." Til smiled warmly up at Cole. "I have a letter here for Lady Harper. Send her my warmest regards. I hope you have a happy pregnancy, Shannon. Take care of yourself. I love you." Til hugged Shannon hard. "Don't let Doctor White walk over you when you take over your new duties in his hospital. Stand up for chloroform in labour and delivery. Start a birth control program immediately; bring relief to the masses."

Shannon threw back her head and howled with laughter. "Save all this energy you are spending on bossing me around! Grayson needs to talk to you, don't forget. I think you have put him off as long as possible."

Til took a deep breath and let it out slowly. "He's going to resign from his position, you know. This is all about closing the file and then I hear he's taking a year off and raising his daughter. He told Cora he would go back to the constabulary but with less responsibility. It's... surreal. I can't believe he would do such a thing."

"I hear Melinda left Ella at his house in the night to follow Archie." Shannon's eyes hardened in judgement.

"His men think he's gone off his rocker." Cole interrupted. "They are shaking their heads and laying bets. They give him seven days at home with a baby before he runs back to the constabulary."

"If I'm holding up the investigation I better go tomorrow," Til conceded.

"It wouldn't hurt to smooth things over. It's not good to burn a bridge with a man like Detective Grayson, you never know when you'll need his service." Shannon teased her aunt. "You're not the easiest..."

"I'm not that bad!" Til interrupted. "I'm trying hard to be delightful!"

"Aunty Til." Shannon placed a hand on Til's cheek. "You are terrible. You really are."

"I'm trying!" Til sputtered, eyes narrowed at Shannon.

"We all appreciate it, very much. Please. Try harder." Shannon patted Til's cheek.

"Well," Til huffed. "I intended to weep when you got on the train, terrible child, I guess I will not! Good riddance!"

Shannon grinned at her aunt and Til grinned back.

"You keep calling me a terrible child. I'm a grown woman." Shannon shook her head.

"You will always be my terrible child." Til smiled fondly at her niece. "I love you Shann. Be happy."

Shannon swallowed hard.

Til's eyes misted with tears as Shannon slid her hand into Cole's. They would have to get on the train and Til suddenly wasn't ready.

"You know Shannon, I would like to catch up with Lady Harper. I'd like to tell her in person what all her jewellery bought and pay her back," Til said. "Please tell her that when I am well, when things have settled, I may just make a trip out to Oakland to see her."

"She would love that." With a smile, Shannon stepped onto the train. She ignored the crowd Cole kept from pressing in on her. She turned to speak to TIl. "I'll alert the press, Oakland and Brandon, get ready... Doctor Til Stone in the prairies! It will never be the same."

Til grinned. "Tell them to brace themselves."

"Apologise to Grayson," Shannon commanded. "This city isn't big enough for you to be at odds with each other. You might need him someday. Go. Settle things."

Til rolled her eyes. It was on the tip of her tongue to say she didn't need a man but the scene in the ship where he beat the three men sent by Alys off of her was fresh in her mind. Til conceded, for the first time in her life, that Shannon might be correct. Promoting birth control in a new land where it was barely legal could present a raft of problems, the more powerful allies the better.

Shannon waved and allowed Cole to drag her safely into a train carriage. The crowd swallowed them both.

Til put thoughts of Grayson away as she watched Shannon and Cole move further away from her until she couldn't see them any longer.

"I love you, Shannon. I love you," Til whispered as the train pulled away. Til stood on the empty platform and watched as her heart left on a train to Oakland.

Chapter Forty-Nine

The next day, Til folded the telegram from Detective Grayson asking to see her at the constabulary at two in the afternoon. He had kindly added if she was not well, he and Sol would see her at her residence. He requested a meeting with her before Friday as he was leaving his position and wanted all loose ends tied up.

So it's true. You are leaving your position for your daughter.

Promptly at two p.m.Til waited in the hall outside his office. Men bustled around her dragging people in irons down corridors. When Grayson and Sol came toward her, her heart pounded in expectation.

What is this about?

"Thank you for meeting with us here. If you would step into my office, I just want to take your statement and be sure that this investigation is completely closed before I leave this position." Grayson held open the door to an interrogation room.

Taking a deep breath, Til proceeded Grayson and Sol into the room.

"Here we are again." Til sat down and clasped her hands in her lap.

"Yes, here we are again. No irons this time though." Grayson smiled at her warmly as he sat down and opened a file. His eyes flicked over her. "Are you well?"

"I am as well as can be expected." Til leaned back in her chair.

"I just have a few questions." Grayson pulled out a sheet of paper. "Your full name, please."

"Matilda May Bertram." Til stated her full name without trepidation. The name Matilda Bertram meant nothing now. No longer running from the Bristols. Having placed the shame of the night she ran firmly on her father, she felt no further crippling shame. Til spoke her old name with a lightening of spirit.

Grayson looked at her and she held his gaze. "Good for you."

"It's over now." Til smiled.

"I am glad of that." Grayson adjusted the paper and kept writing. "Just a few questions regarding your relationship with Mirabel Salter. Did you know Mirabel Salter prior to October 28, 1906?"

"No."

Grayson carefully wrote her reply. "Are you aware that Mirabel Salter is wanted for conspiracy to commit murder?"

"I wasn't aware she was formally charged with that crime." Til shifted in her seat as she stretched the truth.

Grayson continued. "Do you know where Mirabel Salter is living in Toronto?"

"No." Til's palms slicked with sweat as she realised where this line of questioning was going.

"To your knowledge, has she left Toronto?" Grayson asked.

"I last saw Mirabel at the train station at Merritt Street." Til's breath caught with worry for Mirabel.

Please let her get away safe.

Grayson shot a glance at Sol. Sol swiftly left the room.

"Did any money pass from you to her?" Grayson poised with his pen over the paper.

Til swallowed hard. "When Mirabel killed Royce in self defence I promised to give her ten thousand pounds if she would tell me where Shannon McDougall was being kept."

"You paid the ten thousand pounds, is that correct?" Grayson wrote down her response.

"Grayson, am I in trouble here?" Til's stomach churned in worry.

Grayson stopped writing, he got up and checked the corridor and then returned to the table. "You have powerful enemies and so do I. When Alys was apprehended in the clearing and you were upset, I held you. Well, it turns out; one of my men accused me of being romantically involved with you. He reports that we looked like a man and woman who are in love with each other. Sol has testified that he has seen nothing inappropriate between us, but Garrett has lodged a complaint."

Til gasped.

"He wants my position." Grayson's jaw clenched. "I have resigned as of Friday. If he can somehow slant things so that it looks like I have compromised for you, and Sol has covered it up, he is next in line after Sol for the job. My superiors are well aware of the situation, but I don't want trouble for you or me, now or in the future. I need this statement to be very clear. We need them to know the truth, that you didn't know Mirabel Salter and that you are not conspiring with her. That I am not covering up a conspiracy between the two of you because of any inappropriate romantic feelings. I will be honest though. You at a train station giving her money looks very bad for you. For both of us." Grayson's dark eyes were troubled. "Garrett has been following you. He has photographs of you handing her an envelope."

"Gracious." Til's chest tightened with worry. Being accused of conspiring with Mirabel was a grave accusation. "But, I never, ever heard of Mirabel before I arrived in Toronto."

"That is what Sol and I have both sworn to. You are innocent of this charge and I will be sure my superiors see this."

"Grayson, are we off the record?" Til whispered.

"Yes." His eyes flicked over her face in concern.

"May I ask you something?" Til leaned forward.

"Anything," Grayson whispered back.

"Do you have feelings for me?" Til's eyes widened as she waited for the answer.

"I do," Grayson said quietly.

"You do?" Til's breath caught in her throat.

"I say this with no intention of acting on those desires though, Til." Grayson leaned forward in his chair and kept his voice down. "You are grieving a man that you loved very much. I am still technically married to Melinda."

"I know that this is not the right time for us. However, if the right time should present itself, I hope there may be a possibility for us. At a later date of course." Grayson spoke softly.

Til took a deep breath and let it out slowly. "I still wake up crying and now that the crisis seems averted... I will need time and patience to heal, Grayson."

"Of course you do. I would have said nothing of my thoughts or feelings if it weren't for this accusation. I just thought you should know because we were partners in taking down this ring. Partners tell each other everything."

"We were good partners." Til smiled as she placed her hand on his. "I never dreamed I could trust and respect anyone other than Malcolm and at the end of this ordeal I have found that same trust and respect for you, Grayson."

"This might change your mind, Til. I know how you feel about work and you should hear it from me, I am taking a year off to spend with Ella and then I will apply to resume this position. That is my intention. I need to focus on my daughter right now."

"May I ask..." Til leaned forward and then clamped her mouth shut as Sol reentered the room.

Grayson took his hand away.

Worry snaked through Til, if Grayson had to be this proper in front of Sol, the accusation was very bad indeed.

"Mirabel has left for Winnipeg. We'll send notification to the police department there," Sol informed Grayson.

Grayson nodded. "Very good, thanks Sol."

Poor Mirabel!

"Do you know where she planned to reside in Winnipeg?" Grayson asked Til, his mask of professionalism pulled back down.

"No," Til said quietly. "As I said, I don't know her. I didn't know where the train was going."

"Have you had further contact with Miss Salter since she left?"

"No. We are not friends and I am not an acquaintance. We were in the same room with the same white slaver. I paid her to find my niece. No more, no less."

Grayson carefully wrote down every word.

"I will have this statement typed up so you can sign it. Sol, can I ask you to take this to a typist."

Sol reached for the statement and left them in the interrogation room alone.

"About Melinda and Ella," Grayson said softly.

Til held her breath at the obvious pain that flashed across his face.

"Yes," she prompted gently.

"Two nights ago, Melinda came to my home late at night. She had Ella and all Ella's things with her. She left Ella with me. I..." Grayson scrubbed his hands over his face.

"I don't know what to say about that." Til stiffened. "Since we are being honest here, I am not sure how you could have let her take her in the first place."

"I made a massive mistake, Til. Massive." Grayson shot Til a tortured look.

"Why did you let Melinda take your daughter?" Til couldn't take the harshness out of her tone.

Grayson stood up, crossed his arms over his chest. "How could I take a nursing baby from her mother? I watched my mother break apart and never recover when Katherine was taken. I couldn't do that to Melinda."

Til stood up too. "I thought maybe because she was a girl. You wouldn't let Melinda take your son, but a daughter was somehow..."

"Disposable?" Grayson interrupted, jaw tightening. "You think that low of me?"

"Would you have let her take a son?" Til couldn't stop the question from bursting out of her.

Grayson's lips thinned. "Son or daughter makes no difference to me, Til. No difference at all. I love Ella. Only a few short months ago, I thought I was doing the right thing. I stood on a dock and kissed my baby daughter goodbye." Grayson shook as he confessed. "I ran halfway across the world to find Nora Blackburn. I was wrong! My little Ella would have left my life, and I'd never see her again. I had no idea Archie couldn't hold down a job and the only work he could get would be with family in Baltimore. I believed they would stay in Toronto and I would get to see Ella. Things changed. Ella would have grown up watching Archie beat Melinda." Grayson's eyes flashed in fury. "Raised to believe that is acceptable. She would have taken Archie's last name. So, I was wrong. Completely wrong. Ella is back in my care. I resigned so I can stay home, and be sure she knows she is the most important person in the world to me. I just hope she stops being afraid of me."

"She's afraid of you?" Sympathy washed through Til.

"She looks at me and hides her eyes." Grayson's shoulders slumped in defeat. "I took her to Cora today, beside myself, because she isn't sleeping and I am not sleeping. She looks up at me and then buries her face in my chest and wails. I can't tell you how much that devastates me, Til."

"It will get better, Grayson. She's a baby." Til reached out to him.

Grayson took a step back. "So, for now, I will put her first and she will know she is worth it. The job, everything has to come second until that little girl is happy."

"Grayson, you have just restored my faith in men. Not all men, mind you. But a select few." Til pressed her hand to her heart.

"You taught me that, Til." Grayson spoke intensely. "I will never, ever lose her again. I can go back to the constabulary any day of the week, there will be a stack of missing girls, but there is one, right here, that I won't lose again. This incessant search for Katherine has destroyed me and robbed me of the good in my life. I have to let that go. Not because I don't care, but because my care must shift now."

"Good for you." Til echoed back to him.

"What about you?" Grayson asked. He indicated she should sit back down; he sat down across from her.

"You've heard about the clinic at Hope House?" Excitement bubbled up in Til as she said the words.

"Quite a bit actually."

"It's desperately needed, and I love the idea of educating women and girls. It's selfish too, if I'm honest..." Til pressed her lips together as she thought of what to say next.

"How is it selfish?" Grayson leaned forward in his chair.

"I can't believe I am saying this." Til's voice caught. "You'll think I'm weak."

"I think you're a lot of things, Til. Difficult, fussy, particular, but never weak." Grayson grinned at her.

"I can't manage those slums in the East End anymore." Til shook her head. "It's as if I woke up one day and my heart said, that's enough of that. I can't do it."

"Til, that's all right," Grayson whispered.

Til swallowed hard. "Is it?"

"Of course, it's time for new challenges. A fresh start. No more Bristols and tenements and suffering." Grayson smiled warmly. "You've done your time."

"I think so." Til nodded. "I think whatever penance I was paying there is over, Grayson. Finally over. I did my best in a bad situation and it's time to move forward. What happened to me and my sisters, Jimmy, and especially Alys, all falls squarely on my father. As a forty-year-old woman, I see that. Saving myself let me eventually save Shannon, but even if I only saved myself, it's all right. I was worth that." Til bit her lip. "I think I was worth that all along."

Grayson's eyes softened in sympathy. "Of course you were."

"It took a long time to believe it." Tears prickled at the back of Til's eyes. "What you are doing for Ella is... just outstanding. This is how a father should love a daughter. She should be everything to him. I'm very proud of you and I am happy for her. Ella Grayson will never have to question her worth; she won't spend years of her life answering for your actions."

"Thank you, Til. I know you'll do great things at Hope House." Grayson straightened up as he heard footsteps near the door.

Til kept her tone professional. "I like that Hope House is educating, and assisting, not just charity. I hope to be busy there."

"I'm sure you will be."

A knock at the door interrupted them. Sol entered the room and handed Til the statement. Grayson and Til carefully read through it before all three signed their names.

"That's it. All over." Grayson shook Sol's hand and turned to face Til.

Sol reached out and shook Til's hand. "I hear you are staying on at Hope House. Welcome to Toronto." Sol left them in the interrogation room.

"Well, this is it, then." Til stood and slid the handle of her handbag over her wrist. "I guess this is a goodbye of sorts."

"It is." Grayson stood near her and held his hand out. Til and Grayson shook hands over the closed file on the table. "It was a pleasure working with you most of the time."

A grin tugged at Til's. "It was a rocky start for certain, but I will say this. I don't trust men..."

"Really!" Grayson teased her.

Til waved her hand to shush him. "Let me say this! I trust you, Asher Grayson. I really do. So, please... be a little bit careful with me."

"I will be very careful, Til." A smile broke out across Grayson's face. "Before I forget, I will need your itinerary for next week. What days do you intend to work at Hope House?"

"I... I had told Cora only afternoons from 1:30 to 4 o'clock because I find mornings very difficult." Til frowned in confusion.

"I'll pick you up at one then." Grayson grinned at Til.

"I don't understand." Til tilted her head to the side in surprise.

"With the expansion at Hope House and the nature of your work, Cora is concerned about security. If you agree to allow me to protect you and your clinic, I am hired to work the same hours as you as head of security for the family planning wing. She expects some resistance because Canada's laws are stricter than England's. You have been known to bend rules here and there. If any enraged husband comes after you, I am to make short work of him. Also, with hired men about the place adding on the extra rooms, the safety of the women sheltered there is in jeopardy. So, I will tuck Ella in for her afternoon nap in the nursery and keep you out of trouble."

"Really!" Til exclaimed.

"Really," Grayson confirmed. "Cora said if I stay home all day every day I will be bored to death. She's right. So, unless you would prefer someone else, Til. This is your clinic and..." Grayson stood up straighter as if ready to be disappointed.

Tilting her head to the side, her eyes met his. "You would be working for me then? Just so I have this straight."

"I thought you might ask that. I have a contract here for you to sign, ensuring I get to keep some of my rights while we work together. As partners." Grayson handed Til a piece of paper.

"You have a contract for me?" Til's jaw dropped in surprise. She took the paper from him and read it outloud. "This is called the Grayson/Stone code of conduct... did Cora write this?" Til howled with laughture.

"She did," Grayson confirmed. "Keep reading, Til. This is not a joke. I know about suffragettes, I know about your kind."

"I told you, they don't have a category for me." Til's eyes flicked up to his. "Women like me are not typical."

"Too right, and all the more reason for the contract to protect my rights and sensibilities," Grayson asserted. "This would have come in handy on the ship."

Til shook her head. "I never trampled your rights!"

"You trampled them constantly. Read it," Grayson commanded.

"I, Doctor Til Stone, formerly Matilda Bertram, do so solemnly swear to treat Asher Grayson with the rights and freedoms I expect him to afford to me.

Grayson and Stone start this partnership at Hope House on *equal footing*.

Under no circumstances will Stone ever request Grayson's presence in a birthing room, whether that birth be in a clinic, carriage, home, street, wooded glen or any seafaring vessel. Ever." Til laughed harder. "I am to sign this?"

"Sign it here and initial the part about never being in a birthing room. Ever." Grayson grinned at her.

Til poised with her pen over the paper. "I think my name should have come first."

"It's in alphabetical order," Grayson said dryly.

Til signed and smirked at him as Grayson signed and then filed the contract away.

"Now Til." Grayson stepped closer. Til looked up at him. "We are equal partners promoting the safety of women and birth control. Are you happy about this? Are you sure this is what you want?"

Til held out her hand, Grayson took it in his own. They shook hands as partners, and grinned at each other as friends with a glimmering promise of the possibility of more to come.

"I think I would like that very much." Til smiled at Grayson.

Epilogue

Hillcrest, Oakland, Manitoba, April 1910

Shannon sighed as she settled down on the settee in Lady Harper's drawing room of Hillcrest. Sun slanted in through the windows and lit up the warm tones of the wool rug.

"We are gathered here today to read a letter from Til," Shannon said. With great ceremony she opened the big envelope and handed Priscilla Hartwell, Lucy Rood, and Lady Harper an envelope each. Shannon slid her fingertips over the last envelope with her name scrawled across it.

"The note of instruction reads as follows; 'Shannon, please ensure you are together with Priscilla, Lucy and Lady Harper before reading this letter. It is of utmost importance — Til.'" Shannon read to the women assembled for tea and quilting.

"Should we leave?" Ada Bennett grinned as she threaded her quilting needle.

"I think so."Lily Holt giggled as she adjusted her thimble. "This all sounds very ominous to me!"

Ada and Lily chuckled like old conspirators as they waited to hear what the mysterious envelopes contained. "What do you think this is about?" Lady Harper frowned as she slid her finger under the flap of the envelope.

"It's Til, it could be anything," Shannon said dryly. She placed a cushion at the small of her back to ease the tension there. Her second baby was due next month and she was increasingly uncomfortable and warned Cole at length, this was the last pregnancy. They had one beautiful daughter, one more baby would be quite enough.

"It's odd that she has requested we read this note together." Lady Harper's eyebrows raised in surprise.

"Very odd, but it's Til. She is coming in a month to deliver this baby, one wonders why not just speak to us then?" Shannon frowned.

"Shall we? I'm burning with curiosity!" Lucy's finger slid under the flap.

"Now," Shannon commanded as she slid her envelope open.

A hushed quiet fell over the drawing room as each woman swiftly read her letter. Shannon's eyes filled with tears as she read her note out loud.

"Dear Cousin Shannon,

We are excited to be coming to see you on the train. Mama tells us you have a baby in your stomach and she is helping you get the baby out. She says it is only one baby, not two like when she had us in her stomach.

Can you tell Annabel we are bringing her a gift for when the new baby gets here?

Mummy says we get to play with Annabel only a little bit because she is still very small. Mummy says she probably doesn't like trains and we are bringing our big train set. But we are bringing her a really nice doll so she won't feel left out.

While we are visiting you, Mummy is going to marry Mr. Grayson."

Shannon gasped as her eyes filled with tears. Ada sat down beside her and put her arm around her shoulders.

"Mummy is sending a letter to Aunty Cora's friends to see where a good place would be for the ceremony. Mr. Grayson is coming with us on the train and bringing our friend Ella. We are really happy that our friend Silas Stein is coming out for the wedding with his parents, he likes trains too.

After they get married we are all going to live in the same house. Ella hates trains, so we don't have to share our train set with her. We think living all together might be all right.

When Mr. Grayson comes to see us, Mummy smiles a lot. Sometimes when Ella cries, Mummy holds her and rocks her to sleep. Cousin Shannon, at first we didn't like that at all, but Mummy says she has enough love for all of us. Mr. Grayson teaches us how to wrestle and we like that very much.

We will see you on May 15th.

Your cousins,

Malcolm and Maddox

Every woman in the drawing room blinked back tears as Shannon folded the note and placed it on her lap.

"Cora has sent Til's measurements. I am commissioned to make her wedding dress and super scandalous lingerie." Priscilla grinned at Shannon.

"I am to clear out the summer cottage to make room for Cora, Sol and Silas." Lucy smiled. "Cora is due around the same time as you, Shannon! She says she isn't letting Til out of her sight until this new baby is with us, so have a big pot ready to boil water when she gets here. Gracious! Wilbur and I will relocate to the summer cottage and give them our home. More room for them that way."

"I'll organise the food," Ada promised.

"I will help you with that." Lily Holt smiled across the quilt at her friend.

"Thank you, Ada and Lily. May I ask, what does your note say, Lady Harper?" Shannon asked as the women planned Til's wedding as if they were sisters of the bride.

***

Lady Harper looked at the sum Til had offered to host the wedding and her breath caught, she knew that was the exact amount she had handed Til all those years ago in England.

Lady Harper read the letter silently.

> 'My dearest Lady Madeline Harper, I wanted to return the money you so generously lent me in England, in person. I have wanted to see you and settle this account for a long time. The gratitude I feel for you is overwhelming.
>
> To save any embarrassment for both of us, I thought I would offer what I owe you as payment to borrow your grand home, Hillcrest, as the venue of my wedding.
>
> If this is not possible, I completely understand, but I would like to request a tea date so we can catch up in person and I can thank you from the bottom of my heart, again.
>
> Please advise me of a time convenient for you.
>
> With warmest wishes,
>
> Til Stone'

"What has she asked of you, Lady Harper?" Shannon held her breath.

"Til has asked if I would host the wedding on the grounds of Hillcrest." Lady Harper smiled with delight. "We have never had a wedding here. She is offering to pay..." Lady Harper stopped speaking as she was overcome with emotion.

Shannon looked at her carefully. "Pay?"

"Silly Til." Lady Harper shook her head and wiped a tear from her eye. "She thinks she owes me for some money from long ago... when we were in school together."

"Oh?" Shannon sat up a little straighter as Lady Harper blinked tears out of her eyes.

"She's mistaken, Shannon. Honestly, I had quite forgotten about it!" Lady Harper reached for a handkerchief. "I'll send her correspondence today. She will be married at Hillcrest with lilacs, roses, sunshine and happiness. Lord Harper and I will be delighted to host this event. She can put that money straight back into the Hope House initiative with my warmest wishes."

"That is very kind of you, Lady Harper." Shannon's eyes lit up with excitement.

"I'll send confirmation today." Lady Harper nodded at Jaffrey to pour more tea for the women in the drawing room. "We saved each other," Lady Harper said softly to Shannon. "Til Stone doesn't owe me a thing."

Shannon reached out and rested her hand on Lady Harper's forearm. "I'm glad you had each other."

Lady Harper nodded.

"Hold on," Shannon said to the women as she noticed the back of the boy's letter. "There is a post script here. Til is asking if Cole would give her away!" Shannon laughed. "Give her away! This is coming a few years too late! Cole would have happily shot her out of a cannon when they first met! He will be delighted to hand her over to Asher Grayson with his sympathies!"

The ladies of Oakland laughed with Shannon, settled down with fresh cups of tea, and planned a wedding for the one woman who had brought them all together.

The End

Wait! Before you go! Did you read the first two books in this series?
Book one: Hope in Oakland
Book Two: The Night They Came For Til
are available on Amazon.

Please leave me a review on Amazon! Thank you!

The Night They Came For Til

Chapter One

I woke up on a ship sailing west with a note from Malcolm, money, clothes, and my doctor's bag. That was it. The list of what I didn't have was longer. My eyes slid shut as I tried to block out the thought.

A week and a half at sea and I still couldn't bring myself to open the note. I was afraid of what it said. My hands shook with terror thinking that Til may be dead. There was no way to manage that thought. The fragile grip holding my sanity would slip; I would be lost. Wincing with pain, I went to my doctor's bag and pulled out the laudanum and the note. A slow, long sip of laudanum, much more than the suggested fifteen drops, swirled through my veins and unlocked the pain, taking the sharp edges away from my thoughts.

I ran my fingers over Malcolm's handwriting, anything to be close to him. I picked up the note to see if I could smell his aftershave.

A knock on the door interrupted my thoughts.

"Your supper, Miss Stone," the steward shouted through the door.

I put the laudanum bottle on top of the note and went to the door to retrieve my tray. I wondered how much Malcolm had paid this little man to serve me my meals so I could stay alone in my berth.

"Thank you." I gave him a tip. I tipped him every day because he was the only thing preventing me from starving to death. Most days I couldn't stand the thought of facing anyone.

I alternated between worrying about where the ship was taking me and not caring. Some were speaking about Canada— I shut their voices out. I was so sick I wanted to die, then I wanted to fight something, and in the end, I lay there day after day, as my body slowly healed. The bruises were fading; the cuts were healing. Before long, I could sit without wincing in pain. My body was young and resilient; inexorably it healed and left my mind far behind, still broken.

Fragments of the past came back to me, often when I was sleeping. The memories would make me wake screaming. If I thought of the attack, it made me sick to my stomach and I would immediately vomit.

After calculating dates to figure out how long I had been at sea, my mind stubbornly refused to acknowledge the fact that my time of menstruation had not occurred yet. My hands shook as I carefully went through the numbers again. Cold sweat of sheer terror soaked through my bodice as the realization sunk in that I was pregnant. My mind raced back to the attack; I couldn't stop it.

***

The night they came for Til, Malcolm found me half in the gutter and half on the street. He closed his eyes and turned away so I couldn't see the horror on his face. Then he pulled off his coat, bundled me up, and carried me to a hospital where he knew a doctor.

"Where's Til?" he asked through clenched teeth before placing me on a gurney.

"She told me to run. I shouldn't have," I wept.

His eyes met the doctor's.

"I trust you, Joshua," Malcolm said in a voice so low the doctor leaned in to hear him. "She's been beaten and raped. I dare say by more than one man."

I drifted in and out of consciousness. I wanted to scream and never stop.

"No expense spared. Do you understand what I'm saying?" Malcolm demanded.

Joshua must have nodded because I didn't hear him say anything at all to that except, "I'll look after it."

***

Can I prove Lady Constance Carstairs ordered the attack? No, I cannot. My body doesn't care; my mind can't comprehend it.

Pregnant with my attacker's baby, my mind was fragmented with disbelief. The dates did not lie. Finally, I took another deep swig of laudanum and opened the letter.

September 30th, 1904

Dear Shannon,

It is with a heavy heart that I send this letter to you. Putting you on that ship with no one to assist you is one of the hardest things I've ever done. I wish we were right there with you. Someday we will all be together again. It's a promise.

In July, Til received a letter from a close friend, Lady Madeline Harper. She had asked Til to send a midwife to Oakland, Manitoba, Canada. At the time Til was going to say no, as you were already enrolled for the school year. In light of recent events, I have sent instruction that you are to be that midwife. I have already sent your qualifications, including your two years of training at the London School of Medicine for Women and date of arrival. Lord Harper has assured me the town constable has been retained to ensure you are protected at every step of this journey. You will have your own home, so you will have privacy to study and heal in the months ahead.

Til has been incarcerated on charges of abortion. Her trial date has not yet been set. I have established a legal team, and she will be exonerated in due time and with due process. Do not worry yourself for her. She has the finest legal minds at her disposal.

It is Til's wish that you are not here for this "circus" as she calls it. It is her sincere desire that you have a long and prestigious medical career. She is concerned that your reputation as a doctor would be muddied by this attack. It is her wish that you remain in Canada until we have this settled.

The clinic was burned to the ground at the time of attack, so there is no need to worry about who will care for the premises.

I know that you have been through a horrendous ordeal and I am so sorry, Shannon. I am hoping that Lady Harper will take care of you as you take care of her in her time of need. I will find the men who did this and I will deal with them to the fullest extent of the law.
Know that we love you and care for you. I will keep you apprised of all matters relating to your aunt. If you want for anything, do not hesitate to ask. I understand Lady Harper's husband is most reasonable and generous. I trust they will care for you, as you are so easy to love.

I'm so sorry about the interruption of your education. We will arrange for you to continue your studies next year after Lady Harper's baby is born.

I hope your travel has been as pleasant as possible. A letter will be ready for you when you arrive.

With Love,
Malcolm

Pain sliced through my heart. Right then, in that moment, I needed Malcolm. He was the only father I knew. I understood his whole life would revolve around Til's trial, and I couldn't help with that. Grudgingly, I saw the wisdom in getting me out of England.

I reread the letter, the part about how my attackers would be prosecuted to the fullest extent of the law. I wished that promise healed my heart.

***

I arrived in Brandon after traveling across Canada. I was weary and so thin my clothes didn't fit. Two long weeks ago, I had run out of nux vomica and I couldn't keep anything down. During the day, I refused to think about it. Only at night, when I had no control over my thoughts, the images came back. I desperately tried to push it out of my mind.

I sat, freezing to death in a train station, in what looked like the middle of a frozen wilderness. How could it be this cold? It was only the middle of November! I put my head between my legs since I worried I would throw up again. My throat was raw from the frequent vomiting. When my stomach finally settled, I got up and wandered to the window.

As I did so, a man approached. He was wearing a uniform and stood over six feet tall with broad shoulders. I hoped this wasn't the constable. The sheer size of him terrified me, until he smiled; his hazel eyes crinkled at the corners. He came closer, that smile genuine and warm. I tried to smile back, but instead I vomited. All over his shoes. I groaned with mortification and wished for the ground to open up and swallow me.

It didn't.

Hope in Oakland

Chapter One

Toronto, Canada, 1904.

Canada's first female lawyer, Cora Rood, knew that anyone who dared represent Eli Pitman's wife in divorce court would face brutal and depraved retaliation from his hitman.

File in hand, trembling with anxiety, Cora knocked on Mr. Roth's office door. She chose him because of all the partners she worked for she believed he hated her the least. She tried to pull a mask of indifference over her face, because fear, like any other emotion, was not permissible in a lawyer.

"Come in." His voice sounded like ice on iron.

"There must be some mistake." Cora willed her hands to stop shaking while she presented the file for him to review.

Mr. Roth pulled his spectacles down onto the bridge of his nose and ignored the file in her hand. His eyes hardened. "What do you want, Miss Rood?"

"I think I have been handed this divorce case by accident, Mr. Roth. The Pitman divorce...I am sure you intended that for one of the other lawyers. A more experienced lawyer." Cora's voice sounded shrill in her ears.

"You wanted family law — we are giving you what you want." Mr. Roth leaned back into his chair.

You enjoy this. Seeing my fear, you're like all the others.

"Eli Pitman is the biggest crime boss in Toronto." Cora's voice shook with fear. "No one who goes up against him survives. This is career suicide at best, but I fear for my life..."

"Then you better be clever." Mr. Roth looked down his nose at her and held her gaze with his own. "If you want a man to take this case, maybe it's time you came to the realization that women aren't cut out for the practice of law. No shame in giving up. You fought hard for what, five years? Screaming and shouting about equality? Only the suffragettes support you. Decent women think you are incurable. Hand that file in and admit defeat, give up on being a barrister, and go to work as a clerk."

Cora didn't reply. This was an all too familiar rant she had heard too many times. She let the words slide off her.

"I have a suggestion for you." Mr. Roth put down his pencil and looked at her hard. "Get married, Miss Rood, have some children, let the men practice law. There is a reason you are the only woman standing here, asking for a lighter case load. The intellectual powers of women are inferior to men. You do not possess the intelligence or strength of will to be a lawyer. Women are emotional, not logical, and the law is all about logic."

There was a time I would have fought you, but I lost my will to fight in a jail cell. You know as well as I do that I have to put up with your hatred and contempt for two more months until I finish my term so I can be sworn in as a barrister. I have no choices here, I can't turn this down.

"It sounds like the decision is final." She hated the defeat in her voice.

"I'm a busy man, Miss Rood. If you can't handle this, if you're too *delicate* for this, maybe we should reassign all your cases. We had no idea when we assigned this petition to you that your case load was so *taxing*." He sneered at her. "None of the men are complaining about their work."

"I can handle the case load." She straightened her narrow shoulders and tried to sound hard, like him.

"We'll see." Mr. Roth looked back down at his paperwork, effectively dismissing her.

Cora crept back to her office. She closed the door and took a deep breath. Her mind raced as she thought about how she would talk Mrs. Adeline Pitman out of filing for divorce before she showed up for her two o'clock appointment.

She frowned at herself in the mirror. Her reflection revealed a broken woman — unruly chestnut hair, a drab olive green dress, and worn shoes. Her green eyes at one time gleamed with brilliance and excitement at the cases assigned to her. Now, disillusioned by her failures, her eyes had long ago lost their sparkle.

I'm tired of losing.

She shook her head at her sad appearance and turned around in time to see Mrs. Pitman standing at the entrance to the law office.

Mrs. Pitman checked her watch and tapped her foot while the front desk clerk, Jonathan, scampered around his desk to lead the way to Cora's office.

Adeline Pitman was a beautiful woman, in her mid-forties, with masses of dark copper hair piled high on her head and topped with an outrageous hat. She looked regal, refined, and determined. Sweeping by men who salivated at the sight of her, she made eye contact with no one. Mrs. Pitman wore a wool creation the colour of amber with contrast piping of jet black. Her left eye was hidden by the brim of her hat. Cora didn't have the first clue about ornithology, so she had no idea what poor bird had died and given up its feathers so that Mrs. Pitman could sweep in here, half cat, half bird, one hundred percent predator on the prowl.

Cora felt like a mud hen about to interview a peacock.

Mrs. Pitman swept into Cora's office, and they locked eyes. Cora was first to look away. "I am the lawyer assigned to your case," she said. "How can I help you?"

Mrs. Pitman cut straight to the point. "I need a divorce immediately." She pulled her gloves off and adjusted herself in the chair across from Cora.

"I looked over your petition, Mrs. Pitman. Have you spoken to another lawyer?" She settled in her chair across from Mrs. Pitman.

"I'm here for a second opinion. I disagreed with the first one. What can you do with this?" Mrs. Pitman gestured to the file marked "Pitman Petition."

"Very little," Cora responded cautiously.

"Oh?" Mrs. Pitman's eyes narrowed in disapproval.

"The law in Canada is very clear, Mrs. Pitman." Cora tried to head off a temper tantrum. "A party must be at fault. Men can divorce their wives on the grounds of adultery alone. For women, you cannot legally petition for divorce unless he has committed adultery *and* you can prove he is cruel. You have evidence of adultery, but this file does not meet the burden of proof for cruelty. I have to advise you to drop this petition. You won't win."

"I have to win." Mrs. Pitman's teeth clenched in anger. "I won't stop until I win."

"Adultery is not enough." Cora spoke sternly.

Mrs. Pitman's hands clenched into fists, her lips thinned. "This is an outrage. This is a double standard."

"I agree, and I sympathize." Cora leaned away from the petition as if it might burn her. "Outrage or not, it's the law. I can't change the law."

"My husband has been paying for an apartment in the upper west side." Mrs. Pitman held her chin high. "I was confused about why. Imagine my surprise when I went to that apartment to see for myself what exactly was going on. I watched him with binoculars. He exited her apartment bold as brass. Mirabel Salter, a daughter of a friend of mine, kissed him goodbye in her... well... unmentionables."

Cora shifted uncomfortably at the blatant pain on Mrs. Pitman's face.

"An apartment?" Cora moved closer to the petition.

"Yes. He's had this apartment for a while."

"How long?" Cora pulled the petition back in front of her and picked up a pencil to jot down the length of time Eli had maintained a separate residence.

"More than a year." Mrs. Pitman adjusted her gloves on her skirt.

Cora wrote down Mrs. Pitman's statement. "Is he cruel to you? Has he ever hit you?"

Cora couldn't imagine in her wildest dreams any man laying a hand on Mrs. Pitman. She carried herself like a queen. She would never permit it.

"Eli has never hit me." Mrs. Pitman frowned in confusion.

I have been hit by a man, and it's terrible. You will feel it for the rest of your life.

"Has he ever denied you money for basic essentials?" Cora grasped at this last straw.

"No." Mrs. Pitman's tone was cold.

"Mrs. Pitman, I am not unsympathetic. I understand the pain of adultery is very difficult. Even with a separate residence, though, I have to advise you to turn a blind eye and try to…"

"You, a woman, are advising me to turn a blind eye to adultery?" Mrs. Pitman interrupted as her voice escalated with anger. "I expected better from you!"

Cora wished fervently that she could crawl under her desk. Mrs. Pitman was not about to back down. This divorce was going to be filed, and Cora was going to have to argue it.

Conceding, Cora gathered her thoughts and tried to buy some time to come up with some sort of plan. "I just received this case today. Can you give me a day to research and try to think up some way to assist you? Would you mind coming back tomorrow afternoon?"

"Certainly! I am not unreasonable, Miss Rood." Mrs. Pitman hovered on the verge of a temper tantrum.

Mrs. Pitman wouldn't stop until she got her way; Cora had a day to come up with a miracle.

Acknowledgements

Editors:

Alex McGilvery at www.celticfrogpublishing.com. Wow! Three books! Thank you for your hard work on these books in content, line by line editing, and formatting.

Nicky Galliers for her work in copy editing. Thank you for checking British vernacular, and proofing. Til sounds authentic now because of you!

Ev Marshall, Shannon Kohut, and Wendy Holmstrom for their work in proof reading.

Book Cover Design:

Josephine Blake of Covers and Cupcakes LLC. (www.coversandcupcakes.wordpress.com)

Beta Readers:

Thank you Becky-Jo Fluker and Kari Cowan

Arc Readers:

Thank you Christina Lindsay, Tammy Bertram, and Myrna Watkins.

Book launch team:

Thank you very much Mom, for dressing up as Mrs. Daindridge all over this province and making hundreds of butter tarts, literally. I appreciate it! Dad, I appreciate the grant money! Henderson's, Trent for building a lemonade stand for the three cutest lemonade peddlers in the land: Sophia, Olivia, and Meika. Jody thank you for coming to launches as Priscilla. Trevor and Melanie Jenkins, Wayne Fehr and kids who provided live music, Azelin for coming as Shannon, Wes Jenkins for handing me books and organizing stock. Betty Levandoski, Tammi Amundsen (Costumes) Julie and Ashley Racher (photography), Lezlie and Marlee Scebenski (catering) Ev Marshall, Shannon Kohut, and Wendy Holmstrom for proof reading.

Thank you all for your hard work on the launch. These launches are not possible without all of you!

Thank you to the Hillcrest Museum board for allowing me to launch at Hillcrest three times!

Lastly, thank you Peter, there would be no books without you. I appreciate your love and support!

Inspiration:

Carson Jenkins, your work ethic and tenacity inspired the character Asher Grayson.

Research

Criminal Code of Canada, Revised statutes 1906, printed by Samuel Edward Dawson, Law Printer to the Kings. Legislative Assembly, Winnipeg, Manitoba

A big thanks to Fran Saler for helping me research shipping times and immigration for this book and for finding real life Priscilla from the book Hope in Oakland.

Thank you Ferg Devins for helping me with telegraphs, telegrams, and cables.

Author Bio

Historical Fiction author Rebekah Lee Jenkins writes about true Manitoba and Canadian events involving the suffrage movement. Rebekah published The Night They Came For Til in 2017, Hope in Oakland in 2018, and Taking Til in 2019.

Thrilled to be the first writer in resident at Margaret Laurence House in Neepawa in 2017, she finished the first draft of Hope in Oakland there.

Rebekah lives in Souris, Manitoba.

You are welcome to read more of her work and contact her on her website: rebekahleejenkins.wordpress.com or follow her at RebekahLeeJenkinsAuthor on facebook.

45885371R00215

Made in the USA
Middletown, DE
23 May 2019